Jerry Pournelle

BAEN BOOKS

FALKENBERG'S LEGION

Copyright © 1990 by Jerry Pournelle

A Baen Book

Baen Publishing Enterprises
260 Fifth Avenue
New York, N.Y. 10001

First printing, October 1990

ISBN: 0-671-72018-X

Portions of this book were previously published as *The Mercenary* and *West of Honor*.

Cover art by Keith Parkinson

Printed in the United States of America

Distributed by
SIMON & SCHUSTER
1230 Avenue of the Americas
New York, N.Y. 10020

I REFUSE TO
BE ARRESTED

Cordova put his hand on the pistol holstered at his belt. "You're under arrest, Colonel Falkenberg."

"Indeed?"

"This is absurd," President Budreau shouted. "Colonel Cordova, take your hand off that weapon! I will not have my Cabinet meeting turned into a farce."

For a moment nothing happened. The room was very still, and Cordova looked from Budreau to Bradford, wondering what to do now.

Then Bradford faced the President. "You too, old man? Arrest Mr. Budreau as well, Colonel Cordova. As for you, Mr. Traitor George Hamner, you'll get what's coming to you. I have men all through this Palace. I knew I might have to do this."

"You knew—what is this, Ernest?" President Budreau seemed beilwdered, and his voice was plaintive. "What are you doing?"

"Oh, shut up, old man," Bradford snarled. "I suppose you'll have to be shot as well."

"I think we have heard enough," Falkenberg said distinctly. His voice rang through the room although he hadn't shouted. "And I refuse to be arrested."

"Kill him!" Bradford shouted. He reached under his tunic.

Cordova drew his pistol. It had not cleared the holster when there were shots from the doorway. Their sharp barks filled the room, and Hamner's ears rang from the muzzle blast. . . .

TO: Sergeant Herman Liech, Regular Army, U.S.A.;
and Second Lieutenant Zeneke Asfaw,
Kagnew Battalion, Imperial Guard of Ethiopia.

To junior officers
everywhere

Author's Note

This novel is part of the series of "future histories" in which *The Mote in God's Eye* takes place, and it gives the early history of the events in that novel.

The battle in Part II, Chapter XIX is based in large part on the actual experience of Lieutenant Zeneke Asfaw, Ethiopian Imperial Guard, during the Korean War.

ARRARAT: INHABITED AREAS
INCLUDING CAPITAL CITY OF
HARMONY GARRISON

N

HIGH DESERT

BADLANDS

FOREST

FOREST

WESTERN
BADLANDS

ALLAN RIVER
VALLEY

FOREST

ALLANSPORT

BADLANDS

DENISBURG

ESCARPMENT

FORT
BEERSHEBA

JORDAN
VALLEY

FOREST

FARM AREAS

GREEN SEA

HARMONY GARRISON

MOUTHS OF
THE JORDAN

FORT REEDY

NEW WASHINGTON

MT. RAINIER

RAINIER
PENINSULA

ALLANSPORT

CAPE
TITAN

FORD
HEIGHTS

COLUMBIA RIVER

DOAK'S FERRY

ASTORIA

GRAND
FORKS

0   500   1000   1500
KILOMETERS

Chronology

1969   Neil Armstrong sets foot on Earth's Moon.

1990–2000 Series of treaties between U.S. and Soviet Union creates the CoDominium. Military research and development outlawed.

1995   Nationalist movements intensify.

1996   French Foreign Legion forms the basic element of the CoDominium Armed Services.

2004   Alderson Drive perfected at Cal Tech.

2008   First Alderson Drive exploratory ships leave the Solar System.

2010–2100 CoDominium Intelligence Services engage in serious effort to suppress all research into technologies with military applications. They are aided by zero-growth organizations. Most scientific research ceases.

2010   Inhabitable planets discovered. Commercial exploitation begins.

2020   First interstellar colonies are founded. The CoDominium Space Navy and Marines are created, absorbing the original CoDominium Armed Services.

2020	Great Exodus period of colonization begins. First colonists are dissidents, malcontents, and voluntary adventurers.
2030	Sergei Lermontov is born in Moscow.
2040	Bureau of Relocations begins mass outsystem shipment of involuntary colonists.
2043	John Christian Falkenberg II is born in Rome, Italy.
2060	Nationalistic revival movements continue.

Prologue

An oily, acrid smell assaulted him, and the noise was incessant. Hundreds of thousands had passed through the spaceport. Their odor floated through the embarcation hall to blend with the yammer of the current victims crammed into the enclosure.

The room was long and narrow. White painted concrete walls shut out bright Florida sunshine; but the walls were dingy with film and dirt that had been smeared about and not removed by the Bureau of Relocation's convict laborers. Cold luminescent panels glowed brightly above.

The smell and sounds and glare blended with his own fears. He didn't belong here, but no one would listen. No one wanted to. Anything he said was lost in the brutal totality of shouted orders, growls of surly trustee guards in their wire pen running the full length of the long hall; screaming children; the buzz of frightened humanity.

They marched onward, toward the ship that would take them out of the solar system and toward an unknown fate. A few colonists blustered and argued. Some suppressed rage until it might be of use. Most were ashen-faced, shuffling forward without visible emotion, beyond fear.

There were red lines painted on the concrete floor, and the colonists stayed carefully inside them. Even the children had learned to cooperate with BuRelock's

1

guards. The colonists had a sameness about them: shabbily dressed in Welfare Issue clothing mixed with finery cast off by taxpayers and gleaned from Reclamation Stores or by begging or from a Welfare District Mission.

John Christian Falkenberg knew he didn't look much like a typical colonist. He was a gangling youth, already at fifteen approaching six feet in height and thin because he hadn't yet filled out to his latest spurt of growth. No one would take him for a man, no matter how hard he tried to act like one.

A forelock of sand-colored hair fell across his forehead and threatened to blind him, and he automatically brushed it aside with a nervous gesture. His bearing and posture set him apart from the others, as did his almost comically serious expression. His clothing was also unusual: it was new, and fit well, and obviously not reclaimed. He wore a brocaded tunic of real wool and cotton, bright flared trousers, a new belt, and a tooled leather purse at his left hip. His clothes had cost more than his father could afford, but they did him little good here. Still he stood straight and tall, his lips set in defiance.

John stalked forward to keep his place in the long line. His bag, regulation space duffel without tags, lay in front of him and he kicked it forward rather than stoop to pick it up. He thought it would look undignified to bend over, and his dignity was all he had left.

Ahead of him was a family of five, three screaming children and their apathetic parents—or, possibly, he thought, not parents. Citizen families were never very stable. BuRelock agents often farmed out their quotas, and their superiors were seldom concerned about the precise identities of those scooped up.

The disorderly crowds moved inexorably toward the end of the room. Each line terminated at a wire cage containing a plastisteel desk. Each family group moved into a cage, the doors were closed, and their interviews began.

The bored trustee placement officers hardly listened to their clients, and the colonists did not know what to say to them. Most knew nothing about Earth's outsystem worlds. A few had heard that Tanith was hot, Fulson's World cold, and Sparta a hard place to live, but free. Some understood that Hadley had a good climate and was under the benign protection of American Express and the Colonial Office. For those sentenced to transportation without confinement, knowing that little could make a lot of difference to their futures; most didn't know and were shipped off to labor-hungry mining and agricultural worlds, or the hell of Tanith, where their lot would be hard labor, no matter what their sentences might read.

The fifteen-year-old boy—he liked to consider himself a man, but he knew many of his emotions were boyish no matter how hard he tried to control them—had almost reached the interview cage. He felt despair.

Once past the interview, he'd be packed into a BuRelock transportation ship. John turned again toward the gray-uniformed guard standing casually behind the large-mesh protective screen. "I keep trying to tell you, there's been a mistake! I shouldn't—"

"Shut up," the guard answered. He motioned threateningly with the bell-shaped muzzle of his sonic stunner. "It's a mistake for everybody, right? Nobody belongs here. Tell the interview officer, sonny."

John's lip curled, and he wanted to attack the guard, to make him listen. He fought to control the rising flush of hatred. "Damn you, I—"

The guard raised the weapon. The Citizen family in front of John huddled together, shoving forward to get away from this mad kid who could get them all tingled. John subsided and sullenly shuffled forward in the line.

Tri-V commentators said the stunners were painless, but John wasn't eager to have it tried on him. The Tri-V people said a lot of things. They said most colonists were volunteers, and they said transportees were treated with dignity by the Bureau of Relocation.

No one believed them. No one believed anything the government told them. They did not believe in the friendship among nations that had created the Co-Dominium, or in the election figures, or—

He reached the interview cage. The trustee wore the

same uniform as the guards, but his gray coveralls had numbers stenciled across back and chest. There were wide gaps between the man's jaggedly pointed teeth, and the teeth showed yellow stains when he smiled. He smiled often, but there was no warmth in the expression.

"Whatcha got for me?" the trustee asked. "Boy dressed like you can afford anything he wants. Where you want to go, boy?"

"I'm not a colonist," John insisted. His anger rose. The trustee was no more than a prisoner himself—what right had he to speak this way? "I demand to speak with a CoDominium officer."

"One of those, huh?" The trustee's grin vanished. "Tanith for you." He pushed a button and the door on the opposite side of the cage opened. "Get on," he snapped. "Fore I call the guards." His finger poised menacingly over the small console on his desk.

John took papers out of an inner pocket of his tunic. "I have an appointment to CoDominium Navy Service," he said. "I was ordered to report to Canaveral Embarcation Station for transport by BuRelock ship to Luna Base."

"Get movin!—uh?" The trustee stopped himself and the grin reappeared. "Let me see that." He held out a grimy hand.

"No." John was more sure of himself now. "I'll show them to any CD officer, but you won't get your hands on them. Now call an officer."

"Sure." The trustee didn't move. "Cost you ten credits."

"What?"

"Ten credits. Fifty bucks if you ain't got CD credits. Don't give me that look, kid. You don't pay, you go on the Tanith ship. Maybe they'll put things straight there, maybe they won't, but you'll be late reporting. Best you slip me something."

John held out a twenty-dollar piece. "That all you got?" the trustee demanded. "OK, OK, have to do." He punched a code into the phone, and a minute later a petty officer in blue CoDominium Space Navy coveralls came into the cage.

"What you need, Smiley?"

"Got one of yours. New middy. Got himself mixed up with the colonists." The trustee laughed as John struggled to control himself.

The petty officer eyed Smiley with distaste. "Your orders, sir?" he said.

John handed him the papers, afraid that he would never see them again. The Navy man glanced through them. "John Christian Falkenberg?"

"Yes."

"Thank you, sir." He turned to the trustee. "Gimme."

"Aw, he can afford it."

"Want me to call the Marines, Smiley?"

"Jesus, you hardnosed—" The trustee took the coin from his pocket and handed it over.

"This way, please, sir," the Navy man said. He bent to pick up John's duffel. "And here's your money, sir."

"Thanks. You keep it."

The petty officer nodded. "Thank you, sir. Smiley, you bite one of *our* people again and I'll have the Marines look you up when you're off duty. Let's go, sir."

John followed the spacer out of the cubicle. The petty officer was twice his age, and no one had ever called John "sir" before. It gave John Falkenberg a sense of belonging, a sense of having found something he had searched for all his life. Even the street gangs had been closed to him, and friends he had grown up with had always seemed part of someone else's life, not his own. Now, in seconds, he seemed to have found— found what, he wondered.

They went through narrow whitewashed corridors, then into the bright Florida sunshine. A narrow gangway led to the forward end of an enormous winged landing ship that floated at the end of a long pier crowded with colonists and cursing guards.

The petty officer spoke briefly to the Marine sentries at the officers' gangway, then carefully saluted the officer at the head of the boarding gangway. John wanted to do the same, but he knew that you didn't salute in civilian clothing. His father had made him read books on military history and the customs of the Service as soon as he decided to find John an appointment to the Academy.

Babble from the colonists filled the air until they were inside the ship. As the hatch closed behind him the last sounds he heard were the curses of the guards.

"If you please, sir. This way." The petty officer led him through a maze of steel corridors, airtight bulkheads, ladders, pipes, wire races, and other unfamiliar sights. Although the CD Navy operated it, most of the ship belonged to BuRelock, and she stank. There were no viewports and John was lost after several turns in the corridors.

The petty officer led on at a brisk pace until he came to a door that seemed no different from any other. He pressed a button on a panel outside it.

"Come in," the panel answered.

The compartment held eight tables, but only three men, all seated at a single booth. In contrast to the gray steel corridors outside, the compartment was almost cheerful, with paintings on the walls, padded furniture, and what seemed like carpets.

The CoDominium seal hung from the far wall—American eagle and Soviet sickle and hammer, red, white, and blue, white stars and red stars.

The three men held drinks and seemed relaxed. All wore civilian clothing not much different from John's except that the older man wore a more conservative tunic. The others seemed about John's age, perhaps a year older; no more.

"One of ours, sir," the petty officer announced. "New middy got lost with the colonists."

One of the younger men laughed, but the older cut him off with a curt wave. "All right, Cox'n. Thank you. Come in, we don't bite."

"Thank you, sir," John said. He shuffled uncertainly in the doorway, wondering who these men were. Probably CD officers, he decided. The petty officer wouldn't act that way toward anyone else. Frightened as he was, his analytical mind continued to work, and his eyes darted around the compartment.

Definitely CD officers, he decided. Going back up to Luna Base after leave, or perhaps a duty tour in normal gravity. Naturally they'd worn civilian clothing. Wearing the CD uniform off duty earthside was an invitation to be murdered.

"Lieutenant Hartmann, at your service," the older man introduced himself. "And Midshipmen Rolnikov and Bates. Your orders, please?"

"John Christian Falkenberg, sir," John said. "Midshipman. Or I guess I'm a midshipman. But I'm not sure. I haven't been sworn in or anything."

All three men laughed at that. "You will be, Mister," Hartmann said. He took John's orders. "But you're one of the damned all the same, swearing in or no."

He examined the plastic sheet, comparing John's face to the photograph, then reading the bottom lines. He whistled. "Grand Senator Martin Grant. Appointed by the Navy's friend, no less. With him to bat for you, I wouldn't be surprised to see you outrank me in a few years."

"Senator Grant is a former student of my father's," John said.

"I see," Hartmann returned the orders and motioned John to sit with them. Then he turned to one of the other midshipmen. "As to you, Mister Bates, I fail to see the humor. What is so funny about one of your brother officers becoming lost among the colonists? You have never been lost?"

Bates squirmed uncomfortably. His voice was high-pitched, and John realized that Bates was no older than himself. "Why didn't he show the guards his taxpayer status card?" Bates demanded. "They would have taken him to an officer. Wouldn't they?"

Hartman shrugged.

"I didn't have one," John said.

"Um." Hartmann seemed to withdraw, although he didn't actually move. "Well," he said. "We don't usually get officers from Citizen families—"

"We are not Citizens," John said quickly. "My father

is a CoDominium University professor, and I was born in Rome."

"Ah," Hartman said. "Did you live there long?"

"No, sir. Father prefers to be a visiting faculty member. We have lived in many university towns." The lie came easily now, and John thought that Professor Falkenberg probably believed it after telling it so many times. John knew better: he had seen his father desperate to gain tenure, but always, always making too many enemies.

He is too blunt and too honest. One explanation. He is a revolving S.O.B. and can't get along with anyone. That's another. I've lived with the situation so long I don't care anymore. But, it would have been nice to have a home, I think.

Hartmann relaxed slightly, "Well, whatever the reason, Mister Falkenberg, you would have done better to arrange to be born a United States taxpayer. Or a Soviet party member. Unfortunately, you, like me, are doomed to remain in the lower ranks of the officer corps."

There was a trace of accent to Hartmann's voice, but John couldn't place it exactly. German, certainly; there were many Germans in the CD fighting services. This was not the usual German though; John had lived in Heidelberg long enough to learn many shades of the German speech. East German? Possibly.

He realized the others were waiting for him to say something. "I thought, sir, I thought there was equality within the CD services."

Hartmann shrugged. "In theory, yes. In practice— the generals and admirals, even the captains who command ships, always seem to be Americans or Soviets. It is not the preference of the officer corps, Mister. We have no countries of origin among ourselves and no politics. Ever. The Fleet is our fatherland, and our only fatherland." He glanced at his glass. "Mister Bates, we need more to drink, and a glass for our new comrade. Hop it."

"Aye, aye, sir." The pudgy middy left the compartment, passing the unattended bar in the corner on his way. He returned a moment later with a full bottle of American whiskey and an empty glass.

Hartmann poured the glass full and pushed it toward John. "The Navy will teach you many things, Mister Midshipman John Christian Falkenberg. One of them is to drink. We all drink too much. Another thing we will teach you is why we do, but before you learn why, you must learn to do it."

He lifted the glass. When John raised his and took only a sip, Hartmann frowned. "More," he said. The tone made it an order.

John drank half the whiskey. He had been drinking beer for years, but his father did not often let him drink spirits. It did not taste good, and it burned his throat and stomach.

"Now, why have you joined our noble band of brothers?" Hartmann asked. His voice carried a warning: he used bantering words, but under that was a more serious mood—perhaps he was not mocking the Service at all when he called it a band of brothers.

John hoped he was not. He had never had brothers. He had never had friends, or a home, and his father was a harsh schoolmaster, teaching him many things, but never giving him any affection—or friendship.

"I—"

"Honesty," Hartmann warned. "I will tell you a secret, the secret of the Fleet. We do not lie to our own." He looked at the other two midshipmen, and they nodded, Rolnikov slightly amused, Bates serious, as if in church.

"Out there," Hartmann said, "out there they lie, and they cheat, and they use each other. With us this is not true. We are used, yes. But we know that we are used, and we are honest with each other. That is why the men are loyal to us. And why we are loyal to the Fleet."

And that's significant, John thought, because Hartmann had glanced at the CoDominium banner on the wall, but he said nothing about the CD at all. Only the Fleet. "I'm here because my father wanted me out of the house and was able to get an appointment for me," John blurted.

"You will find another reason, or you will not stay with us," Hartmann said. "Drink up."

"Yes, sir."

"The proper response is 'aye aye, sir.' "

"Aye aye, sir." John drained his glass.

Hartmann smiled. "Very good." He refilled his glass, then the others. "What is the mission of the CoDominium Navy, Mister Falkenberg?"

"Sir? To carry out the will of the Grand Senate—"

"No. It is to exist. And by existing, to keep some measure of peace and order in this corner of the galaxy. To buy enough time for men to get far enough away from Earth that when the damned fools kill themselves they will not have killed the human race. And that is our only mission."

"Sir?" Midshipman Rolnikov spoke quietly and urgently. "Lieutenant, sir, should you drink so much?"

"Yes. I should," Hartmann replied. "I thank you for your concern, Mister Rolnikov. But as you see, I am, at present, a passenger. The Service has no regulation against drinking. None at all, Mister Falkenberg. There is a strong prohibition against being unfit for one's duties, but none against drinking. And I have no duties at the moment." He raised his glass. "Save one. To speak to you, Mister Falkenberg, and to tell you the truth, so that you will either run from us or be damned with us for the rest of your life, for we never lie to our own."

He fell silent for a moment, and Falkenberg wondered just how drunk Hartmann was. The officer seemed to be considering his words more carefully than his father ever had when he was drinking.

"What do you know of the history of the CoDominium Navy, Mister Falkenberg?" Hartmann demanded.

Probably more than you, John thought. Father's lecture on the growth of the CoDominium was famous. "It began with *détente*. That collapsed, but was revived, and soon there was a web of formal treaties between the United States and the Soviet Union. The treaties did not end the basic enmity between these great powers, but their common interest was greater than their differences; for it was obviously better that there be only two great powers, than for there to be . . ." No. Hartmann did not want to hear Professor Falkenberg's lecture. "Very little, sir."

"We were created out of the French Foreign Legion," Hartmann said. "A legion of strangers, to fight for an artificial alliance of nations that hate each other. How can a man give his soul and life to that, Mister Falkenberg? What heart has an alliance? What power to inspire men's loyalty?"

"I don't know, sir."

"Nor do they." Hartmann waved at the other middies, who were carefully leaning back in their seats, acting as if they were listening, as if they were not listening—John couldn't tell. Perhaps they thought Hartmann was crazy drunk. Yet it had been a good question.

"I don't know," John repeated.

"Ah. But no one knows, for there is no answer. Men cannot die for an alliance. Yet we do fight. And we do die."

"At the Senate's orders," Midshipman Rolnikov said quietly.

"But we do not love the Senate," Hartmann said. "Do you love the Grand Senate, Mister Rolnikov? Do you, Mister Bates? We know what the Grand Senate is. Corrupt, politicians who lie to each other, and who use us to gather wealth for themselves, power for their own factions. If they can. They do not use us as much as they once did. Drink, gentlemen. *Drink.*"

The whiskey had taken its effect, and John's head buzzed. He felt sweat break out at his temples and in his armpits, and his stomach rebelled, but he lifted the glass and drank again, in unison with Rolnikov and Bates, and it was more meaningful than the Communion cup had ever been. He tried to ask himself why, but there was only emotion, no thought. He belonged here, with this man, with these men, and he was a man with them.

As if he had read John's thoughts, Lieutenant Hartmann put his arms out, across the shoulders of the three boys, two on his left, John alone on his right, and he lowered his voice to speak to all of them. "No. We are here because the Fleet is our only fatherland, and our brothers in the Service are our only family. And if the Fleet should ever demand our lives, we give them as men because we have no other place to go."

PART ONE:
THE CODOMINIUM
YEARS

"Chap named Falkenberg," Lufkin said. "Professional"

I

THE STUDENT LOUNGE was noisy as usual. Students in bright tunics sipped coffee paid for by their taxpayer parents, and spoke of the Rights of Man and the Citizen. Others pretended to read while looking to see if anyone interesting had come in. In one corner three young men and a girl—she detested being called a 'young lady'—sat playing bridge. They were typical students, children of taxpayers, well dressed in the latest fashions of subdued colors. Their teeth were straight, their complexions were good. Two of the boys wore contact lenses. The girl, in keeping with fashion, wore large brightly colored glasses with small jewels at the hinges. The remains of their afternoon snack probably contained as many calories as the average Citizen would have for the day.

"Three No Trump, made four. That's game and rubber," Donald Etheridge said. He scribbled for a moment on the score sheet. "Let's see, I owe twenty-two fifty. Moishe, you owe eleven and a quarter. Richie gets nine bucks, and Bonnie wins the rest."

"You always win," Richard Larkin said accusingly.

Bonnie Dalrymple smiled. "Comes of clean living."

"You?" Donald smirked.

"Don't you just wish," Richie said. He glanced at his watch. "Getting on for class time. Visiting lecturer today."

Moishe Ellison frowned. "Who?"

"Chap named Falkenberg," Larkin said. "Professor at

15

the CD University in Rome. Going to lecture on problems of the CoDominium. Today it's military leadership."

"Oh, I know him," Bonnie Dalrymple said.

"Is he interesting?" Moishe asked. "I've got a lot to do this afternoon."

"He's dense," Bonnie said. She grinned at the blank looks. "Packs a lot into what he says. Makes every paragraph count. I think you better come listen."

"What did you take from him?" Richard Larkin asked.

"Oh, I wasn't old enough to take his classes. Actually, I didn't know Professor Falkenberg very well, I used to be friends with his son. John Christian Falkenberg the Third. It was when Daddy was stationed at the Embassy in Rome. Johnny Falkenberg and I wandered all over the city. He knew everything about it, it was really fun. The Capitoline Hill, with the statues, and up there is the Tarpeian Rock where they threw traitors off—it's not so high, really. And we'd go to the Via Flaminia. We used to tramp down that and Johnny sang this old Roman marching song. 'When you go by the Via Flaminia, by the Legion's road from Rome—' "

"Fun date."

"Wasn't really dating. He was about fourteen and I was twelve, we were just kids out playing around. But we had fun, really. I guess I was studious, then."

"Heh. You still are. You aced me in that last test," Moishe Ellison said.

"Well, if you'd work more instead of running around with *that* girl—"

Ellison winked, and the others laughed. They got up and walked together toward the lecture hall. The smog was bad outside, but it always was, so they didn't notice. "So how do you know about old man Falkenberg's lectures?"

Bonnie laughed. "Johnny used to take me to his house. Usually there wasn't anyone there but this old black housekeeper, but sometimes the Professor would come home early, and when he did, he'd ask where we'd been. Then he'd tell us all about it. *All* about it, wherever we'd been."

"Oh."

"Actually, it was interesting. Rome was nice then,

there were a lot of old buildings I guess they've let fall down now, and the Professor knew about all of them. But he wasn't as interesting as when Johnny told me—I guess I had quite a crush on him." Bonnie laughed.

"That's what's wrong with her," Richie said. "She's never got over her youthful affair with—what was his name?"

"John Christian Falkenberg, the Fourth." Moishe Ellison let the name roll off his tongue.

"Third," Bonnie said. "And maybe you're right."

They reached Smith Hall and went up the marble stairs to the lecture theatre.

Professor Falkenberg was tall and thin, with a surprisingly deep voice that carried authority. Hasn't changed a bit, Bonnie thought. He could read the phone book and make it sound important.

Falkenberg nodded to the students. "Good afternoon. I am pleased to see that there are still a few students in the United States who are interested in history.

"I wish to examine the origins of the CoDominium. To do that, we will have to look at just what happened to the United States and the Soviet Union whose uneasy alliance has produced our modern world. Friends in the Second World War, enemies in the Cold War—how did it happen that these two divided the world between them?

"There are many aspects to this problem. One is the decline of military power in both nations. That in itself has many facets.

"Today we will discuss military leadership, both as a general case and in the specifics of the powers at the time of interest. I begin with a few brief paragraphs by Joseph Maxwell Cameron, a writer of the last century, who said, in his *Anatomy of Military Merit:*"

Professor Falkenberg opened his pocket computer and touched a key, then began to read.

" 'Armies are controlled by the actions of two classes of men in authority that are distinct on the surface by levels of rank, but whose significant difference is in the sources of their authority. One class acts on the authority vested in it by the sovereign power. The other acts

by authority derived of appointment by the first. This is
not a chance relationship but one directed by a natural
ruling principle. The 'commissioned' officer acts in the
name of sovereign power and, or, by order of its commissioned superiors to himself. The 'non-commissioned'
officer exercises equally valid and at times absolute
authority, but he holds it from the commissioned officer
who appointed him and who can at his discretion remove the office. Few controlling principles are as little
understood in current times as these that define the
relationships of commissioned and non-commissioned
ranks to each other, the government, and to the ordinary
soldier. Promotion given as reward, rank seen as caste
and pay as incentive in the profession, occupation, or
career in arms are the villains that cloud the issues. A
private soldier can prove himself of equal value to a general
officer, in fact has often done so; and always by being
the soldier who knew his business, whatever his immediate motivation. A hierarchy of ranks invented to increase
prestige and pay can rob a military body of much of its
power while enjoying general approval of what are considered benefits. One of the sure signs of a military system
in decay is the appearance of an excess ratio of persons
in designated authority over the numbers of those who
serve to follow. The optimum ratio may vary a little
according to current armaments, but with little else.

" 'Because of its specific roles and purposes an army
has an optimum design and structure of control mecha-
nisms, instrumentation, and appendages. It is at best
simple, devoted to the smooth and graceful application
of power to motion and impact. In an almost totally
industrial and technocratic time, however, the existence of a natural pattern tends to be forgotten as
normal members and appendages are tortured and dis-
torted to conform to the caprices of machines. Military
monstrosities analogous to anencephalic and three legged
children are born and nursed toward ultimate impo-
tence. They are quite horribly obvious except to minds
bemused by the magic of technology. . . .' "

Falkenberg closed his computer and smiled thinly.
"Those words were written shortly before the United

States acquired, in what was supposed to be peace time, approximately twice as many general officers as it had employed during the conflict known as the Second World War, despite having a much smaller military establishment. Nor was this all. The ratio of officers to men began to creep upward, inexorably; and since the optimum ratio is perhaps five percent, and some elite organizations have done with less, it should be no surprise that as the United States military establishment moved toward one officer for each dozen men—and one general officer for each fifteen hundred—the effectiveness of the system declined accordingly.

"Military managers are easy enough to come by. Real leaders are rare."

"You were right about the density," Moishe Ellison said.

Bonnie giggled. "He hasn't changed much, that's for sure."

"And you only heard him at home? Wonder his kid didn't go nuts. Whatever happened to him, anyway?"

"He got in some kind of trouble," Bonnie said.

"And no wonder." Richie chuckled.

"I don't know what it was," Bonnie said. "But the next thing I knew, Johnny was off to the CoDominium Academy. We used to write, but when he graduated and was sent off on a ship, well—"

"You sound like you miss him," Moishe said.

"Yeah, hey, you never get that tone of voice when you talk about me," Richie said.

"That'll be the day," Moishe said. "You ever hear from him?"

Bonnie shook her head.

II

ANGELA NILES FOUGHT for wakefulness. It seemed to take a long time. At one level she knew she was dreaming, but it was still real: the crowded alleys of High Shanghai, thousands of men and women in blue canvas clothing, not quite uniforms but so alike they looked like blue ants. They were shouting, screaming words she could not understand, but what they intended was clear enough. The blue ants were coming to kill her. She ran, and suddenly she wasn't alone, there were blue and gold uniforms, a different blue, CoDominium blue, and the tiny squad of CoDominium troops clustered around her. They pulled her away from the mob, then turned, fired a volley, then another, and the blue ants screamed and halted for a moment.

"Fall back." The Navy lieutenant spoke calmly. "First squad. Fall back toward the harbor. Kewney."

"Sir."

Cousin Harold. How did Cousin Harold get here? But he was here, in the uniform of a Navy middie.

"Can you fly that boat?"

"No, sir."

"The cox'n was killed."

"Yes, sir, I know."

"Right. All right, Midshipman. Fall back with the first squad. Halt while we're still in sight, and take defensive positions. Signal when you're ready. We'll hold here. Miss, you go with him—"

"But, yes, but, Harold, what are you doing here, who is this, what—"

20

"No time, Angie. Let's go!"

They ran, and now it was certainly a dream, because she couldn't move, her legs wouldn't work, she tried to run and couldn't—

"Try to remember," a voice said. Whose? "What happened then?"

Running. A Marine was holding her arm. Suddenly he stopped. His eyes grew very wide, and he stood, stock still, in the middle of the street. A long thin steel rod grew out of his chest, and blood came out of his mouth, and he crumpled, slowly, slowly—

"Come on Angie, run, dammit!"

Run. Then they were at the end of the block, and turned the corner, and she could see the harbor, not far away, with the long slender shape of the landing craft, and three sailors at the landing with guns, and the turret on top swiveled.

Harold touched his sleeve and spoke rapidly into the communicator card. There was more gunfire, and more people screaming, then the CoDominium lieutenant and his party came running down the street.

"Almost there," Harold said.

"Get her into the ship," the Lieutenant said.

"Sir, you can fly the damn thing. You get her on the ship."

He was very young, that lieutenant, no more than a boy, he looked so thin and so very young, no older than Harold. "Three minutes," he said. "Three minutes, Kewney, then run like hell."

Harold grinned. "You know it. Ready? Go for it!"

And the lieutenant took her hand and ran with her, pulling her along, and the turret guns fired over their heads, and there was more shooting, and noise everywhere. Something exploded close to them and one of the dockside sailors went down. The lieutenant shouted into his sleeve mike. "Mortars! Run for it, Kewney. NOW!" And dragged her on, to the boarding port, threw her into the cabin.

"Sound Board Ship!"

Recorded bugle notes blared into the bright afternoon. The lieutenant ran forward and moments later there were rumbles. Something exploded outside the hatchway, and a swarm of angry bees came through the open hatch, whipped past her and clattered against the bulkheads. There was another explosion.

"We're hulled!" a sailor shouted.

The engine sounds were louder now. She ran to the hatchway to look out, and shouted for Harold. She couldn't see anyone.

"Clear the hatch!" someone shouted. There were whirs and the hatchway began to close. She felt motion as the ship began to move.

"Harold! Harold!" And there was Harold, only he was an old man, and his face was melting, and then he was gone, and there was another man, and the ship began to fade and she was in a white room in bed, a hospital room, and the men beside the bed were a doctor in a white coat and a CoDominium Navy Commander, very thin. She knew them both. How? Who were they? Lermontov. That was his name. How did she know that?

"Did you ever see Midshipman Kewney again?" Commander Lermontov asked.

"No. I never saw him after we left him at the corner, on the street of—the Street of Three Moons." Her throat was dry, and her left arm hurt. She couldn't move it, and when she looked she saw that it was strapped to a board, and there was an IV inserted at the elbow. And she remembered. Pentothal, something like that. They wanted to question her. What had she told them?

"I've told you everything," she said. "Three times, and whatever I said when I was drugged. Why do we have to go over this again?"

"Your Uncle has demanded thorough investigation," Commander Lermontov said. "And that he will have." He used his stylus on the screen of his pocket computer. "So. You last saw Midshipman Kewney at corner, where he was ordered by Lieutenant Falkenberg to hold for three minutes before retreating."

"Actually Harold volunteered—"

"Yes. Thank you. How long after that order was given did ship begin to move?"

"I don't know—"

"Doctor says you believe was less than three minutes."

"How does he know?"

"I don't know," the white-coated man said. "I can only try to construct events from your memories. Based on what we heard, I conclude that you don't really know, but you suspect that Falkenberg took off as soon as he got you to the ship."

"What does he say?" Angela asked.

"You already know that," Doctor Wittgenstein said.

"He told me Harold was hit by mortar fire before we got to the boat."

"But you don't believe him."

"I don't—I don't know what to believe," she said.

"Boat lifted," Lermontov said. "It had not enough fuel to go to orbit, and was damaged."

Angela shuddered. "More damage than—I was shocked when we landed and I could look. It was amazing that it would fly."

"*Buna* class boat is designed to take damage. So. Falkenberg landed boat at offshore island. What happened there?"

"Nothing. It was perfectly safe there, the people were Thai, no Chinese. Very friendly. It was—nice there, safe and peaceful. So we waited, three weeks until the Navy could send another ship down with a repair crew. Then I was taken to Government House, and John—Lieutenant Falkenberg was sent to his ship. Nothing happened."

"Something happened," Lermontov said.

She frowned at his tone. "What do you mean?"

"Doctor—"

"Miss Niles, you are a month pregnant."

"Oh."

"You do not seem surprised. You took no precautions?"

She felt herself blushing.

"Miss Niles, I have daughter nearly your age," Lermontov said. "You took no precautions?"

She tried to sound casual. "I wasn't thinking about that at the time."

"Nor, apparently, was Lieutenant," Lermontov said. "In this era of disease you were perhaps foolhardy."

Angela shrugged. "Actually, there were no precautions to take—"

"On Navy ship there will always be kits," Lermontov said. "But you are in fact correct. Medical cabinet was damaged along with much other equipment."

"Commander, I fail to see how my condition is relevant—"

"Your uncle will not fail to see," Lermontov said. "Foolhardy young Falkenberg, sacrifices promising Midshipman grandson of Grand Senator, in order to save himself. Then seduces Grand Senator's niece." Lermontov stared pointedly at her midriff. "Evidence will be unmistakable in few weeks."

"Oh. Do you— I guess Uncle Adrian would see it that way."

"At least you're safe," Dr. Wittgenstein said. "That ought to make him grateful."

Angela shook her head. "I'm afraid he won't be, not very. He doesn't like my mother much, and Harold was special. A niece is not a grandson, Doctor. He'd have gladly traded me for Harold." She shrugged. "I think he planned for Harold to become Grand Admiral one day."

"So. What will you do now?" Lermontov asked.

"About—" She rubbed her belly. "It takes getting used to. Does John—does Lieutenant Falkenberg know?"

"Not unless you told him," Dr. Wittgenstein said.

But I didn't know— "You mean, he won't learn unless I tell him?"

Lermontov nodded. "I was told you are intelligent."

"What is that supposed to mean?"

"I think I need not explain. What will Lieutenant Falkenberg do if he learns?"

She blushed again. "I suppose—I suppose he'd marry me, if I wanted him to."

"Is my prediction also," Lermontov said. "Under other circumstances would be good thing for young man's career, marriage to Bronson family. Now—"

"Now it would be ruin for both of us," Angela said. "What—what should I do?"

"You don't have to be pregnant," Dr. Wittgenstein said.

"Damn you! I was waiting for that! Why didn't—while I was still under, while you had me out, why didn't you just do it then, and I'd never have known? But no, you had to wake me up and tell me—"

"You want us to make decision for you?" Lermontov said. When she didn't answer, he turned to Wittgenstein. "Doctor, prepare operating room."

"Wait—no, wait—" She felt tears welling up in her eyes. "What is it?"

"What is what— Oh," Wittgenstein said. "A girl."

"Commander—I want to see John Falkenberg."

"I cannot prevent," Lermontov said. "But I ask you do not. Not until you have decided what you will do. He is not stupid—"

"Do you know him?" she asked. "That's a strange thing to ask, isn't it? Do you know the—father of my unborn daughter? We had three weeks. A lifetime. I think I know him, but do I? I—oh, damn."

Lermontov's expression softened. "He is—was—considered promising young officer. Well regarded." He shrugged. "Pity no one sees Midshipman Kewney die. Now I do not know what we can do for Falkenberg."

"And I can't help—I can only make it worse," she said. "Oh, damn—what should I do?"

"Get rid of it," Lermontov said. "Then, in year, two years, when Senator has forgotten, you will meet again—"

"He'll never forget. And we'll never meet again."

Lermontov was going to speak but she cut him off. "You can't be sure, and I can't be sure," she said. "The only thing that is sure is that—we can kill my daughter."

"Fetus," Wittgenstein said. "Not—"

"I've studied embryology," Angela said. "You don't need to tell me the details." She was silent for a long time. Then she brushed the tears from her eyes and looked directly at Lermontov. "Commander, can you get me passage to Churchill?"

"Yes, but why Churchill?"

"I have relatives there. My branch of the family didn't get the big money, but we're not broke, you know. I'll get by—"

"If you do this, I cannot permit you to see Falkenberg again."

"You couldn't stop me if I demanded it, and you know it," she said. "But—maybe it's better this way. Tell him—" The words caught in her throat, and she felt the tears welling up again. "Tell him I thank him for saving my life, and I wish him well."

The young man marched stiffly into the compartment and saluted. "Lieutenant Falkenberg reporting to Commander Lermontov as ordered, sir."

The thin man behind the desk returned the salute. "Thank you. Have a seat."

"Sir?"

"I said, Sit Down."

"Aye, aye, sir." Falkenberg sat stiffly.

"You believe I am calling you in for punishment?"

Falkenberg fingered the dispatch case under his left arm. "I have orders—"

"I know," Lermontov interrupted. "Not orders I wished to issue, but there is nothing to be done."

"So I'm leaving the Fleet."

"No. Only Navy," Lermontov said. "Unless you prefer to leave Fleet entirely." The older man leaned forward and examined Falkenberg minutely. "I could not blame you if you did, but I hope you will not. I have arranged to transfer you to Marines. As lieutenant with seniority and brevet captain. Also, I have sent message to Senator Grant recommending that he obtain Grand Senate confirmation of Order of Merit, First Class, for you. I expect that will ensure permanent promotion to Marine captain." Lermontov sighed. "If we had better communications, if I could speak to Grant directly, perhaps none of this will be necessary. Perhaps. I do not gauge well the politics of Grand Senate."

Falkenberg glanced at his dispatch case. "Clearly I don't either. Sir."

"This is obvious," Lermontov said. "Yet you did right. Losing one squad of landing party to save others is difficult, but we are all satisfied there was nothing else to be done." He shrugged. "Is unfortunate that squad you lose is commanded by Bronson grandson, but you cannot know this."

"He was a good troop," Falkenberg said. "And actually I did know his connection to—"

Lermontov held up a hand, cutting him off. He glanced involuntarily around the room, then eyed Falkenberg narrowly. "You will never admit that to anyone else," he said. "That your actions cause this young man to be killed is regrettable but justified, and perhaps Bronson will forget. But if Grand Senator Bronson is reminded that you knew of his interest in Midshipman Kewney, it will be much more serious. He will never forget that. I suggest you avoid Senator in future."

"Yes, sir. Only—"

"Yes?"

"Sir, I have asked about Miss Niles, and no one seems to know where she is."

"She requested that she be sent to Churchill, where she has money and relatives. She left two days ago on message boat to rendezvous with ship bound for Churchill."

"Oh— I'd have thought— Did she have a message for me?"

"She says she is very grateful that you have saved her life."

"I see." He was silent for a moment. "Sir, what is my assignment?"

Lermontov smiled thinly. "You have several choices. As usual there is no end of trouble which must be attended to."

III

Crofton's Encyclopedia of Contemporary History and Social Issues (1st Edition)

THE EXODUS

THE ERA OF exploration following the development of the Alderson Drive was predictably followed by a wave of colonization. The initial colonists tended to be both wealthy and discontented with Earth's civilization. Many were motivated by religion: both the more traditional religions, and the secular religion that grew out of what was known in the Twentieth Century as "The Ecology Movement," or "The Greens."

Many of the early colonists were quite sophisticated, and had good reason to expect success in establishing their cultures on new planets. Unfortunately, they did not reckon with the intense pressures on the governments of Earth . . .

2064 A.D.
The bright future she sang of was already stiffened in blood, but Kathryn Malcolm didn't know that, any more than she knew that the sun was orange-red and too bright, or that the gravity was too low.

She had lived all of her sixteen standard years on Arrarat, and although her grandfather often spoke of

Earth, humanity's birthplace was no home to her. Earth
was a place of machines and concrete roads and automobiles and great cities, a place where people crowded
together far from the land. When she thought of Earth
at all, it seemed an ugly place, hardly fit for people to
live on.

Mostly she wondered how Earth would smell. With
all those people huddled together—certainly it must be
different from Arrarat. She inhaled deeply, filling her
lungs with the pleasing smell of newly turned soil. The
land here was good. It felt right beneath her feet. Dark
and crumbly, moist enough to take hold of the seeds
and nurture them, but not wet and full of clods: good
land, perfect land for the late-season crop she was
planting.

She walked steadily behind the plow, using a long
whip to guide the oxen. She flicked the whip near the
leaders, but never close enough to touch them. There
was no need for that. Horace and Star knew what she
wanted. The whip guided them and assured them that
she was watching, but they knew the spiral path as well
as she did. The plow turned the soil inward so that the
center of the field would be higher than the edges. That
helped to drain the field and made it easier to harvest
two crops each year.

The early harvest was already gathered into the stone
barn. Wheat and corn, genetically adapted for Arrarat;
and in another part of the barn were Arrarat's native
breadfruit melons, full of sugar and ready to begin
fermentation. It had been a good year, with more than
enough for the family to eat. There would be a surplus
to sell in town, and Kathryn's mother had promised to
buy a bolt of printed cloth for a new dress that Kathryn
could wear for Emil.

At the moment, though, she wore coveralls and high
boots, and she was glad enough that Emil couldn't see
her. He should know that she could plow as straight a
furrow as any man, and that she could ride as well as
her brother—but knowing it and seeing her here on the
fields were two different things entirely, and she was
glad that he couldn't see her just now. She laughed at

herself when she thought this, but that didn't stop the thoughts.

She twitched the whip to move the oxen slightly outward, then frowned imperceptibly. The second pair in the string had never pulled a wagon across the plains, and Kathryn thought that she could no longer put off their training. Emil would not want to live with Kathryn's grandfather. A man wanted land of his own, even though there were more than a thousand hectares in the Malcolm station.

The land here was taken. If she and Emil were to have land of their own, they would have to move westward, toward the other sea, where the satellite pictures showed good land. We could go, she thought; go so far that the convicts will never find us, and the city will be a place to see once in a lifetime. It would be exciting, although she would hate to leave this valley.

The field she plowed lay among low hills. A small stream meandered along one edge. Most of the crops and trees that she could see had come from Earth as seeds, and they had few predators. Most crop-eaters left Earth plants alone, especially if the fields were bordered with spearmints and marigolds to give off odors that even Earth insects detested.

She thought of what she would need if they struck west to found a new settlement. Seeds they would have; and a mare and stallion, and two pairs of oxen; chickens and swine; her grandfather was rich by local standards. There would be her father's blacksmithing tools, which Emil could learn to use.

They would need a television. Those were rare. A television, and solar cells, and a generator for the windmill; such manufactured goods had to be bought in the city, and that took money. The second crop would be needed this year, and a large one next spring, as well— and they would have to keep all the money they earned. She thrust that thought away, but her hand strayed toward the big sheath knife she wore on her belt.

We will manage, she thought. We will find the money. Children should not go without education. Television was not for entertainment. The programs relayed by the satellites gave weather reports and taught farming, ecology, engineering, metalwork—all the skills needed to live on Arrarat. They also taught reading and mathematics. Most of Kathryn's neighbors despised television and wouldn't have it in their houses, but their children had to learn from others who watched the screen.

And yet, Kathryn thought, there is cause for concern. First it is television. Then light industry. Soon there is more. Mines are opened. Larger factories are built, and around them grow cities. She thought of Arrarat covered with cities and concrete, the animals replaced by tractors and automobiles, the small villages grown into cities; people packed together the way they were in Harmony and Garrison; streams dammed and lakes dirty with sewage; and she shuddered. Not in my time, or my grandchildren's. And perhaps we will be smarter than they were on Earth, and it will never happen here. We know better now. We know how to live with the land.

Her grandfather had been a volunteer colonist, an engineer with enough money to bring tools and equipment to Arrarat, and he was trying to show others how to live with technology. He had a windmill for electricity. It furnished power for the television and the radio. He had radio communications with Denisburg, forty kilometers away, and although the neighbors said they despised all technology, they were not too proud to ask Amos Malcolm to send messages for them.

The Malcolm farm had running water and an efficient system for converting sewage to fertilizer. To Amos, technology was something to be used so long as it did not use you, and he tried to teach his neighbors that.

The phone buzzed to interrupt her thoughts, and Kathryn halted the team. The phone was in the center of the plowed land, where it was plugged into a portable solar reflector that kept its batteries charged. There were very few radio-phones in the valley. They cost a great deal and could only be bought in Harmony. Even her grandfather Amos couldn't manufacture the phone's microcircuits, although he often muttered about buying the proper tools and making something that would be as good. "After all," he was fond of saying, "we do not need the very latest. Only something that will do."

Before she reached the phone, she heard the gun-shots. They sounded far away, but they came from the direction of her home. She looked toward the hill that hid the ranch from her, and a red trail streaked sky-ward. It exploded in a cloud of bright smoke. Amos had sent up a distress rocket. "God, no!" Kathryn screamed. She ran for the phone, but she dropped it in her haste. She scrabbled it up from the freshly plowed dirt and shouted into it. "Yes!"

"Go straight to the village, child," her grandfather's voice told her. He sounded very old and tired. "Do not come home. Go quickly."

"Grandfather—"

"Do as I say! The neighbors will come, and you cannot help."

"But—"

"Kathryn." He spoke urgently, but there were centu-ries in the voice. "They are here. Many of them."

"Who?" she demanded.

"Convicts. They claim to be sheriffs, executing a writ for collection of taxes. I will not pay. My house is strong, Kathryn, and the neighbors will come. The convicts will not get in, and if they kill me now it is no great matter—"

"And mother!" Kathryn shouted.

"They will not take her alive," Amos Malcolm said. "We have talked of this, and you know what I will do. Please. Do not make my whole life meaningless by letting them get you as well. Go to the village, and God go with you. I must fight now."

There were more sounds of firing in the distance. The phone was silent. Then there were rifle shots, plus the harsh stammer of a machine gun. Amos had good defenses for his stone ranch house.

Kathryn heard grenades, sharp explosions, but not loud, and she prayed that she would not hear the final explosion that meant Amos had set off the dynamite under his house. He had often sworn that before he would let anyone take his home, he would blow it and them to hell.

Kathryn ran back to unhitch the oxen. They would be safe enough. The sounds of firing would keep them from going home until the next day, and here on the plains there were no animals large enough to be a threat to healthy oxen. None except men.

She left the team standing beside the plow, their eyes puzzled because the sun was high and the field was not yet plowed, and she ran to the shade trees by the creek. A horse and dog waited patiently there. The dog jumped up playfully, but he sank onto the ground and cringed as he sensed her mood.

Kathryn hurled the saddle onto the horse and fumbled with the leather straps. Her hands were moving so quickly that even familiar motions were difficult, and she was clumsy in her haste. She tied the phone and solar reflector in place behind the saddle and mounted. There was a rifle in the saddle scabbard, and she took it out and fingered it longingly.

Then she hesitated. The guns were still firing. She still heard her grandfather's machine gun and more grenades, and that meant that Amos was alive. *I should help*, she thought. *I should go.*

Emil will be there. He was to plow the field next to our boundary, and he will have heard. He will be there. She turned the horse toward the ranch.

One rider can do no good, she realized. But though she knew that, she knew she must go to her home before it was too late. They would have a good chance, Emil and her grandfather. The house was strong, made of good stone, low to the ground, much of it buried in the earth, sod roof above waterproof plastic. It would withstand raiders. It had before, many times, but there were very many rifles firing now and she could not remember that large a raid before. Not here, and not anywhere.

The phone buzzed again. "Yes!" she shouted. "What is happening?"

"Ride, girl! Ride! Do not disobey my last command. You are all I have—" The voice broke off before Amos said more, and Kathryn held the silent phone and stared at it.

"All I have," Amos had said. Her mother and her brother were dead, then.

She screamed words of hatred and rode toward the sound of the guns. As she crossed over the creek she heard mortars firing, then louder explosions.

Two hundred riders converged on the Malcolm ranch. They rode hard, their horses drenched in sweat, and they came by families, some with their women, all with their oldest boys. Brown dogs ran ahead of them. Their panting tongues hung out between bared fangs as the dogs sensed the anger their masters projected. As the families of riders saw each other, they waved and kicked their horses into an even faster pace.

The riders approached the final rise before the Malcolm ranch and slowed to a trot. There were no sounds from over the hill. Shouted commands sent the dogs ahead. When the loping brown forms went over the hill without halting, the riders kicked their horses back to the gallop and rode on.

"He didn't use the dynamite," George Woodrow said. "I heard explosions, but not Amos's magazines." His neighbors didn't answer. They rode down the hill toward the ranch house.

There was the smell of explosives in the air, mixed with the bright copper smell of fresh blood. The dogs loped among dead men who lay around the stone house. The big front door stood open, and more dead lay in front of that. A girl in bloodstained coveralls and muddy boots sat in the dirt by the open door. She cradled a boy's head in her arms. She rocked gently, not aware of the motion, and her eyes were dry and bright.

"My God!" George Woodrow shouted. He dismounted and knelt beside her. His hand reached out toward the boy, but he couldn't touch him. "Kathryn—"

"They're all dead," Kathryn said. "Grandfather, mother, my brother, and Emil. They're all dead." She spoke calmly, telling George Woodrow of his son's death as she might tell him that there would be a dance at the church next Saturday.

George looked at his dead son and the girl who would have borne his grandchildren. Then he stood and leaned his face against his saddle. He remained that way for a long time. Gradually he became aware that others were talking.

"—caught them all outside except Amos," Harry Seeton said. He kept his voice low, hoping that Kathryn and George Woodrow wouldn't hear. "I think Amos shot Jeanine after they'd grabbed her. How in hell did anyone sneak up on old Amos?"

"Found a dog with an arrow in him back there," Wan Loo said. "A crossbow bolt. Perhaps that is how."

"I still don't understand it," Seeton insisted.

"Go after them!" Kathryn stood beside her dead fiancé. "Ride!"

"We will ride," Wan Loo said. "When it is time."

"Ride now!" Kathryn demanded.

"No." Harry Seeton shook his head sadly. "Do you think this was the only place raided today? A dozen more. Most did not even fight. There are hundreds more raiders, and they will have joined together by now. We cannot ride until there are more of us."

"And then what?" George Woodrow asked. His voice was bitter. "By the time there are enough of us, they will be in the hills again." He looked helplessly at the line of high foothills just at the horizon. "God! Why?"

"Do not blaspheme." The voice was strident. Roger Dornan wore dark clothing, and his face was lean and narrow. *He looks like an undertaker,* Kathryn thought. "The ways of the Lord are not to be questioned," Dornan intoned.

"We don't need that talk, Brother Dornan," Kathryn said. "We need revenge! I thought we had *men* here! George, will you ride with me to hunt your son's murderer?"

"Put your trust in the Lord," Dornan said. "Lay this burden on His shoulders."

"I cannot allow you to ride," Wan Loo said. "You and George would be killed, and for what? You gain no revenge by throwing yourself at their guns." He motioned, and two of his sons went to hold Kathryn's horse. Another took George Woodrow's mount and led it away. "We need all our farmers," Wan Loo said. "And what would become of George's other children? And his wife with the unborn child? You cannot go."

"Got a live one," a rider called. Two men lifted a still figure from the ground. They carried him over to where the others had gathered around Kathryn and George Woodrow, then dropped him into the dirt. Wan Loo knelt and felt for the pulse. Then he seized the raider's hair and lifted the head. Methodically he slapped the face. His fingers left vivid red marks on the too-white flesh. Smack, smack! Forehand, backhand, methodically, and the raider's head rocked with each blow.

"He's about gone," Harry Seeton said.

"All the more reason he should be awakened," Wan Loo said. He ignored the spreading bloodstains on the raider's leather jacket, and turned him face down into the dirt. He seized an arm and twisted violently. The raider grunted.

The raider was no older than twenty. He had a short scraggly beard, not well developed. He wore dark trousers and a leather jacket and soft leather boots much like Kathryn's. There were marks on his fingers, discolorations where rings had been, and his left earlobe was torn.

"They stripped their own dead and wounded," Woodrow grunted. "What all did they get?"

"The windmill generator," Harry Seeton reported. "And all the livestock, and some of the electronics. The phone's gone, too. Wonder why Amos didn't blow the place?"

"Shaped charge penetrated the wall," one of the riders said. "Killed Amos at his gun."

"Leggo. Stop." The young raider moaned. "That hurts."

"He is coming awake," Wan Loo told them. "But he will not last long."

"Pity," George Woodrow said. He bent down and slapped the boy's face. "Wake up, damn you! I want you to feel the rope around your neck! Harry, get a rope."

"You must not," Brother Dornan said. "Vengeance is the Lord's—"

"We'll just help the Lord out a bit," Woodrow said. "Get a rope!"

"Yeah," Seeton said. "I guess. Kathryn?"

"Get it. Give it to me. I want to put it around his neck." She looked down at the raider. "Why?" she demanded. "Why?"

For a moment the boy's eyes met hers. "Why not?"

Three men dug graves on the knoll above the valley. Kathryn came up the hill silently, and they did not see her at first. When they did they stopped working, but she said nothing, and after a while they dug again. Their shovels bit into the rich soil.

"You're digging too many graves," Kathryn said. "Fill one in."

"But—"

"My grandfather will not be buried here," Kathryn said.

The men stopped digging. They looked at the girl and her bloodstained coveralls, then glanced out at the horizon where the rest of the commandos had gone. There was dust out there. The riders were coming home. They wouldn't have caught the raiders before they went into the hills.

One of the gravediggers made a silent decision. Next spring he would take his family and find new lands. It would be better than this. But he wondered if the convicts would not follow wherever he went. When men work the earth, others will come to kill and steal.

"Where?" he asked finally.

"Bury Amos in his doorway," Kathryn said.

"That is a terrible thing, to bury a man in his own door. He will not rest—"

"I don't want him to rest," Kathryn said. "I want him to walk! I want him to walk and remind us all of what Earth has done to us!"

IV

"HEAR THIS. ALL hands brace for reentry. Hear this."

"Seat straps, Lieutenant," Sergeant Cernan said.

"Right." I pulled the shoulder straps down into place and latched them, then looked out at Ararat.

The planet had a bleak look, not like Earth. There were few clouds, and lots of desert. There were also heavy jungle forests near the equator. The only cultivated lands I could see were on a narrow strip at the northern edge of a nearly landlocked sea. South of the sea was another continent. It looked dry and dusty, desert land where men had left no mark in passing—if anyone had ever been there at all.

Northward and westward from the cultivated strip were hills and forests, high desert plateaus, high mountains, and ragged canyons. There were streaks through the forests and across the hills, narrow roads not much more than tracks. When the troopship got lower I could see villages and towns, and every one of them had walls or a stockade and ditch. They looked like tiny fortresses.

The ship circled until it had lost enough speed to make a landing approach. Then it ran eastward, and we could see the city. My briefing folio said it was the only city on Ararat. It stood on a high bluff above the sea, and it seemed huddled in on itself. It looked like a medieval walled town, but it was made of modern concrete, and adobe with plastic waterproofing, and other materials medieval craftsmen probably wouldn't have used if they'd had them.

As the ship passed over the city at two thousand meters, it became obvious that there were really two cities run together, with only a wall between them. Neither was very large. The oldest part of the city, Harmony, showed little evidence of planning: there were little narrow streets running at all angles, and the public squares were randomly placed. The northern part, Garrison, was smaller, but it had streets at precise right angles, and a big public plaza stood opposite the square fort at the northern edge.

All the buildings were low, with only a couple more than two stories high. The roofs were red tile, and the walls were whitewashed. Harmony reminded me of towns I'd seen in Mexico. Bright sun shone off the bay below the city bluff. Garrison was a harsher place, all right angles, neat and orderly, but everything strictly functional. There was a square fortress at its northern edge. My new home.

I was a very junior lieutenant of CoDominium Marines, only three months out of the Academy and green as grass. It was Academy practice to commission the top thirty graduates in each class. The rest went out as cadets and midshipmen for more training. I was proud of the bars on my epaulets, but I was also a bit scared. I'd never been with troops before, and I'd never had any friends from the working classes, so I didn't know much about the kind of people who enlist in the Line Marines. I knew plenty of stories, of course. Men join to get away from their wives, or because some judge gives them a chance to enlist before passing sentence. Others are recruited out of Bureau of Relocation ships. Most come from Citizen classes, and my family's always been taxpayer.

It was just as well for me that my father was a taxpayer. I grew up in the American Southwest, where things haven't changed so much since the CoDominium. We still think we're free men. When my father died, Mom and I tried to run the ranch the way he had, as if it still belonged to us. It did, on paper, but we didn't have his contacts in the bureaucracy. We didn't understand all the regulations and labor restrictions, and we didn't know who to bribe when we broke the rules. When we got in real trouble, I tried to keep the government people from taking possession, and that wasn't too good an idea. The judge was an old friend of my father's and offered to get me into the Academy. U.S. courts don't have jurisdiction over CoDominium officers.

I didn't have a lot of choices, and CD Fleet service looked pretty good just then. I'd not only get out of trouble; I'd leave Earth. Mom was getting married again, so she'd be all right. The government had the ranch and we'd never get it back. I was young enough to think soldiering was a romantic idea, and Judge Hamilton made it pretty clear I was going to have to do something.

"Look, Hal," he told me, "your dad should have left. There's no place for people like us. They want people who want security, who'll obey the rules—people who *like* the welfare state, not ornery cusses like you and your father. Even if I can get you off this time, you'll get in trouble again. You're going to have to leave, and you'll be better off as a CD officer than as a colonist."

He was right. I wondered why he stayed. Same reason my father did, I supposed. Getting older, used to his home, not ready to go make a new start somewhere else. I hadn't said anything, but he must have guessed what I was thinking.

"I can still do some good here. I'm a judge for life— they can't take that away from me without damned good reasons—and I can still help kids like you. There's nothing here for you, Hal. The future's out there. New worlds, new ones found every year. Serve out a hitch in the Fleet service. See what's out there, and decide where you want your kids to grow up. Someplace free."

I couldn't think of anything else to do, so I let him get me into the Academy. It had been all right there. The Fleet has its own brotherhood. I'd been a loner most of my life, not because I wanted to be—God knows I would have liked to have friends!—but because I didn't fit in anywhere. The Academy was different.

It's hard to say how. One thing, though, there aren't any incompetents whining to have the world take care of them. Not that we didn't look out for each other. If a classmate's soft on math, you help him, and if somebody has trouble with electronics—I did—a sharper classmate sits up nights boning up with him. But if after all that he can't cut it, he's out. There's more to it than that, though. I can't explain the Fleet's sense of brotherhood, but it's real enough, and it was what I'd been looking for all my life.

I was there two and a half years, and we worked all the time, cramming everything from weapons maintenance to basic science to civil engineering and road construction. I finished seventh in the class and got my commission. After a month's leave to say goodbye to my mother and my girl—only I didn't really have a girl; I just liked to pretend I did—I was on an Olympic Lines passenger ship headed for another star system.

And now I'm here, I thought. I looked down at the planet, trying to spot places I'd seen on the maps in our briefing kit. I was also listening to the troopers in the compartment. The instructors at the Academy had told us that officers could learn a lot by listening to the men, and I hadn't had much opportunity to listen to these. Three weeks before I'd been on the passenger ship, and now I was at the end of nowhere on an ancient troop carrier, with a detachment commander who'd kept us training so hard there'd been no time for talk or anything else.

There were only a few viewports in the compartment, and those were taken by officers and senior enlisted men. Behind me, Sergeant Cernan was describing what he saw. A number of younger Marines, recruits mostly, were crowded around him. The older troopers were catching naps in their seats.

"Not much outside the city walls," Cernan said. "Trees, look like scrub oaks. And I think those others are olives. There's palms, too. Must be from Earth. Never saw palm trees that didn't come from Earth."

"Hey, Sarge, can you see the fort?" Corporal Roff asked.

"Yeah. Looks like any CD post. You'll be right at home."

"Sure we will," Roff said. "Sure. Christ, why us?"

"Your birthday present," Cernan said. "Just be damned glad you'll be leavin' someday. Think of them poor bastards back aft in the can."

The ship circled the harbor, then glided in on its stubby wings to settle into the chop outside the breakwater. The waves were two meters high and more, and the ship rolled badly. One of the new recruits was sick. His seatmate handed him a plastic bag.

"Hey, Dietz!" Roff called. "Want some fried bacon? A little salt pork?" He grinned. "Maybe some sow belly—"

"Sergeant Cernan."

"Sir!"

The captain didn't say anything else. He sat forward, a dozen rows in front of me, and I hadn't expected him to be listening, but I wasn't surprised. I'd learned in the past three weeks that not much went on without Captain John Christian Falkenberg finding out.

Behind me, Cernan said, very tight-lipped, "Roff, one more word out of you—"

Dietz's buddy found another bag. No one else kidded the sick recruits. Soon the shuttle moved into the inner harbor, where there were no waves, and everyone felt better. A lone tugboat came alongside and eased the spacecraft toward a concrete pier. There was no other traffic in the harbor except for a few small fishing boats.

A Navy officer came into the compartment and looked around until he found Falkenberg. "Sir, the Governor requests that you turn your men out under arms to assist in the prisoner formation."

Falkenberg turned toward the Navy man and raised an eyebrow. Then he nodded. "Sergeant Major!"

"Sir!" Ogilvie shouted from the rear of the compartment.

"Personal weapons for all troops. Rifles and cartridge belts. And bayonets, Sergeant Major. Bayonets, by all means."

"Sir." There was a bustle of activity as Sergeant Major Ogilvie and his weapons sergeants unlocked the arms chest and began passing out rifles.

"What about our other gear?" Falkenberg asked.

"You'll have to make arrangements with the garrison," the ship's officer said.

"Right. That's all, then?"

"Yes. That's all, Major."

I grinned as the Navyman left the compartment. To the Navy there's only one captain aboard ship, and that's the skipper. Marine captains in transit get a very temporary and utterly meaningless "promotion" to major for the duration of the voyage.

Falkenberg went to the forward hatchway. "Lieutenant Slater. A moment, please."

"Sir." I went forward to join him. I hadn't really noticed the low gravity until I stood up, but now it was obvious. It was only eighty-five-percent Earth standard, and on the trip out, Falkenberg had insisted the Navy skipper keep the outer rim of the old troopship at 110 percent spin gravity for as much of the trip as possible. The Navy hadn't liked it, but they'd done it, and Falkenberg had trained us in the high-gravity areas. Now we felt as if we could float away with no trouble.

I didn't know much about Falkenberg. The Service List showed he'd had Navy experience, then transferred to Fleet Marines. Now he was with a Line outfit. Moving around like that, two transfers, should have meant he was being run out, but then there was his rank. He also had a Military Cross, but the List hadn't said what it was for. It did tell me he'd gone into the Academy at fifteen and left as a midshipman.

I first saw him at Betio Transfer Station, which is an airless rock the Fleet keeps as a repair base and supply depot. It's convenient to several important star systems, but there's nothing there. I'd been on my way from graduation to Crucis Sector Headquarters, with assignment to the Fleet Marines. I was proud of that. Of the three Marine branches, Fleet is supposed to be the technical elite. Garrison outfits are mostly for riot suppression. The Line Marines get the dirty jobs left over. Line troops say theirs is the real elite, and they certainly do more than their share of the actual fighting when things are tough. I didn't know if we'd be fighting on Arrarat. I didn't even know why we were sent here. I just knew that Falkenberg had authority to change orders for all unassigned officers, and I'd been yanked off my comfortable berth—first class, damn it!—to report to him at Betio. If he knew what was up, he wasn't telling the junior officers.

Falkenberg wasn't a lot older than I was. I was a few weeks past my twenty-first birthday, and he was maybe five years older, a captain with the Military Cross. He must have had something going for him—influence, possibly, but if that was it, why was he with the Line Marines and not on staff at headquarters? I couldn't ask him. He didn't talk very much. He wasn't unfriendly, but he seemed cold and distant and didn't encourage anyone to get close to him.

Falkenberg was tall, but he didn't reach my height, which is 193 centimeters according to my ID card. We called it six-four where I grew up. Falkenberg was maybe two inches shorter. His eyes were indeterminate in color, sometimes gray and sometimes green, depending on the light, and they seemed very bright when he looked at you. He had short hair the color of sand, and no moustache. Most officers grow them after they make captain, but he hadn't.

His uniforms always fit perfectly. I thought I cut a good military figure, but I found myself studying the way Falkenberg dressed. I also studied his mannerisms, wondering if I could copy any of them. I wasn't sure I liked him or that I really wanted to imitate him, but I told myself that anybody who could make captain before he was thirty was worth at least a bit of study. There are plenty of forty-year-old lieutenants in the service.

He didn't look big or particularly strong, but I knew better. I'm no forty-four-kilo weakling, but he threw me easily in unarmed combat practice, and that was in 100 percent gravity.

He was grinning when I joined him at the forward

hatchway. "Ever think, Lieutenant, that every military generation since World War One has thought theirs would be the last to carry bayonets?" He waved toward where Ogilvie was still passing out rifles.

"No, sir, I never did."

"Few do," Falkenberg said. "My old man was a CoDominium University professor, and he thought I ought to learn military history. Think about it: a weapon originally designed to convert a musket into a pike, and it's still around when we're going to war in starships."

"Yes, sir—"

"Because it's useful, Lieutenant—as you'll find out someday." The grin faded, and Falkenberg lowered his voice. "I didn't call you up here to discuss military history, of course. I want the men to see us in conference. Give them something to worry about. They know they're going ashore armed."

"Yes, sir—"

"Tell me, Harlan Slater, what do they call you?"

"Hal, sir." We had been aboard ship for twenty-one days, and this was the first time Falkenberg had asked. It says a lot about him.

"You're senior lieutenant," Falkenberg said.

"Yes, sir." Which wasn't saying much: the other lieutenants had all been classmates at the Academy, and I outranked them only because I'd graduated higher in the class.

"You'll collect the other officers and stay here at the gangway while we go through this prisoner formation. Then bring up the rear as we take the troops up the hill to the fort. I doubt there's transport, so we'll have to march."

"Yes, sir."

"You don't understand. If you don't understand something, ask about it. Have you noticed our troopers, Mr. Slater?"

"Frankly, Captain, I haven't had enough experience to make any kind of judgment," I said. "We have a lot of recruits—"

"Yes. I'm not worried about them. Nor about the regulars I brought with me to Betio. But for the rest, we've got the scrapings out of half the guardhouses in the Sector. I doubt they'll desert during their first hours ashore, but I'm going to make damned sure. Their gear will stay aboard this ship, and we'll march them up in formation. By dark I'll have turned this command over to Colonel Harrington and it will be his worry, but until then I'm responsible, and I'll see that every man gets to the fort."

"I see. Yes, sir." And that's why he's a captain at his age, on independent assignment at that. Efficient. I wanted to be like that, or thought I did. I wasn't quite sure what I really wanted. The CD Armed Services wasn't my idea, but now that I was in it, I wanted to do it right if I could. I had my doubts about some of the things the CoDominium did—I was glad that I hadn't been assigned to one of the regiments that puts down riots on Earth—but I didn't know what ought to replace the CD and the Grand Senate, either. After all, we did keep the peace, and that has to be worth a lot.

"They're opening the gangway," Falkenberg said. "Sergeant Major."

"Sir!"

"Column of fours in company order, please."

"Sir." Ogilvie began shouting orders. The troops marched down the gangway and onto the concrete pier below. I went out onto the gangway to watch.

It was hot outside and within minutes I was sweating. The sun seemed red-orange, and very bright. After the smells of the troopship, with men confined with too little water for adequate washing, the planetary smells were a relief. Arrarat had a peculiar odor, slightly sweet, like flowers, with an undertone of wet vegetation. All that was mixed with the stronger smells of a salt sea and the harbor.

There were few buildings down at sea level. The city wall stood high above the harbor at the top of its bluff. Down on the level strip just above the sea were piers and warehouses, but the streets were wide and there were large spaces between buildings.

My first alien world. It didn't seem all that strange. I looked for something exotic, like sea creatures, or strange plants, but there weren't any visible from the gangway. I told myself all that would come later.

There was one larger structure at sea level. It was two stories high, with no windows facing us. It had big gates in the center of the wall facing the ship, with a guard tower at each of its corners. It looked like a prison, and I knew that was what it had to be, but there seemed no point in that. The whole planet was a prison.

There was a squad of local militiamen on the pier. They wore drab coveralls, which made quite a contrast to the blue and scarlet undress of the CoDominium Marines marching down the pier. Falkenberg talked with the locals for a moment, and then Sergeant Major Ogilvie shouted orders, and the Marines formed up in a double line that stretched up the dock to the aft gangway. The line went from the gangway to the big gates in the prison building. Ogilvie shouted more orders, and the Marines fixed bayonets.

They did it well. You'd never have known most of them were recruits. Even in the cramped quarters of the troop carrier, Falkenberg had drilled them into a smart-looking unit. The cost had been high. There were twenty-eight suicides among the recruits, and another hundred had been washed out and sent back among the convicts. They told us at the Academy that the only way to make a good Marine is to work him in training until he can have some pride in surviving it, and God knows Falkenberg must have believed that. It had seemed reasonable enough back in the lecture theater at Luna Base.

One morning we had four suicides, and one had been an old Line regular, not a recruit at all. I'd been duty officer when the troops found the body. It had been cut down from where he'd hanged himself to a light fixture, and the rope was missing. I tried to find the rope and even paraded all the men in that compartment, but nobody was saying anything.

Later Sergeant Major Ogilvie came to me in confidence. "You'll never find the rope, Lieutenant," he said. "It's cut up in a dozen pieces by now. That man had won the military medal. The rope he hanged himself with? That's lucky, sir. They'll keep the pieces."

All of which convinced me I had a lot to learn about Line Marines.

The forward companionway opened, and the convicts came out. Officially they were all convicts, or families of transportees who had voluntarily accompanied a convict; but when we'd gone recruiting in the prison section of the ship, we found a number of prisoners who'd never been convicted of anything at all. They'd been scooped up in one of Bureau of Relocation's periodic sweeps and put on the involuntary colonist list.

The prisoners were ragged and unwashed. Most wore BuRelock coveralls. Some carried pathetically small bundles, everything they owned. They milled around in confusion in the bright sunlight until ship's petty officers screamed at them and they shuffled down the gangway and along the pier. They tended to huddle together, shrinking away from the bayonets of the lines of troops on either side. Eventually they were herded through the big square gates of the prison building. I wondered what would happen to them in there.

There were more men than women, but there were plenty of women and girls. There were also far more children than I liked to see in that condition. I didn't like this. I hadn't joined the CoDominium Armed Services for this kind of duty.

"Heavy price, isn't it?" a voice said behind me. It was Deane Knowles. He'd been a classmate at the Academy. He was a short chap, not much above the minimum height for a commission, and had features so fine that he was almost pretty. I had reason to know that women liked him, and Deane liked them. He should have graduated second in the class, but he'd accumulated so many demerits for sneaking off bounds to see his girlfriends that he was dropped twenty-five places in class rank, which was why I outranked him and would until one of us was promoted above the other. I figured he'd make captain before I did.

"Heavy price for what?" I asked.

"For clean air and lower population and all the other

goodies they have back on Earth. Sometimes I wonder if it's worth it."

"But what choices do we have?" I asked.

"None. Zero. Nothing else to do. Ship out the surplus and let 'em make their own way somewhere. In the long run it's not only all to the good, it's all there is; but the run doesn't look so long when you're watching the results. Look out. Here comes Louis."

Louis Bonneyman, another classmate, joined us. Louis had finished a genuine twenty-fourth in class rank. He was part French-Canadian, although he'd been raised in the U.S. most of his life. Louis was a fanatic CD loyalist and didn't like to hear any of us question CD policy, although, like the rest of us in the service, it didn't really matter what the policies were. "No politics in the Fleet" was beaten into our heads at the Academy, and later the instructors made it clear that what that really translated to was: "The Fleet is Our Fatherland." We could question anything the Grand Senate did—as long as we stood by our comrades and obeyed orders.

We stood there watching as the colonists were herded into the prison building. It took nearly an hour to get all two thousand of them inside. Finally the gates were closed. Ogilvie gave more orders and the Marines scabbarded their bayonets, then formed into a column of eight and marched down the road.

"Well, fellow musketeers," I said, "here we go. We're to follow up the hill, and there's apparently no transport."

"What about my ordnance?" Deane asked.

I shrugged. "Apparently arrangements will be made. In any event, it's John Christian Falkenberg's problem. Ours not to reason why—"

"Ours but to watch for deserters," Louis Bonneyman said. "And we'd best get at it. Is your sidearm loaded?"

"Oh, come on, Louis," Deane said.

"Notice," Louis said. "See how Falkenberg has formed up the troops. Recall that their baggage is still aboard. You may not like Falkenberg, Deane, but you will admit that he is thorough."

"As it happens, Louis is right," I said. "Falkenberg

did say something about deserters. But he didn't think there'd be any."

"There you are," Louis said. "He takes no chances, that one."

"Except with us," Deane Knowles said.

"What do you mean by that?" Louis let the smile fade and lifted an eyebrow at Deane.

"Oh, nothing," Deane said. "Not much Falkenberg could do about it, anyway. But I don't suppose you chaps know what the local garrison commander asked for?"

"No, of course not," Louis said.

"How did you find out?" I asked.

"Simple. When you want to know something military, talk to the sergeants."

"Well?" Louis demanded.

Deane grinned. "Come on, we'll get too far behind. Looks as if we really will march all the way up the hill, doesn't it? Not even transport for officers. Shameful."

"Damn your eyes, Deane!" I said.

Knowles shrugged. "Well, the Governor asked for a full regiment and a destroyer. Instead of a regiment and a warship, he got us. Might be interesting if he really needed a regiment, eh? Coming, fellows?"

V

"I'VE A HEAD like a concertina,
   And I think I'm going to die,
   And I'm here in the clink for a thunderin' drink,
   And blackin' the corporal's eye. . . ."

"Picturesque," Louis said. "They sing well, don't they?"

"Shut up and walk," Deane told him. "It's bloody hot."

I didn't find it so bad. It was hot. No question about that, and undress blues were never designed for route marches on hot planets. Still, it could have been worse. We might have turned out in body armor.

There was no problem with the troops. They marched and sang like regulars, even if half of them were recruits and the rest were guardhouse cases. If any of them had ideas of running, they never showed them.

"With another man's cloak underneath my head,
   And a beautiful view of the yard,
   It's thirty day's fine,
   With bread and no wine,
   For Drunk and Resistin' the Guard!
   Mad-drunk and Resistin' the Guard!"

"Curious," Louis said. "Half of them have never seen a guardhouse."

51

"I expect they'll find out soon enough," Deane said. "Lord love us, will you look at that?"

He gestured at a row of cheap adobe houses along the riverbank. There wasn't much doubt about what they sold. The girls were dressed for hot weather, and they sat on the windowsills and waved at the troopers going by.

"I thought Arrarat was full of holy Joes," Louis Bonneyman said. "Well, we will have no difficulty finding any troopers who run—not for the first night, anyway."

The harbor area was just north of a wide river that fanned into a delta east of the city. The road was just inland from the harbor, with the city a high bluff to our right as we marched inland. It seemed a long way before we got to the turnoff to the city gate.

There were facilities for servicing the space shuttle, and some riverboat docks and warehouses, but it seemed to me there wasn't a lot of activity, and I wondered why. As far as I could remember, there weren't any railroads on Arrarat, nor many highways, and I couldn't remember seeing any airfields, either.

After a kilometer of marching inland, we turned sharply right and followed another road up the bluff. There was a rabbit warren of crumbling houses and alleys along the bluff, then a clear area in front of the high city wall. Militiamen in drab coveralls manned a guardhouse at the city gate. Other militiamen patrolled the wall. Inside the gate was Harmony, another warren of houses and shops not a lot different from those outside, but a little better kept up.

The main road had clear area for thirty meters on each side, and beyond that was chaos. Market stalls, houses, tailor shops, electronics shops, a smithy with hand bellows and forge, a shop that wound electric motors and another that sold solar cells, a pottery with kick-wheel where a woman shaped cups from clay, a silversmith, a scissors grinder—the variety was overwhelming, and so was the contrast of modern and the kinds of things you might see in Frontierland.

There were anachronisms everywhere, but I was used

to them. The military services were shot through with contrasts. Part of it was the state of development out in the colonies—many of them had no industrial base, and some didn't want any to begin with. If you didn't bring it with you, you wouldn't have it. There was another reason, too. CoDominium Intelligence licensed all scientific research and tried to suppress anything that could have military value. The U.S.-Soviet alliance was on top and wasn't about to let any new discoveries upset the balance. They couldn't stop everything, but they didn't have to, so long as the Grand Senate controlled everyone's R&D budget and could tinker with the patent laws.

We all knew it couldn't last, but we didn't want to think about that. Back on Earth the U.S. and Soviet governments hated each other. The only thing they hated more was the idea that someone else—like the Chinese or Japanese or United Emirates—would get strong enough to tell them what to do. The Fleet guards an uneasy peace built on an uneasy alliance.

The people of Harmony came in all races and colors, and I heard a dozen languages shouted from shop to shop. Everyone either worked outside his house or had market stalls there. When we marched past, people stopped work and waved at us. One old man came out of a tailor shop and took off his broad-brimmed hat. "God bless you, soldiers!" he shouted. "We love you!"

"Now, that's what we joined up for," Deane said. "Not to herd a bunch of losers halfway across the Galaxy."

"Twenty parsecs isn't halfway across the Galaxy," I told him.

He made faces at me.

"I wonder why they're all so glad to see us?" Louis asked. "And they look hungry. How does one become so thin in an agricultural paradise?"

"Incredible," Deane said. "Louis, you really must learn to pay attention to important details. Such as reading the station roster of the garrison here."

"And when could I have done that?" Bonneyman demanded. "Falkenberg had us working twelve hours a day—"

"So you use the other twelve," Deane said.

"And what, O brilliant one, didst thou learn from the station roster?" I asked.

"That the garrison commander is over seventy, and he has one sixty-three-year-old major on his staff, as well as a sixty-two-year-old captain. Also, the youngest Marine officer on Arrarat is over sixty, and the only junior officers are militia."

"Bah. A retirement post," Bonneyman said. "So why did they ask for a regiment?"

"Don't be silly, Louis," Deane said. "Because they've run into something they can't handle with their militia and their superannuated officers, of course."

"Meaning we'll have to," I said. Only, of course, we didn't have a regiment, only less than a thousand Marines, three junior officers, a captain with the Military Cross, and—well, and nothing, unless the local militia were capable of something. "The heroes have arrived."

"Yes. Nice, isn't it?" Deane said. "I expect the women will be friendly."

"And is that all you ever think about?" Louis demanded.

"What else is there? Marching in the sun?"

A younger townman in dark clerical clothing stood at his table under the awning of a sidewalk café. He raised a hand in a gesture of blessing. There were more cheers from a group of children.

"Nice to be loved," Deane said.

Despite the way he said it, Deane meant that. It was nice to be loved. I remembered my last visit to Earth. There were a lot of places where CD officers didn't dare go without a squad of troopers. Out here the people wanted us. The paladins, I thought, and I laughed at myself because I could imagine what Deane and Louis would say if I'd said that aloud, but I wondered if they didn't think it, too.

"They don't seem to have much transport," Louis said.

"Unless you count those." Deane pointed to a watering trough where five horses were tied. There were also two camels, and an animal that looked like a clumsy combination of camel, moose, and mule, with big splayed feet and silly antlers.

That had to be an alien beast, the first thing I was certain was native to this planet. I wondered what they called it, and how it had been domesticated.

There was almost no motor transport: a few pickup trucks, and one old ground-effects car with no top; everything else was animal transport. There were wagons, and men on horseback, and two women dressed in coveralls and mounted on mules.

Bonneyman shook his head. "Looks as if they stirred up a brew from the American Wild West, medieval Paris, and threw in scenes from the Arabian Nights."

We all laughed, but Louis wasn't far wrong.

Arrarat was discovered soon after the first private exploration ships went out from Earth. It was an inhabitable planet, and although there are a number of those in the regions near Earth, they aren't all that common. A survey team was sent to find out what riches could be taken.

There weren't any. Earth crops would grow, and men could live on the planet, but no one was going to invest money in agriculture. Shipping foodstuffs through interstellar space is a simple way of going bankrupt unless there are nearby markets with valuable minerals and no agriculture. This planet had no nearby market at all.

The American Express Company owned settlement rights through discovery. AmEx sold the planet to a combine of churches. The World Federation of Churches named it Arrarat and advertised it as "a place of refuge for the unwanted of Earth." They began to raise money for its development, and since this was before the Bureau of Relocation began involuntary colonies, they had a lot of help. Charity, tithes, government grants, all helped, and then the church groups hit on the idea of a lottery. Prizes were free transportation to Arrarat for winners and their families; and there were plenty of people willing to trade Earth for a place where there was free land, plenty to eat, hard work, no government harrassment, and no pollution. The World Federation of Churches sold tens of millions of one-credit lottery tickets. They soon had enough money to charter ships and sent people out.

There was plenty of room for colonists, even though the inhabitable portion of Arrarat is comparatively small. The planet has a higher mean temperature than Earth, and the regions near the equator are far too hot for men to live in. At the very poles it is too cold. The southern hemisphere is nearly all water. Even so, there is plenty of land in the north temperate zone. The delta area where Harmony was founded was chosen as the best of the lot. It had a climate like the Mediterranean region of Earth. Rainfall was erratic, but the colony thrived.

The churches had very little money, but the planet didn't need heavy industry. Animals were shipped instead of tractors, on the theory that horses and oxen can make other horses and oxen, but tractors make only oil refineries and smog. Industry wasn't wanted; Arrarat was to be a place where each man could prune his own vineyard and sit in the shade of his fig tree. Some of the Federation of Churches' governing board actively hated industrial technology, and none loved it; and there was no need, anyway. The planet could easily support far more than the half to three-quarters of a million people the churches sent out as colonists.

Then the disaster struck. A survey ship found thorium and other valuable metals in the asteroid belt of Arrarat's system. It wasn't a disaster for everyone, of course. American Express was happy enough, and so was Kennicott Metals after they bought mining rights; but for the church groups it was disaster enough. The miners came, and with them came trouble. The only convenient place for the miners to go for recreation was Arrarat, and the kinds of establishments asteroid miners liked weren't what the Federation of Churches had in mind. The "Holy Joes" and the "Goddamns" shouted at each other and petitioned the Grand Senate for help, while the madams and gamblers and distillers set up for business.

That wasn't the worst of it. The Federation of

Churches' petition to the CoDominium Grand Senate ended up in the CD bureaucracy, and an official in Bureau of Corrections noticed that a lot of empty ships were going from Earth to Arrarat. They came back full of refined thorium, but they went out deadhead . . . and BuCorrect had plenty of prisoners they didn't know what to do with. It cost money to keep them. Why not, BuCorrect reasoned, send the prisoners to Arrarat and turn them loose? Earth would be free of them. It was humane. Better yet, the churches could hardly object to setting captives free. . . .

The BuCorrect official got a promotion, and Arrarat got over half a million criminals and convicts, most of whom had never lived outside a city. They knew nothing of farming, and they drifted to Harmony, where they tried to live as best they could. The result was predictable. Harmony soon had the highest crime rate in the history of man.

The situation was intolerable for Kennicott Metals. Miners wouldn't work without planet leave, but they didn't dare go to Harmony. Their union demanded that someone do something, and Kennicott appealed to the Grand Senate. A regiment of CoDominium Marines was sent to Arrarat. They couldn't stay long, but they didn't have to. They built walls around the city of Harmony, and for good measure they built the town of Garrison adjacent to it. Then the Marines put all the convicts outside the walls.

It wasn't intended to be a permanent solution. A CoDominium Governor was appointed, over the objections of the World Federation of Churches. The Colonial Bureau began preparations for sending a government team of judges and police and technicians and industrial-development specialists so that Arrarat could support the streams of people BuCorrect had sent. Before they arrived, Kennicott found an even more valuable source of thorium in a system nearer to Earth, the Arrarat mines were put into reserve, and there was no longer any reason for the CoDominium Grand Senate to be interested in Arrarat. The Marine garrison pulled out, leaving a cadre to help train colonial militia to defend the walls of Harmony-Garrison.

"What are you so moody about?" Deane asked.

"Just remembering what was in the briefing they gave us. You aren't the only one who studies up," I said.

"And what have you concluded?"

"Not a lot. I wonder how the people here like living in a prison. It's got to be that way, convicts outside and citizens inside. Marvelous."

"Perhaps they have a city jail," Louis said. "That would be a prison within a prison."

"Fun-ny," Deane said.

We walked along in silence, listening to the tramp of the boots ahead of us, until we came to another wall. There were guards at that gate, too. We passed through into the smaller city of Garrison.

"And why couldn't they have had transportation for officers?" Louis Bonneyman said. "There are trucks here."

There weren't many, but there were more than in Harmony. Most of the vehicles were surplus military ground-effects troop carriers. There were also more wagons.

"March or die, Louis. March or die." Deane grinned.

Louis said something under his breath. "March or Die" was a slogan of the old French Foreign Legion, and the Line Marines were direct descendants of the Legion, with a lot of their traditions. Bonneyman couldn't stand the idea that he wasn't living up to the service's standards.

Commands rattled down the ranks of marching men. "Look like Marines, damn you!" Ogilvie shouted.

"Falkenberg's showing off," Deane said.

"About time, too," Louis told him. "The fort is just ahead."

"Sound off!" Ogilvie ordered.

"We've left blood in the dirt of twenty-five worlds,
We've built roads on a dozen more,

And all that we have at the end of our hitch
Buys a night with a second-class whore.
The Senate decrees, the Grand Admiral calls,
The orders come down from on high.
It's 'On Full Kits' and 'Sound Board Ships,'
We're sending you where you can die."

Another Legion tradition, I thought. Over every orderly room door in Line regiments is a brass plaque. It
says: YOU ARE LINE MARINES IN ORDER TO DIE,
AND THE FLEET WILL SEND YOU WHERE YOU
CAN DIE. An inheritance from La Légion Etrangère.
The first time I saw it, I thought it was dashing and
romantic, but now I wondered if they meant it.

The troops marched in the slow cadence of the Line
Marines. It wasn't a fast pace, but we could keep it up
long after quick-marching troops keeled over from
exhaustion.

"The lands that we take, the Senate gives back,
Rather more often than not,
But the more that are killed, the less share the loot,
And we won't be back to this spot.
We'll break the hearts of your women and girls,
We may break your arse, as well,
Then the Line Marines with their banners unfurled
Will follow those banners to hell.
We know the devil, his pomps, and his works,
Ah, yes! We know them well!
When you've served out your hitch in the Line
Marines,
You can bugger the Senate of Hell!"

"An opportunity we may all have," Deane said. "Rather
sooner than I'd like. What *do* they want with us here?"
"I expect we'll find out soon enough," I said.

"Then we'll drink with our comrades and throw down
our packs,
We'll rest ten years on the flat of our backs,
Then it's 'On Full Kits' and out of your racks,

You must build a new road through Hell!
The Fleet is our country, we sleep with a rifle,
No man ever begot a son on his rifle,
They pay us in gin and curse when we sin,
There's not one that can stand us unless we're downwind,
We're shot when we lose and turned out when we win,
But we bury our comrades wherever they fall,
And there's none that can face us, though we've nothing at all."

VI

OFFICERS' ROW STRETCHED along the east side of the parade ground. The fort was nothing special. It hadn't been built to withstand modern weapons, and it looked a bit like something out of *Beau Geste*, which was reasonable, since it was built of local materials by officers with no better engineering education than mine. It's simple enough to lay out a rectangular walled fort, and if that's enough for the job, why make it more complicated?

The officers' quarters seemed empty. The fort had been built to house a regimental combat team with plenty of support groups, and now there were fewer than a dozen Marine officers on the planet. Most of them lived in family quarters, and the militia officers generally lived in homes in the city. It left the rest of us with lots of room to rattle around in. Falkenberg drew a suite meant for the regimental adjutant, and I got a major's rooms myself.

After a work party brought our personal gear up from the landing boat, I got busy and unpacked, but when I finished, the place still looked empty. A lieutenant's travel allowance isn't very large, and the rooms were too big. I stowed my gear and wondered what to do next. It seemed a depressing way to spend my first night on an alien world. Of course, I'd been to the Moon, and Mars, but those are different. They aren't worlds. You can't go outside, and you might as well be in a ship. I wondered if we'd be permitted off post—I was still thinking like a cadet, not an officer on field duty—and what I could do if we were. We'd had no instructions, and I decided I'd better wait for a briefing.

There was a quick knock on my door, and then it opened. An old Line private came in. He might have been my father. His uniform was tailored perfectly, but worn in places. There were hash marks from wrist to elbow.

"Private Hartz reporting, zur." He had a thick accent, but it wasn't pure anything; a lot of different accents blended together. "Sergeant Major sent me to be the lieutenant's dog-robber."

And what the hell do I do with him? I wondered. It wouldn't do to be indecisive. I couldn't remember if he'd been part of the detachment in the ship, or if he was one of the garrison. Falkenberg would never be in that situation. He'd know. The trooper was standing at attention in the doorway. "At ease, Hartz," I said. "What ought I to know about this place?"

"I don't know, zur."

Which meant he was a newcomer, or he wasn't spilling anything to officers, and I wasn't about to guess which. "Do you want a drink?"

"Thank you, yes, zur."

I found a bottle and put it out on the dressing stand. "Always leave two for me. Otherwise, help yourself," I told him.

He went to the latrine for glasses. I hadn't known there were any there, but then I wasn't all that familiar with senior officers' quarters. Maybe Hartz was, so I'd gained no information about him. He poured a shot for himself. "Is the lieutenant drinking?"

"Sure, I'll have one." I took the glass from him. "Cheers."

"*Prosit.*" He poured the whiskey down in one gulp. "I see the lieutenant has unpacked. I will straighten up now. By your leave, zur."

He wandered around the room, moving my spare boots two inches to the left, switching my combat armor from one side of the closet to the other, taking out my dress uniform and staring at it inch by inch.

I didn't need an orderly, but I couldn't just turn him out. I was supposed to get to know him, since he'd be with me on field duty. If any, I thought. To hell with it. "I'm going down to the officers' mess," I told him. "Help yourself to the bottle, but leave me two shots for tonight."

"Zur."

I felt like an idiot, chased out of my own quarters by my own batman, but I couldn't see what else to do. He was clearly not going to be satisfied until he'd gone over every piece of gear I had. Probably trying to impress me with how thorough he was. They pay dog-robbers extra, and it's always good duty for a drinking man. I was pretty sure I could trust him. I'd never crossed Ogilvie that I knew of. It takes a particularly stupid officer to get on the wrong side of the sergeant major.

It wasn't hard to find the officers' club. Like everything else, it had been built for a regiment, and it was a big building. I got a surprise inside. I was met by a Marine corporal I recognized as one of the detachment we'd brought with us. I started to go into the bar, where I saw a number of militia officers, and the corporal stopped me.

"Excuse me, sir. Marine club is that way." He pointed down the hall.

"I think I'd rather drink with the militiamen, Corporal."

"Yes, sir. Sergeant Major told me to be sure to tell all officers, sir."

"I see." I didn't see, but I wasn't going to get into an argument with a corporal, and there wasn't any point in being bullheaded. I went down the hall to the Marine club. Deane Knowles was already there. He was alone except for a waiter—another trooper from our detachment. In the militia bar the waiters were civilians.

"Welcome to the gay and merry life," Deane said. "Will you have whiskey? Or there's a peach brandy that's endurable. For God's sake, sit down and talk to me!"

"I take it you were intercepted by Corporal Hansner," I said.

"Quite efficiently. Now I know it is Fleet practice to

carry the military caste system to extremes, but this seems a bit much, even so. There are, what, a dozen Marine officers here, even including our august selves. So we immediately form our own club."

I shrugged. "Maybe it's the militiamen who don't care for us?"

"Nonsense. Even if they hated our guts, they'd want news from Earth. Meanwhile, we find out nothing about the situation here. What's yours?"

"I'll try your brandy," I told the waiter. "And who's the bartender when you're not on duty?"

"Don't know, sir. Sergeant Major sent me over—"

"Yes, of course." I waited for the trooper to leave. "And Sergeant Major takes care of us, he does, indeed. I have a truly formidable orderly—"

Deane was laughing. "One of the ancients? Yes. I thought so. As is mine. Monitor Armand Kubiak, at my service, sir."

"I only drew a private," I said.

"Well, at least Ogilvie has some sense of propriety," Deane said. "Cheers."

"Cheers. That's quite good, actually." I put the glass down and started to say something else, but Deane wasn't listening to me. He was staring at the door, and after a moment I turned to follow his gaze. "You know, I think that's the prettiest girl I ever saw."

"Certainly a contender," Deane said. "She's coming to our table."

"Obviously." We got to our feet.

She was definitely worth looking at. She wasn't very tall. Her head came about to my chin, so that with the slight heels on her sandals she was just taller than Deane. She wore a linen dress, blue to match her eyes, and it looked as if she'd never been out in the sun at all. The dress was crisp and looked cool. Few of the women we'd seen on the march in had worn skirts, and those had been long, drab cotton things. Her hair was curled into wisps around her shoulders. She had a big golden seal ring on her right hand.

She walked in as if she owned the place. She was obviously used to getting her own way.

"I hope you're looking for us," Deane said.

"As a matter of fact, I am." She had a very nice smile. An expensive smile, I decided.

"Well, you've excellent taste, anyway," Deane said.

I don't know how he gets away with it. I think it's telepathy. There's no particular cleverness to what he says to girls. I know, because I made a study of his technique when we were in the Academy. I thought I could learn it the way I was learning tactics, but it didn't work. What Deane says doesn't matter, and how he says it doesn't seem important. He'll chatter along, saying nothing, even being offensive, and the next thing you know the girl's leaving with him. If she has to ditch a date, that can happen, too.

I was damned if it was going to happen this time, but I had a sinking feeling, because I'd been determined before and it hadn't done me any good. I couldn't think of one thing to say to her.

"I'm Deane Knowles. And this is Lieutenant Slater," Deane said.

You rotten swine, I thought. I tried to smile as she offered her hand.

"And I'm Irina Swale."

"Surely you're the Governor's daughter, then," Deane said.

"That's right. May I sit down?"

"Please do." Deane held her chair before I could get to it. It made me feel awkward. We managed to get seated, and Private Donnelley came over.

"Jericho, please," Irina said.

Donnelley looked blankly at her.

"He came in with us," I said. "He doesn't know what you've ordered."

"It's a wine," she said. "I'm sure there will be several bottles. It isn't usually chilled."

"Yes, ma'am," Donnelley said. He went over to the bar and began looking at bottles.

"We were just wondering what to do," Deane said. "You've rescued us from terminal ennui."

She smiled at that, but there was a shadow behind

the smile. She didn't seem offended by us, but she wasn't really very amused. I wondered what she wanted.

Donnelley brought over a bottle and a wineglass. "Is this it, ma'am?"

"Yes. Thank you."

He put the glass on the table and poured. "If you'll excuse me a moment, Lieutenant Knowles?"

"Sure, Donnelley. Don't leave us alone too long, or we'll raid your bar."

"Yes, sir." Donnelley went out into the hall.

"Cheers," Deane said. "Tell us about the night life on Arrarat."

"It's not very pleasant," Irina said.

"Rather dull. Well, I guess we expected that—"

"It's not so much dull as horrible," Irina said. "I'm sorry. It's just that . . . I feel guilty when I think about my own problems. They're so petty. Tell me, when are the others coming?"

Deane and I exchanged glances. I started to say something, but Deane spoke first. "They don't tell us very much, you know."

"Then it's true—you are the only ones coming," she said.

"Now, I didn't say that," Deane protested. "I said I didn't know—"

"You needn't lie," she said. "I'm hardly a spy. You're all they sent, aren't you? No warship, and no regiment. Just a few hundred men and some junior officers."

"I'd have thought you'd know more than we do," I said.

"I just don't give up hope quite as quickly as my father does."

"I don't understand any of this," I said. "The Governor sent for a regiment, but nobody's told us what that regiment was supposed to do."

"Clean up the mess we've made of this planet," Irina said. "And I really thought they'd do something. The CoDominium has turned Arrarat into sheer hell, and I thought they'd have enough . . . what? Pride? Shame? Enough elementary decency to put things right before we pull out entirely. I see I was wrong."

"I take it things are pretty bad outside the walls," Deane said.

"Bad? They're horrible!" Irina said. "You can't even imagine what's happening out there. Criminal gangs setting themselves up as governments. And my father recognizes them as governments! We make treaties with them. And the colonists are ground to pieces. Murder's the least of it. A whole planet going to barbarism, and we don't even *try* to help them."

"But surely your militia can do something," Deane said.

"Not really." She shook her head, slowly, and stared into the empty wineglass. "In the first place, the militia won't go outside the walls. I don't suppose I blame them. They aren't soldiers. Shopkeepers, mostly. Once in a while they'll go as far as the big river bend, or down to the nearest farmlands, but that doesn't do any good. We tried doing something more permanent, but it didn't work. We couldn't protect the colonists from the convict gangs. And now we recognize convict gangsters as legal governments!"

Donnelley came back in and went to the bar. Deane signaled for refills.

"I noticed people came out to cheer us as we marched through the city," I said.

Irina's smile was bitter. "Yes. They think you're going to open up trade with the interior, rescue their relatives out there. I wish you could."

Before we could say anything else, Captain Falkenberg came in. "Good afternoon," he said. "May I join you?"

"Certainly, sir," Deane said. "This is Captain Falkenberg. Irina Swale, Captain, the Governor's daughter."

"I see. Good afternoon. Brandy, please, Donnelley. And will the rest of you join me? Excellent. Another round, please. Incidentally, my name is John. First names in the mess, Deane—except for the colonel."

"Yes, sir. Excuse me. John. Miss Swale has been telling us about conditions outside the walls. They're pretty bad."

"I gather. I've just spent the afternoon with the colonel. Perhaps we can do something, Miss Swale."

"Irina. First names in the mess." She laughed. It was a very nice laugh. "I wish you could do something for those people, but—well, you only have a thousand men."

"A thousand Line Marines," Falkenberg said. "That's not quite the same thing."

And we don't even have a thousand Marines, I told myself. Lot of recruits with us. I wondered what Falkenberg had in mind. Was he just trying to impress the Governor's daughter? I hoped not, because the way he'd said it made me feel proud.

"I gather you sympathize with the farmers out there," Falkenberg said.

"I'd have to, wouldn't I?" Irina said. "Even if they didn't come to me after Hugo—my father—says he can't help them. And I've tried to do something for the children. Do you really think—" She let her voice trail off.

Falkenberg shrugged. "Doubtless we'll try. We can put detachments out in some of the critical areas. As you said, there's only so much a thousand men can do, even a thousand Marines."

"And after you leave?" Irina said. Her voice was bitter. "They are pulling out, aren't they? You've come to evacuate us."

"The Grand Senate doesn't generally discuss high policy with junior captains," Falkenberg said.

"No, I suppose not. But I do know you brought orders from the Colonial Office, and Hugo took them into his office to read them—and he hasn't spoken to anyone since. All day he's been in there. It isn't hard to guess what they say." Irina sipped at the wine and stared moodily at the oak table. "Of course it's necessary to understand the big picture. What's one little planet with fewer than a million people? Arrarat is no threat to the peace, is it? But they are people, and they deserve something better than— Sorry. I'm not always like this."

"We'll have to think of something to cheer you up," Deane said. "Tell me about the gay social life of Arrarat."

She gave a half smile. "Wild. One continuous whirl

of grand balls and lewd parties. Just what you'd expect on a church-settled planet."

"Dullsville," Deane said. "But now that we're here—"

"I expect we can manage something," Irina said. "I tend to be Dad's social secretary. John, isn't it customary to welcome new troops with a formal party? We'll have to have one in the Governor's palace."

"It's customary," Falkenberg said. "But that's generally to welcome a regiment, not a random collection of replacements. On the other hand, since the replacements are the only military unit here—"

"Well, we do have our militia," Irina said.

"Sorry. I meant the only Line unit. I'm certain everyone would be pleased if you'd invite us to a formal ball. Can you arrange it for, say, five days from now?"

"Of course," she said. She looked at him curiously. So did the rest of us. It hadn't occurred to me that Falkenberg would be interested in something like that. "I'll have to get started right away, though."

"If that's cutting it too close," Falkenberg said, "we—"

"No, that will be all right."

Falkenberg glanced at his watch, then drained his glass. "One more round, gentlemen, and I fear I have to take you away. Staff briefing. Irina, will you need an escort?"

"No, of course not."

We chatted for a few minutes more, then Falkenberg stood. "Sorry to leave you alone, Irina, but we do have work to do."

"Yes. I quite understand."

"And I'll appreciate it if you can get that invitation made official as soon as possible," Falkenberg said. "Otherwise, we're likely to have conflicting duties, but, of course, we could hardly refuse the Governor's invitation."

"Yes, I'll get started right now," she said.

"Good. Gentlemen? We've a bit of work. Administration of the new troops and such. Dull, but necessary."

VII

THE CONFERENCE ROOM had a long table large enough
for a dozen officers, with chairs at the end for twice that
many more. There were briefing screens on two walls.
The others were paneled in some kind of rich wood
native to Ararat. There were scars on the paneling
where pictures and banners had hung. Now the panels
were bare, and the room looked empty and cold. The
only decoration was the CoDominium flag, American
eagle and Soviet hammer and sickle. It stood between
an empty trophy case and a bare corner.

Louis Bonneyman was already there. He got up as
we came in.

"There won't be many here," Falkenberg said. "You
may as well take places near the head of the table."

"Will you be regimental adjutant or a battalion commander?" Deane asked me. He pointed to senior officers' places.

"Battalion commander, by all means," I said. "Line
over staff any day. Louis, you can be intelligence officer."

"That may not seem quite so amusing in a few minutes," Falkenberg said. "Take your places, gentlemen."
He punched a button on the table's console. "And give
some thought to what you say."

I wondered what the hell he meant by that. It hadn't
escaped me that he'd known where to find us. Donnelley
must have called him. The question was, why?

"Ten-hut!"

70

We got up as Colonel Harrington came in. Deane had told me Harrington was over seventy, but I hadn't really believed it. There wasn't any doubt about it now. Harrington was short and his face had a pinched look. The little hair he had left was white.

Sergeant Major Ogilvie came in with him. He looked enormous when he stood next to the Colonel. He was almost as tall as Falkenberg, anyway, and a lot more massive, a big man to begin with. Standing next to Harrington, he looked liked a giant.

The third man was a major who couldn't have been much younger than the Colonel.

"Be seated, gentlemen," Harrington said. "Welcome to Arrarat. I'm Harrington, of course. This is Major Lorca, my Chief of Staff. We already know who you are."

We muttered some kind of response while Harrington took his seat. He sat carefully, the way you might in high gravity, only, of course, Arrarat isn't a high-gravity planet. Old, I thought. Old and past retirement, even with regeneration therapy and geriatric drugs.

"You're quite a problem for me," the Colonel said. "We asked for a regiment of military police. Garrison Marines. I didn't think we'd get a full regiment, but I certainly didn't ask for Line troops. Now what am I to do with you?"

Nobody said anything.

"I cannot integrate Line Marines into the militia," the Colonel said. "It would be a disaster for both units. I don't even want your troops in this city! That's all I need, to have Line troopers practicing system D in Harmony!"

Deane looked blankly at me, and I grinned. It was nice to know something he didn't. System D is a Line troop tradition. The men organize themselves into small units and go into a section of town where they all drink until they can't hold any more. Then they tell the saloon owners they can't pay. If any of them causes trouble, they wreck his place, with the others converging onto the troublesome bar while more units delay the guard.

"I'm sorry, but I want your Line troopers out of this city as soon as possible," Harrington said. "And I can't give you any officers. There's no way I can put Marines under militia officers, and I can't spare any of the few Fleet people I have. That's a break for you, gentlemen, because the four of you will be the only officers in the 501st Provisional Battalion. Captain Falkenberg will command, of course. Mr. Slater, as senior lieutenant you will be his second, and I expect you'll have to take a company, as well. You others will also be company commanders. Major Lorca will be able to assist with logistics and maintenance services, but for the rest of it, you'll be on your own."

Harrington paused to let that sink in. Deane was grinning at me, and I answered it with one of my own. With any luck we'd do pretty well out of this miserable place. Experience as company commanders could cut years off our time as lieutenants.

"The next problem is, what the hell can I do with you after you're organized?" Harrington demanded. "Major Lorca, if you'll give them the background?"

Lorca got up and went to the briefing stand. He used the console to project a city map on the briefing screen. "As you can see, the city is strongly defended," he said. "We have no difficulty in holding it with our militia. However, it is the only part of Arrarat that we have ever been required to hold, and as a result there are a number of competing gangs operating pretty well as they please in the interior. Lately a group calling itself the River Pack has taken a long stretch along the riverbanks and is levying such high passage fees that they have effectively cut this city off from supply. River traffic is the only feasible way to move agricultural goods from the farmlands to the city."

Lorca projected another map showing the river stretching northwestward from Harmony-Garrison. It ran through a line of hills; then upriver of that were more farmlands. Beyond them was another mountain chain. "In addition," Lorca said, "the raw materials for whatever industries we have on this planet come from these mines." A light pointer indicated the distant mountains. "It leaves us with a delicate political situation."

The Colonel growled like a dog. "Delicate. Hell, it's impossible!" he said. "Tell 'em the rest of it, Lorca."

"Yes, Colonel. The political responsibilities on this planet have never been carefully defined. Few jurisdictions are clear-cut. For example, the city of Garrison is under direct military authority, and Colonel Harrington is both civil and military commander within its walls. The city of Harmony is under direct CoDominium rule, with Governor Swale as its head. That is clear, but Governor Swale also holds a commission as planetary executive, which in theory subordinates Colonel Harrington to him. In practice they work together well enough, with the Governor taking civil authority and Colonel Harrington exercising military authority. In effect we have integrated Garrison and Harmony."

"And that's about all we've agreed on," Harrington said. "There's one other thing that's bloody clear. Our orders say we're to hold Garrison at all costs. That, in practice, means we have to defend Harmony as well, so we've an integrated militia force. There's plenty enough strength to defend both cities against direct attack. Supply's another matter."

"As I said, a delicate situation," Major Lorca said. "We cannot hold the city without supply, and we cannot supply the city without keeping the river transport lines open. In the past, Governor Swale and Colonel Harrington were agreed that the only way to do that was to extend CoDominium rule to these areas along the river." The light pointer moved again, indicating the area marked as held by the River Pack.

"They resisted us," Lorca said. "Not only the convicts, but the original colonists as well. Our convoys were attacked. Our militiamen were shot down by snipers. Bombs were thrown into the homes of militia officers— the hostiles don't have many sympathizers inside the city, but it doesn't take many to employ terror tactics. The Governor would not submit to military rule in the city of Harmony, and the militia could not sustain the effort needed to hold the riverbanks. On orders from the Governor, all CoDominium-controlled forces were withdrawn to within the walls of Harmony-Garrison."

"We abandoned those people," Harrington said. "Well, they got what they deserved. As you'd expect, there was a minor civil war out there. When it was over, the River Pack was in control. Swale recognized them as a legal government. Thought he could negotiate with them. Horse puckey. Go on, Lorca. Give 'em the bottom line."

"Yes, sir. As the Colonel said, the River Pack was recognized as a legal government, and negotiations were started. They have not been successful. The River Pack has made unacceptable demands as a condition of opening the river supply lines. Since it is obvious to the Governor that we cannot hold these cities without secure supplies, the Governor directed Colonel Harrington to reopen the supply lines by military force. The attempt was not successful."

"They beat our arses," Harrington said. His lips were tightly drawn. "I've got plenty of explanations for it. Militia are just the wrong kind of troops for the job. That's all burned hydrogen anyway. The fact is, they beat us, and we had to send back to Headquarters for Marine reinforcements. I asked for a destroyer and a regiment of military police. The warship and the Marines would have taken the goddam riverbanks, and the MPs could hold it for us. Instead, I got you people."

"Which seems to have turned the trick," Major Lorca said. "At 1630 hours this afternoon, Governor Swale received word that the River Pack wishes to reopen negotiations. Apparently they have information sources within the city—"

"In the city, hell!" Harrington said. "In the Governor's palace, if you ask me. Some of his clerks have sold out."

"Yes, sir," Lorca said. "In any event, they have heard that reinforcements have come, and they wish to negotiate a settlement."

"Bastards," Colonel Harrington said. "Bloody criminal butchers. You can't imagine what those swine have done out there. And His Excellency will certainly negotiate a settlement that leaves them in control. I guess he has to. There's not much doubt that with the 501st as a spearhead we could retake that area, but we can't hold it with Line Marines! Hell, Line troops aren't any use as military government. They aren't trained for it and they won't do it."

Falkenberg cleared his throat. Harrington glared at him for a moment. "Yes?"

"Question, sir."

"Ask it."

"What would happen if the negotiations failed so that the 501st was required to clear the area by force? Would that produce a more desirable result?"

Harrington nodded, and the glare faded. "I like the way you think. Actually, Captain, it wouldn't, not really. The gangs would try to fight, but when they saw it was hopeless, they'd take their weapons and run. Melt into the bush and wait. Then we'd be back where we were a couple of years ago, fighting a long guerrilla war with no prospect for ending it. I had something like that in mind, Captain, but that was when I was expecting MPs. I think we could govern with a regiment of MPs."

"Yes, sir," Falkenberg said. "But even if we must negotiate a settlement with the River Pack, surely we would like to be in as strong a bargaining position as possible."

"What do you have in mind, Falkenberg?" Harrington asked. He sounded puzzled, but there was genuine interest in his voice.

"If I may, sir." Falkenberg got up and went to the briefing screen. "At the moment I take it we are technically in a state of war with the River Pack?"

"It's not that formal," Major Lorca said. "But, yes, that's about the situation."

"I noticed that there was an abandoned CD fort about 240 kilometers upriver," Falkenberg said. He used the screen controls to show that section of the river. "You've said that you don't want Line Marines in the city. It seemed to me that the old fort would make a good base for the 501st, and our presence there would certainly help keep river traffic open."

"All right. Go on," Harrington said.

"Now we have not yet organized the 501st Battalion, but no one here knows that. I have carefully isolated my officers and troops from the militia. Sergeant Major, have any of the enlisted men talked with anyone on this post?"

"No, sir. Your orders were pretty clear, sir."

"And I know the officers have not," Falkenberg said. He glanced at us and we nodded. "Therefore, I think it highly unlikely that we will run into any serious opposition if we march immediately to our new base," Falkenberg said. "We may be able to do some good on the way. If we move fast, we may catch some River Pack gangsters. Whatever happens, we'll disrupt them and make it simpler to negotiate favorable terms."

"Immediately," Harrington said. "What do you mean by immediately?"

"Tonight, sir. Why not? The troops haven't got settled in. They're prepared to march. Our gear is all packed for travel. If Major Lorca can supply us with a few trucks for heavy equipment, we'll have no other difficulties."

"By God," Harrington said. He looked thoughtful. "It's taking a hell of a risk—" He looked thoughtful again. "But not so big a risk as we'd have if you stayed around here. As you say. Right now nobody knows what we've got. Let the troops get to talking, and it'll get all over this planet that you've brought a random collection of recruits, guardhouse soldiers, and newlies. That wouldn't be so obvious if you hit the road."

"You'd be pretty much on your own until we get the river traffic established again," Major Lorca said.

"Yes, sir," Falkenberg answered. "But we'd be closer to food supply than you are. I've got three helicopters and a couple of Skyhooks. We can bring in military stores with those."

"By God, I like it," Harrington said. "Right now those bastards have beaten us. I wouldn't mind paying them out." He looked at us, then shook his head. "What do you chaps think? I can spare only the four of you. That stands. Can you do it?"

We all nodded. I had my doubts, but I was cocky enough to think I could do anything. "It will be a cakewalk, sir," I said. "I can't think a gang of criminals wants to face a battalion of Line Marines."

"Honor of the corps and all that," Harrington said. "I was never with Line troops. You haven't been with 'em long enough to know anything about them, and here you're talking like one of them already. All right. Captain Falkenberg, you are authorized to take your battalion to Fort Beersheba at your earliest convenience. Tell 'em what you can give 'em, Lorca." The Colonel sounded ten years younger. That defeat had hurt him, and he was looking forward to showing the River Pack what regular troops could do.

Major Lorca told us about logistics and transport. There weren't enough trucks to carry more than a bare minimum of supplies. We could tow the artillery, and there were two tanks we could have. For most of us it would be march or die, but it didn't look to me as if there'd be very much dying.

Finally Lorca finished. "Questions?" he said. He looked at Falkenberg.

"I'll reserve mine for the moment, sir." Falkenberg was already talking like a battalion commander.

"Sir, why is there so little motor transport?" Louis Bonneyman asked.

"No fuel facilities," Lorca told him. "No petroleum refineries. We have a small supply of crude oil and a couple of very primitive distillation plants, but nowhere near enough to support any large number of motor vehicles. The original colonists were quite happy about that. They didn't want them." Lorca reminded me of one of the instructor officers at the Academy.

"What weapons are we facing?" Deane Knowles asked.

Lorca shrugged. "They're better armed than you think. Good rifles. Some rocket launchers. A few mortars. Nothing heavy, and they tend to be deficient in communications, in electronics in general, but there are exceptions to that. They've captured gear from our militia"—Colonel Harrington winced at that—"and, of course, anything we sell to the farmers eventually ends up in the hands of the gangs. If we refuse to let the farmers buy weapons, we condemn them. If we do sell weapons, we arm more convicts. A vicious circle."

I studied the map problem. It didn't look difficult. A thousand men need just over a metric ton of dried food every day. There was plenty of water along the route, though, and we could probably get local forage, as well. We could do it, even with the inadequate transport Lorca could give us. It did look like a cakewalk.

I worried with the figures until I was satisfied, then suddenly realized it wasn't an exercise for a class. This was real. In a few hours we'd be marching into hostile territory. I looked over at my classmates. Deane was punching numbers into his pocket computer and frowning at the result. Louis Bonneyman was grinning like a thief. He caught my eye and winked. I grinned back at him, and it made me feel better. Whatever happened, I could count on them.

Lorca went through a few more details on stores and equipment available from the garrison, plus other logistic support available from the fort. We all took notes, and of course the briefing was recorded. "That about sums it up," he said.

Harrington stood, and we got up. "I expect you'll want to organize the 501st before you'll have any meaningful questions," Harrington said. "I'll leave you to that. You may consider this meeting your formal call on the commanding officer, although I'll be glad to see any of you in my office if you've anything to say to me. That's all."

"Ten-hut!" Ogilvie said. He stayed in the briefing room as Colonel Harrington and Major Lorca left.

"Well. We've work to do," Falkenberg said. "Sergeant Major."

"Sir!"

"Please run through the organization we worked out."

"Sir!" Ogilvie used the screen controls to flash charts onto the screens. As the Colonel had said, I was second in command of the battalion, and also A Company commander. My company was a rifle outfit. I noticed it was heavy with experienced Line troopers, and I had less than my share of recruits.

Deane had drawn the weapons company, which figured. Deane had taken top marks in weapons technology at the Academy, and he was always reading up on artillery tactics. Louis Bonneyman had another rifle company with a heavy proportion of recruits to worry about. Falkenberg had kept a large headquarters platoon under his personal command.

"There are reasons for this structure," Falkenberg said. "I'll explain them later. For the moment, have any of you objections?"

"Don't know enough to object, sir," I said. I was studying the organization chart.

"All of you will have to rely heavily on your NCO's," Falkenberg said. "Fortunately, there are some good ones. I've given the best, Centurion Lieberman, to A Company. Bonneyman gets Sergeant Cernan. If he works out, we can get him a Centurion's badges. Knowles has already worked with Gunner-Centurion Pniff. Sergeant Major Ogilvie stays with Headquarters Platoon, of course. In addition to your command duties, each of you will have to fill some staff slots. Bonneyman will be intelligence." Falkenberg grinned slightly. "I told you it might not seem such a joke."

Louis answered his grin. He was already sitting in the regimental intelligence officer's chair at the table. I wondered why Falkenberg had given that job to Louis. Of the four of us, Louis had paid the least attention to his briefing packet, and he didn't seem cut out for the job.

"Supply and logistics stay with Knowles, of course," Falkenberg said. "I'll keep training myself. Now, I have a proposition for you. The Colonel has ordered us to occupy Fort Beersheba at the earliest feasible moment. If we simply march there with no fighting and without accomplishing much beyond getting there, the Governor will negotiate a peace. We will be stationed out in the middle of nowhere, with few duties beyond patrols. Does anyone see any problems with that?"

"Damned dull," Louis Bonneyman said.

"And not just for us. What have you to say, Sergeant Major?"

Ogilvie shook his head. "Don't like it, sir. Might be all right for the recruits, but wouldn't recommend it for the old hands. Especially the ones you took out of the brig. Be a lot of the bug, sir."

The bug. The Foreign Legion called it *le cafard*, which means the same thing. It had been the biggest single cause of death in the Legion, and it was still that among Line Marines. Men with nothing to do. Armed men, warriors, bored stiff. They get obsessed with the bug until they commit suicide, or murder, or desert, or plot mutiny. The textbook remedy for *le cafard* is a rifle and plenty of chances to use it. Combat. Line troops on garrison duty lose more men to *cafard* than active outfits lose in combat. So my instructors had told us, anyway.

"It will be doubly bad in this case," Falkenberg said. "No regimental pride. No accomplishments to brag about. No battles. I'd like to avoid that."

"How, sir?" Bonneyman asked.

Falkenberg seemed to ignore him. He adjusted the map until the section between the city and Fort Beersheba filled the screen. "We march up the Jordan," he said. "I suppose it was inevitable that the Federation of Churches would call the planet's most important river 'Jordan,' wasn't it? We march northwest, and what happens, Mr. Slater?"

I thought about it. "They run, I suppose. I can't think they'll want to fight. We've much better equipment than they have."

"Equipment and men," Falkenberg said. "And a damned frightening reputation. They already know we've landed, and they've asked for negotiations. They've got sources inside the palace. You heard me arrange for a social invitation for five days from now."

We all laughed. Falkenberg nodded. "Which means that if we march tonight, we'll achieve *real* surprise.

We can catch a number of them unaware and disarm them. What I'd like to do, though, is disarm the lot of them."

I was studying the map, and I thought I saw what he meant. "They'll just about have to retreat right past Fort Beersheba," I said. "Everything narrows down there."

"Precisely," Falkenberg said. "If we held the fort, we could disarm everyone coming through. Furthermore, it is our fort, and we've orders to occupy it quickly. I remind you also that we're technically at war with the River Pack."

"Yes, but how do we get there?" I asked. "Also, Captain, if we're holding the bottleneck, the rest of them will fight. They can't retreat."

"Not without losing their weapons," Falkenberg said. "I don't think the Colonel would be unhappy if we *really* pacified that area. Nor do I think the militia would have all that much trouble holding it if we defeated the River Pack and disarmed their survivors."

"But as Hal asked, how do we get there?" Louis demanded.

Falkenberg said, "I mentioned helicopters. Sergeant Major has found enough fuel to keep them flying for a while."

"Sir, I believe there was something in the briefing kit about losses from the militia arsenal," Deane said. "Specifically including Skyhawk missiles. Choppers wouldn't stand a chance against those."

"Not if anyone with a Skyhawk knew they were coming," Falkenberg agreed. "But why should they expect us? The gear's at the landing dock. Nothing suspicious about a work party going down there tonight. Nothing suspicious about getting the choppers set up and working. I can't believe they expect us to take Beersheba tonight, not when they've every reason to believe we'll be attending a grand ball in five days."

"Yes, sir," Deane agreed. "But we can't put enough equipment into three choppers! The men who take Beersheba will be doomed. Nobody can march up that road fast enough to relieve them."

Falkenberg's voice was conversational. He looked up at the ceiling. "I did mention Skyhooks, didn't I? Two of them. Lifting capacity in this gravity and atmosphere, six metric tons each. That's forty-five men with full rations and ammunition. Gentlemen, by dawn we could have ninety combat Marines in position at Fort Beersheba, with the rest of the 501st marching to their relief. Are you game?"

VIII

IT WAS COLD down by the docks. A chill wind had blown in just after sundown, and despite the previous heat of the day I was shivering. Maybe, I thought, it isn't the cold.

The night sky was clear, with what seemed like millions of stars. I could recognize most of the constellations, and that seemed strange. It reminded me that although we were so far from Earth that a man who began walking in the time of the dinosaurs wouldn't have gotten here yet, it was still an insignificant distance to the universe. That made me feel small, and I didn't like it.

The troops were turned out in work fatigues. Our combat clothing and armor were still tucked away in the packs we were loading onto the Skyhook platforms. We worked under bright lights, and anyone watching would never have known we were anything but a work party, Falkenberg was sure that at least one pair of night glasses was trained on us from the bluff above.

The Skyhook platforms were light aluminum affairs, just a flat plate eight meters on a side with a meter-high railing around the perimeter. We stowed packs onto them. We also piled on other objects: light machine guns, recoilless cannon, mortars, and boxes of shells and grenades. Some of the boxes had false labels on them, stenciled on by troops working inside the warehouse, so that watchers would see what looked like office supplies and spare clothing going aboard.

A truck came down from the fort and went into the warehouse. It seemed to be empty, but it carried rifles for ninety men. The rifles went into bags and were stowed on the Skyhooks.

Arrarat has only one moon, smaller than Earth's and closer. It was a bloody crescent sinking into the highlands to the west, and it didn't give much light. It would be gone in an hour. I wandered over to where Deane was supervising the work on the helicopters.

"Sure you have those things put together right?" I asked him.

"Nothing to it."

"Yeah. I hope not. It's going to be hard to find those landing areas."

"You'll be all right." He wasn't really listening to me. He had two communications specialists working on the navigation computers, and he kept glaring at the squiggles on their scopes. "That's good," he said. "Now feed in the test problem."

When I left to go find Falkenberg, Deane didn't notice I'd gone. Captain Falkenberg was inside the warehouse. "We've about got the gear loaded, sir," I told him.

"Good. Come have some coffee." One of the mess sergeants had set up the makings for coffee in one corner of the big high-bay building. There was also a map table, and Sergeant Major Ogilvie had a communications center set up there. Falkenberg poured two cups of coffee and handed one to me. "Nervous?" he asked me.

"Some."

"You can still call it off. No discredit. I'll tell the others there were technical problems. We'll still march in the morning."

"It'll be all right, sir."

He looked at me over the lip of his coffee cup. "I expect you will be. I don't like sending you into this, but there's no other way we can do it."

"Yes, sir," I said.

"You'll be all right. You've got steady troopers."

"Yes, sir." I didn't know any of the men, of course. They were only names and service records, not even that, just a statistical summary of service records, a tape spewed out by the personal computer. Thirty had been let out of the brig for voluntary service in Arrarat. Another twenty were recruits. The rest were Line Marines, long service volunteers.

Falkenberg used the controls to project a map of the area around Beersheba onto the map table. "Expect you've got this memorized," he said.

"Pretty well, sir."

He leaned over the table and looked at the fort, then at the line of hills north of it. "You've some margin for error, I think. I'll have to leave to you the final decision on using the chopper in the actual assault. You can risk one helicopter. Not both. I must have one helicopter back, even if that costs you the mission. Is that understood?"

"Yes, sir." I could feel a sharp ball in my guts, and I didn't like it. I hoped it wouldn't show.

"Getting on for time," Falkenberg said. "You'll need all the time you can get. We could wait a day to get better prepared, but I think surprise is your best edge."

I nodded. We'd been through all this before. Was he talking because he was nervous, too? Or to keep me talking so I wouldn't brood?

"You may get a commendation out of this."

"If it's all the same to you, I'd rather have a guarantee that you'll show up on time." I grinned when I said it, to show I didn't mean it, but I did. Why the hell wasn't he leading this assault? The whole damned idea was his, and so was the battle plan. It was his show, and he wasn't going. I didn't want to think about the reasons. I had to depend on him to bail me out, and I couldn't even let myself think the word "coward."

"Time to load up," Falkenberg said.

I nodded and drained the coffee cup. It tasted good. I wondered if that would be the last coffee I'd ever drink. It was certain that some of us wouldn't be coming back.

Falkenberg clapped his hand on my shoulder. "You'll give them a hell of a shock, Hal. Let's get on with it."

"Right." But I sure wish you were coming with me.

I found Centurion Lieberman. We'd spent several hours together since Falkenberg's briefing, and I was sure I could trust him. Lieberman was about Falkenberg's height, built somewhere between wiry and skinny. He was about forty-five, and there were scars on his neck. The scars ran down under his tunic. He'd had a lot of regeneration therapy in his time.

His campaign ribbons made two neat rows on his undress blues. From his folder I knew he was entitled to another row he didn't bother to wear.

"Load 'em up," I told him.

"Sir." He spoke in a quiet voice, but it carried through the warehouse. "First and second platoons A Company, take positions on the Skyhook platforms."

The men piled in on top of the gear. It was crowded on the platforms. I got in with one group, and Lieberman boarded the other platform. I'd rather have been up in the helicopter, flying it or sitting next to the pilot, but I thought I was needed down here. Louis Bonneyman was flying my chopper. Sergeant Doty of Headquarters Platoon had the other.

"Bags in position," Gunner-Centurion Pniff said. "Stand ready to inflate Number One." He walked around the platform looking critically at the lines that led from it to the amorphous shape that lay next to it. "Looks good. Inflate Number One."

There was a loud hiss, and a great ghostly bag formed. It began to rise until it was above my platform. The plastic gleamed in the artificial light streaming from inside the warehouse. The bag billowed up until it was huge above us, and still it grew as the compressed helium poured out of the inflating cylinders. It looked bigger than the warehouse before Pniff was satisfied. "Good," he said. "Belay! Stand by to inflate Number Two."

"Jeez," one of the recruits said. "We going up in this

balloon? Christ, we don't have parachutes! We can't go up in a balloon!"

Some of the others began to chatter. "Sergeant Ardwain," I said.

"Sir!"

I didn't say anything else. Ardwain cursed and crawled over to the recruits. "No chutes means we don't have to jump," he said. "Now shut up."

Number Two Skyhook was growing huge. It looked even larger than our own, because I could see all of it, and all I could see of the bag above us was this bloated thing filling the sky above me. The choppers started up, and after a moment they lifted. One rose directly above us. The other went to hover above the other Skyhook. The chopper looked dwarfed next to that huge bag.

The choppers settled onto the bags. Up on top the helicopter crews were floundering around on the billowing stuff to make certain the fastenings were set right. I could hear their reports in my helmet phones. Finally they had it all right.

"Everything ready aboard?" Falkenberg asked me. His voice was unemotional in the phones. I could see him standing by the warehouse doors, and I waved. "All correct, sir," I said.

"Good. Send Number One along, Gunner."

"Sir!" Pniff said. "Ground crews stand by. Let go Number One."

The troops outside were grinning at us as they cut loose the tethers holding the balloons. Nothing happened, of course; the idea of Skyhook is to have almost neutral buoyancy, so that the lift from the gas bags just balances the weight of the load. The helicopters provide all the motive power.

The chopper engines rose in pitch, and we lifted off. A gust of wind caught us and we swayed badly as we lifted. Some of the troops cursed, and their non-coms glared at them. Then we were above the harbor, rising to the level of the city bluff, then higher than that. We moved northward toward the fort, staying high above the city until we got to Garrison's north edge, then dipping low at the fortress wall.

Anyone watching from the harbor area would think we'd just ferried a lot of supplies up onto the bluff. They might wonder about carrying men as well, but we could be pretty sure they wouldn't suspect we were doing anything but ferrying them.

We dropped low over the fields north of the city and continued moving. Then we rose again, getting higher and higher until we were at thirty-three hundred meters.

The men looked at me nervously. They watched the city lights dwindle behind us.

"All right," I said. It was strange how quiet it was. The choppers were ultra-quiet, and what little noise they made was shielded by the gas bag above us. The railings cut off most of the wind. "I want every man to get his combat helmet on."

There was some confused rooting around as the men found their own packs and got their helmets swapped around. We'd been cautioned not to shift weight on the platforms, and nobody wanted to make any sudden moves.

I switched my command set to lowest power so it couldn't be intercepted more than a kilometer away. We were over three klicks high, so I wasn't much worried that anyone was listening. "By now you've figured that we aren't going straight back to the fort," I said.

There were laughs from the recruits. The older hands looked bored.

"We've got a combat mission," I said. "We're going 250 klicks west of the city. When we get there, we take a former CD fort, dig in, and wait for the rest of the battalion to march out and bring us home."

A couple of troopers perked up at that. I heard one tell his buddy, "Sure beats hell out of marching 250 klicks."

"You'll get to march, though," I said. "The plan is to land about eight klicks from the fort and march overland to take it by surprise. I doubt anyone is expecting us."

"Christ Johnny strikes again," someone muttered. I couldn't see who had said that.

"Sir?" a corporal asked. I recognized him: Roff, the man who'd been riding the seasick recruit in the landing boat.

"Yes, Corporal Roff?"

"Question, sir."

"Ask it."

"How long will we be there, Lieutenant?"

"Until Captain Falkenberg comes for us," I said.

"Aye, aye, sir."

There weren't any other questions. I thought that was strange. They must want to know more. Some of you will get killed tonight, I thought. Why don't you want to know more about it?

They were more interested in the balloon. Now that it didn't look as if it would fall, they wanted to look out over the edge. I had the non-coms rotate the men so everyone got a chance.

I'd had my look over the edge, and I didn't like it. Below the level of the railing it wasn't so bad, but looking down was horrible. Besides, there wasn't really anything to see, except a few lights, way down below, and far behind us a dark shape that sometimes blotted out stars: Number Two, about a klick away.

"Would the lieutenant care for coffee?" a voice asked me. "I have brought the flask."

I looked up to see Hartz with my Thermos and a mess-hall cup. I'd seen him get aboard with his communications gear, but I'd forgotten him after that. "Thanks, I'll have some," I said.

It was about half brandy. I nearly choked. Hartz didn't even crack a smile.

We took a roundabout way so that we wouldn't pass over any of the river encampments. The way led far north of the river, then angled southwest to our landing zone. I turned to look over the edge again, and I hoped that Deane had gotten the navigation computers tuned up properly, because there wasn't anything to navigate by down there. Once in a while there was an orange-yellow light, probably a farmhouse, possibly an outlaw encampment, but otherwise all the hills looked the same.

This has got to be the dumbest stunt in military history, I told myself, but I didn't really believe it. The Line Marines had a long reputation for going into battle in newly formed outfits with strange officers. Even so, I doubted if any expedition had ever had so little going for it: a newlie commander, men who'd never served together, and a captain who'd plan the mission but wouldn't go on it. I told myself the time to object had been back in the briefing. It was a bit late now.

I looked at my watch. Another hour of flying time. "Sergeant Ardwain."

"Sir?"

"Get them out of those work clothes and into combat leathers and armor. Weapons check after everyone's dressed." Dressed to kill, I thought, but I didn't say it. It was an old joke, never funny to begin with. I wondered who thought of it first. Possibly some trooper outside the walls of Troy.

Hartz already had my leathers out of my pack. He helped me squirm out of my undress blues and into the synthi-leather tunic and trousers. The platform rocked as men tried to pull on their pants without standing up. It was hard to dress because we were sprawled out on our packs and other equipment. There was a lot of cursing as troopers moved around to find their own packs and rifles.

"Get your goddam foot out of my eye!"

"Shut up, Traeger."

Finally everyone had his armor on and his fatigues packed away. The troopers sat quietly now. Even the old hands weren't joking. There's something about combat armor that makes everything seem real.

They looked dangerous in their bulky leathers and armor, and they were. The armor alone gave us a big edge on anything we'd meet here. It also gives a feeling of safety, and that can be dangerous. Nemourlon will stop most fragments and even pistol bullets, but it won't stop a high-velocity rifle slug.

"How you doing down there?" Louis's voice in my phones startled me for a moment.

"We're all armored up," I told him. "You still think you know where you're going?"

"Nope. But the computer does. Got a radar check five minutes ago. Forking stream that shows on the map. We're right on the button."

"What's our ETA?" I asked.

"About twenty minutes. Wind's nice and steady, not too strong. Piece of cake."

"Fuel supply?" I asked.

"We're hip-deep in spare cans. Not exactly a surplus, but there's enough. Quit worrying."

"Yeah."

"You know," Louis said, "I never flew a chopper with one of those things hanging off it."

"Now you tell me."

"Nothing to it," Louis said. "Handles a bit funny, but I got used to it."

"You'd better have."

"Just leave the driving to us. Out."

The next twenty minutes seemed like a week. I guarantee one way to stretch time is to sit on an open platform at thirty-three hundred meters and watch the night sky while you wait to command your first combat mission. I tried to think of something cheerful to say, but I couldn't, and I thought it was better just to be quiet. The more I talked, the more chance I'd show some kind of strain in my voice.

"Your job is to look confident," Falkenberg had told me. I hoped I was doing that.

"Okay, you can get your first look now," Louis said.

"Rojj." I got my night glasses from Hartz. They were better than issue equipment, a pair of ten-cm Leica light-amplifying glasses I bought myself when I left the Academy. A lot of officers do, because Leica makes a special offer for graduating cadets. I clipped them onto my helmet and scanned the hillside. The landing zone was the top of a peak which was the highest point on a ridge leading from the river. I turned the glasses to full power and examined the area carefully.

It looked deserted. There was some kind of scrubby chaparral growing all over it, and it didn't look as if anybody had ever been to the peak.

"Looks good to me," I told Louis. "What do you have?"

"Nothing on IR, nothing on low-light TV," he said. "Nothing barring a few small animals and some birds roosting in the trees. I like that. If there're animals and birds, there's probably no people."

"Yeah—"

"Okay, that's passive sensors. Should I take a sweep with K-band?"

I thought about it. If there were anyone down there, and that theoretical someone had a radar receiver, the chopper would give itself away with the first pulse. Maybe that would be better. "Yes."

"Rojj," Louis said. He was silent a moment. "Hal, I get nothing. If there's anybody down there, he's dug in good and expecting us."

"Let's go in," I said.

And now, I thought, I'm committed.

IX

"OVER THE SIDE!" Ardwain shouted. "Get those tethers planted! First squad take perimeter guard! Move, damn you!"

The men scrambled off the platform. Some of them had tether stakes, big aluminum corkscrews, which they planted in the ground. Others lashed the platform to the stakes. The first squad, two maniples, fanned out around the area with their rifles ready.

There wasn't much wind, but that big gas bag had a lot of surface area, and I was worried about it. I got off and moved away to look at it. It didn't seem to be too much strain on the tether stakes. The hillside was quiet and dark. We'd set down on top of some low bushes with stiff branches. The leaves felt greasy when they were crushed. I listened, then turned my surveillance amplifier to high gain. Still nothing, not even a bird. Nothing but my own troops moving about. I switched to general command frequency. "Freeze," I said.

The noise stopped. There was silence except for the low "whump!" of the chopper blades, and a fainter sound from Number Two out there somewhere.

"Carry on," I said.

Ardwain came up to me. "Nobody here, sir. Area secure."

"Thank you." I thumbed my command set onto the chopper's frequency. "You can cut yourself loose, and bring in Number Two."

"Aye, aye, sir," Louis said.

We began pulling gear off the platform. After a few moments, Number Two chopper came in. We couldn't see the helicopter at all, only the huge gas bag with its platform dangling below it. The Skyhook settled onto the chaparral and men bailed out with tether stakes. Centurion Lieberman watched until he was sure the platform was secure, then ran over to me.

"All's well?" I asked him.

"Yes, sir." His tone made it obvious he'd wanted to say "of course."

"Get 'em saddled up," I said. "We're moving out."

"Aye, aye, sir. I still think Ardwain would be all right here, sir."

"No. I'll want an experienced man in case something happens. If we don't send for the heavy equipment, or if something happens to me, call Falkenberg for instructions."

"Aye, aye, sir." He still didn't like it. He wanted to come with us. For that matter, I wanted him along, but I had to leave a crew with the Skyhooks and choppers. If the wind came up so tethers wouldn't hold, those things had to get airborne fast, and the rest of us would be without packs and supplies. There were all kinds of contingencies, and I wanted a reliable man I could trust to deal with them.

"We're ready, sir," Ardwain said.

"Right. Let's move out." I switched channels. "Here we go, Louis."

"I'll be ready," Bonneyman said.

"Thanks. Out." I moved up toward the head of the column. Ardwain had already gone up. "Let's get rolling," I said.

"Sir. Question, sir," Ardwain said.

"Yeah?"

"Men would rather take their packs, sir. Don't like to leave their gear behind."

"Sergeant, we've got eight kilometers to cover in less than three hours. No way."

"Yes, sir. Could we take our cloaks? Gets cold without 'em— "

"Sergeant Ardwain, we're leaving Centurion Lieberman and four maniples of troops here. Just what's going to happen to your gear? Get them marching."

"Sir. All right, you bastards, move out."

I could hear grumbling as they started along the ridge. Crazy, I thought. They want to carry packs in this.

The brush was thick, and we weren't making any progress at all. Then the scouts found a dry stream bed, and we moved into that. It was filled with boulders the size of a desk, and we hopped from one to another, moving slightly downhill. It was pitch-black, the boulders no more than shapes I could barely see. This wasn't going to work. I was already terrified.

But thank God for all that exercise in high gravity, I thought. We'll make it, but we've got to have light. I turned my set to low-power command frequency. "NCO's turn on lowest-power infrared illumination," I said. "No visible light."

I pulled the IR screen down in front of my eyes and snapped on my own IR helmet light. The boulders became pale green shapes in front of me, and I could just see them well enough to hop from one to another. Ahead of me the screen showed bright green moving splotches, my scouts and NCO's with their illuminators.

I didn't think anybody would be watching this hill with IR equipment. It didn't seem likely, and we were far from the fort where the only equipment would be—if the River Pack had any to begin with. I told myself it would take extremely good gear to spot us from farther than a klick.

Eight klicks to go and three hours to do it. Shouldn't be hard. Men are in good condition, no packs—damned fools wanted to carry them!—only rifles and ammunition. And the weapons troops, of course. They'd be slowest. Mortarmen with twenty-two kilos each to carry, and the recoilless riflemen with twenty-four.

We were sweating in no time. I opened all the vents in my armor and leathers and wondered if I ought to tell the troops to do the same. Don't be stupid, I told myself. Most of them have done this a dozen times. I can't tell them anything they don't know.

But it's my command, I kept thinking. Anything goes wrong, it's your responsibility, Hal Slater. You asked for it, too, when you took the commission.

I kept thinking of the millions of things that could go wrong. The plan didn't look nearly so good from here as it had when we were studying maps. Here we are, seventy-six men, about to try to take a fort that probably has us outnumbered. Falkenberg estimated 125 men in there. I'd asked him how he got the number.

"Privies, Mr. Slater. Privies. Count the number of outhouses, guess the number of bottoms per hole, and you've got a good estimate of the number of men." He hadn't even cracked a grin.

One hell of a way to guess, and Falkenberg wasn't coming along. We'd find out the hard way how accurate his estimate was.

I kept telling myself what we had going for us. The satellite photos showed nobody lived on this ridge. No privies, I thought, and grinned in the dark. But I'd gone over the pix, and I hadn't seen any signs that people were ever here. Why should they be? There was no water except for the spring inside the fort itself. There was nothing up here, not even proper firewood, only these pesky shrubs that stab at your ankles.

I came around a bend in the stream bed and found a monitor waiting. His maniple stood behind him. He had three recruits in it: one NCO, one long-term private, and three recruits. The usual organization is only one or two recruits to a maniple, and I wondered why Lieberman had set this one up this way.

The monitor motioned uphill. We had to leave the stream bed here. Far ahead of me I could see the dull green glow of my lead men's lanterns. They were pulling ahead of me, and I strained to keep up with them. I left the stream, and after a few meters the only man near me was Hartz. He struggled along with twenty kilos of communications gear on his back and a rifle in his right hand, but if he had any trouble keeping up

with me, he didn't say anything. I was glad I didn't
have to carry all that load.

The ridge flattened out after a hundred meters. The
cover was only about waist-high. The green lights went
out on my IR screen as up ahead the scouts cut their
illuminators. I ordered the others turned off, as well.
Then I crouched under a bush and used the map projector to show me where we were. The helmet projected the map onto the ground, a dim patch of light
that couldn't have been seen except from close up and
directly above.

I was surprised to see we'd come better than halfway.

Fort Beersheba hadn't been much to start with. It
had a rectangle of low walls with guard towers in the
corners, a miniature of the larger fort at Garrison. Then
somebody had improved it, with a ditch and parapet
out in front of the walls, and a concertina of rusting
barbed wire outside of that. I couldn't see inside the
walls, but I knew there were four above-ground buildings and three large bunkers. The buildings were adobe.
The bunkers were logs and earth. They wouldn't burn.
The logs were a local wood with a high metallic content.

The bunkers were going to be a problem, but they'd
have to wait. Right now we had to get inside the walls
of the fort. There was a gate in the wall in front of me.
It was made of the same wood as the bunkers. It had a
ramp across the ditch, and it looked like our best bet,
except that inside the fort one of the bunkers faced the
gate, and it would be able to fire through the opening
once the gate was gone.

I had seventy-five men lying flat in the scrub brush
three hundred meters from the fort. The place looked
deserted. My IR pickups didn't show anyone in the
guard towers or on the walls. Nothing. I glanced at my
watch. Less than an hour before dawn.

I hadn't the faintest idea of what to do, but it was
time to make up my mind.

"Don't get fancy," Falkenberg had told me. "Get the
men to the fort and turn them loose. They'll take it for
you."

Sure, I thought. Sure. You're not here, you bloody coward, and I am, and it's my problem, and I don't know what the hell I'm doing.

I didn't like the looks of that ditch and barbed-wire concertina. It would take a while getting through it. If we crawled up to the ditch, we'd be spotted. They couldn't be that sloppy; if there weren't any guards, there had to be a surveillance system. Body capacitance, maybe. Or radar. Something. They'd have guards posted unless they had reason to believe nobody could sneak up on them.

To hell with it. We've got to do something, I thought. I nodded to Hartz and he handed me a mike. His radio was set to a narrow-beam directional antenna, and we'd left relays along the line of sight back to the landing area. I could talk to the choppers without alerting the fort's electronic watchdogs.

"Nighthawk, this is Blackeagle," I said.

"Blackeagle go."

"We can see the place, Louis. Nothing moving at all. I'd say it was deserted if I didn't know better."

"Want me to come take a look?"

It was a thought. The chopper could circle high above the fort and scan with IR and low-light TV. We'd know who was in the open. But there was a good chance it would be spotted, and we'd throw away our best shot.

"Don't get fancy," Falkenberg had said. "Surprise— that's your big advantage. Don't blow it."

But he wasn't here. There didn't seem to be any right decision. "No," I told Louis. "That's a negative. Load up with troops and get airborne, but stay out of line of sight. Be ready to dash. When I want you, I'll want you bad."

"Aye, aye, sir."

"Blackeagle out." I gave Hartz the mike. Okay, I told myself, this is it. I waved forward to Sergeant Ardwain.

He half rose from the ground and waved. The line moved ahead, slowly. Behind us the mortar and recoilless rifle teams had set up their weapons and lay next to them waiting for orders.

Corporal Roff was just to my left. He was directly in

front of the gate. He waved his troops on and we crawled toward the gate.

We'd gotten to within a hundred meters when there appeared a light at the top of the wall by the gate. Someone up there was shining a spot out onto the field. There was another light, and then another, all hand-held spotlights, powerful, but not very wide beams.

Corporal Roff stood up and waved at them "Hello, there!" he shouted. "Whatcha doin'?" He sounded drunk. I wanted to tell him to get down, but it was too late.

"You guys okay in there?" Roff shouted. "Got anything to drink?"

The others were crouched now, up from a crawl, and running forward.

"Who the hell are you?" someone on the wall demanded.

"Who the flippin' hell are you?" Roff answered. "Gimme a drink!" The lights converged toward him.

I thumbed on my command set. "Nighthawk, this is Blackeagle. Come a-runnin'!"

"Roger dodger."

I switched to the general channel. "Roff, hit the dirt! Fire at will. Charge!" I was shouting into the helmet radio loud enough to deafen half the command.

Roff dove sideways into the dirt. There were orange spurts from all over the field as the troopers opened fire. The lights tumbled off the walls. Two went out. One stayed on. It lay in the dirt just outside the gate.

Troopers rose from the field and ran screaming toward the fort. They sounded like madmen. Then a light machine gun opened from behind me, then another.

Trumpet notes sounded. I hadn't ordered it. I didn't even know we had a trumpet with us. The sound seemed to spur the men on. They ran toward the wire as the mortars fired their first rounds. Seconds later I saw spurts of fire from inside the walls as the shells hit. Just as they did, the recoilless opened behind me and I heard the shell pass not more than a couple of meters to my left. It hit the gates and there was a flash, then another hit the gates, and another. The trumpeter was sounding the charge over and over again, while mortars dropped more V.T. fused to go off a meter above ground into the fort itself. The recoilless fired again.

The gates couldn't take that punishment and fell open. There was smoke inside. One of the mortarmen must have dropped smoke rounds between the gates and the bunker. Streams of tracers came out of the gates, but the men avoided them easily. They ran up on either side of the gates.

Others charged directly at the wire. The first troopers threw themselves onto the concertina. The next wave stepped on their backs and dived into the ditch. More waves followed, and men in the ditches heaved their comrades up onto the narrow strip between the ditch and the walls.

They stopped just long enough to throw grenades over the wall. Then two men grabbed a third and flung him up to where he could catch the top of the wall. They stood and boosted him on until he pulled himself up and could stand on top of it. More men followed, then leaned down to pull up their mates from below. I couldn't believe it was happening so quickly.

The men on the wire were struggling to get loose before there was no one below to boost them over. Those were recruits, I thought. Of course. The monitors had sent the recruits first, with a simple job. Lie down and get walked on.

The helicopter came roaring in, pouring streams of twenty-mm cannon fire into the fort. The tracers were bright against the night sky.

And I was still standing there, watching, amazed at how fast it was all happening. I shook myself and turned on my command set. "I.F.F. beacons on! General order, turn on I.F.F. beacons." I changed channels. "Nighthawk, this is Blackeagle. For God's sake, Louis, be careful! Some of ours are already inside!"

"I see the beacons," Louis said. "Relax, Hal, we watched them going in."

The chopper looped around the fort in a tight orbit, still firing into the fort. Then it plunged downward.

"Mortarmen, hold up on that stuff," Sergeant Ardwain's

voice said. "We're inside the fort now and the chopper's going in."

Christ, I thought, something else I forgot. One hell of a commander I've made. I can't even remember the most elementary things.

The chopper dropped low and even before it vanished behind the walls it was spewing men.

I ran up to the gate, staying to one side to avoid the tracers that were still coming out. Corporal Roff was there ahead of me. "Careful here, sir." He ducked around the gatepost and vanished. I followed him into the smoke, running around to my right, where other troopers had gone over the wall.

The scene inside was chaotic. There were unarmored bodies everywhere, probably cut down by the mortars. Men were running and firing in all directions. I didn't think any of the defenders had helmets. "Anybody without a helmet is a hostile," I said into the command set. Stupid. They know that. "Give 'em hell, lads!" That was another silly thing to say, but at least it was a better reason for shouting in their ears than telling them something they already knew.

A satchel charge went off at one of the bunkers. A squad rushed the entrance and threw grenades into it. That was all I could see from where I stood, but there was firing all over the enclosure.

Now what? I wondered. Even as I did, the firing died out until there were only a few rifle shots now and then, and the futile fire of the machine gun in the bunker covering the gate.

"Lieutenant?" It was Ardwain's voice.

"Yes, Sergeant."

"There's some people in that main bunker, sir. You can hear 'em talking in there. Sound like women. We didn't want to blow it in, not just yet, anyway."

"What about the rest of the fort?"

"Cleared out, sir. Bunkers and barracks, too. We got about twenty prisoners."

That quick. Like automatic magic. "Sergeant, make sure there's nothing that can fire onto the area northwest of the fort. I want to bring the Skyhook in there."

"Aye, aye, sir."

I thumbed my command set to the chopper frequency. "We've got the place, all except one bunker, and it'll be no problem. Bring Number Two in to land in the area northwest of the fort, about three hundred meters out from the wall. I want you to stay up there and cover Number Two. Anything that might hit it, you take care of. Keep scanning. I can't believe somebody won't come up here to see what's happening."

X

THAT WAS MY first fire fight. I wasn't too proud of my part in it. I hadn't given a single order once the rush started, and I was very nearly the last man into the fort. Some leader.

But there was no time to brood. Dawn was a bright smear off in the east. The first thing was to check on the butcher's bill. Four men killed, two of them recruits. Eleven wounded. After a quick conference with our paramedic I sent three to the helicopters. The others could fight, or said they could. Then I sent the two choppers east toward Harmony, while we ferried the rest of our gear into the fort. We were on our own.

Sergeant Doc Crisp had another dozen patients, defenders who'd been wounded in the assault. We had thirty prisoners, thirty-seven wounded, and over fifty dead. One of the wounded was the former commander of the fort.

"Got bashed with a rifle butt outside his quarters," Ardwain told me. "He's able to talk now."

"I'll see him."

"Sir." Ardwain went into the hospital bunker and brought out a man about fifty, dark hair in a ring around a bald head. He had thin, watery eyes. He didn't look like a soldier or an outlaw.

"He says his name's Flawn, sir," Ardwain told me.

"Marines," Flawn said. "CoDominium Marines. Didn't know there were any on the planet. Just why the hell is this place worth the Grand Senate's attention again?"

"Shut up," Ardwain said.

"I've got a problem, Flawn," I said. We were standing in the open area in the center of the fort. "That bunker over there's still got some of your people in it. It'd be no problem to blast it open, but the troopers think they heard women talking in there."

"They did," Flawn said. "Our wives."

"Can you talk them into coming out, or do we set fire to it?"

"Christ!" he said. "What happens to us now?"

"*Machts nichts* to me," I told him. "My orders are to disarm you people. You're free to go anywhere you want to without weapons. Northwest if you like."

"Without weapons. You know what'll happen to us out there without weapons?"

"No, and I don't really care."

"I know," Flawn said. "You bastards never have cared—"

"Mind how you talk to the lieutenant," Ardwain said. He ground his rifle on the man's instep. Flawn gasped in pain.

"Enough of that, Sergeant," I said. "Flawn, you outlaws—"

"Outlaws. Crap!" Flawn said. "Excuse me. Sir, you are mistaken." He eyed Ardwain warily, his lip curled in contempt. "You brought me here as a convict for no reason other than my opposition to the CoDominium. You turned me loose with nothing. Nothing at all, Lieutenant. So we try to build something. Politics here aren't like at home. Or maybe they are, same thing, really, but here it's all out in the open. I managed something, and now you've come to take it away and send me off unarmed, with no more than the clothes on my back, and you expect me to be respectful." He glanced up at the CoDominium banner that flew high above the fort. "You'll excuse me if I don't show more enthusiasm."

"My orders are to disarm you," I said. "Now, will you talk your friends out of that bunker, or do we blow it in?"

"You'll let us go?"

"Yes."

"Your word of honor, Lieutenant?"

I nodded. "Certainly."

"I guess I can't ask for any other guarantees." Flawn looked at Sergeant Ardwain and grimaced. "I wish I dared. All right, let me talk to them."

By noon we had Fort Beersheba to ourselves. Flawn and the others had left. They insisted on carrying their wounded with them, even when Doc Crisp told them most would probably die on the road. The women had been a varied assortment, from teenagers to older women. All had gone with Flawn, to my relief and the troopers' disappointment.

Centurion Lieberman organized the defenses. He put men into the bunkers, set up revetments for the mortars, found material to repair the destroyed gates, stationed more men on the walls, got the mess tents put up, put the liquor we'd found into a strong room and posted guards over it—

I was feeling useless again.

In another hour there were parties coming up the road. I sent Sergeant Ardwain and a squad down there to set up a roadblock. We could cover them from the fort, and the mortars were set up to spray the road. The river was about three hundred meters away and one hundred meters below us, and the fort had a good field of fire all along the road for a klick in either direction. It was easy to see why this bluff had been chosen for a strong point.

As parties of refugees came through, Ardwain disarmed them. At first they went through, anyway, but after a while they began to turn back rather than surrender their weapons. None of them caused any problems, and I wouldn't let Ardwain pursue any that turned away. We had far too few men to risk any in something senseless like that.

"Good work," Falkenberg told me when I made the afternoon report. "We've made forty kilometers so far, and we've got a couple of hours of daylight left. It's a bit hard to estimate how fast we'll be able to march."

"Yes, sir. The first party we disarmed had three Skyhawk missiles. There were five here at the fort, but nobody got them out in time to use them. Couple of guys who tried were killed by the mortars. It doesn't look good for helicopters in this area, though, not now that they're warned."

"Yes," Falkenberg said. "I suspected as much. We'll retire the choppers for a while. You've done well, Slater. I caution you not to relax, though. At the moment we've had no opposition worth mentioning, but that will change soon enough, and after that there may be an effort to break past your position. They don't seem to want to give up their weapons."

"No, sir." And who can blame them? I thought. Eric Flawn had worried me. He hadn't seemed like an outlaw. I don't know what I'd expected here at Beersheba. Kidnapped girls. Scenes of rape and debauchery, I suppose. I'd never seen a thieves' government in operation. Certainly I hadn't expected what I'd found, a group of middle-aged men in control of troops who looked a lot like ours, only theirs weren't very well equipped.

"I understand you liberated some wine," Falkenberg said.

"Yes, sir."

"That'll help. Daily ration of no more than half a liter per man, though."

"Sir? I wasn't planning on giving them any of it until you got here."

"It's theirs, Slater," Falkenberg said. "You could get away with holding on to it, but it wouldn't be best. It's your command. Do as you think you should, but if you want advice, give the troops half a liter each."

"Yes, sir." There's no regulation against drinking in the Line Marines, not even on duty. There are severe penalties for rendering yourself unfit for duty. Men have even been shot for it. "Half a liter with supper, then."

"I think it's wise," Falkenberg said. "Well, sounds as if you're doing well. We'll be along in a few days. Out."

There were a million other details. At noon I'd been startled to hear a trumpet sound mess call, and I went out to see who was doing it. A corporal I didn't recognize had a polished brass trumpet.

"Take me a few days to get everyone's name straight, Corporal," I said. "Yours?"

"Corporal Brady, sir."

"You play that well."

"Thank you, sir."

I looked at him again. I was sure his face was familiar. I thought I remembered that he'd been on Tri-v. Had his own band and singing group. Nightclub performances, at least one Tri-v special. I wondered what he was doing as an enlisted man in the Line Marines, but I couldn't ask. I tried to remember his real name, but that escaped me, too. It hadn't been Brady, I was sure of that. "You'll be sounding all calls here?"

"Yes, sir. Centurion says I'm to do it."

"Right. Carry on, Brady."

All through the afternoon the trumpet calls sent men to other duties. An hour before the evening meal there was a formal retreat. The CoDominium banner was hauled down by a color guard while all the men not on sentry watch stood in formation and Brady played Colors. As they folded the banner I remembered a lecture in Leadership class back at the Academy.

The instructor had been a dried-up Marine major with one real and one artificial arm. We were supposed to guess which was which, but we never did. The lecture I remembered had been on ceremonials. "Always remember," he'd said, "the difference between an army and a mob is tradition and discipline. You cannot enforce discipline on troops who do not feel that they are being justly treated. Even the man who is wrongly punished must feel that what he is accused of deserves punishment. You cannot enforce discipline on a mob, and so your men must be reminded that they are soldiers. Ceremonial is one of your most powerful tools for doing that. It is true that we are perpetually accused of wasting money. The Grand Senate annually wishes to take away our dress uniforms, our badges and colors, and all the so-called nonfunctional items we employ. They are fortunate, because they have never been able to do that. The day that they do, they will find themselves with an army that cannot defend them.

"Soldiers will complain about ceremonials and spit-and-polish, and such like, but they cannot live as an army without them. Men fight for pride, not for money, and no service that does not give them pride will last very long."

Maybe, I thought. But with a thousand things to do, I could have passed up a formal retreat on our first day at Fort Beersheba. I hadn't been asked about it. By the time I knew it was to happen, Lieberman had made all the arrangements and given the orders.

By suppertime we were organized for the night. Ardwain had collected about a hundred weapons, mostly obsolete rifles—there were even muzzle-loaders, handmade here on Arrarat—and passed nearly three hundred people through the roadblock.

We closed the road at dusk. Searchlights played along it, and we had a series of roadblocks made of log stacks. Ardwain and his troops were dug in where they could cover the whole road area, and we could cover them from the fort. It looked pretty good.

Tattoo sounded, and Fort Beersheba began to settle in for the night.

I made my rounds, looking into everything. The body-capacitance system the previous occupants had relied on was smashed when we blew open their bunker, but we'd brought our own surveillance gear. I didn't really trust passive systems, but I needn't have worried. Lieberman had guards in each of the towers. They were equipped with light-amplifying binoculars. There were more men to watch the IR screens.

"We're safe enough," Lieberman said. "If the lieutenant would care to turn in, I'll see the guard's changed properly."

He followed me back to my quarters. Hartz had already fixed the place up. There were fresh adobe patches over the bullet holes in the walls. My gear was laid out where I could get it quickly. Hartz had his cloak and pack spread out in the anteroom.

There was even coffee. A pot was kept warm over an alcohol lamp.

"You can leave it to us," Lieberman said.

Hartz grinned. "Sure. Lieutenants come out of the Academy without any calluses, and we make generals out of them."

"That may take some doing," I said. I invited Lieberman into my sitting room. There was a table there, with a scale model of the fort on it. Flawn had made it, but it hadn't done him much good. "Have a seat, Centurion. Coffee?"

"Just a little, sir. I'd best get back to my duties."

"Call me for the next watch, Centurion."

"If the lieutenant orders it."

"I just—what the hell, Lieberman, why don't you want me to take my turn on guard?"

"No need, sir. May I make a suggestion?"

"Sure."

"Leave it to us, sir. We know what we're doing."

I nodded and stared into my coffee cup. I didn't feel I was really in command here. They tell you everything in the Academy: leadership, communications, the precise form of a regimental parade, laser range-finding systems, placement of patches on uniforms, how to compute firing patterns for mortars, wine rations for the troops, how to polish a pair of boots, servicing recoilless rifles, delivery of calling cards to all senior officers within twenty-four hours of reporting to a new post, assembly and maintenance of helicopters, survival on rocks with poisonous atmosphere or no atmosphere at all, shipboard routines, and a million other details. You have to learn them all, and they get mixed up until you don't know what's trivial and what's important. They're just things you have to know to pass examinations. "You know what you're doing, Centurion, but I'm not sure I do."

"Sir, I've noticed something about young officers," Lieberman said. "They all take things too serious."

"Command's a serious business." Damn, I thought. That's pompous. Especially from a young kid to an older soldier.

He didn't take it that way. "Yes, sir. Too damned

serious to let details get in the way. Lieutenant, if it was just things like posting the guard and organizing the defense of this place, the service wouldn't need officers. We can take care of that. What we need is somebody to tell us what the hell to do. Once that's done, we know *how*."

I didn't say anything. He looked at me closely, probably trying to figure out if I was angry. He didn't seem very worried.

"Take me, for instance," he said. "I don't know why the hell we came to this place, and I don't care. Everybody's got his reasons for joining up. Me, I don't know what else to do. I've found something I'm good at, and I can do it. Officers tell me where to fight, and that's one less damn thing to worry about."

The trumpet sounded outside. Last Post. It was the second time we'd heard it today. The first was when we'd buried our dead.

"Got my rounds to make," Lieberman said. "By your leave, sir."

"Carry on, Centurion." A few minutes later Hartz came in to help me get my boots off. He wouldn't hear of letting me turn in wearing them.

"We'll hold 'em off long enough to get your boots on, zur. Nobody's going to catch a Marine officer in the sack."

He'd sleep with his boots on so that I could take mine off. It didn't make a lot of sense, but I wasn't going to win any arguments with him about it. I rolled into the sack and stared at the ceiling. My first day of command. I was still thinking about that when I went to sleep.

The attacks started the next day. At first it was just small parties trying to force the roadblock, and they never came close to doing that. We could put too much fire onto them from the fort.

That night they tried the fort itself. There were a dozen mortars out there. They weren't very accurate, and our radar system worked fine. They would get off a couple of rounds, and then we'd have them backtracked to the origin point and our whole battery would drop in on them. We couldn't silence them completely, but we could make it unhealthy for the crews servicing their mortars, and after a while the fire slackened. There were rifle attacks all through the night, but nothing in strength.

"Just testing you," Falkenberg said in the morning when I reported to him. "We're pressing hard from this end. They'll make a serious try before long."

"Yes, sir. How are things at your end?"

"We're moving," Falkenberg said. "There's more resistance than the colonel expected, of course. With you stopping up their bolt hole, they've got no route to retreat through. Fight or give up—that's all the choice we left them. You can look for their real effort to break past you in a couple of days. By then we'll be close enough to really worry them."

He was right. By the fourth day we were under continuous attack from more than a thousand hostiles.

It was a strange situation. No one was really worried. We were holding them off. Our ammunition stocks were running low, but Lieberman's answer to that was to order the recruits to stop using their weapons. They were put to serving mortars and recoilless rifles, with an experienced NCO in charge to make sure there was a target worth the effort before they fired. The riflemen waited for good shots and made each one count.

As long as the ammunition held out, we were in no serious danger. The fort had a clear field of fire, and we weren't faced by heavy artillery. The best the enemy had was mortars, and our counterbattery radar and computer system was more than a match for that.

"No discipline," Lieberman said. "They got no discipline. Come in waves, run in waves, but they never press the attack. Damned glad there's no Marine deserters in that outfit. They'd have broke through if they'd had good leadership."

"I'm worried about our ammunition supplies," I said.

"Hell, Lieutenant, Cap'n Falkenberg will get here. He's never let anybody down yet."

"You've served with him before?"

"Yes, sir, in that affair on Domingo. Christian Johnny, we called him. He'll be here."

Everyone acted that way. It made the situation unreal. We were under fire. You couldn't put your head above the wall or outside the gate. Mortars dropped in at random intervals, sometimes catching men in the open and wounding them despite their body armor. We had four dead and nine more in the hospital bunker. We were running low on ammunition, and we faced better than ten-to-one odds, and nobody was worried.

"Your job is to look confident," Falkenberg had told me. Sure.

On the fifth day things were getting serious for Sergeant Ardwain and his men at the roadblock. They were running out of ammunition and water.

"Abandon it, Ardwain," I told him. "Bring your troops up here. We can keep the road closed with fire from the fort."

"Sir. I have six casualties that can't walk, sir."

"How many total?"

"Nine, sir—two walking and one dead."

Nine out of a total of twelve men. "Hold fast, Sergeant. We'll come get you."

"Aye, aye, sir."

I wondered who I could spare. There wasn't much doubt as to who was the most useless man on the post. I sent for Lieberman.

"Centurion, I want a dozen volunteers to go with me to relieve Ardwain's group. We'll take full packs and extra ammunition and supplies."

"Lieutenant—"

"Damn it, don't tell me you don't want me to go. You're capable enough. You told me that you need officers to tell you what to do, not how to do it. Fine. Your orders are to hold this post until Falkenberg comes. One last thing—you will not send or take any relief forces down the hill. I won't have this command further weakened. Is that understood?"

"Sir."

"Fine. Now get me a dozen volunteers."

* * *

I decided to go down the hill just after moonset. We got the packs loaded and waited at the gate. One of my volunteers was Corporal Brady. He stood at the gate, chatting with the sentry there.

"Quiet tonight," Brady said.

"They're still there, though," the sentry said. "You'll know soon enough. Bet you tomorrow's wine ration you don't make it down the hill."

"Done. Remember, you said *down* the hill. I expect you to save that wine for me."

"Yeah. Hey, this is a funny place, Brady."

"How's that?"

"A holy Joe planet, and no Marine chaplain."

"You want a chaplain?"

The sentry shrugged. He had a huge black beard that he fingered, as if feeling for lice. "Good idea, isn't it?"

"They're all right, but we don't need a chaplain. What we need is a good Satanist. No Satanist in this battalion."

"What do you need one of them for?"

Brady laughed. "Stands to reason, don't it? God's good, right? He'll treat you okay. It's the other guy you have to watch out for." He laughed again. "Got three days on bread and no wine for saying that once. Told it to Chaplain Major McCrory, back at Sector H.Q. He didn't appreciate it."

"Time to move out," I said. I shouldered my heavy pack.

"Do we run or walk, zur?" Hartz asked.

"Walk until they know we're there. And be quiet about it."

"Zur."

"Move out, Brady. Quietly."

"Sir." The sentry opened the gate, just a crack. Brady went through, then another trooper, and another. Nothing happened, and finally it was my turn. Hartz was last in the line.

The trail led steeply down the side of the cliff. It was about two meters wide, just a slanting ledge, really. We were halfway down when there was a burst of machine-gun fire. One of the troopers went down.

"Move like hell!" I said.

Two men grabbed the fallen trooper and hauled him along. We ran down the cliff face, jumping across short-cuts at the switchbacks. There was nothing we could see to shoot at, but more bullets sent chips flying from the granite cliff.

The walls above us spurted flame. It looked like the whole company was up there covering us. I hoped not. One of our recoilless men found a target and for a few moments we weren't under fire. Then the rifles opened up. Something zinged past my ear. Then I felt a hard punch in the gut and went down.

I lay there sucking air. Hartz grabbed one arm and shouted to another private. "Jersey! Lieutenant's down. Give me a hand."

"I'm all right," I said. I felt my stomach area. There wasn't any blood. "Armor stopped it. Just knocked the wind out of me." I was still gasping, and I couldn't get my breath.

They dragged me along to Ardwain's command post. "How would we explain to the Centurion if we didn't get you down?" Hartz asked.

The CP was a trench roofed over with ironwood logs. There were three wounded men at one end. Brady took our wounded trooper there. He'd been hit in both legs. Brady put tourniquets on them.

Hartz had his own ideas about first aid. He had a brandy flask. It was supposed to be a universal cure. After he poured two shots down me, he went over to the other end of the bunker to pass the bottle among the other wounded.

"Only three of them, Ardwain?" I said. I was still gasping for air. "I thought you had six."

"Six who cannot walk, sir. But three of them can still fight."

XI

"WE'RE NOT GOING to get up that bluff. Not carrying wounded," I said.

"No, sir." Ardwain had runners carrying ammunition to his troopers. "We're dug in good, sir. With the reinforcements you brought, we'll hold out."

"We damned well have to," I said.

"Not so bad, sir. Most of our casualties came from recoilless and mortars. They've stopped using them. Probably low on ammunition."

"Let's hope they stay that way." I had another problem. The main defense for the roadblock was mortar fire from the fort. Up above they were running low on mortar shells. In another day we'd be on our own. No point in worrying about it, I decided. We'll just have to do the best we can.

The next day was the sixth we'd been in the fort. We were low on rations. Down at the roadblock we had nothing to eat but a dried meat that the men called "monkey." It didn't taste bad, but it had the peculiar property of expanding when you chewed it, so that after a while it seemed as if you had a mouthful of rubber bands. It was said that Line Marines could march a thousand kilometers if they had coffee, wine, and monkey.

We reached Falkenberg by radio at noon. He was still forty kilometers away, and facing the hardest fighting yet. They had to go through villages practically house by house.

"Can you hold?" he asked me.

"The rest of today and tonight, easily. By noon tomorrow we'll be out of mortar shells. Sooner, maybe. When that happens, our outpost down at the roadblock will be without support." I hadn't told him where I was.

"Can you hold until 1500 hours tomorrow?" he asked.

"The fort will hold. Don't know about the roadblock."

"We'll see what we can do," Falkenberg said. "Good luck."

"Christian Johnny'll get us out," Brady said.

"You know him?"

"Yes, sir. He'll get us out."

I wished I were as sure as he was.

They tried infiltrating during the night. I don't know how many crept up along the riverbank, but there were a lot of them. Some went on past us. The others moved in on our bunkers. The fighting was hand to hand, with knives and bayonets and grenades doing most of the work, until we got our foxholes clear and I was able to order the men down into them. Then I had Lieberman drop mortar fire in on our own positions for ten minutes. When it lifted, we went out to clear the area.

When morning came we had three more dead, and every man in the section was wounded. I'd got a grenade fragment in my left upper arm just below where the armor left off. It was painful, but nothing to worry about.

There were twenty dead in our area, and bloody trails were leading off where more enemies had crawled away.

An hour after dawn they rushed us again. The fort had few mortar shells left. We called each one in carefully. They couldn't spare us too much attention, though, because there was a general attack on the fort, as well. When there were moments of quiet in the firing around Fort Beersheba, we could hear more distant sounds to the east. Falkenberg's column was blasting its way through another village.

Ardwain got it just at noon. A rifle bullet in the neck. It looked bad. Brady dragged him into the main bunker and put a compress on. Ardwain's breath rattled in his throat, and his mouth oozed blood. That left Roff and Brady as NCO's, and Roff was immobile, with fragments through his left leg.

At 1230 hours we had four effectives, and no fire support from the fort. We'd lost the troops down by the riverbank, and we could hear movement there.

"They're getting past us, damn it!" I shouted. "All this for nothing! Hartz, get me Lieberman."

"Zur." Hartz was working one-handed. His right arm was in shreds. He insisted on staying with me, but I didn't count him as one of my effectives.

"Sergeant Roszak," the radio said.

"Where's Lieberman?"

"Dead, sir. I'm senior NCO."

"What mortar ammunition have you?"

"Fourteen rounds, sir."

"Drop three onto the riverbank just beyond us, and stand by to use more."

"Aye, aye, sir. One moment." There was silence. Then he said, "On the way."

"How is it up there?"

"We're fighting at the walls, sir. We've lost the north section, but the bunkers are covering that area."

"Christ. You'll need the mortars to hold the fort. But there's no point in holding that fort if the roadblock goes. Stand by to use the last mortar rounds at my command."

"Aye, aye, sir. We can hold."

"Sure you can." Sure.

I looked out through the bunker's firing slit. There were men coming up the road. Dozens of them. I had one clip left in my rifle, and I began trying to pick them off with slow fire. Hartz used his rifle with his left hand, firing one shot every two seconds, slow, aimed fire.

There were more shots from off to my left. Corporal Brady was in a bunker over there, but his radio wasn't working. Attackers moved toward his position. I couldn't hear any others of my command.

Suddenly Brady's trumpet sounded. The brassy notes cut through the battle noises. He played "To Arms!," then settled into the Line Marine march. "We've left blood in the dirt of twenty-five worlds—"

There was a movement in the bunker. Recruit Dietz, hit twice in the stomach, had dragged himself over to Sergeant Ardwain and found Ardwain's pistol. He crawled up to the firing slit and began shooting. He coughed blood with each round. Another trooper staggered out of the bush. He reeled like a drunk as he lurched toward the road. He carried a rack of grenades strung around his neck and threw them mechanically, staggering forward and throwing grenades. He had only one arm. He was hit a dozen times and fell, but his arm moved to throw the last grenade before he died.

More attackers moved toward Brady's bunker. The trumpet call wavered for a moment as Brady fired, and then the notes came as clear as ever.

"Roszak! I've got a fire mission," I said.

"Sir."

"Let me describe the situation down here." I gave him the positions of my CP, Brady's bunker, and the only other one I thought might have any of our troops in it. "Everyplace else is full of hostiles, and they're getting past us along the riverbank. I want you to drop a couple of mortar rounds forty meters down the road from the CP, just north of the road, but not too far north. Corporal Brady's in there and it would be a shame to spoil his concert."

"We hear him up here, sir. Wait one." There was silence. "On the way."

The mortar shells came in seconds later. Brady was still playing. I remembered his name now. It was ten years ago on Earth. He'd been a famous man until he dropped out of sight. Roszak had left his mike open, and in the background I could hear the men in the fort cheering wildly.

Roszak's voice came in my ears. "General order from battalion headquarters, sir. You're to stay in your bunkers. No one to expose himself. Urgent general order, sir."

I wondered what the hell Falkenberg was doing giving me general orders, but I used my command set to pass them along. I doubted if anyone heard, but it didn't matter. No one was going anywhere.

Suddenly the road exploded. The whole distance from fifty meters away down as far as I could see vanished in a line of explosions. They kept coming, pounding the road; then the riverbank was lifted in great clods of mud. The road ahead was torn to bits; then the pieces were lifted by another salvo, and another. I drove into the bottom of the bunker and held my ears while shells dropped all around me.

Finally it lifted. I could hear noises in my phones, but my ears were ringing, and I couldn't understand. It wasn't Roszak's voice. Finally it came through. "Do you need more fire support, Mr. Slater?"

"No. Lord, what shooting—"

"I'll tell the gunners that," Falkenberg said. "Hang on, Hal. We'll be another hour, but you'll have fire support from now on."

Outside, Brady's trumpet sang out another march.

XII

THEY SENT ME back to Garrison to get my arm fixed. There's a fungus infection on Arrarat that makes even minor wounds dangerous. I spent a week in surgery getting chunks cut out of my arm, then another week in regeneration stimulation. I wanted to get back to my outfit, but the surgeon wouldn't hear of it. He wanted me around to check up on the regrowth.

Sergeant Ardwain was in the next bay. It was going to take a while to get him back together, but he'd be all right. With Lieberman dead, Ardwain would be up for a Centurion's badges.

It drove me crazy to be in Garrison while my company, minus its only officer and both its senior NCO's, was out at Fort Beersheba. The day they let me out of sick bay I was ready to mutiny, but there wasn't any transportation, and Major Lorca made it clear that I was to stay in Garrison until the surgeon released me. I went to my quarters in a blue funk.

The place was all fixed up. Private Hartz was there grinning at me. His right arm was in an enormous cast, bound to his chest with what seemed like a mile of gauze.

"How did you get out before I did?" I asked him.

"No infection, zur. I poured brandy on the wounds." He winced. "It was a waste, but there was more than enough for the few of us left."

There was another surprise. Irina Swale came out of my bedroom.

"Miss Swale has been kind enough to help with the work here, zur," Hartz said. He seemed embarrassed. "She insisted, zur. If the lieutenant will excuse me, I have laundry to pick up, zur."

I grinned at him and he left. Now what? I wondered. "Thanks."

"It's the least I could do for Arrarat's biggest hero," Irina said.

"Hero? Nonsense—"

"I suppose it's nonsense that my father is giving you the military medal, and that Colonel Harrington has put in for something else; I forget what, but it can't be approved here—it has to come from Sector Headquarters."

"News to me," I said. "And I still don't think—"

"You don't have to. Aren't you going to ask me to sit down? Would you like something to drink? We have everything here. Private Hartz is terribly efficient."

"So are you. I'm not doing well, am I? Please have a seat. I'd get you a drink, but I don't know where anything is."

"And you couldn't handle the bottles, anyway. I'll get it." She went into the other room and came out with two glasses. Brandy for me and that Jericho wine she liked. Hartz at work, I thought. I'll be drinking that damned brandy the rest of my life.

"It was pretty bad, wasn't it?" she said. She sat on the couch that had appeared while I was gone.

"Bad enough." Out of my original ninety, there were only twelve who hadn't been wounded. Twenty-eight dead, and another dozen who wouldn't be back on duty for a long time. "But we held." I shook my head. "Not bragging, Irina. Amazed, mostly. We held."

"I've been wondering about something," she said. "I asked Louis Bonneyman, and he wouldn't answer me. Why did you have to hold the fort? It was much the hardest part of the campaign, wasn't it? Why didn't Captain Falkenberg do it?"

"Had other things to do, I suppose. They haven't let

me off drugs long enough to learn anything over in sick bay. What's happening out there?"

"It went splendidly," she said. "The Harmony militia are in control of the whole river. The boats are running again, grain prices have fallen here in the city—"

"You don't sound too happy."

"Is it that obvious?" She sat quietly for a moment. She seemed to be trying to control her face. Her lips were trembling. "My father says you've accomplished your mission. He won't let Colonel Harrington send you out to help the other farmers. And the River Pack weren't the worst of the convict governments! In a lot of ways they weren't even so bad. I thought . . . I'd hoped you could go south, to the farmlands, where things are really bad, but Hugo has negotiated a steady supply of grain and he says it's none of our business."

"You're certainly anxious to get us killed."

She looked at me furiously. Then she saw my grin. "By the way," she said, "you're expected at the palace for dinner tonight. I've already cleared it with the surgeon. And this time I expect you to come! All those plans for my big party, and it was nothing but a trick your Captain Falkenberg had planned! You will come, won't you? Please?"

We ate alone. Governor Swale was out in the newly taken territory trying to set up a government that would last. Irina's mother had left him years before, and her only brother was a Navy officer somewhere in Pleiades Sector.

After dinner I did what she probably expected me to. I kissed her, then held her close to me and hoped to go to something a bit more intimate. She pushed me away. "Hal, please."

"Sorry."

"Don't be. I like you, Hal. It's just that—"

"Deane Knowles," I said.

She gave me a puzzled look. "No, of course not. But . . . I do like your friend Louis. Can't we be friends, Hal? Do we have to—"

"Of course we can be friends."

I saw a lot of her in the next three weeks. Friends. I found myself thinking about her when I wasn't with her, and I didn't like that. The whole thing's silly, I told myself. Junior officers have no business getting involved with Governors' daughters. Nothing can come of it, and you don't want anything to come of it to begin with. Your life's complicated enough as it is.

I kept telling myself that right up to the day the surgeon told me I could rejoin my outfit. I was glad to go.

It was still my company. I hadn't been with most of them at all, and I'd been with the team at the fort only a few days, but A Company was mine. Every man in the outfit thought so. I wondered what I'd done right. It didn't seem to me that I'd made any good decisions, or really any at all.

"Luck," Deane told me. "They think you're lucky."

That explained it. Line Marines are probably the most superstitious soldiers in history. And we'd certainly had plenty of luck.

I spent the next six weeks honing the troops into shape. By that time Ardwain was back, with Centurion's badges. He was posted for light duty only, but that didn't stop him from working the troops until they were ready to drop. We had more recruits, recently arrived convicts, probably men who'd been part of the River Pack at one time. It didn't matter. The Marine Machine takes over, and if it doesn't break you, you come out a Marine.

Falkenberg had a simple solution to the problem of deserters. He offered a reward, no questions asked, to anyone who brought in a deserter—and a larger reward for anyone bringing in the deserter's head. It wasn't an original idea, but it was effective.

Or had been effective. As more weeks went by with nothing to do but make patrols along the river, drill and train, stand formal retreat and parades and inspections, men began to think of running.

They also went berserk. They'd get drunk and shoot

a comrade. Steal. We couldn't drill them forever, and when we gave them any time off, they'd get the bug.

The day the main body had reached Fort Beersheba, the 501st had been combat-weary, with a quarter of its men on the casualty list. It was an exhausted battalion, but it had high spirits. Now, a few months later, it was up to strength, trained to perfection, well-organized and well-fed—and unhappy.

I found a trooper painting I.H.T.F.P. on the orderly room wall. He dropped the paint bucket and stood to attention as I came up.

"And what does that mean, Hora?"

He stood straight as a ramrod. "Sir, it means 'I Have Truly Found Paradise.' "

"And what's going to happen to you if Sergeant Major truly finds Private Hora painting on the orderly room wall?"

"Cells, Lieutenant."

"If you're lucky. More likely you'll get to dig a hole and live in it a week. Hora, I'm going to the club for a drink. I don't expect to see any paint on that wall when I come back."

Deane laughed when I told him about it. "So they're doing that already. 'I hate this fucking place.' He means it, too."

"Give us another six weeks and I'll be painting walls," I said. "Only I'll put mine on the Governor's palace."

"You'll have to wait your turn," Deane said.

"Goddamn it, Deane, what can we do? The NCO's have gotten so rough I think I'll have to start noticing it, but if we relax discipline at all, things will really come apart."

"Yeah. Have you spoken to Falkenberg about it?"

"Sure I have," I told him. "But what can he do? What we need is some combat, Deane. I never thought I'd say that. I thought that was all garbage that they gave us at the Academy, that business about *le cafard* and losing more men to it than to an enemy, but I believe it now."

"Cheer up," Deane said. "Louis is officer of the day, and I just heard the word from him. We've got a break in the routine. Tomorrow Governor Hugo Swale, Hisself, is coming to pay a visit to the gallant troops of the 501st. He's bringing your medal, I make no doubt."

"How truly good," I said. "I'd rather he brought us a good war."

"Give him time," Deane said. "The way those damned merchants from Harmony are squeezing the farmers, they're all ready to revolt."

"Just what we need. A campaign to put down the farmers," I said. "Poor bastards. They get it from everybody, don't they? Convicts that call themselves tax collectors. Now you say the Harmony merchants—"

"Yeah," Deane said. "Welcome to the glory of CoDominium Service."

Sergeant Major Ogilvie's baritone rang out across the Fort Beersheba parade ground. "Battalion, *attenhut!* A Company color guard, front and center, *march!*"

That was a surprise. Governor Swale had just presented me with the military medal, which isn't the Earth, but I was a bit proud of it. Now our color guard marched across the hard adobe field to the reviewing stand.

"Attention to orders," Ogilvie said. "For conspicuous gallantry in the face of the enemy, A Company, 501st Provisional Battalion, is awarded the Unit Citation of Merit. By order of Rear Admiral Sergei Lermontov, Captain of the Fleet, Crucis Sector Headquarters. A Company, *pass in review!*"

Bits of cloth and metal, and men will die for them, I thought. The old military game. It's all silly. And we held our heads high as we marched past the reviewing stand.

Falkenberg had found five men who could play bagpipes, or claimed they could—how can you tell if they're doing it right?—and they had made their own pipes. Now they marched around the table in the officers' mess at Fort Beersheba. Stewards brought whiskey and brandy.

Governor Hugo Swale sat politely, trying not to show

any distress as the pipers thundered past him. Eventually they stopped. "I think we should join the ladies," Swale said. He looked relieved when Falkenberg stood.

We went into the lounge. Irina had brought another girl, a visitor from one of the farm areas. She was about nineteen, I thought, with red-brown hair and blue eyes. She would have been beautiful if she didn't have a perpetual haunted look. Irina had introduced her as Kathryn Malcolm.

Governor Swale was obviously embarrassed to have her around. He was a strange little man. There was no resemblance between him and Irina, nothing that would make you think he was her father. He was short and dumpy, almost completely bald, with wrinkles on his high forehead. He had a quick nervous manner of speaking and gesturing. He so obviously disliked Kathryn that I think only the bagpipes could have driven him to want to get back to her company. I wondered why. There'd been no chance to talk to any of them at dinner.

We sat around the fireplace. Falkenberg gave a curt nod, and all the stewards left except Monitor Lazar, Falkenberg's own orderly. Lazar brought a round of drinks and went off into the pantry.

"Well. Here's to A Company and its commander," Falkenberg said. I sat embarrassed as the others stood and lifted their glasses.

"Good work, indeed," Hugo Swale said. "Thanks to this young man, the Jordan Valley is completely pacified. It will take a long time before there's any buildup of arms here again. I want to thank you gentlemen for doing such a thorough job."

I'd had a bit too much to drink with dinner, and there'd been brandy afterward, and the pipers with their wild war sounds. My head was buzzing. "Perhaps too thorough," I muttered as the others sat down. I honestly don't know whether I wanted the others to hear me or not. Deane and Louis threw me sharp looks.

"What do you mean, Hal?" Irina asked.

"Nothing."

"Spit it out," Falkenberg said. The tone made it an order.

"I've a dozen good men in cells and three more in a worse kind of punishment, half my company is on extra duty, and the rest of them are going slowly mad," I said. "If we'd left a bit of the fighting to do, we'd at least have employment." I tried to make it a joke.

Governor Swale took it seriously. "It's as much a soldier's job to prevent trouble as to fight," he said.

You pompous ass, I thought. But of course he was right.

"There's plenty that needs doing," Kathryn Malcolm said. "If your men are spoiling to fight somebody, loan them to us for a while." She wasn't joking at all.

Governor Swale wasn't pleased at all. "That will do, Kathryn. You know we can't do that."

"And why not?" she demanded. "You're supposed to be Governor of this whole planet, but the only people you care about are the merchants in Harmony—those sanctimonious hymn-singers! You know the grain they're buying is stolen. Stolen from us, by gangsters who claim to be our government, and if we don't give them what they want, they take it anyway, and kill everyone who tries to stop them. And then you buy it from them!"

"There is nothing I can do," Swale protested. "I don't have enough troops to govern the whole planet. The Grand Senate explicitly instructed me to deal with local governments—"

"The way you did with the River Pack," Kathryn said. Her voice was bitter. "All they did was try to make some money by charging tolls for river traffic. They wouldn't deal with your damned merchants, so you sent the Marines to bargain with them. Just how many people in the Jordan Valley thanked you for that, Governor? Do they think you're their liberator?"

"Kathryn, that's not fair," Irina protested. "There are plenty of people glad to be free of the River Pack. You shouldn't say things like that."

"All I meant was that the River Pack wasn't so bad.

Not compared to what *we* have to live with. But his Excellency isn't concerned about us, because his merchants can buy their grain at low prices. He doesn't care that we've become slaves."

Swale's lips tightened, but he didn't say anything.

"Local governments," Kathryn said. "What you've done, Governor, is recognize one gang. There's another gang, too, and both of them collect taxes from us! It's bad enough with just one, but it can't even protect us from the other! If you won't give us our land back, can't you at least put down the rival gangsters so we only have one set of crooks stealing from us?"

Swale kept his voice under control. He was elaborately polite as he said, "There is nothing we can do, Miss Malcolm. I wish there were. I suggest you people help yourselves."

"That isn't fair, either," Irina said. "You know it isn't. They didn't ask for all those convicts to be sent here. I think Kathryn has a very good idea. Loan her the 501st. Once those hills are cleaned out and the gangsters are disarmed, the farmers can protect themselves. Can't they, Kathryn?"

"I think so. We'd be ready, this time."

"See? And Hal says his men are spoiling for a good fight. Why not let them do it?"

"Irina, I have to put up with that from Miss Malcolm because she is a guest, but I do not have to take it from you, and I will not. Captain, I thought I was an invited guest on this post."

Falkenberg nodded. "I think we'd best change the subject," he said.

There was an embarrassed silence. Then Kathryn got up and went angrily to the door. "You needn't bother to see me to my room," she said. "I can take care of myself. I've had to do it often enough. I'm not surprised that Captain Falkenberg isn't eager to lead his troops into the hills. I notice that he sent a newly commissioned lieutenant to do the tough part of Governor Swale's dirty work. I'm not surprised at all that he doesn't want any more fighting." She left, slamming the door behind her.

Falkenberg acted as if he hadn't heard her. I don't suppose there was anything else he could do. The party didn't last much longer.

I went to my rooms alone. Deane and Louis offered to stay with me, but I didn't want them. I told them I'd had enough celebrating.

Hartz had left the brandy bottle on the table, and I poured myself another drink, although I didn't want it. The table was Arrarat ironwood, and God knows how the troops had managed to cut planks out of it. My company had built it, and a desk, and some other furniture, and put them in my rooms while I was in hospital. I ran my hand along the polished tabletop.

She should never have said that, I thought. And I expect it's my fault. I remembered Irina saying much the same thing back in Garrison, and I hadn't protested. My damned fault. Falkenberg never explained anything about himself, and I'd never learned why he hadn't come with us the night we attacked the fort, but I was damned sure it wasn't cowardice. Louis and Deane had straightened me out about that. No one who'd been with him on the march up the river could even suspect it.

And why the hell didn't I tell Irina that? I wondered. Cocky kid, trying to impress the girl. Too busy being proud of himself to—

There was a knock on the door. "Come in," I said.

It was Sergeant Major Ogilvie. There were some others in the hall. "Yes, Sergeant Major?"

"If we could have a word with the lieutenant. We have a problem, sir."

"Come in."

Ogilvie came inside. When his huge shoulders were out of the doorway, I saw Monitor Lazar and Kathryn Malcolm behind him. They all came in, and Kathryn stood nervously, her hands twisted together. "It's all my fault," she said.

Ogilvie ignored her. "Sir, I have to report that Monitor Lazar has removed certain orders from the battalion files without authorization."

"Why tell me?" I asked. "He's Captain Falkenberg's orderly."

"Sir, if you'll look at the papers. He showed them to this civilian. If you say we should report it to the captain, we'll have to." Ogilvie's voice was carefully controlled. He handed me a bound stack of papers.

They were orders from Colonel Harrington to Falkenberg as commander of the 501st, and they were dated the first day we'd arrived on Arrarat. I'd never seen them myself. No reason I should, unless Falkenberg were killed and I had to take over as his deputy.

Lazar stood at rigid attention. He wasn't looking at me, but seemed fascinated with a spot on the wall above me.

"You say Miss Malcolm has read these, Sergeant Major?"

"Yes, sir."

"Then it will do no harm if I read them, I suppose." I opened the order book. The first pages were general orders commanding Falkenberg to organize the 501st. There was more, about procedures for liaison with Major Lorca and the Garrison supply depot. I'd seen copies of all those. "Why the devil did you think Miss Malcolm would be interested in this stuff, Lazar?" I asked.

"Not that, sir," Ogilvie said. "Next page."

I thumbed through the book again. There it was.

Captain John Christian Falkenberg, Commanding Officer, 501st Provisional Battalion of Line Marines:

1. These orders are written confirmation of verbal orders issued in conference with above-named officer.

2. The 501st Bn. is ordered to occupy Fort Beersheba at earliest possible moment consistent with safety of the command and at the discretion of Bn. CO.

3. Immediate airborne assault on Fort Beersheba is

authorized, provided that assault risks no more than 10% of effective strength of 501st Bn.

4. Any assault on Fort Beersheba in advance of main body of 501st Bn. shall be commanded by officer other than CO 501st Bn., and request of Captain Falkenberg to accompany assault and return to Bn. after Fort Beersheba is taken is expressly denied.

NOTE: It is the considered judgment of undersigned that officers assigned to 501st would not be competent to organize Bn. and accomplish main objective of pacification of Jordan Valley without supervision of experienced officer. It is further considered judgment of undersigned that secondary objective of early capture of Fort Beersheba does not justify endangering main mission of occupation of Jordan Valley. Captain Falkenberg is therefore ordered to refrain from exposing himself to combat risks until such time as primary mission is assured.

By Order of Planetary Military Commander

Nicholas Harrington, Colonel, CoDominium Marines

"Lazar, I take it you were listening to our conversation earlier," I said.

"No way to avoid it, sir. The lady was shouting." Lazar's expression didn't change.

I turned the book over and over in my hands. "Sergeant Major."

"Sir."

"I'm finished with this order book. Would you please see that it's returned to the battalion safe? Also, I think I forgot to log it out. You may do as you see fit about that."

"Sir."

"Thank you. You and Lazar may go now. I see no

reason why the captain should be disturbed because I wanted a look at the order book."

"Yes, sir. Let's go, Monitor." Ogilvie started to say something else, but he stopped himself. They left, closing the door behind them.

"That was nice of you," Kathryn said.

"About all I could do," I said. "Would you like a drink?"

"No, thank you. I feel like a fool—"

"You're not the only one. I was just thinking the same thing, and for about the same reasons, when Ogilvie knocked. Won't you sit down? I suppose we should open the door."

"Don't be silly." She pulled a chair up to the big table. She was wearing a long plaid skirt, like a very long kilt, with a shiny blouse of some local fabric, and a wool jacket that didn't close at the front. Her hair was long, brown with red in it, but I thought it might be a wig. A damned pretty girl, I thought. But there was that haunted look in her eyes, and her hands were scarred, tiny scars that showed regeneration therapy by unskilled surgeons.

"I think Irina said you're a farmer. You don't look like a farmer."

She didn't smile. "I own a farm . . . or did. It's been confiscated by the government—one of our governments." Her voice was bitter. "The Mission Hills Protective Association. A gang of convicts. We used to fight them. My grandfather and my mother and my brother and my fiancé were all killed fighting them. Now we don't do anything at all."

"How many of these gangsters are there?"

She shrugged. "I guess the Protectionists have about four thousand. Something like that, anyway. Then there is the True Brotherhood. They have only a few hundred, maybe a thousand. No one really knows. They aren't really very well organized."

"Seems like they'd be no problem."

"They wouldn't be, if we could deal with them, but the Protective Association keeps our farmers disarmed and won't let us go on commando against the Brotherhood. They're afraid we'll throw the Association out, as well. The Brotherhood isn't anything real—they're closer to savages than human beings—but we can't do anything about them because the Association won't let us."

"And how many of you are there?"

"There are twenty thousand farmers in the Valley," she said. "And don't tell me we ought to be able to run both gangs off. I know we should be able to. But we tried it, and it didn't work. Whenever they raided one of our places, we'd turn out to chase them down, but they'd run into the hills, where it would take weeks to find them. Then they'd wait until we came down to grow crops again, then come down and kill everyone who resisted them, families and all."

"Is that what happened to your grandfather?"

"Yes. He'd been one of the Valley leaders. They weren't really trying to loot his place; they just wanted to kill him. I tried to organize resistance after that, and then—" She looked at her hands. "They caught me. I guess I will have that drink, after all."

"There's only brandy, I'm afraid. Or coffee."

"Brandy is all right."

I got another glass and poured. Her hands didn't shake as she lifted it.

"Aren't you going to ask?" she said. "Everyone wants to know, but they're afraid to ask." She shuddered. "They don't want to embarrass me. Embarrass!"

"Look, you don't want to talk about—"

"I don't want to, but I have to. Can you understand that?"

"Yes."

"Hal, there's very little you can imagine that they didn't do to me. The only reason I lived through it was that they wanted me to live. Afterward, they put me in a cage in the village square. As an example. A warning."

"I'd have thought that would have the opposite effect." I was trying to speak calmly, but inside I was boiling with hatred.

"No. I wish it had. It would have been worth it. Maybe—I don't know. The second night I was there, two men who'd been neighbors killed one of their guards and got me out. The Protectionists shot thirty people the next day in reprisal." She looked down at her hands. "My friends got me to a safe place. The doctor wasn't very well trained, they tell me. He left scars. If they could see what I was like when I got to him, they wouldn't say that."

I didn't know what to say. I didn't trust myself to say anything. I wanted to take her in my arms and hold her, not anything else, just hold her and protect her. And I wanted to get my hands on the people who'd done this, and on anyone who could have stopped it and didn't. My God, what are soldiers for, if not to put a stop to things like that? But all I could do was pour her another drink. I tried to keep my voice calm. "What will you do now?"

"I don't know. When Father Reedy finally let me leave his place, I went to Harmony. I guess I hoped I could get help. But . . . Hal, why won't Governor Swale do something? Anything?"

"More a matter of why should he," I said. "God, Kathryn, how can I say it? From his view, things are quiet. He can report that all's well here. They don't promote troublemakers in BuColonial, and Hugo Swale doesn't strike me as the kind of man who wants to retire on Arrarat." I drained my brandy glass. "Maybe I'm not being fair to him. Somehow I don't even want to be."

"But you'd help us if you could. Wouldn't you?"

"My God, yes. At least you're safe now."

She had a sad little smile. "Yes, nothing but a few scars. Come here. Please." She stood. I went to her. "Put your hands on my shoulders," she said.

I reached out to her. She stood rigidly. I could feel her trembling as I touched her.

"It happens every time," she said. "Even now, and I like you. I . . . Hal, I'd give anything if I could just relax and let you hold me. But I can't. It's all I can do to sit here and talk to you."

"Then I'd better let you go."

"No. Please. Please understand. I like you. I want to talk with you. I want to show myself there are men I can trust. Just . . . don't expect too much . . . not for a while. I keep telling myself I'm going to get over it. I don't want to be alone, but I'm afraid to be with anyone, and I'm going to get over that."

XIII

WE HAD MORE weeks of parades and training. Falkenberg had a new scheme. He bought two hundred mules and assigned my company the job of learning to live with them. The idea was to increase our marching capability by using pack mules, and to teach the men to hang on to the pack saddles so they could cover more kilometers each day. It worked fine, but it only increased the frustration because there was nothing to march toward.

Governor Swale had gone back to Garrison, but Irina and Kathryn stayed as guests of the battalion. The men were pleased to have them on the post, and there was much less of a problem with discipline. They particularly adopted Kathryn. She was interested in everything they did, and the troops thought of her as a mascot. She was young and vulnerable, and she didn't talk down to them, and they were half in love with her.

I was more than that. I saw so much of her that Falkenberg thought it worthwhile to remind me that the service does not permit lieutenants to marry. That isn't strictly true, of course, but it might as well be. There's no travel allowance and it takes an appeal to Saint Peter or perhaps an even higher level to get married quarters. The rule is, "Captains may marry, Majors should marry, Colonels must marry," and there aren't many exceptions to it.

"Not much danger of that," I told him.

"Yes?" He raised an eyebrow. It was an infuriating gesture.

I blurted out her story.

He only nodded. "I was aware of most of it, Mr. Slater."

"How in God's name can you be so cool about it?" I demanded. "I know you don't like her after that outburst—"

"Miss Malcolm has been very careful to apologize and to credit you with the explanation," Falkenberg said. "And the next time you take the order book out of the safe, I'll expect you to log it properly. Now tell me why we have three men of your company sleeping under their bunks without blankets."

He didn't really want an explanation, of course, and for that matter he probably already knew. There wasn't much about the battalion that he didn't know. It made a smooth change of subject, but I wasn't having any. I told him, off the record, what the charges would have been if I'd officially heard what the men had done. "Centurion Ardwain preferred not to report it," I said. "Captain, I still cannot understand how you can be so calm when you know that not two hundred kilometers from here—"

"Mr. Slater, I remain calm because at the moment there is very little I can do. What do you want? That we lead the 501st in a mutiny? If it is any comfort to you, I do not think the situation will last. It is my belief that Governor Swale is living in a fool's paradise. You cannot deal with criminal gangs on any permanent basis, and I believe the situation will explode. Until it does, there is not one damned thing we can do, and I prefer not to be reminded of my helplessness."

"But, sir—"

"But nothing, Mr. Slater. Shut up and soldier."

Falkenberg had guessed right. Although we didn't know it, about the time we had that conversation the Protective Association had decided to raise the price of grain. Two weeks later they hiked the price again and held up the shipments to show the Governor they meant it.

It wasn't long after that the Governor paid another visit to Fort Beersheba.

Deane Knowles found me in the club. "His Excellency has arrived," he said. "He's really come with full kit this time. He's brought Colonel Harrington and a whole company of militia."

"What the devil are they for?" I asked.

"Search me."

"I thought you knew everything, well, well. I suppose we will know soon enough. There's Officers' Call."

The Governor, Colonel Harrington, and Falkenberg were all in the staff conference room. There was also a colonel of militia. He didn't look very soldierly. His uniform was baggy, and he had a bulge around his middle. The Governor introduced him as Colonel Trevor.

"I'll come right to the point, gentlemen," Swale said. "Due to certain developments in the southern areas, I am no longer confident that food supply for the cities of Harmony and Garrison is assured. The local government down there has not negotiated in good faith. It's time to put some pressure on them."

"In other words," Colonel Harrington said, "he wants to send the Marines down to bash heads so the Harmony merchants won't have to pay so much."

"Colonel, that remark was not called for," Governor Swale said.

"Certainly it was." There was no humor in Harrington's voice. "If we can send my lads down to get themselves killed, we can tell them why they're going. It's hardly a new mission for the Line Marines."

"Your orders are to hold the cities," Swale said. "That cannot be done without adequate food supplies. I think that justifies using your troops for this campaign."

"Sure it does," Harrington said. "And after the CD pulls both of us out of here, what happens? Doesn't that worry you a bit, Colonel Trevor?"

"The CoDominium won't abandon Arrarat." Trevor sounded very positive.

"You're betting a lot on that," Colonel Harrington told him.

"If you two are quite through," Swale said. "Captain, how soon can your battalion be ready to march?"

Falkenberg looked to Colonel Harrington. "Are we to hold the Jordan area, as well, sir?"

"You won't need much here," Harrington said. "The militia can take over now."

"And what precisely are we to accomplish in the southern farm area?" Falkenberg asked.

"I just told you," Swale said. "Go down and put some pressure on the Protective Association so they'll see reason."

"And how am I to do that?"

"For heaven's sake, Falkenberg, it's a punitive expedition. Go hurt them until they're ready to give in."

"Burn farms and towns. Shoot livestock. Destroy transport systems. That sort of thing?"

"Well . . . I'd rather you didn't do it that way."

"Then, Governor, exactly what am I to do?" Falkenberg demanded. "I remind you that the Protective Association is itself an occupying power. They don't really care what we do to the farmers. They don't work that land; they merely expropriate from those who do."

"Then confine your punitive actions to the Protective Association—" Swale's voice trailed off.

"I do not even know how to identify them, sir. I presume that anyone I find actually working the land is probably not one of the criminal element, but I can hardly shoot everyone who happens to be idle at the moment I pass through."

"You needn't be sarcastic with me, *Captain*."

"Sir, I am trying to point out the difficulties inherent in the orders you gave me. If I have been impertinent, you have my apology."

Sure you do, I thought. Deane and Louis grinned at each other and at me. Then we managed to get our faces straight. I wondered what Falkenberg was trying to do. I found out soon enough.

"Then what the devil do you suggest?" Swale demanded.

"Governor, there is a way I can assure you a reasonable and adequate grain supply. It requires your cooperation. Specifically, you must withdraw recognition from the Protective Association."

"And recognize whom? An unorganized bunch of farmers who couldn't hold on to the territory in the first place? Captain, I have sympathy for those people, even if all of you here do suspect me of being a monster with no feelings. My sympathy is of no matter. I must feed the people of Harmony, and to do that I'll deal with the devil himself if that's what it takes."

"And you very nearly have," I muttered.

"What's that, Lieutenant Slater?"

"Nothing, Governor. Excuse me."

"I expect I know what you said. Captain, let's suppose I do what you ask and withdraw recognition from the Protective Association. Now what do I do? We are not in the democracy-building business. My personal sympathies may well lie with what we are pleased to call 'free and democratic institutions,' but I happen to be an official of the CoDominium, not of the United States. So, by the way, do you. If this planet had been settled by Soviets, we wouldn't even be having this conversation. There would be an assured grain supply, and no nonsense about it."

"I hardly think the situations are comparable," Colonel Harrington said.

"Nor I," Trevor added. That surprised me.

"I ask again, what do we do?" the Governor said.

"Extend CoDominium protection to the area," Harrington said. "It needn't be permanent. I make no doubt that Colonel Trevor's people have friends among the farmers. *We* may not be in the democracy-building business, but there are plenty who'd like to try."

"You are asking for all-out war on the Protective Association," Swale said. "Colonel Harrington, have you any idea of what that will cost? The Senate is very reluctantly paying the basic costs of keeping these Marines on Arrarat. They have not sent one deci-credit to pay for combat actions. How am I supposed to *pay* for this war?"

"You'll just have to tax the grain transactions, that's all," Harrington said.

"I can't do that."

"You're going to have to do it. Captain Falkenberg is right. We can drive out the Protective Association—with enough local cooperation—but we sure as hell can't grow wheat for you. I suppose we could exterminate everyone in the whole damned valley and repopulate it—"

"Now *you're* being impertinent."

"My apologies," Harrington said. "Governor, just what *do* you want? Those farmers aren't going to grow crops just to have a bunch of gangsters take the profits. They'll move out first, or take the land out of cultivation. Then what happens to your grain supply?"

"The situation is more complex than you think, Colonel. Believe me, it is. Your business is war and violence. Mine is politics, and I tell you that things aren't always what they seem. The Protective Association can keep Harmony supplied with grain at a reasonable price. That's what we must have, and it's what you're going to get for me. Now you tell me that my only alternatives are a war I can't pay for, or starvation in the city. Neither is acceptable. I order you to send an expeditionary force to Allansport. It will have the limited objective of demonstrating our intent and putting sufficient pressure on the Protective Association to make them reasonable, and that is the whole objective."

Harrington studied his fingernails for a moment. "Sir, I cannot accept the responsibility."

"Damn you. Captain Falkenberg, you will—"

"I can't accept the responsibility, either, Governor."

"Then, by God, I'll have Colonel Trevor lead it. Trevor, if you say you can't accept responsibility, I damned well know a dozen militia officers who can."

"Yes, sir. Who'll command the Marines sir? They won't take orders from me. Not directly."

"The lieutenants will—" He stopped, because one by one, Deane, Louis, and I all shook our heads.

"This is blackmail! I'll have every one of you cashiered!"

Colonel Harrington laughed. "Now, you know, I really doubt that. Me you might manage to get at. But junior officers for refusing an assignment their colonel turned down? Try peddling that to Admiral Lermontov and he'll laugh like hell."

Swale sat down. He struggled for a moment until he was in control of his voice. "Why are you doing this?"

Colonel Harrington shook his head slowly. "Governor, everything you said about the service is true. We're used. They use us to bash heads so that some senator's nephew can make a mega-credit. They hand people a raw deal and then call on us to make the victims stay in the game. Most of the time we have to take it. It doesn't mean we like it much. Once in a while, just every now and then, the Fleet gets a chance to put something right after you civilians mess it up. We don't pass up such chances." Harrington's voice had been quiet, but now he let it rise slightly. "Governor, just what the hell do you think men become soldiers for? So that you can get promoted to a cushy job?"

"I have told you, I would like to help those farmers. I can't do it. Cannot you understand? We can't *pay* for a long campaign. *Can't*. Not won't. Can't."

"Yes, sir," Colonel Harrington said. "I expect I'd better get back to Garrison. The staff's going to have to work out a pretty strict rationing plan."

"You think you have won," the Governor said. "Not yet, Colonel. Not yet. Colonel Trevor, I asked you to put a battalion of militia on riverboats. How long will it take for them to get here?"

"Be here tomorrow, sir."

"When they arrive, I want you to have made arrangements for more fuel and supplies. We are taking that battalion to Allansport, where I will personally direct operations. I've no doubt we can make the Protective Association see reason. As to the rest of you, you will sit in this fort and rot for all I care. Good afternoon, gentlemen."

I told Kathryn about the conference when I met her for supper that night. She listened with bewilderment.

"I don't understand, Hal," she finally blurted. "All that fuss about costs. *We'd* pay for the campaign and be happy to do it."

"Do you think the Governor knows that?" I asked.

"Of course he knows it. I've told him, and I've brought him offers from some of the other farmers. Don't you remember I asked him to loan us the 501st?"

"Sure, but you weren't serious."

"I wasn't then, but it sounded like such a good idea that later on we really tried to hire you. He wasn't interested."

"Wasn't interested in what?" Louis Bonneyman asked. "Is this an intimate conversation, or may I join you?"

"Please do," Kathryn said. "We're just finishing—"

"I've had my dinner, also," Louis said. "But I'll buy you a drink. Hal, did you ever think old Harrington had that kind of guts?"

"No. Surprised me. So what happens next?"

"Beats me," Louis said. "But I'll give you a hint. I just finished helping Sergeant Major cut orders putting this whole outfit on full field alert as of reveille tomorrow."

"Figures. I wonder just how much trouble His Excellency will get himself into."

Louis grinned. "With any luck, he'll get himself killed and Colonel Harrington becomes Acting Governor. Then we can really clean house."

"You can't wish that on Irina's father," Kathryn protested. "I thought you liked her, Louis."

"Her, yes. Her old man I can live without. I'd have thought you'd share the sentiment."

"He was kind enough to let me live in his home," Kathryn said. "I don't understand him at all. He seems like a good man. It's only when—"

"When he puts on his Governor's hat," I said. "I keep wondering if we blew it, Kathryn. If we'd taken the Governor up on his offer, we could at least have gotten down there to do *something*. I might even have caught the bastard that— You know who I mean."

"I'm glad you didn't, Hal. It would have been horrible. Anything you did to those gangsters they'd take out on my friends as soon as you'd left. I wouldn't have helped you, and I don't think anyone else would, because anybody that did would be signing death warrants for his whole family, and all his friends, too."

"Sounds like a rough gang," Louis said. "Thorough. If you're going to use terror, go all the way. Unfortunately, it works."

Kathryn nodded. "Yes. I've tried to explain it to Governor Swale. If he sends an expedition there, a lot of my friends will try to help. They'll be killed if he leaves those hoodlums in control when it's over. It would be better if none of you ever went there."

"But the Harmony merchants don't like the prices," Louis said. "They want their grain cheaper, and Swale's got to worry about them, too. A complaint from the Harmony city council wouldn't look too good on his record. Somebody at BuColonial might take it seriously."

"Politics," Kathryn said. "Why can't—"

"Be your age," Louis said. "There's politics in the CoDominium, sure, but we still keep the peace. And it's not all that bad, anyway. Swale was appointed by Grand Senator Bronson's people."

"An unsavory lot," I said.

"Maybe," Louis admitted. "Anyway, of course that means that Bronson's enemies will be looking for reasons to discredit Swale. He's got to be careful. The Harmony merchants still have friends at American Express—and AmEx hates Bronson with a passion."

"I'd say our Governor has problems, then," I said. "From the looks of the troops he took with him, he won't scare the Association much. The militia have pretty uniforms, but they're all city kids. All right for holding walls and cruising along the Jordan now that we've disarmed everybody here, but they're unlikely to scare anybody with real combat experience."

XIV

WE PUT THE entire battalion on ready alert, but nothing happened for a week. Colonel Harrington stayed at Fort Beersheba and joined us in the officers' mess in the evenings. Like Falkenberg, he liked bagpipes. To my horror, so did Kathryn. I suppose every woman has some major failing.

"What the hell is he doing?" Colonel Harrington demanded. "I'd have sworn he'd have gotten himself into trouble by now. Maybe we've overestimated the Mission Hills Protective Association. Why the hell did they come up with that name? There aren't any Mission Hills on this planet, to the best of my knowledge."

"They brought the name with them, Colonel," Louis told him. "There's a Southern California gang with that name. Been around for two or three generations. A number of them happened to be on the same prison ship, and they stuck together when they got there."

"How the hell did you find that out?" Harrington demanded.

"Captain Falkenberg insists that his people be thorough," Louis said. "It was a matter of sifting through enough convicts until I found one who knew, and then finding some corroboration."

"Well, congratulations, Louis," Harrington said. "John, you've done well with your collection of newlies."

"Thank you, Colonel."

"Real test's coming up now, though. What the hell is

happening down there? Steward, another whiskey, all around. If we can't fight, we can still drink."

"Maybe Governor Swale will come to terms with them," I said.

The colonel gave me a sour look. "Doubt it, Hal. He's between a rock and a hard place. The merchants won't stand for the prices those goons want, and they think they've got him by the balls. They're not afraid of us, you know. They've got a good idea of what's going on in Harmony. They know damned well that Fleet isn't sending any more support to Arrarat, and what the hell can a thousand men do? Even a thousand Line Marines?"

"I hope they think that way," Deane said. "If they'll stand and fight, they're finished—"

"But they won't," John Falkenberg said. "They're no fools. They won't stand and fight, they'll run like hell as soon as we get close to them. They've only to sit up in the hills and avoid us. Eventually we'll have to leave, but they won't."

Harrington nodded. "Yeah. In the long run those poor damned farmers will have to cut it for themselves. Maybe they'll make it. At least we can try to set things right for them. John, do you think the pipers have had their drink by now?"

"I'm certain of it, Colonel. Lazar! Have Pipe Major bring us a tune!"

Eight days after the Governor left Fort Beersheba, we still had no word. That night there was the usual drinking with the pipers in the mess. I excused myself early and went up to my rooms with Kathryn. I still couldn't touch her without setting her to trembling, but we were working on it. I'd decided I was in love with her, and I could wait for the physical aspects to develop. I didn't dare think very far ahead. We had no real future that I could see, but for the moment just being together was enough. It wasn't a situation either of us enjoyed, but we hated to be separated.

The phone buzzed. "Slater," I told it.

"Sergeant Major Ogilvie, sir. You're wanted in the staff room immediately."

"Hallelujah. Be right there, Sergeant Major." As I hung up, Brady's trumpet sounded "On Full Kits." I turned to Kathryn. We were both grinning like idiots. "This is it, sweetheart."

"Yes. Now that it's happened, I'm scared."

"So am I. As Falkenberg says, we're all scared, but it's an officer's job not to show it. Be back when I can—"

"Just a second." She came to me and put her hands on my shoulders. Her arms went around me, and she pulled me against herself. "See? I'm hardly shaking at all." She kissed me, quickly, then a long, lingering kiss.

"This is one hell of a time for a miraculous psychiatric cure," I said.

"Shut up and get out of here."

"Aye, aye, ma'am." I went out quickly.

Hartz was in the hallway. "I will have our gear ready, zur," he said. "And now we fight."

"I hope so."

As I walked across the parade ground, I wondered why I felt so good. We were about to go kill and maim a lot of people, and give them the chance to do it to us. For a million reasons we ought to have been afraid, and we ought to dread what was coming, but we didn't.

Is it that what we think we ought to do is so thoroughly alien to what we really feel? I couldn't kid myself that this time was different because our cause was just. We say we love peace, but it doesn't excite us. Even pacifists talk more about the horrors of war than about the glories of peace.

And you're not supposed to solve the problems of the universe, I told myself. But you do get to kill the man that raped your girl.

The others were already in the conference room, with Colonel Harrington at the head of the table.

"The expected has happened," Harrington said. I knew for a fact that he'd drunk four double whiskeys since supper, but there wasn't a trace of it in his speech.

I'd swallowed two quick-sober pills on the way over. I really hadn't needed them. I was sure they hadn't had time to dissolve, but I felt fine.

"Our Governor has managed to get himself besieged in Allansport," Harrington said. "With half of his force outside the town. He wants us to bail him out. I have told him we will march immediately—for a price."

"Then he's agreed to withdraw recognition of the Association?" Deane asked.

"Agreed to, yes. He hasn't done it yet. I think he's afraid that the instant he does, they will get really nasty. However, I have his word on it, and I will hold him to it. Captain Falkenberg, the 501st is hereby ordered to drive the Mission Hills Protective Association out of the Allan River Valley by whatever means you think best. You may cooperate with local partisan forces in the area and make reasonable agreements with them. The entire valley is to be placed under CoDominium protection."

"Aye, aye, sir." Falkenberg's detached calm broke for a moment and he let a note of triumph get into his voice.

"Now, Captain, if you will be kind enough to review your battle plan," Harrington said.

"Sir." Falkenberg used the console to project a map onto the briefing screen.

I'd already memorized the area, but I examined it again. About ten kilometers upriver from Beersheba, the Jordan was joined by a tributary known as the Allan River. The Allan runs southwest through forest lands for about fifty kilometers, then turns and widens in a valley that lies almost due north-south. The east side of the Allan Valley is narrow, because no more than twenty klicks from the river there's a high mountain range and east of that is high desert. Nobody lives there and nobody would want to. The west side, though, is some of the most fertile land on Arrarat. The valley is irregularly shaped, narrowing to no more than twenty-five klicks wide in places, but opening out to more than one hundred klicks in others. It reminded me of the San

Joaquin Valley of California, a big fertile bowl with rugged mountains on both sides of it.

Allansport is 125 klicks upriver from where the Allan runs into the Jordan. Falkenberg left the big valley map on one screen and projected a detail onto the other. He fiddled with the console to bring red and green lines representing friendly and hostile forces onto the map.

"As you can see, Governor Swale and one company of militia have taken a defensive position in Allansport," Falkenberg said. "The other two militia companies are south of him, actually upriver. How the devil he ever got himself into such a stupid situation, I cannot say."

"Natural talent," Colonel Harrington muttered.

"No doubt," Falkenberg said. "We have two objectives. The minor, but most urgent, is to rescue Governor Swale. The major objective is pacification of the area. It seems very unlikely that we can accomplish that without a general uprising of the locals in our favor. Agreed?"

We were all silent for a moment. "Mr. Bonneyman, I believe you're the junior," Colonel Harrington said.

"Agreed, sir," Louis said.

Deane and I spoke at once. "Agreed."

"Excellent. I remind you that this conference is recorded," Falkenberg said.

Of course, I thought. All staff conferences are. It didn't seem like Falkenberg and Harrington to spread responsibility around by getting our opinions on record, but I was sure they had their reasons.

"The best way to stimulate a general uprising would be to inflict an immediate and major defeat on the Protective Association," Falkenberg said. "A defeat, not merely driving them away, but bringing them to battle and eliminating a large number of them. It is my view that this is sufficiently important to justify considerable risks. Is that agreed to?"

Aha! I thought. Starting with Louis, we all stated our agreements.

"Then we can proceed to the battle plan," Falkenberg

said. "It is complex, but I think it is worth a try. You will notice that there is a pass into the hills west of Allensport. Our informants tell us that this is the route the Association forces will take if they are forced to retreat. Furthermore, there is a sizable militia force south of Allansport. If the militia were strengthened with local partisans, and if we can take the pass before the besieging hostiles realize their danger, we will have them trapped. The main body of the battalion will march upriver, approach from the north, and engage them. We won't get them all, but we should be able to eliminate quite a lot of them. With that kind of victory behind us, persuading the other ranchers to rise up and join us should not be difficult."

As he talked he illustrated the battle plan with lights on the map. He was right. It was complex.

"Questions?" Falkenberg asked.

"Sir," I said, "I don't believe those two militia companies can take the pass. I certainly wouldn't count on it."

"They can't," Harrington said. "But they're pretty steady on defense. Give 'em a strong position to hold and those lads will give a good account of themselves."

"Yes," Falkenberg said. "I propose to stiffen the militia outside the city with two sections of Marines. We still have our Skyhooks, and I see no reason why we can't use them again."

"Here we go again," I muttered. "Even so, sir, it all depends on how strongly that pass is held, and we don't know that. Or do we?"

"Only that it will be defended," Falkenberg said. "The attack on the pass will have to be in the nature of a probe, ready to be withdrawn if the opposition is too stiff."

"I see." I thought about that for a while. I'd never done anything like that, of course. I might have a military medal, but I couldn't kid myself about my combat experience. "I think I can manage that, sir," I said.

Falkenberg gave me his half grin, the expression he

used when he was springing one of his surprises. "I'm
afraid you won't have all the fun this time, Mr. Slater. I
intend to lead the Skyhook force myself. You'll have
command of the main body."

There was more to his plan, including a part I didn't
like at all. He was taking Kathryn with him on the
Skyhook. I couldn't really object. She'd already volunteered. Falkenberg had called her in my rooms while I
was on the way over to the conference.

"I really have little choice," Falkenberg said. "We
must have someone reliable who is known to the locals.
The whole plan depends on getting enough local assist-
ance to seal off the valley to the south of Allansport.
Otherwise, there's no point to it."

I had to agree. I didn't have to like it. I could
imagine what she'd say if I tried to stop her.

Falkenberg finished with the briefing. "Any more
questions? No? Then once again I'll ask for your
opinions."

"Looks all right to me," Louis said. Of course he
would. He was going with Falkenberg in the Skyhooks.

"No problem with heavy weapons," Deane said. "I
like it."

"Mr. Slater?"

"My operation looks straightforward enough. No
problems."

"It's straightforward," Colonel Harrington said, "but
not trivial. You've got the trickiest part of the job. You
have to seal off the northern escape route, engage the
enemy, rescue the Governor, and then swing around
like a hammer to smash the hostiles against the anvil
Captain Falkenberg will erect at the passes. The timing
is critical."

"I have confidence in Lieutenant Slater," Falkenberg
said.

"So have I, or I wouldn't approve this plan," Harrington said. "But don't ignore what we're doing here.
In order to carry out the major objective of clearing the
hostiles from the whole valley, we're leaving Governor

Swale in a rather delicate situation. If something goes wrong, Sector will have our heads—with justice, I might add." He stood, and we all got to our feet. "But I like it. No doubt the Association thinks we'll be rushing directly to the Governor's aid, and their people are prepared for that. I hate to be obvious."

"So do I," Falkenberg said.

Harrington nodded curtly. "Gentlemen, you have your orders."

The riverboats looked like something out of the American Civil War as they puffed their way down the dark river. We'd had a rainstorm when we left the fort, but now the sky was clear and dark, with bright stars overhead. My rivercraft were really nothing more than barges with steam engines and enough superstructure to get cargo under cover. They were made of wood, of course; there wasn't enough of a metal industry on Arrarat to build steel hulls, and not much reason to want to.

I had three barges, each about fifty meters long and twenty wide, big rectangular floating platforms with cabins whose roofs served as raised decks, and a central bridge to control them. Every centimeter of available space was covered with troops, mules, guns, supply wagons, ammunition, tentage, and rations. The 501st was going to the Allan Valley to stay.

The barges burned wood, which we had to stop and cut with chain saws. In addition, I had one amphibious hovercraft with light armor. It could make fifty-five kilometers an hour compared to the eleven kilometers an hour the barges got under full steam. Perched on top of the third barge was Number Three helicopter, which could make a couple of hundred kilometers an hour. The discrepancies in speeds would have been amusing if they weren't so frustrating.

"One goddamned DC-45," Deane said. "One. That's all, one Starlifter, and we could be there in an hour."

"We make do with what we got," I told him. "Besides, think how romantic it all is. Pity we don't have a leadsman up in the bows singing out the river depth, instead of a sonar depth finder."

The hovercraft ran interference to be sure there weren't any nasty surprises waiting for us. As we got closer to Allansport, I sent up the chopper to make a high-altitude survey of the landing area. We were landing a good twenty klicks downriver from Allansport. Not only were the banks a lot steeper farther upriver, but we didn't want to scare the Association off by landing too close. Governor Swale was screaming at me hourly, of course. He wanted us in Allansport right now. When I told him where we were putting ashore, he was almost hysterical.

"What the hell are you doing?" he demanded. "All you have to do is show up! They won't stand and fight you. This is all a political maneuver. Put heavy pressure on them and they'll come to terms."

I didn't point out that we didn't intend to come to terms with the Association. "Sir, Colonel Harrington approved the battle plan."

"I don't care if God the Father approved it!" Swale shouted. "What are you doing? I know Falkenberg is south of here with troops he brought in by helicopter, but he won't tell me what he's doing! And now he's withdrawn the militia! I'm trapped in here, and you're playing some kind of game! I demand to know what you intend!"

"Governor, I don't know myself," I said. "I just know what my orders are. We'll have you out of there in a few hours. Out." I switched off the set and turned to Deane.

"Well," I said, "we know Louis and Falkenberg are doing something down south of us. Wish I knew how they're making out."

"If there's something we need to know, they'll tell us," Deane said. "Worried about Kathryn?"

"Some."

"Never get so attached to anyone that you worry about her. Saves a lot of skull sweat."

"Yeah, sure. Helmsman, that looks like our landing area. Look sharp."

"Aye, aye, sir."

"Hartz, get me the chopper pilot."

"Zur." Hartz fiddled with the radio for a moment, then handed me the mike.

"Sergeant Stragoff, sir."

"Stragoff, I want you to make a complete sweep of our landing area. There should be two unarmed people there to meet us. They'll show you a blue light. If they show any other color, spray the whole area and get the hell out of there. If they show blue, tell me about it, but I still want a complete survey."

"Aye, aye, sir."

"And just who is meeting us?" Deane asked.

"Don't know their names," I said. "Falkenberg said he'd try to set up a welcoming committee of local resistance types. If we're satisfied with them, we help 'em arm some of their neighbors. That's why we brought those extra rifles."

The radio came to life again. "Two people with a blue light, sir. Nothing else on radar or IR."

"Good. Okay, now make a wider sweep. I don't want to find out there's an artillery battery registered on our landing area."

"Sir."

"Sergeant Major," I said.

"Sir."

"You can take the hovercraft in to occupy the landing area. Treat the welcoming committee politely, but keep an eye on them. When the area's secure, we'll all go ashore."

"Sir."

I looked up at the stars. There was no moon. About five hours to dawn. With any luck we'd be deployed and ready for combat by first light. "Okay, Deane, you're in charge," I said. "Hartz, you stay with him."

"If the lieutenant orders it."

"Damn it, I did order it. Belay that. All right, come with me."

We went to the deck level. The river was less than a meter below us. It wasn't a river to swim in; there are aquatic snakes on Arrarat, and their poison will finish off anything that has protein in it. It acts as a catalyst to coagulate cell bodies. I had no real desire to be a hard rubber lump.

We had one canoe on board. I'd already found troopers who knew something about handling them. We had a dozen men familiar with the screwy watercraft, which didn't surprise me. The story is that you can find *any* skill in a Line Marine regiment, and it seems to be true. In my own company I had two master masons, an artist, a couple of electronic techs (possibly engineers, but they weren't saying), at least one disbarred lawyer, a drunken psychiatrist, and a chap the men claimed was a defrocked preacher.

Corporal Anuraro showed me how to get into the canoe without swamping it. We don't have those things in Arizona. As they paddled me ashore, I thought about how silly the situation was. I was being paddled in a canoe, a device invented at least ten thousand years ago. I was carrying a pair of light-amplifying field glasses based on a principle not discovered until after I was born. Behind me was a steamboat that might have been moving up the Missouri River at the time of Custer's last stand, and I got to this planet in a starship.

The current was swift, and I was glad to have experienced men at the paddles. The water flowed smoothly alongside. Sometimes an unseen creature made riffles in it. Over on the shore the hovercraft had already landed, and someone was signaling us with a light. When we got to the bank I was glad to be on dry land.

"Where are our visitors, Roszak?" I asked.

"Over here, sir."

Two men, both ranchers or farmers. One was Oriental. They looked to be about fifty years old. As agreed, they weren't armed.

"I'm Lieutenant Slater," I said.

The Oriental answered. "I am Wan Loo. This is Harry Seeton."

"I've heard of you. Kathryn says you helped her, once."

"Yes. To escape from a cage," Wan Loo said.

"You're supposed to prove something," I said.

Wan Loo smiled softly. "You have a scar on your left arm. It is shaped like a scimitar. When you were a boy you had a favorite horse named Candybar."

"You've seen Kathryn," I said. "Where is she?"

"South of Allansport. She is trying to raise a force of ranchers to reinforce Captain Falkenberg. We were sent here to assist you."

"We've done pretty well," Harry Seeton added. "A lot of ranchers will fight if you can furnish weapons. But there's something else."

"Yes?"

"Please do not think we are not grateful," Wan Loo said. "But you must understand. We have fought for years, and we cannot fight any longer. We have an uneasy peace in this valley. It is the peace of submission, and we do not care for it, but we will not throw it away simply to help you. If you have not come to stay, please take your soldiers, rescue your Governor, and go away without involving us."

"That's blunt enough," I said.

"We have to be blunt," Harry Seeton said. "Wan Loo isn't talking for us. We're outlaws, anyway. We're with you no matter what happens. But we can't go ask our friends to join if you people don't mean it when you say you'll stay and protect them."

"It is an old story," Wan Loo said. "You cannot blame the farmers. They would rather have you than the Association, but if you are here only for a little while, and the Association is here forever, what can they do? My ancestors were faced with the same problem on Earth. They chose to support the West, and when the Americans, who had little stake in the war, withdrew their forces, my great-grandfather gave up land his family had held for a thousand years to go with them. He had no choice. Do you think he would have chosen the American side if he had known that would happen?"

"The CoDominium has extended protection to this valley," I said.

"Governments have no honor," Wan Loo said. "Many people have none, either, but at least it is possible for a man to have honor. It is not possible for a government. Do you pledge that *you* will not abandon our friends if we arouse them for you?"

"Yes."

"Then we have your word. Kathryn says you are an honorable man. If you will help us with transportation and radio, by noon tomorrow I believe we will have five hundred people to assist you."

"And God help 'em if we lose," Seeton said. "God help 'em."

"We won't lose," I said.

"A battle is not a war," Wan Loo said. "And wars are not won by weapons, but by the will to win them. We will go now."

XV

It is a basic military maxim that no battle plan ever survives contact with the enemy, but by noon it looked as if this operation would be an exception. Falkenberg's combat team—two platoons of B Company, brought down by Skyhook after we were aboard our barges—struck at the passes just before dawn and in three hours of sharp fighting had taken them over. He brought up two companies of militia to dig in and hold them.

Meanwhile, the ranchers in the south were armed and turned out on command to block any southward retreat. I had only scattered reports from that sector, but all seemed under control. Kathryn had raised a force of nearly five hundred, which ought to be enough to hold the southern defensive line.

Then it was my turn. Two hours after dawn I had a skirmish line stretching eight kilometers into the valley. My left flank was anchored on the river. There'd be no problem there. The right flank was a different story.

"It bothers me," I told Falkenberg when I reported by radio. "My right flank is hanging in thin air. The only thing protecting us is Wan Loo's ranchers, and there's no more than three hundred of them—if that many." Wan Loo hadn't been as successful as Kathryn had been. Of course, he'd had a lot less time.

"And just what do you expect to hit you in the flank?" Falkenberg asked.

"I don't know. I just don't like it when we have to

depend on other people—and on the enemy doing what we want them to do."

"Neither do I, but do you have an alternative to suggest?"

"No, sir."

"Then carry out your orders, Mr. Slater. Advance on Allansport."

"Aye, aye, sir."

It wasn't an easy battle line to control. I had units strung all across the valley, with the major strength on the left wing that advanced along the river. The terrain was open, gently rolling hills with lines of hedges and eucalyptus trees planted as windbreaks. The fields were recently harvested, and swine had been turned loose in the wheat stubble. The fields were muddy, but spread as we were, we didn't churn them up much.

The farmhouses were scattered at wide intervals. These had been huge farm holdings. The smallest were over a kilometer square, and some were much larger. A lot of the land was unworked. The houses were stone and earth, partly underground, built like miniature fortresses. Some had sections of wall blown out by explosives.

Harry Seeton was with me in my ground-effects caravan. When we came to a farmhouse, he'd try to persuade the owner and his children and relatives to join us. If they agreed, he'd send them off to join the growing number on our right wing.

"Something bothers me," I told Seeton. "Sure, you have big families and everybody works, but how did you cultivate all this land? That last place was at least five hundred hectares."

"Rainfall here's tricky," Seeton said. "Half the time we've got swamp, and the other half we have drought. The only fertilizer is manure. We've got to leave a lot of the land fallow, or planted in legumes to be plowed under."

"It still seems like a lot of work for just one family."

"Well, we had hired help. Convicts, mostly. Ungrateful bastards joined the Association gangs first chance they got. Tell me something, Lieutenant."

"Yes?"

"Are your men afraid they'll starve to death? I never saw anything like it, the way they pick up anything they can find." He pointed to one B Company trooper who was just ahead of us. He wasn't a large man to begin with, and he had his pockets stuffed with at least three chickens, several ears of corn, and a bottle he'd liberated somewhere. There were bulges in his pack that couldn't have come from regulation equipment, and he'd even strapped firewood on top of it so that we couldn't see his helmet from behind him. "They're like a plague of locusts," Seeton said.

"Not much I can do about it," I said. "I can't be everywhere, and the Line Marines figure anything that's not actually penned up and watched is fair game. They'll eat well for a few days—it beats monkey and greasy rice." I didn't add that if he thought things were bad now, with the troops on the way to a battle, he'd really be horrified after the troops had been in the field a few weeks.

There were shots from ahead. "It's started," I said. "How many of these farm areas are still inhabited by your people?"

"Not many, this close to Allansport. The town itself is almost all Association people. Or goddamned collaborators, which is the same thing. I expect that's why they haven't blasted it down. They outnumber your Governor's escort by quite a lot."

"Yeah." That bothered me. Why hadn't the Association forces simply walked in and taken Governor Swale? As Seeton said, Swale had only a couple of companies of militia with him, yet the siege had been a stalemate. As if they hadn't really wanted to capture him.

Of course, they had problems no matter what they did. If they killed the Governor, Colonel Harrington would be in control. I had to assume the Protective Association had friends in Harmony, possibly even inside the palace. Certainly there were plenty of leaks. They'd know that Harrington was a tougher nut than Swale.

The resistance was stronger as we approached Allansport. The Association forces were far better armed than we'd expected them to be. They had mortars and light artillery, and plenty of ammunition for both.

We had two close calls with the helicopters. I'd sent them forward as gunships to support the advancing infantry. We found out the Association had target-seeking missiles, and the only reason they didn't get the choppers was that their gunners were too eager. They fired while the helicopters still had time to maneuver. I pulled the choppers back to headquarters. I could use them for reconnaissance, but I wasn't going to risk them in combat.

We silenced their artillery batteries one by one. They had plenty of guns, but their electronics were ineffective. Their counterbattery fire was pathetic. We'd have a couple of exchanges, our radars would backtrack their guns, and that would be the end of it.

"Where the hell did they get all that stuff?" I asked Seeton.

"They've always had a lot of equipment. Since the first time they came out of the hills, they've been pretty well armed. Lately it's gotten a lot worse. One reason we gave up."

"It had to come from off-planet," I said. "How?"

"I don't know. Ask your governor."

"I intend to. That stuff had to come through the spaceport. Somebody's getting rich selling guns to the Protective Association."

We moved up to the outer fringes of Allensport. The town was spread across low hills next to the river. It had a protective wall made of brick and adobe, like the houses. Deane's artillery tore huge gaps in the wall and the troops moved into the streets beyond. The fighting was fierce. Seeton was right about the sentiments of the townspeople. They fought from house to house, and the Marines had to move cautiously, with plenty of artillery support. We were flattening the town as we moved into it.

Governor Swale and two companies of Harmony militia were dug in on the bluffs overlooking the river, very nearly in the center of the semicircular town. They held the riverfront almost to the steel bridge that crossed the Allan. I'd hoped to reach the Governor by dark, but the fighting in the town was too severe. At dusk I called to report that I wouldn't reach him for another day.

"However, we're within artillery range of your position," I told him. "We can give you fire support if there's any serious attempt to take your position by storm."

"Yes. You've done well," he told me.

That was a surprise. I'd expected him to read me off for not getting there sooner. Live and learn, I told myself. "I'm bringing the right flank around in an envelopment," I told Swale. "By morning we'll have every one of them penned in Allansport, and we can deal with them at our leisure."

"Excellent," Swale said. "My militia officers tell me the Association forces have very little strength in the southern part of the town. You may be able to take many of the streets during the night."

We halted at dark. I sent Ardwain forward with orders to take A Company around the edges of the town and occupy sections at the southern end. Then I had supper with the troops. As Seeton had noticed, they'd provisioned themselves pretty well. No monkey and rice tonight! We had roast chicken and fresh corn.

After dark I went back to my map table. I'd parked the caravan next to a stone farmhouse two klicks from the outskirts of Allansport. Headquarters platoon set up the C.P., and there were a million details to attend to: supply, field hospitals, plans to evacuate wounded by helicopter, shuffling ammunition around to make sure each unit had enough of the right kind. The computers could handle a lot of it, but there were decisions to be made and no one to make them but me. Finally I had time to set up our positions into the map table computer and make new plans. By feeding the computer the proper inputs, it would show the units on the map, fight battles and display the probable outcomes, move units around under fire and subtract our casualties. . . .

It reminded me of the afternoon's battles. There'd been fighting going on, but I'd seen almost none of it.

Just more lines on the map table, and later the bloody survivors brought back to the field hospital. Tri-V war, none of it real. The observation satellite had made a pass over the Allan Valley just before dark, and the new pictures were relayed from Garrison. They weren't very clear. There'd been low clouds, enough to cut down the resolution and leave big gaps in my data about the Association forces.

"Number One chopper's coming in, sir," Sergeant Jaski reported. He was a headquarters platoon communications expert, an elderly wizened chap who ran the electronics section with smiles and affection until something went wrong. Then he could be as rough as any NCO in the Fleet.

Number One was Falkenberg's. I wasn't surprised when the captain came in a few minutes later. He'd said he might join the main body if things were quiet up at the pass. I got up from the map table to give him the command seat. It hadn't fit me too well, anyway; I was glad to have someone else take charge.

"Just going over the satellite pix," I told him.

"One reason I came by. Things are going well. When that happens I wonder what I've overlooked." He keyed the map table to give him the current positions of our troops. "Ardwain having any problem with the envelopment?" he asked.

"No, sir."

He grunted and played with the console keys. Then he stared at the satellite pictures. "Mr. Slater, why haven't the Association troops taken the riverbank areas behind the Governor?"

"I don't know, sir."

"Any why didn't His Excellency withdraw by water? He could certainly have gotten out, himself and a few men."

"Didn't want to abandon the militia, sir?"

"Possibly."

I looked at the time. Two hours after dark. The troops were well dug in along the perimeter, except for Ardwain's mobile force moving toward the southern edge of the town.

Falkenberg went through the day's reports and looked up, frowning. "Mr. Slater, why do I have the impression that there's something phony about this whole situation?"

"In what way, sir?"

"It's been too easy. We've been told the Association is a tough outfit, but so far the only opposition has been some infantry screens that withdrew before you made real contact, and the first actual hard fighting was when you reached the town."

"There were the artillery duels, sir."

"Yes. All won by a few exchanges of fire. Doesn't that seem strange?"

"No, sir." I had good reason to know that Deane's lads could do some great shooting. After the support they gave me at the roadblock below. Beersheba, I was ready to believe they could do anything. "I hadn't thought about it, sir, but now that you ask—well, it was easy. A couple of exchanges and their guns are quiet."

Falkenberg was nodding. "Knocked out, or merely taken out of action? Looking at this map, I'd say you aren't ready for the second alternative."

"I—"

"You've done well, Lieutenant. It's my nasty suspicious mind. I don't like surprises. Furthermore, why hasn't the Governor asked to be evacuated by water? Why is he sitting there in Allansport?"

"Sir—"

He wouldn't let me finish. "I presume you've reported your positions and plans to the Governor?"

"Certainly, sir."

"And we took the pass with very little effort. Next to no casualties. Yet the Association is certainly aware that we hold it. Why haven't their town forces done something? Run, storm the bluffs and take the Governor for a hostage—*something*!" He straightened in decision. "Sergeant Major!"

"Sir!"

I want a message taken to Centurion Ardwain. I don't want any possibility of it being intercepted."

"Sir."

"He's to hold up on the envelopment. Send a couple of patrols forward to dig in where they can observe, but keep our forces out of Allansport. He can move around out there and make a lot of noise. I want them to think we've continued the envelopment, but, in fact, Ardwain is to take his troops northwest and dig in no closer than two klicks to the town. They're to do that as quietly and invisibly as possible."

"Yes, sir." Ogilvie went out.

"Insurance, Mr. Slater," Falkenberg said. "Insurance. We didn't need your envelopment."

"Yes, sir."

"Confused, Mister?"

"Yes, sir."

"Just preserving options, Lieutenant. I don't like to commit my forces until I'm certain of my objectives."

"But the objective is to trap the Association forces and neutralize them," I said. "The envelopment would have done that. We wouldn't have to trust to the ranchers to keep them from escaping to the south."

"I understood that, Lieutenant. Now, if you'll excuse me, we've both got work to do."

"Yes, sir." I left the caravan to find another place to work. There was plenty to do. I set up shop in one of the farmhouse rooms and went back to shuffling papers. About an hour later Deane Knowles came in.

"I got the change of orders," he said. "What's up?"

"Damfino. Have a seat? Coffee's over there."

"I'll have some, thanks." He poured himself a cup and sat across from me. The room had a big wooden table, rough-hewn from a single tree. That table would have been worth a fortune on Earth. Except for a few protected redwoods, I doubted there was a tree that size in the United States.

"Don't you think I ought to know what's going on?" Deane asked. His voice was friendly, but there was a touch of sarcasm in it.

"Bug Falkenberg if you really want answers," I said. "He doesn't tell me anything, either. All I know is he's sent A Company out into the boonies, and when I asked him to let me join my company, he said I was needed here."

"Tell me about it," Deane said.

I described what had happened.

Deane blew on the hot coffee, then took a sip. "You're telling me that Falkenberg thinks we've put our heads in a trap."

"Yes. What do you think?"

"Good point about the artillery. I thought things were going too well myself. Let's adopt his theory and see where it leads."

"You do understand there's only one person who could have set this theoretical trap," I said.

"Yes."

"What possible motive could he have?" I demanded.

Deane shrugged. "Even so, let's see where it leads. We assume for the purposes of discussion that Governor Hugo Swale has entered into a conspiracy with a criminal gang to inflict anything from a defeat to a disaster on the 501st—"

"And you see how silly it sounds," I said. "Too silly to discuss."

"Assume it," Deane insisted. "That means that the Protective Association is fully aware of our positions and our plans. What could they do with that information?"

"That's why it's so stupid," I said. "So what if they know where we are? If they come out and fight, they'll still get a licking. They can't possibly expect to grind up professional troops! They may be great against ranchers and women and children, but this is a battalion of Line Marines."

"A provisional battalion."

"Same thing."

"Is it? Be realistic, Hal. We've had one campaign, a short one. Otherwise, we're still what came here—a random assortment of troops, half of them recruits, another quarter scraped out of guardhouses, commanded by three newlie lieutenants and the youngest captain in the Fleet. Our colonel's a superannuated military policeman, and we've not a quarter of the equipment a regular line battalion carries."

"We're a match for anything a criminal gang can put in the field—"

"A well-armed criminal gang," Deane said. "Hold onto your regimental pride, Hal. I'm not downgrading the 501st. The point is that we may know we're a damned good outfit, but there's not much reason for anyone else to believe it."

"They'll soon have reason to think differently."

"Maybe." Deane continued to study the maps. "Maybe."

XVI

THE NIGHT WAS quiet. I went on patrol about midnight, not to inspect the guard—we could depend on the NCO's for all that—but mostly to see what it was like out there. The troops were cheerful, looking forward to the next day's battles. Even the recruits grinned wolfishly. They were facing a disorganized mob, and we had artillery superiority. They'd pitched tents by maniples, and inside each tent they'd set up their tiny field stoves so there was hot coffee and chicken stew—and they'd found wine in some of the farmhouses. Our bivouac had more the atmosphere of a campout than an army just before a battle.

Underneath it all was the edge that men have when they're going to fight, but it was well hidden. You're sure it's the other guy who'll buy the farm. Never you. Deep down you know better, but you never talk about that.

An hour before dawn every house along the southern edge of Allansport exploded in red fire. In almost the next instant a time-on-target salvo fell just outside the walls. The bombardment continued, sharp thunder in the night, with red flashes barely visible through the thick mist rising up off the river. I ran to the command caravan.

Falkenberg was already there, of course. I doubt if

168

he'd ever gone to bed. Sergeant Jaski had gotten communications with one of the forward patrols.

"Corporal Levine, sir. I'm dug in about five hundred meters outside the walls. Looks like it was mines in the houses, Captain. Then they dropped a hell of a load onto where we'd have been if we'd moved up last night."

"What's your situation, Levine?" Falkenberg demanded.

"Dug in deep, sir. They killed a couple of my squad even so. It's thick out here, sir. Big stuff. Not just mortars."

That was obvious from the sound, even as far away as we were. No light artillery makes that kind of booming sound.

"A moment, Captain," Levine said. There was a long silence. "Can't keep my head up long, Captain. They're still pounding the area. I see movement in the town. Looks like assault troops coming out the gate. The fire's lifting now. Yeah, those are assault troops. A lot of 'em."

"Sergeant Major, put the battalion on alert for immediate advance," Falkenberg said. "Jaski, when's the next daylight pass of the spy satellite over this area?"

"Seventy minutes after daylight, sir."

"Thank you. Levine, you still there?"

"Yes, Captain. There's more troops moving out of Allansport. Goddamn, there's a couple of tanks. Medium jobs. Suslov class, I'd say. I didn't know them bastards had tanks! Where'd they get them?"

"Good question. Levine, keep your head down and stay out of sight. I want you to stay alive."

"Won't fight over those orders, Captain."

"They're breaking out toward the south," Falkenberg said. "Jaski, get me Lieutenant Bonneyman."

"Sir."

"While you're at it, see if you can raise Centurion Cernan at the pass."

"Aye, aye, sir." Jaski worked at the radio for a moment. "No answer from Mr. Bonneyman, sir. Here's Cernan."

"Thank you." Falkenberg paused. "Mr. Slater, stay here for a moment. You'll need instructions. Centurion Cernan, report."

"Not much to report, Captain. Some movement up above us."

"Above you. Hostiles coming *down* the pass?"

"Could be, Captain, but I don't know. I have patrols up that way, but they haven't reported yet."

"Dig in, Cernan," Falkenberg said. "I'll try to send you some reinforcements. You've got to hold that pass no matter which direction it's attacked from."

"Aye, aye, sir."

Falkenberg nodded. The map board was crawling with symbols and lights as reports came in to Jaski's people and they were programmed onto the display. "Wish I had some satellite pix," Falkenberg said. "There's only one logical move the Association can be making at this point."

He was talking to himself. Maybe he wasn't. Maybe he thought I understood him, but I didn't.

"In any event, we have the only sizable military force on the entire planet," Falkenberg said. "We can't risk its destruction."

"But we've got to relieve Bonneyman and the ranchers," I protested. I didn't mention Kathryn. Falkenberg might think it was just a personal problem. Maybe it was. "Those tanks are headed south, right for their lines."

"I know. Jaski, keep trying to get Bonneyman."

"Sir!"

Outside the trumpets were sounding. "On Full Kits." Brady's sang louder than the rest.

"And we must rescue the Governor," Falkenberg said. "Indeed, we must." He came to a decision. "Jaski, get me Mr. Wan Loo."

While Jaski used the radio, Falkenberg said, "I want you to talk to him, Mr. Slater. He has met you and he has never met me. His first impulse will be to rush to the aid of his friends in the south. He must not do that. His forces, what there are of them, will be far more useful as reinforcements for Centurion Cernan at the pass."

"Mr. Wan Loo, sir," Jaski said.

Falkenberg handed me the mike.

"I don't have time to explain," I said. "You're to take everything you've got and move up to the pass. There are mixed Marine and militia units holding it, and there's a chance Association forces are moving down the pass toward them. Centurion Cernan is in command up there, and he'll need help."

"But what is happening?" Wan Loo asked.

"The Association forces in Allansport have broken loose and are heading south," I said.

"But our friends to the south—"

Falkenberg took the mike. "This is Captain John Christian Falkenberg. We'll assist your friends, but we can do nothing if the forces coming down the pass are not contained. The best way you can help your friends is to see that no fresh Association troops get into this valley."

There was a long pause. "You would not abandon us, Captain?"

"No. We won't abandon you," Falkenberg said.

"Then I have assurances from two honorable men. We will help your friends, Captain. And go with God."

"Thank you. Out." He gave the mike back to Jaski. "Me, I'd rather have a couple of anti-tank guns—or, better still, tanks of our own. How's Old Beastly?"

"Still running, sir." Old Beastly was the 501st's only tank, a relic of the days when CD regulars had come to Arrarat. It was kept going by constant maintenance.

"Where the devil are the Protective Association people getting fuel for tanks?" Falkenberg said. "To hell with it. Sergeant Major, I want Centurion Ardwain to take two platoons of A Company and Old Beastly. Their mission is to link up with Governor Swale. They're to attack through the north end of the town along the riverbank, and they're to move cautiously."

"Captain, that's my company," I said. "Shouldn't I go with them?"

"No. I have a number of operations to perform, and I'll need help. Don't you trust Ardwain?"

"Of course I trust him, sir—"

"Then let him do his job. Sergeant Major, Ardwain's mission is to simulate at least a company. He's to keep the men spread out and moving around. The longer it takes for the enemy to tumble to how small his force is, the better. And he's not to take chances. If they gang up on him, he can run like hell."

"Sir," Ogilvie said. He turned to a waiting runner.

"Ardwain's got a radio, sir," I said.

"Sure he has." Falkenberg's voice was conversational. "Know much about the theory of the scrambler codes we use, Mr. Slater?"

"Well, no, sir—"

"You know this much: in theory any message can be recorded off the air and unscrambled with a good enough computer."

"Yes, sir. But the only computer on Arrarat that could do that is ours, in Garrison."

"And the Governor's in the palace at Harmony," Falkenberg said. "And those two are the ones we know about."

"Sir, you're saying that Governor—"

"No," he interrupted. "I have said nothing at all. I merely choose to be certain that my orders are not intercepted. Jaski, where the hell is Bonneyman?"

"Still trying to raise him, sir."

"Any word from Miss Malcolm or the other ranchers in the southern area?"

"No, sir."

More information appeared on the map board. Levine was still reporting. There were only the two tanks, but a sizable infantry force had come out of Allansport and was headed south along the riverbank. If Levine was right, there'd been more troops in Allansport than we'd ever suspected.

"I have Lieutenant Bonneyman, sir."

"Thank God." Falkenberg grabbed the mike. "Mr. Bonneyman, nearly one thousand hostiles have broken free from Allansport and are moving south. They have with them at least two medium tanks and an appreciable artillery train. Are you well dug in?"

"Yes, sir. We'll hold them."

"The devil, you will. Not with riflemen against that."

"We have to hold, sir," Louis said. "Miss Malcolm and an escort moved about twenty kilometers south during the night in the hopes of raising more reinforcements. She was not successful, but she has reports of hostile activities south of us. At least two, possibly more, groups of Association forces are moving north. We must hold them or they'll break through and link up with the Allansport groups.

"One moment," Falkenberg said. "Sergeant Major, I want helicopter observation of the area to the south of Lieutenant Bonneyman and his ranchers. Send Stragoff. He's to stay at high altitude, but it's vital that I find out what's coming north at us out of Denisburg. All right, Mr. Bonneyman. At the moment you don't know what you're facing."

"No, sir, but I'm in a pretty good position. Rifle pits, and we're strengthening the southern perimeter."

"All right. You're probably safer there than anywhere else. If you get into trouble, your escape route is east, toward the river. I'm bringing the 501st around the town. We'll skirt it wide to stay away from their artillery. Then we'll cut in toward the river and stay right along the bank until we reach your position. If necessary, our engineers can throw up a pontoon bridge and we'll go out across the river to escape."

"Do we need to run, Captain?" Louis sounded dismayed.

"As I have explained to Mr. Slater, our prime objective is to retain the 501st as a fighting unit. Be prepared to withdraw eastward on command, Mr. Bonneyman. Until then, you're to hold that position no matter what happens, and it's likely to be rough."

"Can do, Captain."

"Excellent. Now, what about Miss Malcolm?"

"I don't know where she is, sir. I can send a patrol—"

"No. You have no forces to spare. If you can get a message to her, have her rejoin you if that's possible.

Otherwise, she's on her own. You understand your orders, Mister?"

"Yes, sir."

"Excellent. Out."

"So Kathryn's expendable," I said.

"Anyone is expendable, Mister. Sergeant Major, have Stragoff listen on Miss Malcolm's frequency. If he can locate her, he can try to evacuate her from the southern area, but he is not to compromise the reconnaissance mission in doing it."

"Sir."

"You are one hard-nosed son-of-a-bitch," I said.

His voice was calm as he said, "Mister, I get paid to take responsibilities, and at the moment I'm earning my keep. I'll overlook that remark. Once."

And if I say anything else, I'll be in arrest while my troops are fighting. Got you. "What are my orders, sir?"

"For the moment you're to lead the forward elements of the 501st. I want the battalion to move in column around the town, staying outside artillery range. When you've reached a point directly southwest of Allansport, halt the lead elements and gather up the battalion as I send it to you. I'll stay here until this has been accomplished. I still must report to the Governor and I want the daylight satellite pictures."

I looked at my watch. Incredibly, it was still a quarter-hour before dawn. A lot had happened in the last forty-five minutes. When I left the caravan, Falkenberg was playing games on the map board. More bloodless battles, with glowing lights and wriggling lines crawling across the map at lightning speed, simulations of hours of bloody combat and death and agony.

And what the hell are you accomplishing? I thought. The computer can't give better results than the input data, and your intelligence about the hostiles is plain lousy. How many Association troops are coming down the pass toward Centurion Cernan? No data. How many more are in those converging columns moving toward Louis and Kathryn and their ranchers? Make a guess. What are their objectives? Another guess. Guess and guess again, and Kathryn's out there, and instead of rescuing her, we're keeping the battalion intact. I wanted to mutiny, to go to Kathryn with all the men I could get to follow me, but I wasn't going to do that. I blinked back tears. We had a mission, and Falkenberg was probably right. He was going to the aid of the ranchers, and that's what Kathryn would want. She'd pledged her honor to those people, and it was up to us to make that good. Maybe Stragoff will find her, I thought. Maybe.

I went to my room and let Hartz hang equipment onto my uniform. It was time to move out, and I was glad of something, anything, to do.

XVII

THE VALLEY WAS filled with a thick white mist. The fog boiled out of the river and flowed across the valley floor. In the two hours since dawn, the 501st had covered nine kilometers. The battalion was strung out in a long column of men and mules and wagons on muddy tracks that had once been roads and now had turned into sloppy gunk. The men strained at ropes to pull the guns and ammunition wagons along, and when we found oxen or mules in the fields, we hitched them up as well. The rainstorm that had soaked us two days before at Beersheba had passed across the Allan Valley, and the fields were squishy marshlands.

Out in the distance we could hear the sound of guns: Ardwain's column, the Allansport garrison trying to get through Louis's position—or someone else a world away. In the fog we couldn't know. The sound had no direction, and out here there was no battle, only mud.

There were no enemies here in the valley. There weren't any friends, either. There were only refugees, pathetic families with possessions piled on their mules and oxen, or carried in their arms. They didn't know where they were going, and I had no place to send them. Sometimes we passed farms, and we could see women and children staring at us from the partly open doors or from behind shuttered windows. Their eyes had no expression in them. The sound of the guns over the horizon, and the curses of the men as they fought to move our equipment through the mud; more curses as men whipped oxen we'd found and hitched to the wagons; shrill cries from farmers protesting the loss of their stock; everything dripping wet in white swirling fog, all blended together into a long nightmare of outraged feelings and senselessness. I felt completely alone, alien to all this. Where were the people we'd come to set free?

We reached the map point Falkenberg had designated, and the troops rested in place while the rest of the column caught up with us. The guns were just moving in when Falkenberg's command caravan roared up. The ground-effects machine could move across the muddy fields with no problems, while we had to sweat through them.

He sent for Deane Knowles and had us both come into the caravan. Then he sent out all the NCO's and enlisted men. The three of us were alone with the map table.

"I've held off explaining what I've been doing until the last minute," he said. "As it is, this is for your ears only. If something happens, I want someone to know I haven't lost my mind."

"Yes, sir," I said. Deane and I looked at each other.

"Some background," Falkenberg said. "There's been something peculiar about the Allan Valley situation for years. The convict groups have been too well armed, for a beginning. Governor Swale was too eager to recognize them as a legitimate local government. I think both of you have remarked on that before."

Deane and I looked at each other again.

"This morning's satellite pictures," Falkenberg said. "There's too much mist to show any great details, but there are some clear patches. This strip was taken in the area south of Mr. Bonneyman. I invite your comments."

He handed us the photos. Most were of patches of mist, with the ground below completely invisible. Others showed patches where the mist was thin, or there wasn't any. "Nothing at all," Deane said.

"Precisely," Falkenberg said. "Yet we have reports of

troop movements in that area. It is as if the hostiles knew when the satellite would be overhead, and avoided clear patches."

"As well they might," Deane said. "It shouldn't be hard to work out the ephemeris of the spy-eye."

"Correct. Now look at the high resolution enlargements of those clear areas."

We looked again. "The roads are chewed up," I said. "Mud and ruts. A lot of people and wagons have passed over them."

"And recently, I'd say." Falkenberg nodded in satisfaction. If this had been a test, we'd passed. "Now another datum. I have had Sergeant Jaski's people monitoring all transmissions from Allansport. It may or may not be significant that shortly after every communication between 501st headquarters and outlying commands, there has been a transmission from the Governor to the palace at Harmony—and, within half an hour, a reply. Not an immediate reply, gentlemen, but a reply within half an hour. And shortly after that, there is traffic on the frequencies the Association forces use."

There wasn't anything to say to that. The only explanation made no sense.

"Now, let's see what the hostiles have in mind," Falkenberg said. "They besiege the Governor in Allansport. Our initial orders are to send a force to relieve him. We don't know what they would have done, but instead we devised a complex plan to trap them. We take the initial steps, and what happens? The hostiles invite us to continue. They do nothing. Later we learn that a considerable force, possibly the major part of their strength, is marching northward. Their evident objective is Mr. Bonneyman's mixed group of Marines and ranchers. I point out that the elimination of those ranchers would be significant to the Association. They would not only be rid of potential opposition to their rule, but I think it would in future be impossible to persuade any significant group of ranchers to rise against them. The Association would be the only possible government in the Allan Valley."

"Yes, sir, but why?" Deane said. "What could be . . . why would Governor Swale cooperate with them?"

"We'll leave that for the moment, Mr. Knowles. One thing at a time. Now for the present situation. Centurion Ardwain has done an excellent job of simulating a large force cautiously advancing into Allansport from the north. Governor Swale seems convinced that we've committed at least half our strength there. I have further informed him that we will now bring the balance of the 501st from its present position directly east to the riverbank, where we will once again divide out troops, half going south to aid Mr. Bonneyman, the other half moving into the town. The Governor thought that a splendid plan. Have you an opinion, Mr. Slater?"

"It's the dumbest thing I ever heard of," I said. "Especially if he thinks you've already divided the force! If you do that, you'll be inviting defeat in detail."

"Precisely," Falkenberg said. "Of course Governor Swale has no military background."

"He doesn't need one to know that plan's a bust," I said. "Lousy traitor—"

"No accusations," Falkenberg said. "We've no proof of anything. In any event, I am making the assumption that the Association is getting decoded copies of all my transmissions. I don't need to know how they get them. You'll remember that whenever you use radio signals that might be overheard."

"Yes, sir." Deane looked thoughtful. "That limits our communications somewhat."

"Yes. I hope that won't matter. Next problem. Under my assumption, the hostiles expect me to send a force eastward toward the river. That expectation must be met. I need Mr. Knowles to handle the artillery. It leaves you, Mr. Slater. I want you to take a platoon and simulate two companies with it. You'll send back a stream of reports, as if you're the main body of the battalion reporting to me at a headquarters left safely out of the combat zone." Falkenberg grinned slightly. "To the best of my knowledge, Irina's opinion of me is shared by her father. He won't find it at all hard to believe that I'm avoiding a combat area."

"But what if I really have a message?" I asked.

"You're familiar with O'Grady drill?" Falkenberg asked.

"Yes, sir." O'Grady drill is a form of torture devised by drill sergeants. You're supposed to obey only the commands that begin with "O'Grady says:." Then the sergeant snaps out a string of orders.

"We'll play that little game," Falkenberg said. "Now your mission is to get to the river, make a short demonstration, as if you're about to attack the southern edge of Allansport, and then move directly south, away from the town, until you link up with Mr. Bonneyman. You will then aid in his defense until you are relieved."

"But—Captain, you're assuming they know your orders."

He nodded. "Of course they'll put out an ambush. In this fog it will be a natural thing for them to do. Since they'll assume you have a much larger force with you, they'll probably use all the force that left Allansport this morning. I can't think they're stupid enough to try it with less."

"And we're to walk into it," I said.

"Yes. With your eyes open, but walk into it. You're bait, Mr. Slater. Get out there and wiggle."

I remembered an old comic strip. I quoted a line from it. "Don't much matter whether you catch a fish or not; once you been used for bait, you ain't much good for nothing else nohow."

"Maybe," Falkenberg said. "Maybe. But I remind you that you'll be keeping a major column of Association forces off Mr. Bonneyman's back."

"We will so long as we survive—"

"Yes. So I'll expect you to survive as long as possible."

"Can't quarrel with those orders, Captain."

The fog was thicker when we reached the river. The troops were strung out along almost a full kilometer route, each maniple isolated from the others in the dripping-white blanket that lay across the valley. The troops were enjoying themselves, with monitors reporting as if they were platoon sergeants, and corporals playing centurion. They kept up a steady stream of chatter on the radio, while two men back at Falkenberg's headquarters sent orders that we paid no attention to. So far it was easy enough, because we hadn't run into anything at all.

"There's the city wall." Roszak pointed leftward. I could barely see a darker shape in the fog. "We'll take a quick look over. All right, Lieutenant?"

"Yes. Be careful."

"Always am, sir. Brady, bring your squad. Let's see what's over there." They vanished into the fog.

It seemed like hours, but it was only a few minutes before Brady returned. "Nothing, sir. Nothing and nobody, at least not close to the walls. May be a lot of them farther in. I got a feeling."

Roszak's voice came into my command set. "Moved fifty meters in. No change from what Brady reported."

"Did he have your feeling, Brady?" I asked.

"Yes, sir."

I switched the set back on. "Thank you, Roszak. Rejoin your company."

"Aye, aye, sir."

There were distant sounds of firing from the north. Ardwain's group was doing a good job of simulating a company. They were still moving into the town house by house. I wondered if he was running into opposition, or if that was all his own doing. He was supposed to go cautiously, and his men might be shooting up everything in sight. They were making a lot of noise.

"Get me Falkenberg," I told Hartz.

"Yes, Mr. Slater?"

"Captain, Monitor O'Grady reports the south end of the town has been abandoned. I can hear the A Company combat team up at the north end, but I don't know what opposition they've encountered."

"Very light, Mister. You leave a company to assist A Company just in case, and continue south. Exactly as planned, Mr. Slater. No change. Got that?"

"Yes, sir."

"Having any trouble with the guns?"

"A little, sir. Roads are muddy. It's tough going, but we're moving."

"Excellent. Carry on, then. Out."

And that, I told myself, is that. I told off a monitor to dig in just outside the town and continue making reports. "You've just become B Company centurion," I said.

He grinned. "Yes, sir. Save a few of 'em for me."

"I'll do that, Yokura. Good luck." I waved the rest of my command down the road. We were strung out in a long column. The fog was a little thinner. Now I could see over twenty meters before the world was blotted out in swirling white mist.

What's the safest way to walk into an ambush? I asked myself. The safest way is not to do it. Bar that solution and you don't have a lot of choices. I used the helmet projector to show me a map of the route.

The first test was a hill just outside of town: Hill 509, called the Rockpile, a warren of jumbled boulders and flinty ledges. It dominated the road into the southern gate of Allansport. Whoever owned it controlled traffic into and out of the town.

If the Association only wanted to block us from moving south, that's where they'd have their strong point. If they were out to ambush the whole battalion, they'd leave it bare and set the trap farther on. Either way, they'd never expected me to go past it without having a look.

Four kilometers past the Rockpile there was a string of low hills. The road ran through a valley below them. It was an ideal place for an ambush. That's where they'll be, I decided. Only they must know we'll expect them to be along there somewhere. Bait should wiggle, but it shouldn't too obviously be bait. How would I act if I really had most of a battalion with me?

Send a strong advance guard, of course. An advance guard about as strong as the whole force I've got. Anything less won't make any sense.

"Roszak, start closing them up. Leave the wagons and half a dozen men with radios strung out along the line of march, and get everyone else up here. We'll form up as an advance guard and move south."

"Aye, aye, sir."

When I had the troops assembled, I led them up on the Rockpile. Nothing there, of course. I'd gauged it right. They were waiting for us up ahead.

Roszak nudged me and turned his head slightly to the right. I nodded, carefully. "Don't point, Sergeant. I saw something move up there myself."

We had reached the hills.

"Christ, what are they waiting for?" Roszak muttered.

"For the rest of the battalion. They don't want us; they want the whole 501st."

"Yes, sir."

We moved on ahead. The fog was lifting; visibility was over fifty meters already. It wouldn't be long before it would be obvious there weren't any troops following me, despite the loud curses and the squeals of wagon wheels back there. It's amazing how much noise a couple of wagons can make if the troops work at it.

To hell with it, I thought. We've got to find a good position and try to hold it. It'll do no good to keep walking farther into their trap. There was a rocky area ahead. It wasn't perfect, but it was the best spot I'd seen in half an hour. I nudged Roszak. "When we get up to there, start waving the men off into the rocks. The fog's thicker there."

"What if there's hostiles there already?" Roszak demanded.

"Then we'll fight for the ground, but I doubt they'll be there. I expect they've been moving out of our way as we advance. They still think there's a column a whole klick long behind us." Sound confident, I told myself. "We'll take up a defensive perimeter in there and wait the war out."

"Sure." Roszak moved to his right and spoke to the next man. The orders were passed along the line.

Three more minutes, I told myself. Three minutes and we'll at least have some cover. The area I'd chosen was a saddle, a low pass between the hills to either side of us. Not good, but better than the road. I could feel rifles aimed at me from the rocks above, but I saw nothing but grotesque shapes, boulders dripping in the fog. We climbed higher, moving steadily toward the place I'd chosen.

Maybe there's nobody up there watching at all. They may be on the other side of the valley. You only saw one man. Maybe not even a man. Just something moving. A wild animal. A dog. A blowing patch of fog.

Whatever it was, I can't take this much longer. You don't have to. Another minute. That boulder up there, the big one. When you reach it, you've finished. Don't run. Keep it slow—

"All right, you can fall out and take a break!" I shouted. "Hartz, tell the column to rest in place. We'll take ten. Companies should close up and gather in the stragglers. They'll assemble here after the break."

"Zur."

"Better get a perimeter guard out, Sergeant."

"Sir," Roszak called.

"Corporal Brady, how about a little coffee? You can set up the stove in the lee of that rock."

"Right, Lieutenant."

The men vanished into the fog. There were scrambling noises as they found hiding places. I moved out of the open and hunkered down in the rocks with Corporal Brady. "You didn't really have to make coffee," I said.

"Why not, Lieutenant? We have a while to wait, don't we?"

"I hope so, Corporal. I hope so. But that fog's lifting fast."

Ten minutes later we heard the guns. It was difficult to tell the direction of the sound in the thick fog, but I thought they were ahead of us, far to the south. There was no way to estimate the range.

"O'Grady message from Captain Falkenberg," Hartz said. "Lieutenant Bonneyman's group is under heavy attack from the south."

"Acknowledge." From the south. That meant the columns coming north out of Denisburg had made contact with Louis's ranchers. Falkenberg had guessed that much right. Maybe this whole screwy plan would work, after all. "Anything new on Ardwain's situation?"

"No messages, zur."

I thumbed my command set to the general frequency. "All units of the 501st, there is heavy fighting to the south. Assemble immediately. We'll be moving south to provide fire support. Get those guns rolling right now."

There was a chorus of radio answers. Only a dozen men, but they sounded like hundreds. I'd have been convinced it was a battalion combat team. I was congratulating myself when a shaft of sunlight broke through the mist and fell on the ground at my feet.

XVIII

ONCE THE SUN had broken through, the fog lifted fast. In seconds visibility went from fifty meters to a hundred, then two hundred. In minutes the road for a kilometer north of us was visible—and empty. One wagon struggled along it, and far back in the distance a single man carried a radio.

"O'Grady says hit the dirt!" I yelled. "Hartz, tell Falkenberg the deception's over."

And still there was nothing. I took out my glasses and examined the rocks above and behind us. They were boiling with activity. "Christ," I said. "Roszak, we've run into the whole Allansport outfit. Damned near a thousand men! Dig in and get your heads down!"

A mortar shell exploded on the road below. Then another, and then a salvo. Not bad shooting, I said to myself. Of course it didn't hit anything, because there was nothing to hit except the one wagon, but they had it registered properly. If we'd been down there, we'd have had it.

Rifle bullets zinged overhead. The Association troops were firing at last. I tried to imagine the feelings of the enemy commander, and I found myself laughing. He'd waited patiently all this time for us to walk into his trap, and all he'd caught was something less than a platoon. He was going to be mad.

He was also going to chew up my sixty men, two mortars, and four light machine guns. It would take him a little time, though. I'd picked a good spot to wait for him. Now that the fog had cleared, I saw it was a better place than I'd guessed from the map. We had reasonably clear fields of fire, and the rocks were large and sturdy. They'd have to come in and get us. All we had to do was keep our heads down.

No point in deception anymore. "O'Grady says stay loose and let 'em come to us."

There was a chorus of shouted responses. Then Brady's trumpet sounded, beginning with "On Full Kits" and running through half the calls in the book before he settled onto the Line Marines' March. A favorite, I thought. Damned right. Then I heard the whistle of incoming artillery, and I dove for the tiny shelter between my rocks as barrage after barrage of heavy artillery dropped onto our position.

Riflemen swarmed down onto the road behind me. My radiomen and the two wagoneers were cut down in seconds. At least a company of Association troops started up the gentle slope toward us.

The Association commander made his first mistake then. His artillery had been effective enough for making us keep our heads down, but the rocks gave us good cover and we weren't taking many casualties. When the Association charged us, their troops held back until the artillery fire lifted. It takes experienced non-coms and a lot of discipline to get troops to take casualties from their own artillery. It pays off, but our attackers didn't know or believe it.

They were too far away when the artillery fire lifted. My lads were out of their hiding places in an instant. They poured fire on the advancing troops—rifles and the light machine guns, then both mortars. Few of the enemy had combat armor, and our fire was devastating.

"Good men," Hartz grunted. "They keep coming."

They were, but not for long. Too many of them were cut down. They swept to within fifty meters, wavered, and dropped back, some dragging their wounded with them, others running for it. When the attack was broken, we dropped back into the rocks to wait for the next barrage. "Score one for the Line Marines," I called.

Brady answered with the final fanfare from the March. "And there's none that can face us—"

"They won't try that again," Roszak said. He grinned with satisfaction. "Lads are doing right well, Mr. Slater."

"Well, indeed."

Our area was quiet, but there were sounds of heavy fighting in the south: artillery, rifle and machine gun fire, mortars and grenades. It sounded louder, as if it were coming closer to us. Louis and his commando of ranchers were facing big odds. I wondered if Kathryn were with him.

"They'll try infiltration next," Roszak predicted.

"What makes you think so?" Hartz asked.

"No discipline. After what happened last time, they'll never get a full attack going."

"No, they will have one more try in force. Perhaps two," Hartz argued.

"Never. Bet on it? Tomorrow's wine ration."

"Done," Hartz said. He was quiet for a moment, then handed me the handset. "Captain Falkenberg."

"Thank you. Yes, Captain?"

"O'Grady says the O'Grady drill is over. Understood?"

"Yes, sir."

"What's your situation?"

"We're in the saddle notch of Hill 239, seven klicks south of Allansport," I said. "Holding all right for now, but we're surrounded. Most of the hostiles are between us and Allansport. They let us right through for the ambush. They've tried one all-out attack and that didn't work. Roszak and Hartz are arguing over what they'll try next."

"How long can you hold?"

"Depends on what losses they're willing to take to get us out of here."

"You don't have to hold long," Falkenberg said. "A lot has happened. Ardwain broke through to the Governor and brought him out, but he ran into a strong force in Allansport. There's more coming over the bridge from the east side of the river."

"Sounds like they're bringing up everything they have."

"They are, and we're beating all of it. The column that moved north from Denisburg ran into Bonneyman's group. They deployed to break through that, and we circled around to their west and hit them in the flank. They didn't expect us. Your maneuver fooled them completely. They thought the 501st was with you until it was too late. They know better now, but we've broken them. Of course, there's a lot more of them than of us, and we couldn't hold them. They've broken through between Bonneyman and the river, and you're right in their path."

"How truly good."

"I think you'd do well to get out of their way," Falkenberg said. "I doubt you can stop them."

"If they link up with the Allansport force, they'll get away across the bridge. I can't hold them, but if you can get some artillery support here, I can spot for the guns. We might delay them."

"I was going to suggest that," Falkenberg said. "I've sent Ardwain and the Governor's escort toward that hill outside Allansport—the Rockpile. It looks like a dominant position."

"It is, sir. I've seen it. If we held that, we could keep this lot from getting into Allansport. We might bag the whole lot."

"Worth a try, anyway," Falkenberg said. "Provided you can hold on. It will be nearly an hour before I can get artillery support to you."

"We'll hold, sir."

"Good luck."

Roszak lost his wine ration. They tried one more assault. Two squads of Association troops got within twenty meters of our position before we threw them back. Of my sixty men, I had fewer than thirty effectives when it was over.

That was their last try, though. Shortly after, they regrouped. The elements which had been south of us had already skirted around the hills to join the main body, and now the whole group was moving north. They were headed for Allansport.

The sounds of fighting to the south were coming

closer all the time. Falkenberg had Deane moving parallel to the Association troops, racing to get close enough to give us support, but it wouldn't arrive in time.

I sent our wounded up the hill away from the road with orders to dig in and lie low. The rest of us followed the retreating force. We were now sandwiched between the group ahead of us and the Denisburg column behind.

The first elements of Association forces were headed up the Rockpile when Deane came in range. He was still six kilometers southeast of us, long range and long time of flight, but we were in a good position to spot for him. I called in the first salvo on the advancing Association troops. The shells went beyond their target, and before I could walk them back down the hill, the Association forces retreated.

"They'll send another group around behind the hill," Roszak said. "We'll never stop them."

"No." So damned near. A few minutes' difference and we'd have bagged them all. The column Falkenberg was chasing was now no more than two kilometers south of us and moving fast.

"Hold one," Deane said. "I've got a Corporal Dangier calling in. Claims to be in position to spot targets for me."

"He's one of the wounded we left behind," I said. "He can see the road from his position, all right, but he won't last long once they know we've got a spotter in position to observe them."

"Do I fire the mission?" Deane demanded.

"Yes." Scratch Corporal Dangier, who had a girl in Harmony and a wife on Earth.

"I'll leave one gun at your disposal," Deane said. "I'm putting the rest on Dangier's mission."

A few minutes later we heard the artillery falling on the road behind us. That would play hell with the Association retreat. It kept up for ten minutes; then Deane called in again. "Can't raise Dangier any longer."

"No. There's nothing we can do here. They're staying out of sight. I'll call in some fire in places that might do some good, but it's shooting blind."

I amused myself with that for a while. It was frustrating. Once that force got to the top of the Rockpile, the route into Allansport would be secure. I was still cursing when Hartz shouted urgently.

"Centurion Ardwain on the line, sir."

"Ardwain, where are you?"

"Less than a klick west of you, Lieutenant. We moved around the edge of the town. Can't get inside without support. Militia won't try it, anyway."

"How many Marines do you have?" I demanded.

"About eighty effective. And Old Beastly."

"By God! Ardwain, move in fast. We'll join you as you come by. We're going right up to the top of the Rockpile and sit there until Falkenberg gets here. With Deane's artillery support we can hold that hill."

"Aye, aye, sir. We're coming."

"Let's go!" I shouted. "Who's been hit and can't run?"

No one answered. "Sergeant Roszak took one in the leg an hour ago, Lieutenant," Hartz said.

"I can still travel," Roszak said.

"Bullshit. You'll stay here and spot artillery for us. All the walking wounded stay with him. The rest of you get moving. We want to be in position when Centurion Ardwain comes."

"But—"

"Shut up and soldier, Roszak." I waved and we moved down from our low hilltop. We were panting when we got to the base of the Rockpile. There were already Association forces up there. I didn't know how many. We had to get up there before more joined them. The way up just ahead of me was clear, because it was in direct view of Roszak and his artillery spotters. We could use it and they couldn't.

I waved the men forward. Even a dozen of us on top of the Rockpile might be enough if Ardwain came up fast. We started up. Two men went down, then another, and my troops began to look around for shelter. I couldn't blame them, but I couldn't let them do it. Getting up that hill had become the only thing in my life. I had to get them moving again.

"Brady!" I shouted. "Corporal, sound the charge!"

The trumpet notes sang out. A monitor whipped out a banner and waved it above his head. I shouted "Follow me!" and ran up the hill. Then a mortar shell exploded two meters away. I had time to see bright red blotches spurt across my trousers legs and to wonder if that was my own blood; then I fell. The battle noises dimmed out.

"Lieutenant! Mr. Slater!"

I was in the bottom of a well. It was dark down there, and it hurt to look up at the light. I wanted to sink back into the well, but someone at the top was shouting at me. "Mr. Slater!"

"He's coming around, Centurion."

"He's got to, Crisp! Mr. Slater!"

There were people all around me. I couldn't see them very clearly, but I could recognize the voice. "Yes, Centurion."

"Mr. Slater," Ardwain said. "The Governor says we shouldn't take the hill! What do we do, sir?"

It didn't make sense. Where am I? I wondered. I had just sense enough not to ask. Everybody asks that, I thought. Why does everybody ask that? But I don't know—

I was pulled to a sitting position. My eyes managed to focus again, just for a moment. I was surrounded by people and rocks. Big rocks. Then I knew where I was. I'd passed these rocks before. They were at the base of the hill. Rocks below the Rockpile.

"What's that? Don't take the hill?" I said.

"Yes, sir—"

"Lieutenant, I have ordered your men to pull back. There are not enough to take this hill, and there's no point in wasting them."

That wasn't the Governor, but I'd heard the voice before. Trevor. Colonel Trevor of the militia. He'd been with Swale at the staff meeting back at Beersheba. Bits of the staff meeting came back to me, and I tried to remember more of them. Then I realized that was silly.

The staff meeting wasn't important, but I couldn't think. What was important? There was something I had to do.

Get up the hill. I had to get up the hill. "Get me on my feet, Centurion."

"Sir—"

"Do it!" I was screaming. "I'm going up there. We have to take the Rockpile."

"You heard the company commander!" Ardwain shouted. "Move out!"

"Slater, you don't know what you're saying!" Trevor shouted.

I ignored him. "I've got to see," I said. I tried to get up, but my legs weren't working. Nothing happened when I tried to move them. "Lift me where I can see," I said.

"Sir—"

"Crisp, don't argue with me. Do it."

"You're crazy, Slater!" Trevor shouted. "Delirious. Sergeant Crisp, put him down. You'll kill him."

The medics hauled me to the edge of the boulder patch. Ardwain was leading men up the hill. Not just Marines, I saw. The militia had followed, as well. Insane, something whispered in the back of my mind. All insane. It's a disease, and they've caught it, too. I pushed the thought away.

They were falling, but they were still moving forward as they fell. I didn't know if they'd get to the top.

"You wanted to see!" Trevor shouted. "Now you've seen it! You can't send them up there. It's suicide, and they won't even listen to me! You've got to call them back, Slater. Make them retreat."

I looked at the fallen men. Some were just ahead of me. They hadn't even gotten twenty meters. There was one body blown in half. Something bright lay near it. I saw what it was and turned to Trevor.

"Retreat, Colonel? See that? Our trumpeter was killed sounding the charge. I don't know how to order a retreat."

XIX

I was deep in the well again, and it was dark, and I was afraid. They reached down into it after me, trying to pull me up, and I wanted to come. I knew I'd been in there a long time, and I wanted out, because I could hear Kathryn calling for me. I reached for her hand, but I couldn't find it. I remember shouting, but I don't know what I said. The nightmare went on for a long time.

Then it was daytime. The light was orange-red, very bright, and the walls were splashed with the orange light. I tried to move my head.

"Doc!" someone shouted. His voice was very loud.

"Hal?"

"I can't see you," I said. "Where are you, Kathryn? Where are you?"

"I'm here, Hal. I'll always be here."

And then it was dark again, but it wasn't so lonely in there.

I woke up several times after that. I couldn't talk much, and when I did I don't suppose I made much sense, but finally things were clear. I was in the hospital in Garrison, and I'd been there for weeks. I wasn't sure just how long. Nobody would tell me anything, and they talked in hushed tones so that I was sure I was dying, but I didn't.

"What the hell's wrong with me?" I demanded.

"Just take it easy, young fellow." He had a white

coat, thick glasses, and a brown beard with white hairs in it.

"Who the hell are you?"

"That's Dr. Cechi," Kathryn told me.

"Well, why won't he tell me what's wrong with me?"

"He doesn't want to worry you."

"Worry me? Do you think not knowing gives peace of mind? Tell me."

"All right," Cechi said. "Nothing permanent. Understand that first. Nothing permanent, although it's going to take a while to fix you up. We almost lost you a couple of times, you know. Multiple perforations of the gut, two broken vertebrae, compound fracture of the left femur, and assorted scrapes, punctures, bruises, abrasions, and contusions. Not to mention almost complete exsanguination when they brought you in. It's nothing we can't fix, but you're going to be here a while, Captain." He was holding my arm, and I felt pressure there, a hypo-spray. "You just go to sleep and we'll tell you the rest tomorrow."

"But—" Whatever I was going to say never got out. I sank back, but it wasn't into the well. It was just sleep, and I could tell the difference.

The next time I awoke, Falkenberg was there. He grinned at me.

I grinned back. "Hi, Captain."

"Major. You're the captain."

"Uh? Run that past—"

"Just brevet promotions, but Harrington thinks they'll stick."

"We must have won."

"Oh, yeah." He sat where I could see him. His eyes looked pale blue in that light. "Lieutenant Ardwain took the Rockpile, but he said it was all your doing."

"Lieutenant Ardwain. Lot of promotions out of this," I said.

"Some. The Association no longer exists as an organized military force. Your girl's friends are in control. Wan Loo is the acting president, or supervisor, or whatever they call him. Governor Swale's not too happy about it, but officially he has to be. He didn't like endorsing Harrington's report, either, but he had no choice."

"But he's a lousy traitor. Why's he still governor?"

"Act your age, Captain." There wasn't any humor in Falkenberg's voice now. "We have no proof. I know the story, if you'd like to hear it. In fact, you'd better. You're popular enough with the Fleet, but there'll be elements of the Grand Senate that'll hate your guts."

"Tell me."

"Swale has always been part of the Bronson faction," Falkenberg said. "The Bronson family is big in Dover Mineral Development Inc. Seems there's more to this place than either American Express or Kennicott ever knew. Dover found out and tried to buy mineral rights. The holy Joes wouldn't sell—especially the farmers like Wan Loo and Seeton. They don't want industrial development here, and it was obvious to Swale that they wouldn't sell any mining rights to Dover. Swale's policy has been to help groups like the Association in return for their signatures on mining rights contracts. If enough of those outfits are recognized as legitimate local governments, there won't be any trouble over the contracts. You can probably figure out the rest."

"Maybe it's my head," I told him, "but I can't. What the devil did he let us into the valley for, then? Why did he go down there at all?"

"Just because they signed over some mining rights didn't make them his slaves. They were trying to jack up the grain prices. If the Harmony merchants complained loud enough, Swale wouldn't be governor here, and what use would he be to Dover then? He had to put some pressure on them—enough to make them sell, not so much that they'd be thrown out."

"Only we threw them out," I said.

"Only we threw them out. This time. Don't imagine that it's over."

"It has to be over," I said. "He couldn't pull that again."

"Probably he won't. Bronson hasn't much use for failures. I expect Governor Swale will shortly be on his way to a post as First Secretary on a mining asteroid. There'll be another governor, and if he's not a Bronson client, he'll be someone else's. I'm not supposed to depress you. You've got a decision to make. I've been assigned to a regular Line Regiment as adjutant. The 42nd. It's on Kennicott. Tough duty. Probably a lot of fighting, good opportunities, regular troops. I've got room on the staff. Want to come along? They tell me you'll be fit to move by the time the next ship gets here."

"I'll think about it."

"Do that. You've got a good career ahead of you. Now *you're* the youngest captain in the Fleet. Couldn't swing the Military Star, but you'll get another medal."

"I'll think about it. I have to talk with Kathryn—"

He shrugged. "Certainly, Captain." He grinned and went out.

Captain. Captains may marry, Majors should marry, Colonels must marry—

But that was soldier talk, and I wasn't sure I was a soldier. Strange, I thought. Everyone says I am. I've done well, and I have a great career, and it all seems like a fit of madness. Corporal Brady won't be playing his trumpet any longer because of me. Dangier, wounded but alive, until he volunteered to be an artillery spotter. And all the others, Levine and Lieberman and recruit—no, Private—Dietz, and the rest, dead and blended together in my memory until I can't remember where they died or what for, only that I killed them.

But we won. It was a glorious victory. That was enough for Falkenberg. He had done his job and done it well. Was it enough for me? Would it be in the future?

When I was up and around, I couldn't avoid meeting Governor Swale. Irina was nursing Louis Bonneyman. Louis was worse off than I was. Sometimes they can grow you a new leg, but it takes time, and it's painful. Irina saw him every day, and when I could leave the hospital she insisted that I come to the palace. It was inevitable that I would meet the Governor.

"I hope you're proud of yourself," Swale said. "Everyone else is."

"Hugo, that's not fair," Irina protested.

"Not fair?" Swale said. "How isn't it fair?"

"I did the job I was paid to do, sir," I said.

"Yes. You did, indeed—and thereby made it impossible for me to do mine. Sit down, Captain Slater. Your Major Falkenberg has told you plenty of stories about me. Now let me tell you my side of it."

"There's no need, Ggovernor," I said.

"No, there isn't. Are you afraid to find out just what you've done?"

"No. I've helped throw out a gang of convicts who pretended to be a government. And I'm proud enough of that."

"Are you? Have you been to the Allan Valley lately, Captain? Of course you haven't. And I doubt Kathryn Malcolm has told you what's happening there—how Wan Loo and Harry Seeton and a religious fanatic named Brother Dornan have established commissions of deacons to inquire into the morals and loyalties of everyone in the valley; how anyone they find deficient is turned off the land to make room for their own people. No, I don't suppose she told you any of that."

"I don't believe you."

"Don't you? Ask Miss Malcolm. Or would you believe Irina? She knows it's true."

I looked to Irina. The pain in her eyes was enough. She didn't have to speak.

"I was governor of the whole planet, Slater. Not just Harmony, not just the Jordan and Allan valleys, but all of the planet. Only they gave me responsibilities and no authority, and no means to govern. What am I supposed to do with the convicts, Slater? They ship them here by the thousands, but they give me nothing to feed them with. You've seen them. How are they supposed to live?"

"They can work—"

"At what? As farmhands on ranches of five hundred hectares? The best land on the planet, doled out as huge ranches with half the land not worked because there's no fertilizer, no irrigation, not even decent drainage systems. They sure as hell can't work in our nonexistent industries. Don't you see that Arrarat *must* industrialize? It doesn't matter what Allan Valley farmers want, or what the other holy Joes want. It's industrialize or face famine, and, by God, there'll be no famines while I can do something about them."

"So you were willing to sell out the 501st. Help the Association defeat us. An honorable way to achieve an honorable end."

"As honorable as yours. Yours is to kill and destroy. War is honorable, but deceit isn't. I prefer my way, Captain."

"I expect you do."

Swale nodded vigorously, to himself, not to me. "Smug. Proud and smug. Tell me, Captain, just how are you better than the Protective Association? They fought. Not for the honor of the corps, but for their land, their families, for friends. They lost. You had better men, better officers, better training. A lot better equipment. If you'd lost, you'd have been returned to Garrison under terms. The Association troops were shot out of hand. All of them. Be proud, Slater. But you make me sick. I'll leave you now. I don't care to argue with my daughter's guests."

"That's true also, isn't it?" I asked Irina. "They shot all the Association troops?"

"Not all," Irina said. "The ones that surrendered to Captain Falkenberg are still alive. He even recruited some of them."

He would. The battalion would need men after those battles. "What's happened to the rest?"

"They're under guard at Beersheba. It was after your Marines left the valley that the real slaughter began."

"Sure. People who wouldn't turn out to fight for their homes when we needed their help got real patriotic after it was over," I said. "I'm going back to my quarters, Irina. Thank you for having me over."

"But Kathryn is coming. She'll be here—"

"I don't want to see anyone just now. Excuse me." I left quickly and wandered through the streets of Harmony. People nodded and smiled as I passed. The Marines were still popular. Of course. We'd opened the trade route up the Jordan, and we'd cleared out the Allan Valley. Grain was cheap, and we'd held the convicts at bay. Why shouldn't the people love us?

Tattoo sounded as I entered the fort. The trumpets and drums sounded through the night, martial and complex and the notes were sweet. Sentries saluted as I passed. Life here was orderly and there was no need to think.

Hartz had left a full bottle of brandy where I could find it. It was his theory that the reason I wasn't healing fast was that I didn't drink enough. The surgeons didn't share his opinion. They were chopping away at me, then using the regeneration stimulators to make me grow better parts. It was a painful process, and they didn't think liquor helped it much.

To hell with them, I thought, and poured a double. I hadn't finished it when Kathryn came in.

"Irina said—Hal, you shouldn't be drinking."

"I doubt that Irina said that."

"You know—what's the matter with you, Hal?"

"Why didn't you tell me?" I asked.

"I was going to. Later. But there never was a right time."

"And it's all true? Your friends are driving the families of everyone who cooperated with the Association out into the hills? And they've shot all the prisoners?"

"It's—yes. It's true."

"Why didn't you stop them?"

"Should I have wanted to?" She looked at the scars on her hands. "Should I?"

There was a knock at the door. "Come in," I said.

It was Falkenberg. "Thought you were alone," he said.

"Come in. I'm confused."

"I expect you are. Got any more of that brandy?"

"Sure. What did you mean by that?"

"I understand you've just learned what's happening out in the Allan Valley."

"Crapdoodle! Has Irina been talking to everyone in

Garrison? I don't need a convention of people to cheer me up."

"You don't eh?" He made no move to leave. "Spit it out, Mister."

"You don't call Captains 'Mister.' "

He grinned. "No. Sorry. What's the problem, Hal? Finding out that things aren't as simple as you'd like them to be?"

"John, what the hell were we fighting for out there? What good do we do?"

He stretched a long arm toward the brandy bottle and poured for both of us. "We threw a gang of criminals out. Do you doubt that's what they were? Do you insist that the people we helped be saints?"

"But the women. And children. What will happen to them? And the Governor's right—something's got to be done for the convicts. Poor bastards are sent here, and we can't just drown them."

"There's land to the west," Kathryn said. "They can have that. My grandfather had to start from the beginning. Why can't the new arrivals?"

"The Governor's right about a lot of things," Falkenberg said. "Industry's got to come to Arrarat someday. Should it come just to make the Bronson family rich? At the expense of a bunch of farmers who bought their land with one hell of a lot of hard work and blood? Hal, if you're having second thoughts about the action here on Arrarat, what'll you do when the Fleet's ordered to do something completely raw?"

"I don't know. That's what bothers me."

"You asked what good we do," Falkenberg said. "We buy time. Back on Earth they're ready to start a war that won't end until billions are dead. The Fleet's the only thing preventing that. The only thing, Hal. Be as cynical about the CoDominium as you like. Be contemptuous of Grand Senator Bronson and his friends—yes, and most of his enemies, too, damn it. But remember that the Fleet keeps the peace, and as long as we do, Earth still lives. If the price of that is getting our hands dirty out here on the frontiers, then it's a price we have to pay. And while we're paying it, just once in a while we do something right. I think we did that here. For all that they've been vicious enough now that the battle's over, Wan Loo and his people aren't evil. I'd rather trust the future to them than to people who'd do . . . that." He took Kathryn's hand and turned it over in his. "We can't make things perfect, Hal. But we can damned sure end some of the worst things people do to each other. If that's not enough, we have our own honor, even if our masters have none. The Fleet is our country, Hal, and it's an honorable fatherland." Then he laughed and drained his glass. "Talking's dry work. Pipe Major's learned three new tunes. Come and hear them. You deserve a night in the club, and the drinks are on the battalion. You've friends here, and you've not seen much of them."

He stood, the half smile still on his lips. "Good evening, Hal. Kathryn."

"You're going with him, aren't you?" Kathryn said when he'd closed the door.

"You know I don't care all that much for bagpipes—"

"Don't be flippant with me. He's offered you a place with his new regiment, and you're going to take it."

"I don't know. I've been thinking about it—"

"I know. I didn't before, but I do now. I watched you while he was talking. You're going."

"I guess I am. Will you come with me?"

"If you'll have me, yes. I can't go back to the ranch. I'll have to sell it. I couldn't ever live there now. I'm not the same girl I was when this started."

"I'll always have doubts," I said. "I'll need—" I couldn't finish the thought, but I didn't have to. She came to me, and she wasn't trembling at all, not the way she'd been before, anyway. I held her for a long time.

"We should go now," she said finally. "They'll be expecting you."

"But—"

"We've plenty of time, Hal. A long time."

As we left the room, Last Post sounded across the fort.

PART TWO
MERCENARY

FROM THE LAST West Point lecture by Professor John Christian Falkenberg, II, delivered at the United States Military Academy immediately prior to the reorganization of the Academy. After the Academy was restructured to reflect rising nationalism in the United States, Falkenberg as a CoDominium Professor was unwelcome in any event; but the content of this lecture would have assured that anyway. *Crofton's Essays and Lectures in Military History, 2nd Edition.*

"All large and important institutions change slowly. It is probably as well that this is true for the military; but well or not, it is inevitable. It takes time to build history and traditions, and military organizations with no history and traditions are generally ineffective.

"There are of course notable exceptions to this rule, although some of the more popular cases do not bear examination. For example, Colonel Michael Hoare's Fifth Commando in Katanga in the 1960s, while rightly studied as a harbinger of the growth of mercenary organizations in this century, owed much of its justly celebrated success to the incompetence—including frequent drunkenness—of its opposition. Moreover, Hoare, by recruiting most of his officers and non-coms, and many of his troopers, from British veterans, was able to draw on the long history and tradition of the British Army.

"I dare say something of this sort will happen in the

future, as many CoDominium military units are disbanded. It is conceivable that entire units will be hired on by one or another patron. Certainly a small cohesive unit accustomed to working together would be preferable to a larger group of mercenaries.

"The building of the CoDominium military forces is itself an illustrative case; once again, by incorporating disbanded units such as the French *L'egion E'trange're*, [['denotes accent mark]] the Cameron Highlanders, and the Cossack Adventurers, was able to appropriate to itself considerable history and tradition. Even so, it has taken decades to build the CoDominium Line Marines into the formidable force they have become.

"However, I bring up the subject of changing institutions for another reason. We are seeing, I believe, the completion of yet another full cycle in the history of violence and civilization. As late as the turn of the Millennium, most military organizations were motivated by national patriotism, and the 'Laws of War' were treated either as a joke, as unwanted restrictions on military action, or, as in the case of the infamous 'War Crimes' trials following World War II, as a means of retaliation against a defeated enemy.

"Then, during the course of this century, the Laws of War have become quite important, and have often been observed; and where they are not observed there is a good chance that the CoDominium Fleet will punish those who violate them—particularly if the violation involves CoDominium citizens, and inevitably if it involves a member of the Fleet.

"Now I believe we are entering a new period; one in which the nationalist forces will pursue a new policy of expediency, while the CoDominium and mercenary units continue to observe and insist on the Laws of War. Now it would appear that the outcome of such a conflict is predictable: that the organizations which recognize no limitations save expediency will always triumph over those which restrict their uses of military power. This is impossible. I do not believe it will be inevitable.

However, many do believe that the Laws of War will go the way of the Rights of Neutrals in the last century.

After all, the United States, having entered World War I ostensibly to protect the rights of neutral vessels on the high seas, within days of entering World War II declared unrestricted submarine warfare against Germany and Japan; while the Allied powers, having denounced Japanese actions against Nanking in the 1930s, had no scruples about bombing civilians and open cities as the war progressed, culminating in Hiroshima, Nagasaki, and the fire raids against Tokyo.

"By the end of World War II, few observed any limits on the use of military power. Allied units regularly took civilian hostages and exposed civilian officials to danger as a means of discouraging partisan activity. Most of these actions had been taken by the German Army and of course had been denounced at the time.

"That expedient view became so widespread that for decades no one could conceive of another.

"However, it has not always been thus. Prior to the present era there were at least three periods in which war became stylized and subject to rules. These eras have been described well enough by Martin Van Creveld in his definitive *Technology and War*.

"The first such era was the Hellenistic period from about 300 to 200 B.C. During that time there were essentially no differences among the successor states. Each was ruled by despotism built around a dynasty and generally ruled by a single man. The ordinary citizen had no stake in this government, and cared not a whit whether this man or that held the throne. The military units were composed of professionals who had no personal stake in the outcome of a campaign. As Creveld says:

" 'Accordingly, there applied among those states a fairly strict code which dictated what was and was not permissible in regard to the treatment of prisoners, the enslavement of captured cities, the robbery for military purposes of temples dedicated to the gods (this was legitimate provided that restitution was subsequently made, or at any rate promised), and so on.

" 'The application of rules to warfare was, however, extended further than this. While it would be imprecise to say that there existed an explicit international agreement concerning the types of military technology that might or might not be used, the various contestants shared a common material civilization and knew what to expect of each other. Since they fielded much the same weapons and equipment, but also because commanders and technical experts frequently transferred from one army to another, they found themselves operating on broadly similar tactical and strategic codes . . .'

"The second period of warfare treated as a game with rules was, of course, the period of feudal chivalry, and probably quite enough has been said about it in previous lectures. For the third, I quote again from Creveld:

" 'The play-element often present in armed conflict was, however, probably never as pronounced as in the eighteenth century, when war became popularly known as the game of kings. It was an age in which, according to Voltaire, all Europeans lived under the same kind of institutions, believed in the same kind of ideas, and fornicated with the same kind of women. Most states were ruled by absolute monarchs. Even those who were not so ruled neither expected nor demanded the lump-in-the-throat type of allegiance later to be associated with the nationalist states. Armies were commanded by members of an international nobility who spoke French as their *lingua franca* and switched sides as they saw fit. There were manned by personnel who, often enlisted by trickery and kept in the ranks by main force, cared nothing for honor, duty, or country . . .'

" 'In each of the three above periods, as well as in many others which witnessed the same phenomenon, the transformation of war into something akin to a game did not pass without comment. What some people took as a sign of piety or reason or progress, other saw as proof of stupidity, effeminacy, and degeneration. During the last years before the French Revolution, Gibbons praised war for its moderation and expressed the hope that it would soon disappear altogether. Simultaneously, a French nobleman, the Comte de Guibet, was cutting a figure among the ladies of the *salons* by denouncing the prevailing military practices as degenerate and calling for a commander and a people who, to use his own words, would tear apart the feeble constitution of Europe like the north wind bending the reeds . . .'

"Gentlemen and ladies, I invite you to reflect on this. We live in a time when the major powers of the Earth are governed by what can only be called self perpetuating oligarchies. While there is more ostensible turnover in the compositions of the Congress of the United States and the Supreme Soviet than there was in the last decade of the twentieth century, there is not a lot more, and what turnover there is happens to be meaningless; the new master is indistinguishable from the old.

"Nor is it important that these oligarchs think themselves important doing important work—indeed that they *are* important and *do* important work. The effect has been to alienate the Citizen entirely; while the taxpayer supports the present system only because he fears the loss of his privileges—because he fears he will be cast into the lot of the Citizen. The same is true in the Soviet system, where Party Members have long ago lost confidence in the possibility of reform, and now do no more than jealously hold onto their privileges.

"Yet—while it is easy to denounce the CoDominium and its endless cynicism, it is not so certain that whatever replaces it will be better. Indeed, we must wonder just what would survive the collapse of the CoDominium . . ."

I
Twenty years later ...

EARTH FLOATED ETERNALLY lovely above bleak lunar mountains. Daylight lay across California and most of the Pacific, and the glowing ocean made an impossibly blue backgound for a vortex of bright clouds swirling in a massive tropical storm. Beyond the lunar crags, man's home was a fragile ball amidst the black star-studded velvet of space; a ball that a man might reach out to grasp and crush in his bare hands.

Grand Admiral Sergei Lermontov looked at the bright viewscreen image and thought how easy it would be for Earth to die. He kept her image on the viewscreen to remind himself of that every time he looked up.

"That's all we can get you, Sergei." His visitor sat with hands carefully folded in his lap. A photograph would have shown him in a relaxed position, seated comfortably in the big visitor's chair covered with leathers from animals that grew on planets a hundred light years from Earth. Seen closer, the real man was not relaxed at all. He looked that way from his long experience as a politician.

"I wish it could be more." Grand Senator Martin Grant shook his head slowly from side to side. "At least it's something."

"We will lose ships and disband regiments. I cannot operate the Fleet on that budget." Lermontov's voice was flat and precise. He adjusted his rimless spectacles to a comfortable position on his thin nose. His gestures, like his voice, were precise and correct, and it was said in Navy wardrooms that the Grand Admiral practiced in front of a mirror.

"You'll have to do the best you can. It's not even certain the United Party can survive the next election. God knows we won't be able to if we give any more to the Fleet."

"But there is enough money for national armies." Lermontov looked significantly at Earth's image on the viewscreen. "Armies that can destroy earth. Martin, how can we keep the peace if you will not let us have ships and men?"

"You can't keep the peace if there's no CoDominium."

Lermontov frowned. "Is there a real chance that the United Party will lose, then?"

Martin Grant's head bobbed in an almost imperceptible movement. "Yes."

"And the United States will withdraw from the CD." Lermontov thought of all that would mean, for Earth and for the nearly hundred worlds where men lived. "Not many of the colonies will survive without us. It is too soon. If we did not suppress science and research it might be different, but there are so few independent worlds— Martin, we are spread thin across the colony worlds. The CoDominium must help them. We created their problems with our colonial governments. We gave them no chances at all to live without us. We cannot let them go suddenly."

Grant sat motionless, saying nothing.

"Yes, I am preaching to the converted. But it is the Navy that gave the Grand Senate this power over the colonies. I cannot help feeling responsible."

Senator Grant's head moved slightly again, either a nod or a tremor. "I would have thought there was a lot you could do, Sergei. The Fleet obeys you, not the Senate. I know my nephew has made that clear enough. The warriors respect another warrior, but they've only contempt for us politicians."

"You are inviting treason?"

"No. Certainly I'm not suggesting that the Fleet try running the show. Military rule hasn't worked very well for us, has it?" Senator Grant turned his head slightly to indicate the globe behind him. Twenty nations on Earth were governed by armies, none of them very well.

On the other hand, the politicians aren't doing a much better job, he thought. Nobody is. "We don't seem to have any goals, Sergei. We just hang on, hoping that things will get better. Why should they?"

"I have almost ceased to hope for better conditions," Lermontov replied. "Now I only pray they do not get worse." His lips twitched slightly in a thin smile. "Those prayers are seldom answered."

"I spoke with my brother yesterday," Grant said. "He's threatening to retire again. I think he means it this time."

"But he cannot do that!" Lermontov shuddered. "Your brother is one of the few men in the U.S. government who understands how desperate is our need for time."

"I told him that."

"And?"

Grant shook his head. "It's the rat race, Sergei. John doesn't see any end to it. It's all very well to play rear guard, but for what?"

"Isn't the survival of civilization a worthwhile goal?"

"If that's where we're headed, yes. But what assurance do we have that we'll achieve even that?"

The Grand Admiral's smile was wintry. "None, of course. But we may be sure that *nothing* will survive if we do not have more time. A few years of peace, Martin. Much can happen in a few years. And if nothing does—why, we will have had a few years."

The wall behind Lermontov was covered with banners and plaques. Centered among them was the CoDominium Seal: American eagle, Soviet sickle and hammer, red stars and white stars. Beneath it was the Navy's official motto: PEACE IS OUR PROFESSION.

We chose that motto for them, Grant thought. The Senate made the Navy adopt it. Except for Lermontov I wonder how many Fleet officers believe it? What would they have chosen if left to themselves?

There are always the warriors, and if you don't give them something worthwhile to fight for. . . . But we can't live without them, because there comes a time when you have to have warriors. Like Sergei Lermontov.

But do we have to have politicians like me? "I'll talk

to John again. I've never been sure how serious he is about retiring anyway. You get used to power, and it's hard to lay it down. It only takes a little persuasion, some argument to let you justify keeping it. Power's more addicting than opiates."

"But you can do nothing about our budget."

"No. Fact is, there's more problems. We need Bronson's votes, and he's got demands."

Lermontov's eyes narrowed, and his voice was thick with distaste. "At least we know how to deal with men like Bronson." And it was strange, Lermontov thought, that despicable creatures like Bronson should be so small as problems. They could be bribed. They expected to be bought.

It was the men of honor who created the real problems. Men like Harmon in the United States and Kaslov in the Soviet Union, men with causes they would die for—they had brought mankind to this.

But I would rather know Kaslov and Harmon and their friends than Bronson's people who support us.

"You won't like some of what he's asked for," Grant said. "Isn't Colonel Falkenberg a special favorite of yours?"

"He is one of our best men. I use him when the situation seems desperate. His men will follow him anywhere, and he does not waste lives in achieving our objectives."

"He's apparently stepped on Bronson's toes once too often. They want him cashiered."

"No." Lermontov's voice was firm.

Martin Grant shook his head. Suddenly he felt very tired, despite the low gravity of the moon. "There's no choice, Sergei. It's not just personal dislike, although there's a lot of that too. Bronson's making up to Harmon, and Harmon thinks Falkenberg's dangerous."

"Of course he is dangerous. He is a warrior. But he is a danger only to enemies of the CoDominium. . . ."

"Precisely." Grant sighed again. "Sergei, I *know*. We're robbing you of your best tools and then expecting you to do the work without them."

"It is more than that, Martin. How do you control warriors?"

"I beg your pardon?"

"I asked, 'How do you control warriors?' " Lermontov adjusted his spectacles with the tips of the fingers of both hands. "By earning their respect, of course. But what happens if that respect is forfeit? There will be no controlling him; and you are speaking of one of the best military minds alive. You may live to regret this decision, Martin."

"Can't be helped. Sergei, do you think I like telling you to dump a good man for a snake like Bronson? But it doesn't matter. The Patriot Party's ready to make a big thing out of this, and Falkenberg couldn't survive that kind of political pressure anyway, you know that. No officer can. His career's finished no matter what."

"You have always supported him in the past."

"Goddamn it, Sergei, I appointed him to the Academy in the first place. I cannot support him, and you can't either. He goes, or we lose Bronson's vote on the budget."

"But why?" Lermontov demanded. "The real reason."

Grant shrugged. "Bronson's or Harmon's? Bronson has hated Colonel Falkenberg ever since that business on Kennicott. The Bronson family lost a lot of money there, and it didn't help that Bronson had to vote in favor of giving Falkenberg his medals either. I doubt there's any more to it than that.

"Harmon's a different matter. He really believes that Falkenberg might lead his troops against Earth. And once he asks for Falkenberg's scalp as a favor from Bronson—"

"I see. But Harmon's reasons are ludicrous. At least at the moment they are ludicrous—"

"If he's that damned dangerous, kill him," Grant said. He saw the look on Lermontov's face. "I don't really mean that, Sergei, but you'll have to do something."

"I will."

"Harmon thinks you might order Falkenberg to march on Earth."

Lermontov looked up in surprise.

"Yes. It's come to that. Not even Bronson's ready to ask for *your* scalp. Yet. But it's another reason why your special favorites have to take a low profile right now."

"You speak of our best men."

Grant's look was full of pain and sadness. "Sure. Anyone who's effective scares hell out of the Patriots. They want the CD eliminated entirely, and if they can't get that, they'll weaken it. They'll keep chewing away, too, getting rid of our most competent officers, and there's not a lot we can do. Maybe in a few years things will be better."

"And perhaps they will be worse," Lermontov said.

"Yeah. There's always that, too."

Sergei Lermontov stared at the viewscreen long after Grand Senator Grant had left the office. Darkness crept slowly across the Pacific, leaving Hawaii in shadow, and still Lermontov sat without moving, his fingers drumming restlessly on the polished wood desktop.

I knew it would come to this, he thought. Not so soon, though, not so soon. There is still so much to do before we can let go.

And yet it will not be long before we have no choice. Perhaps we should act now.

Lermontov recalled his youth in Moscow, when the Generals controlled the Presidium, and shuddered. No, he thought. The military virtues are useless for governing civilians. But the politicians are doing no better.

If we had not suppressed scientific research. But that was done in the name of the peace. Prevent development of new weapons. Keep control of technology in the hands of the government, prevent technology from dictating policy to all of us; it had seemed so reasonable, and besides, the policy was very old now. There were few trained scientists, because no one wanted to live under the restrictions of the Bureau of Technology.

What is done is done, he thought, and looked around the office. Open cabinets held shelves covered with the mementos of a dozen worlds. Exotic shells lay next to reptilian stuffed figures and were framed by gleaming rocks that could bring fabulous prices if he cared to sell.

Impulsively he reached toward the desk console and turned the selector switch. Images flashed across the viewscreen until he saw a column of men marching through a great open bubble of rock. They seemed dwarfed by the enormous cave.

A detachment of CoDominium Marines marching through the central area of Luna Base. Senate chamber and government offices were far below the cavern, buried so deeply into rock that no weapon could destroy the Co-Dominium's leaders by surprise. Above them were the warriors who guarded, and this group was marching to relieve the guard.

Lermontov turned the sound pickup but heard no more than the precise measured tramp of marching boots. They walked carefully in low gravity, their pace modified to accommodate their low weight; and they would, he knew, be just as precise on a high-gravity world.

They wore uniforms of blue and scarlet, with gleaming buttons of gold, badges of the dark rich bronze alloys found on Kennicott, berets made from some reptile that swam in Tanith's seas. Like the Grand Admiral's office, the CoDominium Marines showed the influence of worlds light years away.

"Sound off!"

The order came through the pickup so loud that it startled the Admiral, and he turned down the volume as the men began to sing.

Lermontov smiled to himself. That song was officially forbidden, and it was certainly not an appropriate choice for the guard mount about to take posts outside the Grand Senate chambers. It was also very nearly the official marching song of the Marines. And that, Admiral Lermontov thought, ought to tell something to any Senator listening.

If Senators ever listened to anything from the military people.

The measured verses came through, slowly, in time with the sinister gliding step of the troops.

"We've left blood in the dirt of twenty-five worlds,
we've built roads on a dozen more,
and all that we have at the end our hitch,
buys a night with a second-class whore.

"The Senate decrees, the Grand Admiral calls,
the orders come down from on high,

It's 'On Full Kits' and sound 'Board Ships,'
We're sending you where you can die.

"The lands that we take, the Senate gives back,
rather more often than not,
so the more that are killed, the less share the loot,
and we won't be back to this spot.

"We'll break the hearts of your women and girls,
we may break your arse as well,
Then the Line Marines with their banners unfurled,
will follow those banners to Hell.

"We know the devil, his pomps and his works,
Ah yes! we know them well!
When we've served out our hitch as Line Marines,
we can bugger the Senate of Hell!

"Then we'll drink with our comrades and lay down
    our packs,
we'll rest ten years on the flat of our backs,
then it's 'On Full Kits' and 'Out of Your Racks,'
you must build a new road through Hell!

"The Fleet is our country, we sleep with a rifle,
no one ever begot a son on his rifle,
they pay us in gin and curse when we sin,
there's not one that can stand us unless we're down
    wind,
we're shot when we lose and turned out when we
    win,
but we bury our comrades wherever they fall,
and there's none that can face us though we've
    nothing at all."

The verse ended with a flurry of drums, and Lermontov
gently changed the selector back to the turning Earth.
    Perhaps, he thought. Perhaps there's hope, but only
if we have time.
    Can the politicians buy enough time?

II

THE HONORABLE JOHN Rogers Grant laid a palm across a winking light on his desk console and it went out, shutting off the security phone to Luna Base. His face held an expression of pleasure and distaste, as it always did when he was through talking with his brother.

I don't think I've ever won an argument with Martin, he thought. Maybe it's because he knows me better than I know myself.

Grant turned toward the Tri-V, where the speaker was in full form. The speech had begun quietly as Harmon's speeches always did, full of resonant tones and appeals to reason. The quiet voice had asked for attention, but now it had grown louder and demanded it.

The background behind him changed as well, so that Harmon stood before the stars and stripes covering the hemisphere, with an American eagle splendid over the Capitol. Harmon was working himself into one of his famous frenzies, and his face was contorted with emotion.

"Honor? It is a word that Lipscomb no longer understands! Whatever he might have been—and my friends, we all know how great he once was—he is no longer one of us! His cronies, the dark little men who whisper to him, have corrupted even as great a man as President Lipscomb!

"And our nation bleeds! She bleeds from a thousand

218

wounds! People of America, hear me! She bleeds from the running sores of these men and their CoDominium!

"They say that if we leave the CoDominium it will mean war. I pray God it will not, but if it does, why these are hard times. Many of us will be killed, but we would die as men! Today our friends and allies, the people of Hungary, the people of Rumania, the Czechs, the Slovaks, the Poles, all of them groan under the oppression of their Communist masters. Who keeps them there? We do! Our CoDominium!

"We have become no more than slavemasters. Better to die as men.

"But it will not come to that. The Russians will never fight. They are soft, as soft as we, their government is riddled with the same corruptions as ours. People of America, hear me! People of America, listen!"

Grant spoke softly and the Tri-V turned itself off. A walnut panel slid over the darkened screen, and Grant spoke again.

The desk opened to offer a smal bottle of milk. There was nothing he could do for his ulcer despite the advances in medical science. Money was no problem, but there was never time for surgery and weeks with the regeneration stimulators.

He leafed through papers on his desk. Most were reports with bright red security covers, and Grant closed his eyes for a moment. Harmon's speech was important and would probably affect the upcoming elections. The man is getting to be a nuisance, Grant thought.

I should do something about him.

He put the thought aside with a shudder. Harmon had been a friend, once. Lord, what have we come to? He opened the first report.

There had been a riot at the International Federation of Labor convention. Three killed and the smooth plans for the reelection of Matt Brady thrown into confusion. Grant grimaced again and drank more milk. The Intelligence people had assured him this one would be easy.

He dug through the reports and found that three of Harvey Bertram's child crusaders were responsible.

They'd bugged Brady's suite. The idiot hadn't known better than to make deals in his room. Now Bertram's people had enough evidence of sellouts to inflame floor sentiment in a dozen conventions.

The report ended with a recommendation that the government drop Brady and concentrate support on MacKnight, who had a good reputation and whose file in the CIA building bulged with information. MacKnight would be easy to control. Grant nodded to himself and scrawled his signature on the action form.

He threw it into the "Top Secret: Out" tray and watched it vanish. There was no point in wasting time. Then he wondered idly what would happen to Brady. Matt Brady had been a good United Party man; blast Bertram's people anyway.

He took up the next file, but before he could open it his secretary came in. Grant looked up and smiled, glad of his decision to ignore the electronics. Some executives never saw their secretaries for weeks at a time.

"Your appointment, sir," she said. "And it's time for your nerve tonic."

He grunted. "I'd rather die." But he let her pour a shot glass of evil-tasting stuff, and he tossed it off and chased it with milk. Then he glanced at his watch, but that wasn't necessary. Miss Ackridge knew the travel time to every Washington office. There'd be no time to start another report, which suited Grant fine.

He let her help him into his black coat and brush off a few silver hairs. He didn't feel sixty-five, but he looked it now. It happened all at once. Five years ago he could pass for forty. John saw the girl in the mirror behind him and knew that she loved him, but it wouldn't work.

And why the hell not? he wondered. It isn't as if you're pining away for Priscilla. By the time she died you were praying it would happen, and we married late to begin with. So why the hell do you act as if the great love of your life has gone out forever? All you'd have to do is turn around, say five words, and—and what? She wouldn't be the perfect secretary any longer, and secretaries are harder to find than mistresses. Let it alone.

She stood there a moment longer, then moved away. "Your daughter wants to see you this evening," she told him. "She's driving down this afternoon and says it's important."

"Know why?" Grant asked. Ackridge knew more about Sharon than Grant did. Possibly a lot more.

"I can guess. I think her young man has asked her."

John nodded. It wasn't unexpected, but still it hurt. So soon, so soon. They grow so fast when you're an old man. John Jr. was a commander in the CoDominium Navy, soon to be a captain with a ship of his own. Frederick was dead in the same accident as his mother. And now Sharon, the baby, had found another life . . . not that they'd been close since he'd taken this job.

"Run his name through CIA, Flora, I meant to do that months ago. They won't find anything, but we'll need it for the records."

"Yes, sir. You'd better be on your way now. Your drivers are outside."

He scooped up his briefcase. "I won't be back tonight. Have my car sent around to the White House, will you? I'll drive myself home tonight."

He acknowledged the salutes of the driver and armed mechanic with a cheery wave and followed them to the elevator at the end of the long corridor. Paintings and photographs of ancient battles hung along both sides of the hall, and there was carpet on the floor, but otherwise it was like a cave. Blasted Pentagon, he thought for the hundredth time. Silliest building ever constructed. Nobody can find anything, and it can't be guarded at any price. Why couldn't someone have bombed it?

They took a surface car to the White House. A flight would have been another detail to worry about, and besides, this way he got to see the cherry trees and flower beds around the Jefferson. The Potomac was a sludgy brown mess. You could swim in it if you had a strong stomach, but the Army Engineers had "improved" it a few administrations back. They'd given it concrete banks. Now they were ripping them out, and it brought down mudslides.

They drove through rows of government buildings, some abandoned. Urban renewal had given Washington all the office space the Government would ever need, and more, so that there were these empty buildings as relics of the time when D.C. was the most crime-ridden city in the world. Sometime in Grant's youth, though, they'd hustled everyone out of Washington who didn't work there, with bulldozers quickly following to demolish the tenements. For political reasons the offices had gone in as quickly as the other buildings were torn down.

They passed the Population Control Bureau and drove around the Elipse and past Old State to the gate. The guard carefully checked his identity and made him put his palm on the little scanning plate. Then they entered the tunnel to the White House basement.

The President stood when Grant entered the Oval Office, and the others shot to their feet as if they had ejection charges under them. Grant shook hands around but looked closely at Lipscomb. The President was feeling the strain, no question about it. Well, they all were.

The Secretary of Defense wasn't there, but then he never was. The Secretary was a political hack who controlled a bloc of Aerospace Guild votes and an even larger bloc of aerospace industry stocks. As long as government contracts kept his companies busy employing his men, he didn't give a danm about policy. He could sit in on formal Cabinet sessions where nothing was ever said, and no one would know the difference. John Grant was Defense as much as he was CIA.

Few of the men in the Oval Office were well known to the public. Except for the President any one of them could have walked the streets of any city except Washington without fear of recognition. But the power they controlled, as assistants and deputies, was immense, and they all knew it. There was no need to pretend here.

The servitor brought drinks and Grant accepted Scotch. Some of the others didn't trust a man who wouldn't drink with them. His ulcer would give him hell, and his doctor more, but doctors and ulcers didn't understand the realities of power. Neither, thought Grant, do I or any of us, but we've got it.

"Mr. Karins, would you begin?" the President asked. Heads swiveled to the west wall where Karins stood at the briefing screen. To his right a polar projection of Earth glowed with lights showing the status of the forces that the President ordered, but Grant controlled.

Karins stood confidently, his paunch spilling out over his belt. The fat was an obscenity in so young a man. Herman Karins was the second youngest man in the room, Assistant Director of the Office of Management and Budget, and said to be one of the most brilliant economists Yale had ever produced. He was also the best political technician in the country, but he hadn't learned that at Yale.

He activated the screen to show a set of figures. "I have the latest poll results," Karins said too loudly. "This is the real stuff, not the slop we give the press. It stinks."

Grant nodded. It certainly did. The Unity Party was hovering around thirty-eight percent, just about evenly divided between the Republican and Democratic wings. Harmon's Patriot Party had just over twenty-five. Millington's violently left wing Liberation Party had its usual ten, but the real shocker was Bertram's Freedom Party. Bertram's popularity stood at an unbelievable twenty percent of the population.

"These are figures for those who have an opinion and might vote," Karins said. "Of course there's the usual gang that doesn't give a damn, but we know how they split off. They go to whomever got to 'em last anyway. You see the bad news."

"You're sure of this?" the Assistant Postmaster General asked. He was the leader of the Republican wing of Unity, and it hadn't been six months since he had told them they could forget Bertram.

"Yes, sir," Karins said. "And it's growing. Those riots at the labor convention probably gave 'em another five points we don't show. Give Bertram six months and he'll be ahead of us. How you like them apples, boys and girls?"

"There is no need to be flippant, Mr. Karins," the President said.

"Sorry, Mr. President." Karins wasn't sorry at all and he grinned at the Assistant Postmaster General with triumph. Then he flipped the switches to show new charts.

"Soft and hard," Karins said. "You'll notice Bertram's vote is pretty soft, but solidifying. Harmon's is so hard you couldn't get 'em away from him without you use nukes. And ours is a little like butter. Mr. President, I can't even guarantee we'll be the largest party after the election, much less that we can hold a majority."

"Incredible," the Chairman of the Joint Chiefs muttered.

"Worse than incredible." The Commerce rep shook her head in disbelief. "A disaster. Who will win?"

Karins shrugged. "Toss-up, but if I had to say, I'd pick Bertram. He's getting more of our vote than Harmon."

"You've been quiet, John," the President said. "What are your thoughts here?"

"Well, sir, it's fairly obvious what the result will be no matter who wins as long as it isn't us." Grant lifted his Scotch and sipped with relish. He decided to have another and to hell with the ulcer. "If Harmon wins, he pulls out of the CoDominium, and we have war. If Bertram takes over, he relaxes security, Harmon drives him out with his storm troopers, and we have war anyway."

Karins nodded. "I don't figure Bertram could hold power more'n a year, probably not that long. Man's too honest."

The President sighed loudly. "I can recall a time when men said that about me, Mr. Karins."

"It's still true, Mr. President." Karins spoke hurriedly. "But you're realistic enough to let us do what we have to do. Bertram wouldn't."

"So what do we do about it?" the President asked gently.

"Rig the election," Karins answered quickly. "I give out the popularity figures here." He produced a chart indicating a majority popularity for Unity. "Then we keep pumping out more faked stuff while Mr. Grant's people work on the vote-counting computers. Hell, it's been done before."

"Won't work this time." They turned to look at the youngest man in the room. Larry Moriarty, assistant to the President, and sometimes called the "resident heretic," blushed at the attention. "The people know better. Bertram's people are already taking jobs in the computer centers, aren't they, Mr. Grant? They'll see it in a minute."

Grant nodded. He'd sent the report over the day before; interesting that Moriarty had already digested it.

"You make this a straight rigged election, and you'll have to use CoDominium Marines to keep order," Moriarty continued.

"The day I need CoDominium Marines to put down riots in the United States is the day I resign," the President said coldly. "I may be a realist, but there are limits to what I will do. You'll need a new chief, gentlemen."

"That's easy to say, Mr. President," Grant said. He wanted his pipe, but the doctors had forbidden it. To hell with them, he thought, and took a cigarette from a pack on the table. "It's easy to say, but you can't do it."

The President frowned. "Why not?"

Grant shook his head. "The Unity Party supports the CoDominium, and the CoDominium keeps the peace. An ugly peace, but by God, peace. I wish we hadn't got support for the CoDominium treaties tied so thoroughly to the Unity Party, but it is and that's that. And you know damn well that even in the Party it's only a thin majority that supports the CoDominium. Right, Harry?"

The Assistant Postmaster General nodded. "But don't forget, there's support for the CD in Bertram's group."

"Sure, but they hate our guts," Moriarty said. "They say we're corrupt. And they're right."

"So flipping what if they're right?" Karins snapped. "We're in, they're out. Anybody who's in for long is corrupt. If he isn't, he's not in."

"I fail to see the point of this discussion," the President interrupted. "I for one do not enjoy being reminded of all the things I have done to keep this office. The question is, what are we going to do? I feel it only fair to warn you that nothing could make me happier than to have Mr. Bertram sit in this chair. I've been President for a long time, and I'm tired. I don't want the job anymore."

III

EVERYONE SPOKE AT once, shouting to the President, murmuring to their neighbors, until Grant cleared his throat loudly. "Mr. President," he said using the tone of command he'd been taught during his brief tour in the Army Reserve. "Mr. President, if you will pardon me, that is a ludicrous suggestion. There is no one else in the Unity Party who has even a ghost of a chance of winning. You alone remain popular. Even Mr. Harmon speaks as well of you as he does of anyone not in his group. You cannot resign without dragging the Unity Party with you, and you cannot give that chair to Mr. Bertram because he couldn't hold it six months."

"Would that be so bad?" President Lipscomb leaned toward Grant with the confidential manner he used in his fireside chats to the people. "Are we really so sure that only we can save the human race, John? Or do we only wish to keep power?"

"Both, I suppose," Grant said. "Not that I'd mind retiring myself."

"Retire!" Karins snorted. "You let Bertram's clean babies in the files for two hours, and none of us will retire to anything better'n a CD prison planet. You got to be kidding, retire."

"That may be true," the President said.

"There's other ways," Karins suggested. "General, what happens if Harmon takes power and starts his war?"

227

"Mr. Grant knows better than I do," General Carpenter said. When the others stared at him, Carpenter continued. "No one has ever fought a nuclear war. Why should the uniform make me more of an expert than you? Maybe we could win. Heavy casualties, very heavy, but our defenses are good."

Carpenter gestured at the moving lights on the wall projection. "We have better technology than the Russki's. Our laser gun sought to get most of their missiles. CD Fleet won't let either of us use space weapons. We might win."

"We might." Lipscomb was grim. "John?"

"We might not win. We might kill more than half the human race. We might get more. How in God's name do I know what happens when we throw nuclear weapons around?"

"But the Russians aren't prepared," Commerce said. "If we hit them without warning—people never change governments in the middle of a war."

President Lipscomb sighed. "I am not going to start a nuclear war to retain power. Whatever I have done, I have done to keep peace. That is my last excuse. I could not live with myself if I sacrifice peace to keep power."

Grant cleared his throat gently. "We couldn't do it anyway. If we start converting defensive missiles to offensive, CoDominium Intelligence would hear about it in ten days. The Treaty prevents that, you know."

He lit another cigarette. "We aren't the only threat to the CD, anyway. There's always Kaslov."

Kaslov was a pure Stalinist, who wanted to liberate Earth for Communism. Some called him the last Communist, but of course he wasn't the last. He had plenty of followers. Grant could remember a secret conference with Ambassador Chernikov only weeks ago.

The Soviet was a polished diplomat, but it was obvious that he wanted something desperately. He wanted the United States to keep the pressure on, not relax her defenses at the borders of the U.S. sphere of influence, because if the Communist probes ever took anything from the U.S. without a hard fight, Kaslov would gain more influence at home. He might even win control of the Presidium.

"Nationalism everywhere," the President sighed. "Why?"

No one had an answer to that. Harmon gained power in the U.S. and Kaslov in the Soviet Union; while a dozen petty nationalist leaders gained power in a dozen other countries. Some thought it started with Japan's nationalistic revival.

"This is all nonsense," said the Assistant Postmaster General. "We aren't going to quit and we aren't starting any wars. Now what does it take to get the support away from Mr. Clean Bertram and funnel it back to us where it belongs? A good scandal, right? Find Bertram's dirtier than we are, right? Worked plenty of times before. You can steal people blind if you scream loud enough about how the other guy's a crook."

"Such as?" Karins prompted.

"Working with the Japs. Giving the Japs nukes, maybe. Supporting Meiji's independence movement. I'm sure Mr. Grant can arrange something."

Karins nodded vigorously. "That might do it. Disillusion his organizers. The pro-CoDominium people in his outfit would come to us like a shot."

Karins paused and chuckled. "Course some of them will head for Millington's bunch, too."

They all laughed. No one worried about Millington's Liberation Party. His madmen caused riots and kept the taxpayers afraid, and made a number of security arrangements highly popular. The Liberation Party gave the police some heads to crack, nice riots for Tri-V to keep the Citizens amused and the taxpayers happy.

"I think we can safely leave the details to Mr. Grant." Karins grinned broadly.

"What will you do, John?" the President asked.

"Do you really want to know, Mr. President?" Moriarty interrupted. "I don't."

"Nor do I, but if I can condone it, I can at least find out what it is. What will you do, John?"

"Frame-up, I suppose. Get a plot going, then uncover it."

"That?" Moriarty shook his head. "It's got to be good. The people are beginning to wonder about all these plots."

Grant nodded. "There will be evidence. Hard-core evidence. A secret arsenal of nuclear weapons."

There was a gasp. Then Karins grinned widely again. "Oh, man, that's tore it. Hidden nukes. Real ones, I suppose?"

"Of course." Grant looked with distaste at the fat youth. What would be the point of fake nuclear weapons? But Karins lived in a world of deception, so much so that fake weapons might be appropriate in it.

"Better have lots of cops when you break that story," Karins said. "People hear that, they'll tear Bertram apart."

True enough, Grant thought. It was a point he'd have to remember. Protection of those kids wouldn't be easy. Not since one militant group atom-bombed Bakersfield, California, and a criminal syndicate tried to hold Seattle for a hundred million ransom. People no longer thought of private stocks of atomic weapons as something to laugh at.

"We won't involve Mr. Bertram personally," the President said grimly. "Not under any circumstances. Is that understood?"

"Yes, sir," John answered quickly. He hadn't liked the idea either. "Just some of his top aides." Grant stubbed out the cigarette. It, or something, had left a foul taste in his mouth. "I'll have them end up with the CD for final custody. Sentenced to transportation. My brother can arrange it so they don't have hard sentences."

"Sure. They can be independent planters on Tanith if they'll cooperate," Karins said. "You can see they don't suffer."

Like hell, Grant thought. Life on Tanith was no joy under the best conditions.

"There's one more thing," the President said. "I understand Grand Senator Bronson wants something from the CD. Some officer was a little too efficient at uncovering the Bronson family deals, and they want him removed." The President looked as if he'd tasted sour milk. "I hate this, John. I hate it, but we need Bronson's support. Can you speak to your brother?"

"I already have," Grant said. "It will be arranged."

Grant left the meeting a few minutes later. The others could continue in endless discussion, but Grant saw no point to it. The action needed was clear, and the longer they waited the more time Bertram would have to assemble his supporters and harden his support. If something were to be done, it should be now.

Grant had found all his life that the wrong action taken decisively and in time was better than the right action taken later. After he reached the Pentagon he summoned his deputies and issued orders. It took no more than an hour to set the machinery in motion.

Grant's colleagues always said he was rash, too quick to take action without examining the consequences. They also conceded that he was lucky. To Grant it wasn't luck, and he did consider the consequences; but he anticipated events rather than reacted to crisis. He had known that Bertram's support was growing alarmingly for weeks and had made contingency plans long before going to the conference with the President.

Now it was clear that action must be taken immediately. Within days there would be leaks from the conference. Nothing about the actions to be taken, but there would be rumors about the alarm and concern. A secretary would notice that Grant had come back to the Pentagon after dismissing his driver. Another would see that Karins chuckled more than usual when he left the Oval Office, or that two political enemies came out together and went off to have a drink. Another would hear talk about Bertram, and soon it would be all over Washington: the President was worried about Bertram's popularity.

Since the leaks were inevitable, he should act while this might work. Grant dismissed his aides with a sense of satisfaction. He had been ready, and the crisis would be over before it began. It was only after he was alone that he crossed the paneled room to the teak cabinet and poured a double Scotch.

*   *   *

The Maryland countryside slipped past far below as the Cadillac cruised on autopilot. A ribbon antenna ran almost to Grant's house, and he watched the twilight scene with as much relaxation as he ever achieved lately. House lights blinked below, and a few surface cars ran along the roads. Behind him was the sprawling mass of Columbia Welfare Island where most of those displaced from Washington had gone. Now the inhabitants were third generation and had never known any other life.

He grimaced. Welfare Islands were lumps of concrete buildings and roof parks, containers for the seething resentment of useless lives kept placid by Government furnished supplies of Tanith hashpot and borloi and American cheap booze. A man born in one of those complexes could stay there all his life, and many did.

Grant tried to imagine what it would be like there, but he couldn't. Reports from his agents gave an intellectual picture, but there was no way to identify with those people. He could not feel the hopelessness and dulled senses, burning hatreds, terrors, bitter pride of street gangs.

Karins knew, though. Karins had begun his life in a Welfare Island somewhere in the Midwest. Karins clawed his way through the schools to a scholarship and a ticket out forever. He'd resisted stimulants and dope and Tri-V. Was it worth it? Grant wondered. And of course there was another way out of Welfare, as a voluntary colonist; but so few took that route now. Once there had been a lot of them.

The speaker on the dash suddenly came to life cutting off Beethoven in mid bar. "WARNING. YOU ARE APPROACHING A GUARDED AREA. UNAUTHORIZED CRAFT WILL BE DESTROYED WITHOUT FURTHER WARNING. IF YOU HAVE LEGITIMATE ERRANDS IN THIS RESTRICTED AREA, FOLLOW THE GUIDE BEAM TO THE POLICE CHECK STATION. THIS IS A FINAL WARNING."

The Cadillac automatically turned off course to ride the beam down to State Police headquarters, and Grant cursed. He activated the mike and spoke softly. "This is John Grant of Peachem's Bay. Something seems to be wrong with my transponder."

There was a short pause, then a soft feminine voice came from the dash speaker. "We are very sorry, Mr. Grant. Your signal is correct. Our identification unit is out of order. Please proceed to your home."

"Get that damned thing fixed before it shoots down a taxpayer," Grant said. Ann Arundel County was a Unity stronghold. How long would that last after an accident like that? He took the manual controls and cut across country, ignoring regulations. They could only give him a ticket now that they knew who he was, and his banking computer would pay it without bothering to tell him of it.

It brought a grim smile to his face. Traffic regulations were broken, computers noted it and levied fines, other computers paid them, and no human ever became aware of them. It was only if there were enough tickets accumulated to bring a warning of license suspension that a taxpayer learned of the things—unless he liked checking his bank statements himself.

His home lay ahead, a big rambling early twentieth-century place on the cove. His yacht was anchored offshore, and it gave him a guilty twinge. She wasn't neglected, but she was too much in the hands of paid crew, too long without attention from her owner.

Carver, the chauffeur, rushed out to help Grant down from the Cadillac. Hapwood was waiting in the big library with a glass of sherry. Prince Bismark, shivering in the presence of his god, put his Doberman head on Grant's lap, ready to leap into the fire at command.

There was irony in the situation, Grant thought. At home he enjoyed the power of a feudal lord, but it was limited by how strongly the staff wanted to stay out of Welfare. But he only had to lift the Security phone in the corner, and his real power, completely invisible and limited only by what the President wanted to find out, would operate. Money gave him the visible power, heredity gave him the power over the dog; what gave him the real power of the Security phone?

"What time would you like dinner, sir?" Hapwood asked. "And Miss Sharon is here with a guest."

"A guest?"

"Yes, sir. A young man, Mr. Allan Torrey, sir."

"Have they eaten?"

"Yes, sir. Miss Ackridge called to say that you would be late for dinner."

"All right, Hapwood. I'll eat now and see Miss Grant and her guest afterwards."

"Very good, sir. I will inform the cook." Hapwood left the room invisibly.

Grant smiled again. Hapwood was another figure from Welfare and had grown up speaking a dialect Grant would never recognize. For some reason he had been impressed by English butlers he'd seen on Tri-V and cultivated their manner—and now he was known all over the county as the perfect household manager.

Hapwood didn't know it, but Grant had a record of every cent his butler took in: kickbacks from grocers and caterers, contributions from the gardeners, and the surprisingly well-managed investment portfolio. Hapwood could easily retire to his own house and live the life of a taxpayer investor.

Why? Grant wondered idly. Why does he stay on? It makes life easier for me, but why? It had intrigued Grant enough to have his agents look into Hapwood, but the man had no politics other than staunch support for Unity. The only suspicious thing about his contacts was the refinement with which he extracted money from every transaction involving Grant's house. Hapwood had no children, and his sexual needs were satisfied by infrequent visits to the fringe areas around Welfare.

Grant ate mechanically, hurrying to be through and see his daughter, yet he was afraid to meet the boy she had brought home. For a moment he thought of using the Security phone to find out more about him, but he shook his head angrily. Too much security thinking wasn't good. For once he was going to be a parent, meeting his daughter's intended and nothing more.

He left his dinner unfinished without thinking how much the remnants of steak would have cost, or that

Hapwood would probably sell them somewhere, and went to the library. He sat behind the massive Oriental fruitwood desk and had a brandy.

Behind him and to both sides the walls were lined with book shelves, immaculate dust-free accounts of the people of dead empires. It had been years since he had read one. Now all his reading was confined to reports with bright red covers. The reports told live stories about living people, but sometimes, late at night, Grant wondered if his country was not as dead as the empires in his books.

Grant loved his country but hated her people, all of them: Karins and the new breed, the tranquilized Citizens in their Welfare Islands, the smug taxpayers grimly holding onto their privileges. What, then, do I love? he wondered. Only our history, and the greatness that once was the United States, and that's found only in those books and in old buildings, never in the security reports.

Where are the patriots? All of them have become Patriots, stupid men and women following a leader toward nothing. Not even glory.

Then Sharon came in. She was a lovely girl, far prettier than her mother had ever been, but she lacked her mother's poise. She ushered in a tall boy in his early twenties.

Grant studied the newcomer as they came toward him. Nice-looking boy. Long hair, neatly trimmed, conservative mustache for these times. Blue and violet tunic, red scarf . . . a little flashy, but even John Jr. went in for flashy clothes when he got out of CD uniform.

The boy walked hesitantly, almost timidly, and Grant wondered if it were fear of him and his position in the government, or only the natural nervousness of a young man about to meet his fiancée's wealthy father. The tiny diamond on Sharon's hand sparkled in the yellow light from the fireplace, and she held the hand in an unnatural position.

"Daddy, I . . . I've talked so much about him, this is Allan. He's just asked me to marry him!" She sparkled,

Grant saw; and she spoke trustingly, sure of his approval, never thinking he might object. Grant wondered if Sharon weren't the only person in the country who didn't fear him. Except for John Jr., who didn't have to be afraid. John was out of the reach of Grant's Security phone. The CD Fleet takes care of its own.

At least he's asked her to marry him. He might have simply moved in with her. Or has he already? Grant stood and extended his hand. "Hello, Allan."

Torrey's grip was firm, but his eyes avoided Grant's. "So you want to marry my daughter." Grant glanced pointedly at her left hand. "It appears that she approves the idea."

"Yes, sir. Uh, sir, she wanted to wait and ask you, but I insisted. It's my fault, sir." Torrey looked up at him this time, almost in defiance.

"Yes." Grant sat again. "Well, Sharon, as long as you're home for the evening, I wish you'd speak to Hapwood about Prince Bismark. I do not think the animal is properly fed."

"You mean right now?" she asked. She tightened her small mouth into a pout. "Really, Daddy, this is Victorian! Sending me out of the room while you talk to my fiancé!"

"Yes, it is, isn't it?" Grant said nothing else, and finally she turned away.

Then: "Don't let him frighten you, Allan. He's about as dangerous as that—as that moosehead in the trophy room!" She fled before there could be any reply.

IV

THEY SAT AWKWARDLY. Grant left his desk to sit near the fire with Torrey. Drinks, offer of a smoke, all the usual amenities—he did them all; but finally Hapwood had brought their refreshments and the door was closed.

"All right, Allan," John Grant began. "Let us be trite and get it over with. How do you intend to support her?"

Torrey looked straight at him this time. His eyes danced with what Grant was certain was concealed amusement. "I expect to be appointed to a good post in the Department of the Interior. I'm a trained engineer."

"Interior?" Grant thought for a second. The answer surprised him—he hadn't thought the boy was another office seeker. "I suppose it can be arranged."

Torrey grinned. It was an infectious grin, and Grant liked it. "Well, sir, it's already arranged. I wasn't asking for a job."

"Oh?" Grant shrugged. "I hadn't heard."

"Deputy Assistant Secretary for Natural Resources. I took a master's in ecology."

"That's interesting, but I would have thought I'd have heard of your coming appointment."

"It won't be official yet, sir. Not until Mr. Bertram is elected President. For the moment I'm on his staff." The grin was still there, and it was friendly, not hostile. The boy thought politics was a game. He wanted to win, but it was only a game.

And he's seen real polls, Grant thought. "Just what do you do for Mr. Bertram, then?"

Allan shrugged. "Write speeches, carry the mail, run the Xerox—you've been in campaign headquarters. I'm the guy who gets the jobs no one else wants."

Grant laughed. "I did start as a gopher, but I soon hired my own out of what I once contributed to the Party. They did not try that trick again with me. I don't suppose that course is open to you."

"No, sir. My father's a taxpayer, but paying taxes is pretty tough just now—"

"Yes." Well, at least he wasn't from a Citizen family. Grant would learn the details from Ackridge tomorrow, for now the important thing was to get to know the boy.

It was difficult. Allan was frank and relaxed, and Grant was pleased to see that he refused a third drink, but there was little to talk about. Torrey had no conception of the realities of politics. He was one of Bertram's child crusaders, and he was out to save the United States from people like John Grant, although he was too polite to say so.

And I was once that young, Grant thought. I wanted to save the world, but it was so different then. No one wanted to end the CoDominium when I was young. We were too happy to have the Second Cold War over with. What happened to the great sense of relief when we could stop worrying about atomic wars? When I was young that was all we thought of, that we would be the last generation. Now they take it for granted that we'll have peace forever. Is peace such a little thing?

"There's so much to do," Torrey was saying. "The Baja Project, thermal pollution of the Sea of Cortez! They're killing off a whole ecology just to create estates for the taxpayers.

"I know it isn't your department, sir, you probably don't even know what they're doing. But Lipscomb has been in office too long! Corruption, special interests, it's time we had a genuine two-party system again instead of things going back and forth between the wings of Unity. It's time for a change, and Mr. Bertram's the right man, I know he is."

Grant's smile was thin, but he managed it. "You'll hardly expect me to agree with you," Grant said.

"No, sir."

Grant sighed. "But perhaps you're right at that. I must say I wouldn't mind retiring, so that I could live in this house instead of merely visiting it on weekends."

What was the point? Grant wondered. He'd never convince this boy, and Sharon wanted him. Torrey would drop Bertram after the scandals broke.

And what explanations were there anyway? The Baja Project was developed to aid a syndicate of taxpayers in the six states of the old former Republic of Mexico. The Government needed them, and they didn't care about whales and fish. Shortsighted, yes, and Grant had tried to argue them into changing the project, but they wouldn't, and politics is the art of the possible.

Finally, painfully, the interview ended. Sharon came in, grinning sheepishly because she was engaged to one of Bertram's people, but she understood that no better than Allan Torrey. It was only a game. Bertram would win and Grant would retire, and no one would be hurt.

How could he tell them that it didn't work that way any longer? Unity wasn't the cleanest party in the world, but at least it had no fanatics—and all over the world the causes were rising again. The Friends of the People were on the move, and it had all happened before, it was all told time and again in those aseptically clean books on the shelves above him.

BERTRAM AIDES ARRESTED BY INTER-CONTINENTAL BUREAU OF INVESTIGATION!! IBI RAIDS SECRET WEAPONS CACHE IN BER-TRAM HEADQUARTERS. NUCLEAR WEAP-ONS HINTED!!!

Chicago, May 15, (UPI)—IBI agents here have arrested five top aides to Senator Harvey Bertram in what government officials call one of the most despicable plots ever discovered. . . .

Grant read the transcript on his desk screen without

satisfaction. It had all gone according to plan, and there was nothing left to do, but he hated it.

At least it was clean. The evidence was there. Bertram's people could have their trial, challenge jurors, challenge judges. The Government would waive its rights under the Thirty-first Amendment and let the case be tried under the old adversary rules. It wouldn't matter.

Then he read the small type below. "Arrested were Gregory Kalamintor, nineteen, press secretary to Bertram; Timothy Giordano, twenty-two, secretary; Allan Torrey, twenty-two, executive assistant—" The page blurred, and Grant dropped his face into his hands.

"My God, what have we done?"

He hadn't moved when Miss Ackridge buzzed. "Your daughter on four, sir. She seems upset."

"Yes." Grant punched savagely at the button. Sharon's face swam into view. Her makeup was ruined by long streaks of tears. She looked older, much like her mother during one of their—

"Daddy! They've arrested Allan! And I know it isn't true, he wouldn't have anything to do with nuclear weapons! A lot of Mr. Bertram's people said there would never be an honest election in this country. They said John Grant would see to that! I told him they were wrong, but they weren't, were they? You've done this to stop the election, haven't you?"

There was nothing to say because she was right. But who might be listening? "I don't know what you're talking about. I've only seen the Tri-V casts about Allan's arrest, nothing more. Come home, kitten, and we'll talk about it."

"Oh no! You're not getting me where Dr. Pollard can give me a nice friendly little shot and make me forget about Allan! No! I'm staying with my friends, and I won't be home, Daddy. And when I go to the newspapers, I think they'll listen to me. I don't know what to tell them yet, but I'm sure Mr. Bertram's people will think of something. How do you like that, Mr. God?"

"Anything you tell the press will be lies, Sharon. You know nothing." One of his assistants had come in and now left the office.

"Lies? Where did I learn to lie?" The screen went blank.

And is it that thin? he wondered. All the trust and love, could it vanish that fast, was it that thin?

"Sir?" It was Hartman, his assistant.

"Yes?"

"She was calling from Champaign, Illinois. A Bertram headquarters they think we don't know about. The phone had one of those guaranteed no-trace devices."

"Trusting lot, aren't they?" Grant said. "Have some good men watch that house, but leave her alone." He stood and felt a wave of nausea so strong that he had to hold the edge of the desk. "MAKE DAMNED SURE THEY LEAVE HER ALONE. DO YOU UNDERSTAND?" he shouted.

Hartman went as pale as Grant. The chief hadn't raised his voice to one of his own people in five years. "Yes, sir, I understand."

"Then get out of here." Grant spoke carefully, in low tones, and the cold mechanical voice was more terrifying than the shout.

He sat alone and stared at the telephone. What use was its power now?

What can we do? It wasn't generally known that Sharon was engaged to the boy. He'd talked them out of a formal engagement until the banns could be announced in the National Cathedral and they could hold a big social party. It had been something to do for them at the time, but . . .

But what? He couldn't have the boy released. Not that boy. He wouldn't keep silent as the price of his own freedom. He'd take Sharon to a newspaper within five minutes of his release, and the resulting headlines would bring down Lipscomb, Unity, the CoDominium—and the peace. Newsmen would listen to the daughter of the top secret policeman in the country.

Grant punched a code on the communicator, then another. Grand Admiral Lermontov appeared on the screen.

'Yes, Mr. Grant?"

"Are you alone?"

"Yes."

The conversation was painful, and the long delay while the signals reached the moon and returned didn't make it easier.

"When is the next CD warship going outsystem? Not a colony ship, and most especially not a prison ship. A warship."

Another long pause, longer even than the delay. "I suppose anything could be arranged," the Admiral said. "What do you need?"

"I want . . ." Grant hesitated, but there was no time to be lost. No time at all. "I want space for two very important political prisoners. A married couple. The crew is not to know their identity, and anyone who does learn their identity must stay outsystem for at least five years. And I want them set down on a good colony world, a decent place. Sparta, perhaps. No one ever returns from Sparta. Can you arrange that?"

Grant could see the changes in Lermontov's face as the words reached him. The Admiral frowned. "It can be done if it is important enough. It will not be easy."

"It's important enough. My brother Martin will explain everything you'll need to know later. The prisoners will be delivered tonight, Sergei. Please have the ship ready. And—and it better not be *Saratoga*. My son's in that one and he—he will know one of the prisoners." Grant swallowed hard. "There should be a chaplain aboard. The kids will be getting married."

Lermontov frowned again, as if wondering if John Grant had gone insane. Yet he needed the Grants, both of them, and certainly John Grant would not ask such a favor if it were not vital.

"It will be done," Lermontov said.

"Thank you. I'll also appreciate it if you will see they have a good estate on Sparta. They are not to know who arranged it. Just have it taken care of and send the bill to me."

It was all so very simple. Direct his agents to arrest Sharon and conduct her to CD Intelligence. He wouldn't want to see her first. The attorney general would send

Torrey to the same place and announce that he had escaped.

It wasn't as neat as having all of them convicted in open court, but it would do, and having one of them a fugitive from justice would even help. It would be an admission of guilt.

Something inside him screamed again and again that this was his little girl, the only person in the world who wasn't afraid of him, but Grant refused to listen. He leaned back in the chair and almost calmly dictated his orders.

He took the flimsy sheet from the writer and his hand didn't tremble at all as he signed it.

All right, Martin, he thought. All right. I've bought the time you asked for, you and Sergei Lermontov. Now can you do something with it?

V

2087 A.D.

THE LANDING BOAT fell away from the orbiting warship.
When it had drifted to a safe distance, retros fired,
and after it had entered the thin reaches of the planet's
upper atmosphere, scoops opened in the bows. The
thin air was drawn in and compressed until the stagna-
tion temperature in the ramjet chamber was high enough
for ignition.

The engines lit with a roar of flame. Wings swung out
to provide lift at hypersonic speeds, and the spaceplane
turned to streak over empty ocean toward the continen-
tal land mass two thousand kilometers away.

The ship circled over craggy mountains twelve kilometers high, then dropped low over thickly forested
plains. It slowed until it was no longer a danger to the
thin strip of inhabited lands along the ocean shores.
The planet's great ocean was joined to a smaller sea by
a nearly landlocked channel no more than five kilometers across at its widest point, and nearly all of the
colonists lived near the junction of the waters.

Hadley's capital city nestled on a long peninsula at
the mouth of that channel, and the two natural harbors,
one in the sea, the other in the ocean, gave the city the
fitting name of Refuge. The name suggested a tranquil-
ity the city no longer possessed.

The ship extended its wings to their fullest reach and
floated low over the calm water of the channel harbor.
It touched and settled in. Tugboats raced across clear

blue water. Sweating seamen threw lines and towed the landing craft to the dock where they secured it.

A long line of CoDominium Marines in garrison uniform marched out of the boat. They gathered on the gray concrete piers into neat brightly colored lines. Two men in civilian clothing followed the Marines from the flyer.

They blinked at the unaccustomed blue-white of Hadley's sun. The sun was so far away that it would have been only a small point if either of them were foolish enough to look directly at it. The apparent small size was only an illusion caused by distance; Hadley received as much illumination from its hotter sun as Earth does from Sol.

Both men were tall and stood as straight as the Marines in front of them, so that except for their clothing they might have been mistaken for a part of the disembarking battalion. The shorter of the two carried luggage for both of them, and stood respectfully behind; although older he was obvioualy a subordinate. They watched as two younger men came uncertainly along the pier. The newcomers' unadorned blue uniforms contrasted sharply with the bright reds and golds of the CoDominium Marines milling around them. Already the Marines were scurrying back into the flyer to carry out barracks bags, weapons, and all the other personal gear of a light infantry battalion.

The taller of the two civilians faced the uniformed newcomers. "I take it you're here to meet us?" he asked pleasantly. His voice rang through the noise on the pier, and it carried easily although he had not shouted. His accent was neutral, the nearly universal English of non-Russian officers in the CoDominium Service, and it marked his profession almost as certainly as did his posture and the tone of command.

The newcomers were uncertain even so. There were a lot of ex-officers of the CoDominium Space Navy on the beach lately. CD budgets were lower every year. "I think so," one finally said. "Are you John Christian Falkenberg?"

His name was actually John Christian Falkenberg III,

and he suspected that his grandfather would have insisted on the distinction. "Right. And Sergeant Major Calvin."

"Pleasure to meet you, sir. I'm Lieutenant Banners, and this is Ensign Mowrer. We're on President Budreau's staff." Banners looked around as if expecting other men, but there were none except the uniformed Marines. He gave Falkenberg a slightly puzzled look, then added, "We have transportation for you, but I'm afraid your men will have to walk. It's about eleven miles."

"Miles." Falkenberg smiled to himself. This *was* out in the boondocks. "I see no reason why ten healthy mercenaries can't march eighteen kilometers, Lieutenant." He turned to face the black shape of the landing boat's entry port and called to someone inside. "Captain Fast. There is no transportation, but someone will show you where to march the men. Have them carry all gear."

"Uh, sir, that won't be necessary," the lieutenant protested. "We can get—well, we have horse-drawn transport for baggage." He looked at Falkenberg as if he expected him to laugh.

"That's hardly unusual on colony worlds," Falkenberg said. Horses and mules could be carried as frozen embryos, and they didn't require high-technology industries to produce more, nor did they need an industrial base to fuel them.

"Ensign Mowrer will attend to it," Lieutenant Banners said. He paused again and looked thoughtful as if uncertain how to tell Falkenberg something. Finally he shook his head. "I think it would be wise if you issued your men their personal weapons, sir. There shouldn't be any trouble on their way to barracks, but—anyway, ten armed men certainly won't have any problems."

"I see. Perhaps I should go with my troops, Lieutenant. I hadn't known things were quite this bad on Hadley." Falkenberg's voice was calm and even, but he watched the junior officers carefully.

"No, sir. They aren't, really. . . . But there's no point in taking chances." He waved Ensign Mowrer to the landing craft and turned back to Falkenberg. A large black shape rose from the water outboard of the landing craft. It splashed and vanished. Banners seemed not to notice, but the Marines shouted excitedly. "I'm sure the ensign and your officers can handle the disembarkation, and the President would like to see you immediately, sir."

"No doubt. All right, Banners, lead on. I'll bring Sergeant Major Calvin with me." He followed Banners down the pier.

There's no point to this farce, Falkenberg thought. Anyone seeing ten armed men conducted by a Presidential ensign will know they're mercenary troops, civilian clothes or not. Another case of wrong information.

Falkenberg had been told to keep the status of himself and his men a secret, but it wasn't going to work. He wondered if this would make it more difficult to keep his own secrets.

Banners ushered them quickly through the bustling CoDominium Marine barracks, past bored guards who half-saluted the Presidential Guard uniform. The Marine fortress was a blur of activity, every open space crammed with packs and weapons; the signs of a military force about to move on to another station.

As they were leaving the building, Falkenberg saw an elderly Naval officer. "Excuse me a moment, Banners." He turned to the CoDominium Navy captain. "They sent someone for me. Thanks, Ed."

"No problem. I'll report your arrival to the Admiral. He wants to keep track of you. Unofficially, of course. Good luck, John. God knows you need some right now. It was a rotten deal."

"It's the way it goes."

"Yeah, but the Fleet used to take better care of its own than that. I'm beginning to wonder if anyone is safe. Damn Senator—"

"Forget it," Falkenberg interrupted. He glanced back to be sure Lieutenant Banners was out of earshot. "Pay my respects to the rest of your officers. You run a good ship."

The captain smiled thinly. "Thanks. From you that's quite a compliment." He held out his hand and gripped John's firmly. "Look, we pull out in a couple of days, no more than that. If you need a ride on somewhere I can arrange it. The goddam Senate won't have to know. We can fix you a hitch to anywhere in CD territory."

"Thanks, but I guess I'll stay."

"Could be rough here," the captain said.

"And it won't be everywhere else in the CoDominium?" Falkenberg asked. "Thanks again, Ed." He gave a half-salute and checked himself.

Banners and Calvin were waiting for him, and Falkenberg turned away. Calvin lifted three personal effects bags as if they were empty and pushed the door open in a smooth motion. The CD captain watched until they had left the building, but Falkenberg did not look back.

"Damn them," the captain muttered. "Damn the lot of them."

"The car's here." Banners opened the rear door of a battered ground effects vehicle of no discoverable make. It had been cannibalized from a dozen other machines, and some parts were obviously cut-and-try jobs done by an uncertain machinist. Banners climbed into the driver's seat and started the engine. It coughed twice, then ran smoothly, and they drove away in a cloud of black smoke.

They drove past another dock where a landing craft with wings as large as the entire Marine landing boat was unloading an endless stream of civilian passengers. Children screamed, and long lines of men and women stared about uncertainly until they were ungently hustled along by guards in uniforms matching Banners'. The sour smell of unwashed humanity mingled with the crisp clean salt air from the ocean beyond. Banners rolled up the windows with an expression of distaste.

"Always like that," Calvin commented to no one in particular. "Water discipline in them CoDominium prison ships bein' what it is, takes weeks dirtside to get clean again."

"Have you ever been in one of those ships?" Banners asked.

"No, sir," Calvin replied. "Been in Marine assault boats just about as bad, I reckon. But I can't say I fancy being stuffed into no cubicle with ten, fifteen thousand civilians for six months."

"We may all see the inside of one of those," Falkenberg said. "And be glad of the chance. Tell me about the situation here, Banners."

"I don't even know where to start, sir," the lieutenant answered. "I—do you know about Hadley?"

"Assume I don't," Falkenberg said. May as well see what kind of estimate of the situation the President's officers can make, he thought. He could feel the Fleet Intelligence report bulging in an inner pocket of his tunic, but those reports always left out important details; and the attitudes of the Presidential Guard could be important to his plans.

"Yes, sir. Well, to begin with, we're a long way from the nearest shipping lanes—but I guess you knew that. The only real reason we had any merchant trade was the mines. Thorium, richest veins known anywhere for a while, until they started to run out.

"For the first few years that's all we had. The mines are up in the hills, about eighty miles over that way." He pointed to a thin blue line just visible at the horizon.

"Must be pretty high mountains," Falkenberg said. "What's the diameter of Hadley? About eighty percent of Earth? Something like that. The horizon ought to be pretty close."

"Yes, sir. They are high mountains. Hadley is small, but we've got bigger and better everything here." There was pride in the young officer's voice.

"Them bags seem pretty heavy for a planet this small," Calvin said.

"Hadley's very dense," Banners answered. "Gravity nearly ninety percent standard. Anyway, the mines are over there, and they have their own spaceport at a lake nearby. Refuge—that's this city—was founded by the American Express Company. They brought in the first colonists, quite a lot of them."

"Volunteers?" Falkenberg asked.

"Yes. All volunteers. The usual misfits. I suppose my father was typical enough, an engineer who couldn't keep up with the rat race and was tired of Bureau of

Technology restrictions on what he could learn. They were the first wave, and they took the best land. They founded the city and got an economy going. American Express was paid back all advances within twenty years." Banners' pride was evident, and Falkenberg knew it had been a difficult job.

"That was, what, fifty years ago?" Falkenberg asked.

"Yes."

They were driving through crowded streets lined with wooden houses and a few stone buildings. There were rooming houses, bars, sailors' brothels, all the usual establishments of a dock street, but there were no other cars on the road. Instead the traffic was all horses and oxen pulling carts, bicycles, and pedestrians.

The sky above Refuge was clear. There was no trace of smog or industrial wastes. Out in the harbor tugboats moved with the silent efficiency of electric power, and there were also wind-driven sailing ships, lobster boats powered by oars, even a topsail schooner lovely against clean blue water. She threw up white spume as she raced out to sea. A three-masted, full-rigged ship was drawn up to a wharf where men loaded her by hand with huge bales of what might have been cotton.

They passed a wagonload of melons. A gaily dressed young couple waved cheerfully at them, then the man snapped a long whip at the team of horses that pulled thir wagon. Falkenberg studied the primitive scene and said, "It doesn't look like you've been here fifty years."

"No." Banners gave them a bitter look. Then he swerved to avoid a group of shapeless teenagers lounging in the dockside street. He had to swerve again to avoid the barricade of paving stones that they had masked. The car jounced wildly. Banners gunned it to lift it higher and headed for a low place in the barricade. It scraped as it went over the top, then he accelerated away.

Falkenberg took his hand from inside his shirt jacket.

Behind him Calvin was inspecting a submachine gun that had appeared from the oversized barracks bag he'd brought into the car with him. When Banners said nothing about the incident, Falkenberg frowned and leaned back in his seat, listening. The Intelligence reports mentioned lawlessness, but this was as bad as a Welfare Island on Earth.

"No, we're not much industrialized," Banners continued. "At first there wasn't any need to develop basic industries. The mines made everyone rich, so we imported everything we needed. The farmers sold fresh produce to the miners for enormous prices. Refuge was a service industry town. People who worked here could soon afford farm animals, and they scattered out across the plains and into the forests."

Falkenberg nodded. "Many of them wouldn't care for cities."

"Precisely. They didn't want industry, they'd come here to escape it." Banners drove in silence for a moment. "Then some blasted CoDominium bureaucrat read the ecology reports about Hadley. The Population Control Bureau in Washington decided this was a perfect place for involuntary colonization. The ships were coming here for the thorium anyway, so instead of luxuries and machinery they were ordered to carry convicts. Hundreds of thousands of them, Colonel Falkenberg. For the last ten years there have been better than fifty thousand people a year dumped in on us."

"And you couldn't support them all," Falkenberg said gently.

"No, sir." Banners' face tightened. He seemed to be fighting tears. "God knows we try. Every erg the fusion generators can make goes into converting petroleum into basic protocarb just to feed them. But they're not like the original colonists! They don't know anything, they won't *do* anything! Oh, not really, of course. Some of them work. Some of our best citizens are transportees. But there are so many of the other kind."

"Why'n't you tell 'em to work or starve?" Calvin asked bluntly. Falkenberg gave him a cold look, and the sergeant nodded slightly and sank back into his seat.

"Because the CD wouldn't let us!" Banners shouted. "Damn it, we didn't have self-government. The CD

Bureau of Relocation people told us what to do. They ran everything . . ."

"We know," Falkenberg said gently. "We've seen the results of Humanity League influence over BuRelock. My sergeant major wasn't asking you a question, he was expressing an opinion. Nevertheless, I am surprised. I would have thought your farms could support the urban population."

"They should be able to, sir." Banners drove in grim silence for a long minute. "But there's no transportation. The people are here, and most of the agricultural land is five hundred miles inland. There's arable land closer, but it isn't cleared. Our settlers wanted to get away from Refuge and BuRelock. We have a railroad, but bandit gangs keep blowing it up. We can't rely on Hadley's produce to keep Refuge alive. There are a million people on Hadley, and half of them are crammed into this one ungovernable city."

They were approaching an enormous bowl-shaped structure attached to a massive square stone fortress. Falkenberg studied the buildings carefully, them asked what they were.

"Our stadium," Banners replied. There was no pride in his voice now. "The CD built it for us. We'd rather have had a new fusion plant, but we got a stadium that can hold a hundred thousand people."

"Built by the GLC Construction and Development Company, I presume," Falkenberg said.

"Yes . . . how did you know?"

"I think I saw it somewhere." He hadn't, but it was an easy guess: GLC was owned by a holding company that was in turn owned by the Bronson family. It was easy enough to understand why aid sent by the CD Grand Senate would end up used for something GLC might participate in.

"We have very fine sports teams and racehorses," Banners said bitterly. "The building next to it is the Presidential Palace. Its architecture is quite functional."

The Palace loomed up before them, squat and massive; it looked more fortress than capital building.

The city was more thickly populated as they approached the Palace. The buildings here were mostly stone and poured concrete instead of wood. Few were more than three stories high, so that Refuge sprawled far along the shore. The population density increased rapidly beyond the stadium-palace complex. Banners was watchful as he drove along the wide streets, but he seemed less nervous than he had been at dockside.

Refuge was a city of contrasts. The streets were straight and wide, and there was evidently a good waste-disposal system, but the lower floors of the buildings were open shops, and the sidewalks were clogged with market stalls. Clouds of pedestrians moved through the kiosks and shops.

There was still no motor traffic and no moving pedways. Horse troughs and hitching posts had been constructed at frequent intervals along with starkly functional street lights and water distribution towers. The few signs of technology contrasted strongly with the general primitive air of the city.

A contingent of uniformed men thrust their way through the crowd at a street crossing. Falkenberg looked at them closely, then at Banners. "Your troops?"

"No, sir. That's the livery of Glenn Foster's household. Officially they're unorganized reserves of the President's Guard, but they're household troops all the same." Banners laughed bitterly. "Sounds like something out of a history book, doesn't it? We're nearly back to feudalism, Colonel Falkenberg. Anyone rich enough keeps hired bodyguards. They *have* to. The criminal gangs are so strong the police don't try to catch anyone under organized protection, and the judges wouldn't punish them if they were caught."

"And the private bodyguards become gangs in their own right, I suppose,"

Banners looked at him sharply. "Yes, sir. Have you seen it before?"

"Yes. I've seen it before." Banners was unable to make out the expression on Falkenberg's lips.

VI

THEY DROVE INTO the Presidential Palace and received the salutes of the blue uniformed troopers. Falkenberg noted the polished weapons and precise drill of the Presidential Guard. There were well-trained men on duty here, but the unit was small. Falkenberg wondered if they could fight as well as stand guard. They were local citizens, loyal to Hadley, and would be unlike the CoDominium Marines he was accustomed to.

He was conducted through a series of rooms in the stone fortress. Each had heavy metal doors, and several were guardrooms. Falkenberg saw no signs of government activity until they had passed through the outer layers of the enormous palace into an open courtyard, and through that to an inner building.

Here there was plenty of activity. Clerks bustled through the halls, and girls in the draped to gas fashionable years before on Earth sat at desks in offices. Most seemed to be packing desk contents into boxes, and other people scurried through the corridors. Some offices were empty, their desks covered with fine dust, and there were plastiboard moving boxes stacked outside them.

There were two anterooms to the President's office. President Budreau was a tall, thin man with a red pencil mustache and quick gestures. As they were ushered into the overly ornate room the President looked up from a sheaf of papers, but his eyes did not focus immediately on his visitors. His face was a mask of worry and concentration.

"Colonel John Christian Falkenberg, sir," Lieutenant Banners said. "And Sergeant Major Calvin."

Budreau got to his feet. "Pleased to see you, Falkenberg." His expression told them differently; he looked at his visitors with faint distaste and motioned Banners out of the room. When the door closed he asked, "How many men did you bring with you?"

"Ten, Mr. President. All we could bring aboard the carrier without arousing suspicion. We were lucky to get that many. The Grand Senate had an inspector at the loading docks to check for violation of the anti-mercenary codes. If we hadn't bribed a port official to distract him we wouldn't be here at all. Calvin and I would be on Tanith as involuntary colonists."

"I see." From his expression he wasn't surprised. John thought Budreau would have been more pleased if the inspector had caught them. The President tapped the desk nervously. "Perhaps that will be enough. I understand the ship you came with also brought the Marines who have volunteered to settle on Hadley. They should provide the nucleus of an excellent constabulary. Good troops?"

"It was a demobilized battalion," Falkenberg replied. "Those are the troops the CD didn't want anymore. Could be the scrapings of every guardhouse on twenty Planets. We'll be lucky if there's a real trooper in the lot."

Budreau's face relaxed into its former mask of depression. Hope visibly drained from him.

"Surely you have troops of your own," Falkenberg said.

Budreau picked up a sheaf of papers. "It's all here. I was just looking it over when you came in." He handed the report to Falkenberg. "There's little encouragement in it, Colonel. I have never thought there was any military solution to Hadley's problems, and this confirms that fear. If you have only ten men plus a battalion of forced-labor Marines, the military answer isn't even worth considering."

Budreau returned to his seat. His hands moved restlessly over the sea of papers on his desk. "If I were you, Falkenberg, I'd get back on that Navy boat and forget Hadley."

"Why don't you?"

"Because Hadley's my home! No rabble is going to drive me off the plantation my grandfather built with his own hands. They will not make me run out." Budreau clasped his hands together until the knuckles were white with the strain, but when he spoke again his voice was calm. "You have no stake here. I do."

Falkenberg took the report from the desk and leafed through the pages before handing it to Calvin. "We've come a long way, Mr. President. You may as well tell me what the problem is before I leave."

Budreau nodded sourly. The red mustache twitched and he ran the back of his hand across it. "It's simple enough. The ostensible reason you're here, the reason we gave the Colonial Office for letting us recruit a planetary constabulary, is the bandit gangs out in the hills. No one knows how many of them there are, but they are strong enough to raid farms. They also cut communications between Refuge and the countryside whenever they want to."

"Yes." Falkenberg stood in front of the desk because he hadn't been invited to sit. If that bothered him it did not show. "Guerrilla gangsters have no real chance if they've no political base."

Budreau nodded. "But, as I am sure Vice President Bradford told you, they are not the real problem." The President's voice was strong, but there was a querulous note in it, as if he was accustomed to having his conclusions argued against and was waiting for Falkenberg to begin. "Actually, we could live with the bandits, but they get political support from the Freedom Party. My Progressive Party is larger than the Freedom Party, but the Progressives are scattered all over the planet. The FP is concentrated right here in Refuge, and they have God knows how many voters and about forty thousand loyalists they can concentrate whenever they want to stage a riot."

"Do you have riots very often?" John asked.

"Too often. There's not much to control them with. I have three hundred men in the Presidential Guard, but they're CD recruited and trained like young Banners. They're not much use at riot control, and they're loyal to the job, not to me, anyway. The FP's got men inside the guard."

"So we can scratch the President's Guard when it comes to controlling the Freedom Party," John observed.

"Yes." Budreau smiled without amusement. "Then there's my police force. My police were all commanded by CD officers who are pulling out. My administrative staff was recruited and trained by BuRelock, and all the competent people have been recalled to Earth."

"I can see that would create a problem."

"Problem? It's impossible," Budreau said. "There's nobody left with skill enough to govern, but I've got the job and everybody else wants it. I might be able to scrape up a thousand Progressive partisans and another fifteen thousand party workers who would fight for us in a pinch, but they have no training. How can they face the FP's forty thousand?"

"You seriously believe the Freedom Party will revolt?"

"As soon as the CD's out, you can count on it. They've demanded a new constitutional convention to assemble just after the CoDominium Governor leaves. If we don't give them the convention they'll rebel and carry a lot of undecided with them. After all, what's unreasonable about a convention when the colonial governor has gone?"

"I see."

"And if we do give them the convention they want, they'll drag things out until there's nobody left in it but their people. My Party is composed of working voters. How can they stay on day after day? The FR's unemployed will sit it out until they can throw the Progressives out of office. Once they get in they'll ruin the planet. Under the circumstances I don't see what a military man can do for us, but Vice President Bradford insisted that we hire you."

"Perhaps we can think of something," Falkenberg said smoothly. "I've no experience in administration as such, but Hadley is not unique. I take it the Progressive Party is mostly old settlers?"

"Yes and no. The Progressive Party wants to industrialize Hadley, and some of our farm families oppose that. But we want to do it slowly. We'll close most of the mines and take out only as much thorium as we have to sell to get the basic industrial equipment. I want to keep the rest for our own fusion generators, because we'll need it later.

"We want to develop agriculture and transport, and cut the basic citizen ration so that we'll have the fusion power available for our new industries. I want to close out convenience and consumer manufacturing and keep it closed until we can afford it." Budreau's voice rose and his eyes shone; it was easier to see why he had become popular. He believed in his cause.

"We want to build the tools of a self-sustaining world and get along without the CoDominium until we can rejoin the human race as equals!" Budreau caught himself and frowned. "Sorry. Didn't mean to make a speech. Have a seat, won't you?"

"Thank you." Falkenberg sat in a heavy leather chair and looked around the room. The furnishings were ornate, and the office decor had cost a fortune to bring from Earth; but most of it was tasteless—spectacular rather than elegant. The Colonial Office did that sort of thing a lot, and Falkenberg wondered which Grand Senator owned the firm that supplied office furnishings. "What does the opposition want?"

"I suppose you really do need to know all this." Budreau frowned and his mustache twitched nervously. He made an effort to relax, and John thought the President had probably been an impressive man once. "The Freedom Party's slogan is 'Service to the People.' Service to them means consumer goods now. They want strip mining. That's got the miners' support, you can bet. The FP will rape this planet to buy goods from other systems, and to hell with how they're paid for. Runaway inflation wlll be only one of the problems they'll create."

"They sound ambitious."

"Yes. They even want to introduce internal combustion engine economy. God knows how, there's no support technology here, but there's oil. We'd have to buy all that from off planet, there's no heavy industry here to make engines even if the ecology could absorb them, but that doesn't matter to the FP. They promise cars for everyone. Instant modernization. More food, robotic factories, entertainment . . . in short, paradise and right now."

"Do they mean it, or is that just slogans?"

"I think most of them mean it," Budreau answered. "It's hard to believe, but I think they do."

"Where do they *say* they'll get the money?"

"Soaking the rich, as if there were enough wealthy people here to matter. Total confiscation of everything everyone owns wouldn't pay for all they promise. Those people have no idea of the realities of our situation, and their leaders are ready to blame anything that's wrong on the Progressive Party, CoDominium administrators, anything but admit that what they promise just isn't possible. Some of the Party leaders may know better, but they don't admit it if they do."

"I take it that program has gathered support."

"Of course it has," Budreau fumed. "And every Bu-Relock ship brings thousands more ready to vote the FP line."

Budreau got up from his desk and went to a cabinet on the opposite wall. He took out a bottle of brandy and three glasses and poured, handing them to Calvin and Falkenberg. Then he ignored the sergeant but waited for Falkenberg to lift his glass.

"Cheers." Budreau drained the glass at one gulp. "Some of the oldest families on Hadley have joined the damned Freedom Party. They're worried about the taxes *I've* proposed! The FP won't leave them anything at all, but they still join the opposition in hopes of making deals. You don't look surprised."

"No, sir. It's a story as old as history, and a military man reads history."

Budreau looked up in surprise. "Really?"

"A smart soldier wants to know the causes of wars.

Also how to end them. After all, war is the normal state of affairs, isn't it? Peace is the name of the ideal we deduce from the fact that there have been interludes between wars." Before Budreau could answer, Falkenberg said, "No matter. I take it you expect armed resistance immediately after the CD pulls out."

"I hoped to prevent it. Bradford thought you might be able to do something, and I'm gifted at the art of persuasion." The President sighed. "But it seems hopeless. They don't want to compromise. They think they can get a total victory."

"I wouldn't think they'd have much of a record to run on," Falkenberg said.

Budreau laughed. "The FP partisans claim credit for driving the CoDominium out, Colonel."

They laughed together. The CoDominium was leaving because the mines were no longer worth enough to make it pay to govern Hadley. If the mines were as productive as they'd been in the past, no partisans would drive the Marines away.

Budreau nodded as if reading his thoughts. "Well, they have people believing it anyway. There was a campaign of terrorism for years, nothing very serious. It didn't threaten the mine shipments, or the Marines would have put a stop to it. But they have demoralized the capital police. Out in the bush people administer their own justice, but here in Refuge the FP gangs control a lot of the city."

Budreau pointed to a stack of papers on one corner of the desk. "Those are resignations from the force. I don't even know how many police I'll have left when the CD pulls out." Budreau's fist tightened as if he wanted to pound on the desk, but he sat rigidly still. "Pulls out. For years they ran everything, and now they're leaving us to clean up. I'm President by courtesy of the CoDominium. They put me in office, and now they're leaving."

"At least you're in charge," Falkenberg said. "The BuRelock people wanted someone else. Bradford talked them out of it."

"Sure. And it cost us a lot of money. For what? Maybe it would have been better the other way."

"I thought you said their policies would ruin Hadley."

"I did say that. I believe it. But the policy issues came after the split, I think." Budreau was talking to himself as much as to John. "Now they hate us so much they oppose anything we want out of pure spite. And we do the same thing."

"Sounds like CoDominium politics. Russkis and U.S. in the Grand Senate. Just like home." There was no humor in the polite laugh that followed.

Budreau opened a desk drawer and took out a parchment. "I'll keep the agreement, of course. Here's your commission as commander of the constabulary. But I still think you might be better off taking the next ship out. Hadley's problems can't be solved by military consultants."

Sergeant Major Calvin snorted. The sound was almost inaudible, but Falkenberg knew what he was thinking. Budreau shrank from the bald term "mercenary," as if "military consultant" were easier on his conscience. John finished his drink and stood.

"Mr. Bradford wants to see you," Budreau said. "Lieutenant Banners will be outside to show you to his office."

"Thank you, sir." Falkenberg strode from the big room. As he closed the door he saw Budreau going back to the liquor cabinet.

Vice President Ernest Bradford was a small man with a smile that never seemed to fade. He worked at being liked, but it didn't always work. Still, he had gathered a following of dedicated party workers, and he fancied himself an accomplished politician.

When Banners showed Falkenberg into the office, Bradford smiled even more broadly, but he suggested that Banners should take Calvin on a tour of the Palace guardrooms. Falkenberg nodded and let them go.

The Vice President's office was starkly functional. The desks and chairs were made of local woods with an indifferent finish, and a solitary rose in a crystal vase provided the only color. Bradford was dressed in the same manner, shapeless clothing bought from a cheap store.

"Thank God you're here," Bradford said when the door was closed. "But I'm told you only brought ten men. We can't do anything with just ten men! You were supposed to bring over a hundred men loyal to us!" He bounced up excitedly from his chair, then sat again. "Can you do something?"

"There were ten men in the Navy ship with me," Falkenberg said. "When you show me where I'm to train the regiment I'll find the rest of the mercenaries."

Bradford gave him a broad wink and beamed. "Then you did bring more! We'll show them—all of them. We'll win yet. What did you think of Budreau?"

"He seems sincere enough. Worried, of course. I think I would be in his place."

Bradford shook his head. "He can't make up his mind. About anything! He wasn't so bad before, but lately he's had to be forced into making every decision. Why did the Colonial Office pick him? I thought you were going to arrange for me to be President. We gave you enough money."

"One thing at a time," Falkenberg said. "The Undersecretary couldn't justify you to the Minister. We can't get to everyone, you know. It was hard enough for Professor Whitlock to get them to approve Budreau, let alone you. We sweated blood just getting them to let go of having a Freedom Party President."

Bradford's head bobbed up and down like a puppet's. "I knew I could trust you," he said. His smile was warm, but despite all his efforts to be sincere it did not come through. "You have kept your part of the bargain, anyway. And once the CD is gone—"

"We'll have a free hand, of course."

Bradford smiled again. "You are a very strange man, Colonel Falkenberg. The talk was that you were utterly loyal to the CoDominium. When Dr. Whitlock suggested that you might be available I was astounded."

"I had very little choice," Falkenberg reminded him.

"Yes." Bradford didn't say that Falkenberg had little

more now, but it was obvious that he thought it. His smile expanded confidentially. "Well, we have to let Mr. Hamner meet you now. He's the Second Vice President. Then we can go to the Warner estate. I've arranged for your troops to be quartered there, it's what you wanted for a training ground. No one will bother you. You can say your other men are local volunteers."

Falkenberg nodded. "I'll manage. I'm getting rather good at cover stories lately."

"Sure." Bradford beamed again. "By God, we'll win this yet." He touched a button on his desk. "Ask Mr. Hamner to come in, please." He winked at Falkenberg and said, "Can't spend too long alone. Might give someone the idea that we have a conspiracy."

"How does Hamner fit in?" Falkenberg asked.

"Wait until you see him. Budreau trusts him, and he's dangerous. He represents the technology people in the Progressive Party. We can't do without him, but his policies are ridiculous. He wants to turn loose of everything. If he has his way, there won't be any government. And his people take credit for everything—as if technology was all there was to government. He doesn't know the first thing about governing. All the people we have to keep happy, the meetings, he thinks that's all silly, that you can build a party by working like an engineer."

"In other words, he doesn't understand the political realities," Falkenberg said. "Just so. I suppose he has to go, then."

Bradford nodded, smiling again. "Eventually. But we do need his influence with the technicians at the moment. And of course, he knows nothing about any arrangements you and I have made."

"Of course." Falkenberg sat easily and studied maps until the intercom announced that Hamner was outside. He wondered idly if the office was safe to talk in. Bradford was the most likely man to plant devices in other people's offices, but he couldn't be the only one who'd benefit from eavesdropping, and no place could be absolutely safe.

There isn't much I can do if it is, Falkenberg decided. And it's probably clean.

George Hamner was a large man, taller than Falkenberg and even heavier than Sergeant Major Calvin. He had the relaxed movements of a big man, and much of the easy confidence that massive size usually wins. People didn't pick fights with George Hamner. His grip was gentle when they shook hands, but he closed his fist relentlessly, testing Falkenberg carefully. As he felt answering pressure he looked surprised, and the two men stood in silence for a long moment before Hamner relaxed and waved to Bradford.

"So you're our new colonel of constabulary," Hamner said. "Hope you know what you're getting into. I should say I hope you *don't* know. If you know about our problems and take the job anyway, we'll have to wonder if you're sane."

"I keep hearing about how severe Hadley's problems are," Falkenberg said. "If enough of you keep saying it, maybe I'll believe it's hopeless, but right now I don't see it. So we're outnumbered by the Freedom Party people. What kind of weapons do they have to make trouble with?"

Hamner laughed. "Direct sort of guy, aren't you? I like that. There's nothing spectacular about their weapons, just a lot of them. Enough small problems make a big problem, right? But the CD hasn't permitted any big stuff. No tanks or armored cars, hell, there aren't enough cars of any kind to make any difference. No fuel or power distribution net ever built, so no way cars would be useful. We've got a subway, couple of monorails for in-city stuff, and what's left of the railroad . . . you didn't ask for a lecture on transportation, did you?"

"No."

Hamner laughed. "It's my pet worry at the moment. We don't have enough. Let's see, weapons. . . ." The big man sprawled into a chair. He hooked one leg over the arm and ran his fingers through thick hair just receding from his large brows. "No military aircraft, hardly any aircraft at all except for a few choppers. No artillery, machine guns, heavy weapons in general.

Mostly light-caliber hunting rifles and shotguns. Some police weapons. Military rifles and bayonets, a few, and we have almost all of them. Out in the streets you can find anything, Colonel, and I mean literally anything. Bows and arrows, knives, swords, axes, hammers, you name it."

"He doesn't need to know about obsolete things like that," Bradford said. His voice was heavy with contempt, but he still wore his smile.

"No weapon is ever really obsolete," Falkenberg said. "Not in the hands of a man who'll use it. What about body armor? How good a supply of Nemourlon do you have?"

Hamner looked thoughtful for a second. "There's some body armor in the streets, and the police have some. The President's Guard doesn't use the stuff. I can supply you with Nemourlon, but you'll have to make your own armor out of it. Can you do that?"

Falkenberg nodded. "Yes. I brought an excellent technician and some tools. Gentlemen, the situation's about what I expected. I can't see why everyone is so worried. We have a battalion of CD Marines, not the best Marines perhaps, but they're trained soldiers. With the weapons of a light infantry battalion and the training I can give the recruits we'll add to the battalion, I'll undertake to face your forty thousand Freedom Party people. The guerrilla problem will be somewhat more severe, but we control all the food distribution in the city. With ration cards and identity papers it should not be difficult to set up controls."

Hamner laughed. It was a bitter laugh. "You want to tell him, Ernie?"

Bradford looked confused. "Tell him what?"

Hamner laughed again. "Not doing your homework. It's in the morning report for a couple of days ago. The Colonial Office has decided, on the advice of BuRelock, that Hadley does not need any military weapons. The CD Marines will be lucky to keep their rifles and bayonets. All the rest of their gear goes out with the CD ships."

"But this is insane." Bradford protested. He turned to Falkenberg. "Why would they do that?"

Falkenberg shrugged. "Perhaps some Freedom Party manager got to a Colonial Office official. I assume they are not above bribery?"

"Of course not," Bradford said. "We've got to do something!"

"If we can. I suspect it will not be easy." Falkenberg pursed his lips into a tight line. "I hadn't counted on this. It means that if we tighten up control through food rationing and identity documents, we face armed rebellion. How well organized are these FP partisans, anyway?"

"Well organized and well financed," Hamner said. "And I'm not so sure about ration cards being the answer to the guerrilla problem anyway. The CoDominium was able to put up with a lot of sabotage because they weren't interested in anything but the mines, but we can't live with the level of terror we have right now in this city. Some way or other we have to restore order—and justice, for that matter."

"Justice isn't something soldiers ordinarily deal with," Falkenberg said. "Order's another matter. *That* I think we can supply."

"With a few hundred men?" Hamner's voice was incredulous. "But I like your attitude. At least you don't sit around and whine for somebody to help you. Or sit and think and never make up your mind."

"We will see what we can do," Falkenberg said.

"Yeah." Hamner got up and went to the door. "Well, I wanted to meet you, Colonel. Now I have. *I've* got work to do. I'd think Ernie does too, but I don't notice him doing much of it." He didn't look at them again, but went out, leaving the door open.

"You see," Bradford said. He closed the door gently. His smile was knowing. "He is useless. We'll find someone to deal with the technicians as soon as you've got everything else under control."

"He seemed to be right on some points," Falkenberg said. "For example, he knows it won't be easy to get proper police protection established. I saw an example of what goes on in Refuge on the way here, and if it's that bad all over—"

"You'll find a way," Bradford said. He seemed certain. "You can recruit quite a large force, you know. And a lot of the lawlessness is nothing more than teenage street gangs. They're not loyal to anything. Freedom Party, us, the CD, or anything else. They merely want to control the block they live on."

"Sure. But they're hardly the whole problem."

"No. But you'll find a way. And forget Hamner. His whole group is rotten. They're not real Progressives, that's all." His voice was emphatic, and his eyes seemed to shine. Bradford lowered his voice and leaned forward. "Hamner used to be in the Freedom Party, you know. He claims to have broken with them over technology policies, but you can never trust a man like that."

"I see. Fortunately, I don't have to trust him."

Bradford beamed. "Precisely. Now let's get you started. You have a lot of work, and don't forget now, you've already agreed to train some party troops for me."

VII

THE ESTATE WAS large, nearly five kilometers on a side, located in low hills a day's march from the city of Refuge. There was a central house and barns, all made of local wood that resembled oak. The buildings nestled in a wooded bowl in the center of the estate.

"You're sure you won't need anything more?" Lieutenant Banners asked.

"No, thank you," Falkenberg said. "The few men we have with us carry their own gear. We'll have to arrange for food and fuel when the others come, but for now we'll make do."

"All right, sir," Banners said. "I'll go back with Mowrer and leave you the car, then. And you've the animals. . . ."

"Yes. Thank you, Lieutenant."

Banners saluted and got into the car. He started to say something else, but Falkenberg had turned away and Banners drove off the estate.

Calvin watched him leave. "That's a curious one," he said. "Reckon he'd like to know more about what we're doing."

Falkenberg's lips twitched into a thin smile. "I expect he would at that. You will see to it that he learns no more than we want him to."

"Aye aye, sir. Colonel, what was that Mr. Bradford was saying about Party troopers? We going to have many of them?"

"I think so." Falkenberg walked up the wide lawn

268

toward the big ranch house. Captain Fast and several of
the others were waiting on the porch, and there was a
bottle of whiskey on the table.

Falkenberg poured a drink and tossed it off. "I think
we'll have quite a few Progressive Party loyalists here
once we start, Calvin. I'm not looking forward to it, but
they were inevitable."

"Sir?" Captain Fast had been listening quietly.

Falkenberg gave him a half-smile. "Do you really think
the governing authorities are going to hand over a monop-
oly of military force to us?"

"You think they don't trust us."

"Amos, would *you* trust us?"

"No sir," Captain Fast said. "But we could hope."

"We will not accomplish our mission on hope, Captain. Sergeant Major."

"Sir."

"I have an errand for you later this evening. For the
moment, find someone to take me to my quarters and
then see about our dinner."

"Sir."

Falkenberg woke to a soft rapping on the door of his
room. He opened his eyes and put his hand on the
pistol under his pillow, but made no other movement.

The rap came again. "Yes," Falkenberg called softly.

"I'm back, Colonel," Calvin answered.

"Right, Come in." Falkenberg swung his feet out of
his bunk and pulled on his boots. He was fully dressed
otherwise.

Sergeant Major Calvin came in. He was dressed in
the light synthetic leather tunic and trousers of the CD
Marine battledress. The total black of a night combat
coverall protruded from the war bag slung over his
shoulder. He wore a pistol on his belt and a heavy
trench knife was slung in a holster on his left breast.

A short wiry man with a thin brown mustache came
in with Calvin.

"Glad to see you," Falkenberg said. "Have any trouble?"

"Gang of toughs tried to stir up something as we was
coming through the city, Colonel," Calvin replied. He

grinned wolfishly. "Didn't last long enough to set any records."

"Anyone hurt?"

"None that couldn't walk away."

"Good. Any problem at the relocation barracks?"

"No, sir," Calvin replied. "They don't guard them places. Anybody wants to get away from BuRelock's charity, they let 'em go. Without ration cards, of course. This was just involuntary colonists, not convicts."

As he took Calvin's report, Falkenberg was inspecting the man who had come in with him. Major Jeremy Savage looked tired and much older than his forty-five years. He was thinner than John remembered him.

"Bad as I've heard?" Falkenberg asked him.

"No picnic," Savage replied in the clipped accents he'd learned when he grew up on Churchill. "Didn't expect it to be. We're here, John Christian."

"Yes, and thank God. Nobody spotted you? The men behave all right?"

"Yes, sir. We were treated no differently from any other involuntary colonists. The men behaved splendidly, and a week or two of hard exercise should get us all back in shape. Sergeant Major tells me the battalion arrived intact."

"Yes. They're still at Marine barracks. That's our weak link, Jeremy. I want them out here where we control who they talk to, and as soon as possible."

"You've got the best ones. I think they'll be all right."

Falkenberg nodded. "But keep your eyes open, Jerry, and be careful with the men until the CD pulls out. I've hired Dr. Whitlock to check things for us. He hasn't reported in yet, but I assume he's on Hadley."

Savage acknowledged Falkenberg's wave and sat in the room's single chair. He took a glass of whiskey from Calvin with a nod of thanks.

"Going all out hiring experts, eh? He's said to be the best available. . . . My, that's good. They don't have anything to drink on those BuRelock ships."

"When Whitlock reports in we'll have a full staff meeting," Falkenberg said. "Until then, stay with the plan. Bradford is supposed to send the battalion out tomorrow, and soon after that he'll begin collecting volunteers from his party. We're supposed to train them. Of course, they'll all be loyal to Bradford. Not to the Party and certainly not to us."

Savage nodded and held out the glass to Calvin for a refill.

"Now tell me a bit about those toughs you fought on the way here, Sergeant Major," Falkenberg said.

"Street gang, Colonel. Not bad at individual fightin', but no organization. Hardly no match for near a hundred of us."

"Street gang." John pulled his lower lip speculatively, then grinned. "How many of our battalion used to be punks just like them, Sergeant Major?"

"Half anyway, sir. Includin' me."

Falkenberg nodded. "I think it might be a good thing if the Marines got to meet some of those kids, Sergeant Major. Informally, you know."

"Sir!" Calvin's square face beamed with anticipation.

"Now," Falkenberg continued. "Recruits will be our real problem. You can bet some of them will try to get chummy with the troops. They'll want to pump the men about their backgrounds and outfits. And the men will drink, and when they drink they talk. How will you handle that, Top Soldier?"

Calvin looked thoughtful. "Won't be no trick for a while. We'll keep the recruits away from the men except drill instructors, and DI's don't talk to recruits. Once they've passed basic it'll get a bit stickier, but hell, Colonel, troops like to lie about their campaigns. We'll just encourage 'em to fluff it up a bit. The stories'll be so tall nobody'll believe 'em."

"Right. I don't have to tell both of you we're skating on pretty thin ice for a while."

"We'll manage, Colonel." Calvin was positive. He'd been with Falkenberg a long time, and although any man can make mistakes, it was Calvin's experience that Falkenberg would find a way out of any hole they dropped into.

And if they didn't—well, over every CD orderly room door was a sign. It said, "You are Marines in order

to die, and the Fleet will send you where you can die."
Calvin had walked under that sign to enlist, and thousands of times since.

"That's it, then, Jeremy," Falkenberg said.

"Yes, sir," Savage said crisply. He stood and saluted.
"Damned if it doesn't feel good to be doing this again,
sir." Years fell away from his face.

"Good to have you back aboard," Falkenberg replied.
He stood to return the salute. "And thanks, Jerry. For
everything. . . ."

The Marine battalion arrived the next day. They
were marched to the camp by regular CD Marine officers, who turned them over to Falkenberg. The captain
in charge of the detail wanted to stay around and watch,
but Falkenberg found an errand for him and sent Major
Savage along to keep him company. An hour later there
was no one in the camp but Falkenberg's people.

Two hours later the troops were at work constructing
their own base camp.

Falkenberg watched from the porch of the ranch
house. "Any problems, Sergeant Major?" he asked.

Calvin fingered the stubble on his square jaw. He
shaved twice a day on garrison duty, and at the moment
he was wondering if he needed his second. "Nothing a
trooper's blast won't cure, Colonel. With your permission I'll draw a few barrels of whiskey tonight and let
'em tie one on before the recruits come in."

"Granted."

"They won't be fit for much before noon tomorrow,
but we're on schedule now. The extra work'll be good
for 'em."

"How many will run?"

Calvin shrugged. "Maybe none, Colonel. We got
enough to keep 'em busy, and they don't know this
place very well. Recruits'll be a different story, and
once they get in we may have a couple take off."

"Yes. Well, see what you can do. We're going to
need every man. You heard President Budreau's assess-
ment of the situation."

"Yes, sir. That'll make the troops happy. Sounds like a good fight comin' up."

"I think you can safely promise the men some hard fighting, Sergeant Major. They'd also better understand that there's no place to go if we don't win this one. No pickups on this tour."

"No pickups on half the missions we've been on, Colonel. I better see Cap'n Fast about the brandy. Join us about midnight, sir? The men would like that."

"I'll be along, Sergeant Major."

Calvin's prediction was wrong: the troops were useless throughout the entire next day. The recruits arrived the day after.

The camp was a flurry of activity. The Marines relearned lessons of basic training. Each maniple of five men cooked for itself, did its own laundry, made its own shelters from woven synthetics and rope, and contributed men for work on the encampment revetments and palisades.

The recruits did the same kind of work under the supervision of Falkenberg's mercenary officers and NCO's. Most of the men who had come with Savage on the BuRelock colony transport were officers, centurions, sergeants, and technicians, while there was an unusual number of monitors and corporals within the Marine battalion. Between the two groups there were enough leaders for an entire regiment.

The recruits learned to sleep in their military greatcloaks, and to live under field conditions with no uniform but synthi-leather battledress and boots. They cooked their own food and constructed their own quarters and depended on no one outside the regiment. After two weeks they were taught to fashion their own body armor from Nemourlon. When it was completed they lived in it, and any man who neglected his duties found his armor weighted with lead. Maniples, squads, and whole sections of recruits and veterans on punishment marches became a common sight after dark.

The volunteers had little time to fraternize with the Marine veterans. Savage and Calvin and the other cadres relentlessly drove them through drills, field problems, combat exercises, and maintenance work. The recruit formations were smaller each day as men were driven to leave the service, but from somewhere there was a steady supply of new troops.

These were all younger men who came in small groups directly to the camp. They would appear before the regimental orderly room at reveille, and often they were accompanied by Marine veterans. There was attrition in their formations as well as among the Party volunteers, but far fewer left the service—and they were eager for combat training.

After six weeks Vice President Bradford visited the camp. He arrived to find the entire regiment in formation, the recruits on one side of a square, the veterans on the other.

Sergeant Major Calvin was reading to the men.

"Today is April 30 on Earth." Calvin's voice boomed out; he had no need for a bullhorn. "It is Camerone Day. On April 30, 1863, Captain Jean Danjou of the Foreign Legion, with two officers and sixty-two legionnaires, faced two thousand Mexicans at the farmhouse of Camerone.

"The battle lasted all day. The legionnaires had no food or water, and their ammunition was low. Captain Danjou was killed. His place was taken by Lieutenant Villain. He also was killed.

"At five in the afternoon all that remained were Lieutenant Clement Maudet and four men. They had one cartridge each. At the command each man fired his last round and charged the enemy with the bayonet.

"There were no survivors."

The troops were silent. Calvin looked at the recruits. They stood at rigid attention in the hot sun. Finally Calvin spoke. "I don't expect none of you to ever get it. Not the likes of you. But maybe one of you'll someday know what Camerone is all about.

"Every man will draw an extra wine ration tonight. Combat veterans will also get a half-liter of brandy. Now attention to orders."

Falkenberg took Bradford inside the ranch house. It

was now fitted out as the Officers' Mess, and they sat in one corner of the lounge. A steward brought drinks.

"And what was all that for?" Bradford demanded. "These aren't Foreign Legionnaires! You're supposed to be training a planetary constabulary."

"A constabulary that has one hell of a fight on its hands," Falkenberg reminded him. "True, we don't have any continuity with the Legion in this outfit, but you have to remember that our basic cadre are CD Marines. Or were. If we skipped Camerone Day, we'd have a mutiny."

"I suppose you know what you're doing." Bradford sniffed. His face had almost lost the perpetual half-smile he wore, but there were still traces of it. "Colonel, I have a complaint from the men we've assigned as officers. My Progressive Party people have been totally segregated from the other troops, and they don't like it. I don't like it."

Falkenberg shrugged. "You chose to commission them before training, Mr. Bradford. That makes them officers by courtesy, but they don't know anything. They would look ridiculous if I mixed them with the veterans, or even the recruits, until they've learned military basics."

"You've got rid of a lot of them, too—"

"Same reason, sir. You have given us a difficult assignment. We're outnumbered and there's no chance of outside support. In a few weeks we'll face forty thousand Freedom Party men, and I won't answer for the consequences if we hamper the troops with incompetent officers."

"All right. I expected that. But it isn't just the officers, Colonel. The Progressive volunteers are being driven out as well. Your training is too hard. Those are loyal men, and loyalty is important here!"

Falkenberg smiled softly. "Agreed. But I'd rather have one battalion of good men I can trust than a regiment of troops who might break under fire. After I've a bare minimum of first-class troops, I'll consider taking on others for garrison duties. Right now the need is for men who can fight."

"And you don't have them yet—those Marines seemed well disciplined."

"In ranks, certainly. But do you really think the CD would let go of reliable troops?"

"Maybe not," Bradford conceded. "OK. You're the expert. But where the hell are you getting the other recruits? Jailbirds, kids with police records. You keep them while you let my Progressives run!"

"Yes, sir." Falkenberg signaled for another round of drinks. "Mr. Vice President—"

"Since when have we become that formal?" Bradford asked. His smile was back.

"Sorry. I thought you were here to read me out."

"No, of course not. But I've got to answer to President Budreau, you know. And Hamner. I've managed to get your activities assigned to my department, but it doesn't mean I can tell the Cabinet to blow it."

"Right," Falkenberg said. "Well, about the recruits. We take what we can get. It takes time to train green men, and if the street warriors stand up better than your party toughs, I can't help it. You can tell the Cabinet that when we've a cadre we can trust, we'll be easier on volunteers. We can even form some kind of part-time militia. But right now the need is for men tough enough to win this fight coming up, and I don't know any better way to do it."

After that Falkenberg found himself summoned to report to the Palace every week. Usually he met only Bradford and Hamner; President Budreau had made it clear that he considered the military force as an evil whose necessity was not established, and only Bradford's insistence kept the regiment supplied.

At one conference Falkenberg met Chief Horgan of the Refuge police.

"The Chief's got a complaint, Colonel," President Budreau said.

"Yes sir?" Falkenberg asked.

"It's those damned Marines," Horgan said. He rubbed the point of his chin. "They're raising hell in the city at night. We've never hauled any of them in because Mr. Bradford wants us to go easy, but it's getting rough."

"What are they doing?" Falkenberg asked.

"You name it. They've taken over a couple of taverns and won't let anybody in without their permission, for one thing. And they have fights with street gangs every night.

"We could live with all that, but they go to other parts of town, too. Lots of them. They go into taverns and drink all night, then say they can't pay. If the owner gets sticky, they wreck the place. . . ."

"And they're gone before your patrols get there," Falkenberg finished for him. "It's an old tradition. They call it System D, and more planning effort goes into that operation than I can ever get them to put out in combat. I'll try to put a stop to System D, anyway."

"It would help. Another thing. Your guys go into the roughest parts of town and start fights whenever they can find anyone to mix with."

"How are they doing?" Falkenberg asked interestedly.

Horgan grinned, then caught himself after a stern look from Budreau. "Pretty well. I understand they've never been beaten. But it raises hell with the citizens, Colonel. And another trick of theirs is driving people crazy! They march through the streets fifty strong at all hours of the night playing bagpipes! Bagpipes in the wee hours, Colonel, can be a frightening thing."

Falkenberg thought he saw a tiny flutter in Horgan's left eye, and the police chief was holding back a wry smile.

"I wanted to ask you about that, Colonel," Second Vice President Hamner said. "This is hardly a Scots outfit, why do they have bagpipes anyway?"

Falkenberg shrugged. "Pipes are standard with many Marine regiments. Since the Russki CD outfits started taking up Cossack customs, the Western bloc regiments adopted their own. After all, the Marines were formed out of a number of old military units. Foreign Legion, Highlanders—a lot of men like the pipes. I'll confess I do myself."

"Sure, but not in my city in the middle of the night," Horgan said.

John grinned openly at the chief of police. "I'll try to keep the pipers off the streets at night. I can imagine they're not good for civilian morale. But as to keeping the Marines in camp, how do I do it? We need every one of them, and they're volunteers. They can get on the CD carrier and ship out when the rest go, and there's not one damned thing we can do about it."

"There's less than a month until they haul down that CoDominium flag," Bradford added with satisfaction. He glanced at the CD banner on its staff outside. Eagle with red shield and black sickle and hammer on its breast; red stars and blue stars around it. Bradford nodded in satisfaction. It wouldn't be long.

That flag meant little to the people of Hadley. On Earth it was enough to cause riots in nationalistic cities in both the U.S. and the Soviet Union, while in other countries it was a symbol of the alliance that kept any other nation from rising above second-class status. To Earth the CoDominium Alliance represented peace at a high price, too high for many.

For Falkenberg it represented nearly thirty years of service ended by court martial.

Two weeks to go. Then the CoDominium governor would leave, and Hadley would be officially independent. Vice President Bradley visited the camp to speak to the recruits.

He told them of the value of loyalty to the government, and the rewards they would all have as soon as the Progressive Party was officially in power. Better pay, more liberties, and the opportunity for promotion in an expanding army; bonuses and soft duty. His speech was full of promises, and Bradford was quite proud of it.

When he had finished, Falkenberg took the Vice President into a private room in the Officers' Mess and slammed the door.

"Damn you, you don't *ever* make offers to my troops without my permission." John Falkenberg's face was cold with anger.

"I'll do as I please with my army, Colonel," Bradford

replied smugly. The little smile on his face was completely without warmth. "Don't get snappy with me, *Colonel* Falkenberg. Without my influence Budreau would dismiss you in an instant."

Then his mood changed, and Bradford took a flask of brandy from his pocket. "Here, Colonel, have a drink." The little smile was replaced with something more genuine. "We have to work together, John. There's too much to do, even with both of us working it won't all get done. Sorry, I'll ask your advice in future, but don't you think the troops, should get to know me? I'll be President soon." He looked to Falkenberg for confirmation.

"Yes, sir," John took the flask and held it up for a toast. "To the new president of Hadley. I shouldn't have snapped at you, but don't make offers to troops who haven't proved themselves. If you give men reason to think they're good when they're not, you'll never have an army worth its pay."

"But they've done well in training. You said so."

"Sure, but you don't tell *them* that. Work them until they've nothing more to give, and let them know that's just barely satisfactory. Then one day they'll give you more than they knew they had in them. That's the day you can offer rewards, only by then you won't need to."

Bradford nodded grudging agreement. "If you say so. But I wouldn't have thought—"

"Listen," Falkenberg said.

A party of recruits and their drill masters marched past outside. They were singing and their words came in the open window.

> "When you've blue'd your last tosser,
> on the brothel and the booze,
> and you're out in the cold on your ear,
> you hump your bundle on the rough,
> and tell the sergeant that you're tough,
> and you'll do him the favor of his life.
> He will cry and he will scream,
> and he'll curse his rotten luck,
> and he'll ask why he was ever born.
> If you're lucky he will take you,

and he'll do his best to break you,
and they'll feed you rotten monkey on a knife."

"Double time, heaow!" The song broke off as the men ran across the central parade ground.

Bradford turned away from the window. "That sort of thing is all very well for the jailbirds, Colonel, but I insist on keeping my loyalists as well. In future you will dismiss no Progressive without my approval. Is that understood?"

Falkenberg nodded. He'd seen this coming for some time. "In that case, sir, it might be better to form a separate battalion. I will transfer all of your people into the Fourth Battalion and put them under the officers you've appointed. Will that be satisfactory?"

"If you'll supervise their training, yes."

"Certainly," Falkenberg said.

"Good." Bradford's smile broadened, but it wasn't meant for Falkenberg. "I will also expect you to consult me about any promotions in that battalion. You agree to that, of course."

"Yes, sir. There may be some problems about finding locals to fill the senior NCO slots. You've got potential monitors and corporals, but they've not the experience to be sergeants and centurions."

"You'll find a way, I'm sure," Bradford said carefully. "I have some rather, uh, special duties for the Fourth Battalion, Colonel. I'd prefer it to be entirely staffed by Party loyalists of my choosing. Your men should only be there to supervise training, not as their commanders. Is this agreed?"

"Yes, sir."

Bradford's smile was genuine as he left the camp.

Day after day the troops sweated in the bright blue-tinted sunlight. Riot control, bayonet drill, use of armor in defense and attacks against men with body armor; and more complex exercises as well. There were forced marches under the relentless direction of Major Savage, the harsh shouts of sergeants and centurions, Captain

Amos Fast with his tiny swagger stick and biting sarcasm. . . .

Yet the number leaving the regiment was smaller now, and there was still a flow of recruits from the Marine's nocturnal expeditions. The recruiting officers could even be selective, although they seldom were. The Marines, like the Legion before it, took anyone willing to fight; and Falkenberg's officers were all Marine trained.

Each night groups of Marines sneaked past sentries to drink and carouse with the field hands of nearby ranchers. They gambled and shouted in local taverns, and they paid little attention to their officers. There were many complaints, and Bradford's protests became stronger.

Falkenberg always gave the same answer. "They always come back, and they don't have to stay here. How do you suggest I control them? Flogging?"

The constabulary army had a definite split personality, with recruits treated harsher than veterans. Meanwhile the Fourth Battalion grew larger each day.

VIII

GEORGE HAMNER TRIED to get home for dinner every
night, no matter what it might cost him in night work
later. He thought he owed at least that to his family.

His walled estate was just outside the Palace district.
It had been built by his grandfather with money borrowed from American Express. The old man had been
proud of paying back every cent before it was due. It
was a big comfortable place which cunningly combined
local materials and imported luxuries, and George was
always glad to return there.

At home he felt he was master of something, that at
least one thing was under his control. It was the only
place in Refuge where he could feel that way.

In less than a week the CoDominium Governor would
leave. Independence was near, and it should be a time
of hope, but George Hamner felt only dread. Problems
of public order were not officially his problem. He held
the Ministry of Technology, but the breakdown in law
and order couldn't be ignored. Already half of Refuge
was untouched by government.

There were large areas where the police went only in
squads or not at all, and maintenance crews had to be
protected or they couldn't enter. For now the CoDominium Marines escorted George's men, but what would
it be like when the Marines were gone?

George sat in the paneled study and watched lengthen-
ing shadows in the groves outside. They made dancing

patterns through the trees and across neatly clipped lawns. The outside walls spoiled the view of Raceway Channel below, and Hamner cursed them.

Why must we have walls? Walls and a dozen armed men to patrol them. I can remember when I sat in this room with my father, I was no more than six, and we could watch boats in the Channel. And later, we had such big dreams for Hadley. Grandfather telling why he had left Earth, and what we could do here. Freedom and plenty. We had a paradise, and Lord, Lord, what have we done with it?

He worked for an hour, but accomplished little. There weren't any solutions, only chains of problems that led back into a circle. Solve one and all would fall into place, but none were soluble without the others. And yet, if we had a few years, he thought. A few years, but we aren't going to get them.

In a few years the farms will support the urban population if we can move people out to the agricultural interior and get them working—but they won't leave Refuge, and we can't make them do it.

If we could, though. If the city's population could be thinned, the power we divert to food manufacture can be used to build a transport net. Then we can get more to live in the interior, and we can get more food into the city. We could make enough things to keep country life pleasant, and people will want to leave Refuge. But there's no way to the first step. The people don't want to move and the Freedom Party promises they won't have to.

George shook his head. Can Falkenberg's army make them leave? If he gets enough soldiers can he forcibly evacuate part of the city? Hamner shuddered at the thought. There would be resistance, slaughter, civil war. Hadley's independence can't be built on a foundation of blood. No.

His other problems were similar. The government was bandaging Hadley's wounds, but no more. Treating symptoms because there was never enough control over events to treat causes.

He picked up a report on the fusion generators. They

needed spare parts, and he wondered how long even this crazy standoff would last. He couldn't really expect more than a few years even if everything went well. A few years, and then famine because the transport net couldn't be built fast enough. And when the generators failed, the city's food supplies would be gone, sanitation services crippled . . . famine and plague. Were those horsemen better than conquest and war?

He thought of his interview with the Freedom Party leaders. They didn't care about the generators because they were sure that Earth wouldn't allow famines on Hadley. They thought Hadley could use her own helplessness as a weapon to extract payments from the CoDominium.

George cursed under his breath. They were wrong. Earth didn't care, and Hadley was too far away to interest anyone. But even if they were right they were selling Hadley's independence, and for what? Didn't real independence mean anything to them?

Laura came in with a pack of shouting children.

"Already time for bed?" he asked. The four-year-old picked up his pocket calculator and sat on his lap, punching buttons and watching the numbers and lights flash.

George kissed them all and sent them out, wondering as he did what kind of future they had.

I should get out of politics, he told himself. I'm not doing any good, and I'll get Laura and the kids finished along with me. But what happens if we let go? What future will they have then?

"You look worried." Laura was back after putting the children to bed. "It's only a few days—"

"Yeah."

"And what really happens then?" she asked. "Not the promises we keep hearing. What really happens when the CD leaves? It's going to be bad, isn't it?"

He pulled her to him, feeling her warmth, and tried to draw comfort from her nearness. She huddled against him for a moment, then pulled away.

"George, shouldn't we take what we can and go east? We wouldn't have much, but you'd be alive."

"It won't be *that* bad," he told her. He tried to chuckle, as if she'd made a joke, but the sound was hollow. She didn't laugh with him.

"There'll be time for that later," he told her. "If things don't work. But it should be all right at first. We've got a planetary constabulary. It should be enough to protect the government—but I'm moving all of you into the palace in a couple of days."

"The army," she said with plenty of contempt. "Some army, Georgie. Bradford's volunteers who'd kill you—and don't think he wouldn't like to see you dead, either. And those Marines! You said yourself they were the scum of space."

"I said it. I wonder if I believe it. There's something strange happening here, Laura. Something I don't understand."

She sat on the couch near his desk and curled her legs under herself. He'd always liked that pose. She looked up, her eyes wide with interest. She never looked at anyone else that way.

"I went to see Major Karantov today," George said. "Thought I'd presume on an old friend to get a little information about this man Falkenberg. Boris wasn't in his office, but one of the junior lieutenants, fellow named Kleist—"

"I've met him," Laura said. "Nice boy. A little young."

"Yes. Anyway, we got into a conversation about what happens after independence. We discussed street fighting, and the mob riots, you know, and I said I wished we had some reliable Marines instead of the demobilized outfit they were leaving here. He looked funny and asked just what did I want, the Grand Admiral's Guard?"

"That's strange."

"Yes, and when Boris came in and I asked what Kleist meant, Boris said the kid was new and didn't know what he was talking about."

"And you think he did?" Laura asked. "Boris wouldn't lie to you. Stop that!" she added hastily. "You have an appointment."

"It can wait."

"With only a couple of dozen cars on this whole planet and one of them coming for you, you will not keep it waiting while you make love to your wife, George Hamner!" Her eyes flashed, but not with anger. "Besides, I want to know what Boris told you." She danced away from him, and he went back to the desk.

"It's not just that," George said. "I've been thinking about it. Those troops don't look like misfits to me. Off duty they drink, and they've got the field hands locking their wives and daughters up, but you know, come morning they're out on that drill field. And Falkenberg doesn't strike me as the type who'd put up with undisciplined men."

"But—"

He nodded. "But it doesn't make sense. And there's the matter of the officers. He's got too many, and they're not from Hadley. That's why I'm going out there tonight, without Bradford."

"Have you asked Ernie about it?"

"Sure. He says he's got some Party loyalists training as officers. I'm a little slow, Laura, but I'm not that stupid. I may not notice everything, but if there were fifty Progressives with military experience I'd know. Bradford is lying, and why?"

Laura looked thoughtful and pulled her lower lip in a gesture that Hamner hardly noticed now, although he'd kidded her about it before they were married. "He lies for practice," she said. "But his wife has been talking about independedce, and she let something slip about when Ernie would be President she'd make some changes."

"Well, Ernie expects to succeed Budreau."

"No," Laura said. "She acted like it would be soon. Very soon."

George Hamner shook his massive head. "He hasn't the guts for a coup," he said firmly. "And the technicians would walk out in a second. They can't stand him and he knows it."

"Ernest Bradford has never recognized any limitations," Laura said. "He really believes he can make anyone like him if he'll just put out the effort. No matter how many times he's kicked a man, he thinks a few smiles and apologies will fix it. But what did Boris tell you about Falkenberg?"

"Said he was as good as we can get. A top Marine commander, started as a Navy man and went over to Marines because he couldn't get fast enough promotions in the Navy."

"An ambitious man. How ambitious?"

"Don't know."

"Is he married?"

"I gather he once was, but not for a long time. I got the scoop on the court martial. There weren't any slots open for promotion. But when a review board passed Falkenberg over for a promotion that the admiral couldn't have given him in the first place, Falkenberg made such a fuss about it that he was dismissed for insubordination."

"Can you trust him, then?" Laura asked. "His men may be the only thing keeping you alive—"

"I know. And you, and Jimmy, and Christie, and Peter. . . . I asked Boris that, and he said there's no better man available. You can't hire CD men from active duty. Boris recommends him highly. Says troops love him, he's a brilliant tactician, has experience in troop command and staff work as well—"

"Sounds like quite a catch."

"Yes. But Laura, if he's all that valuable, why did they boot him out? My God, it all sounds so trivial—"

The interphone buzzed, and Hamner answered it absently. It was the butler to announce that his car and driver were waiting. "I'll be late, sweetheart. Don't wait up for me. But you might think about it . . . I swear Falkenberg is the key to something, and I wish I knew what."

"Do you like him?" Laura asked.

"He isn't a man who tries to be liked."

"I asked if *you* like him."

"Yes. And there's no reason to. I like him, but can I trust him?"

As he went out he thought about that. Could he trust Falkenberg? With Laura's life . . . and the kids . . . and for that matter, with a whole planet that seemed headed for hell and no way out.

The troops were camped in an orderly square. Earth ramparts had been thrown up around the perimeter, and the tents were pitched in lines that might have been laid with a transit.

The equipment was scrubbed and polished, blanket rolls were tight, each item in the same place inside the two-man tents . . . but the men were milling about, shouting, gambling openly in front of the campfires. There were plenty of bottles in evidence even from the outer gates.

"Halt! Who's there?"

Hamner started. The car had stopped at the barricaded gate, but Hamner hadn't seen the sentry. This was his first visit to the camp at night, and he was edgy. "Vice President Hamner," he answered.

A strong light played on his face from the opposite side of the car. Two sentries, then, and both invisible until he'd come on them. "Good evening, sir," the first sentry said. "I'll pass the word you're here."

He raised a small communicator to his lips. "Corporal of the Guard. Post Number Five." Then he shouted the same thing, the call ringing clear in the night. A few heads around campfires turned toward the gate, then went back to their other activities.

Hamner was escorted across the camp to officers' row. The huts and tent stood across a wide parade ground from the densely packed company streets of the troops and had their own guards.

Over in the company area the men were singing, and Hamner paused to listen.

"I've a head like a concertina, and I think I'm
        ready to die,
and I'm here in the clink for a thundrin' drink and
        blacking the Corporal's eye,
With another man's cloak underneath of my head
and a beautiful view of the yard,

it's the crapaud for me, and no more System D,
I was Drunk and Resistin' the Guard!
Mad drunk and resistin' the guard!
    It's the crapaud for me, and no more System D,
    I was Drunk and Resistin' the Guard."

Falkenberg came out of his hut. "Good evening, sir.
What brings you here?"

I'll just bet you'd like to know, Hamner thought. "I
have a few things to discuss with you, Colonel. About
the organization of the constabulary."

"Certainly." Falkenberg was crisp and seemed slightly
nervous. Hamner wondered if he were drunk. "Shall
we go to the Mess?" Falkenberg asked. "More comfortable there, and I haven't got my quarters made up for
visitors."

Or you've got something here I shouldn't see, George
thought. Something or someone. Local girl? What difference does it make? God, I wish I could trust this man.

Falkenberg led the way to the ranch house in the
center of officers' row. The troops were still shouting
and singing, and a group was chasing each other on the
parade ground. Most were dressed in the blue and
yellow garrison uniforms Falkenberg had designed, but
others trotted past in synthi-leather battledress. They
carried rifles and heavy packs.

"Punishment detail," Falkenberg explained. "Not as
many of those as there used to be."

Sound crashed from the Officers' Mess building: drums
and bagpipes, a wild sound of war mingled with shouted
laughter. Inside, two dozen men sat at a long table as
white-coated stewards moved briskiy about with whiskey bottles and glasses.

Kilted bandsmen marched around the table with pipes.
Drummers stood in one corner. The deafening noise
stopped as Falkenberg entered, and everyone got to his
feet. Some were quite unsteady.

"Carry on," Falkenberg said, but no one did. They
eyed Hamner nervously, and at a wave from the mess
president at the head of the table the pipers and drummers went outside. Several stewards with bottles fol-

lowed them. The other officers sat and talked in low tones. After all the noise the room seemed very quiet.

"We'll sit over here, shall we?" the colonel asked. He led Hamner to a small table in one corner. A steward brought two glasses of whiskey and set them down.

The room seemed curiously bare to Hamner. A few banners, some paintings; very little else. Somehow, he thought, there ought to be more. As if they're waiting. But that's ridiculous.

Most of the officers were strangers, but George recognized half a dozen Progressives, the highest rank a first lieutenant. He waved at the ones he knew and received brief smiles that seemed almost guilty before the Party volunteers turned back to their companions.

"Yes, sir?" Falkenberg prompted.

"Just who are these men?" George demanded. "I know they're not native to Hadley. Where did they come from?"

"CoDominium officers on the beach," Falkenberg answered promptly. "Reduction in force. Lots of good men got riffed into early retirement. Some of them heard I was coming here and chose to give up their reserve ranks. They came out on the colony ship on the chance I'd hire them."

"And you did."

"Naturally I jumped at the chance to get experienced men at prices we could afford."

"But why all the secrecy? Why haven't I heard about them before?"

Falkenberg shrugged. "We've violated several of the Grand Senate's regulations on mercenaries, you know. It's best not to talk about these things until the CD has definitely gone. After that, the men are committed. They'll have to stay loyal to Hadley." Falkenberg lifted his whiskey glass. "Vice President Bradford knew all about it."

"I'll bet he did." Hamner lifted his own glass. "Cheers."

"Cheers."

And I wonder what else that little snake knows about, Hamner wondered. Without his support Falkenberg would be out of here in a minute . . . and what then?

"Colonel, your organization charts came to my office yesterday. You've kept all the Marines in one battalion with these newly hired officers. Then you've got three battalions of locals, but all the Party stalwarts are in the Fourth. The Second and Third are local recruits, but under your own men."

"That's a fair enough description, yes, sir," Falkenberg said.

And you know my question, George thought. "Why, Colonel? A suspicious man would say that you've got your own little army here, with a structure set so that you can take complete control if there's ever a difference of opinion between you and the government."

"A suspicious man might say that," Falkenberg agreed. He drained his glass and waited for George to do the same. A steward came over with freshly filled glasses.

"But a practical man might say something else," Falkenberg continued. "Do you expect me to put green officers in command of those guardhouse troops? Or your good-hearted Progressives in command of green recruits?"

"But you've done just that—"

"On Mr. Bradford's orders I've kept the Fourth Battalion as free of my mercenaries as possible. That isn't helping their training, either. But Mr. Bradford seems to have the same complaint as you."

"I haven't complained."

"I thought you had," Falkenberg said. "In any event, you have your Party force, if you wish to use it to control me. Actually you have all the control you need anyway. You hold the purse strings. Without supplies to feed these men and money to pay them, I couldn't hold them an hour."

"Troops have found it easier to rob the paymaster than fight for him before now," Hamner observed. "Cheers." He drained the glass, then suppressed a cough. The stuff was strong, and he wasn't used to drinking neat whiskey. He wondered what would happen if he ordered something else, beer, or a mixed drink. Somehow it didn't seem to go with the party.

"I might have expected that remark from Bradford," Falkenberg said.

Hamner nodded. Bradford was always suspicious of something. There were times when George wondered if the First Vice President were quite sane, but that was silly. Still, when the pressure was on, Ernie Bradford did manage to get on people's nerves with his suspicions, and he would rather see nothing done than give up control of anything.

"How am I supposed to organize this coup?" Falkenberg demanded. "I have a handful of men loyal to me. The rest are mercenaries, or your locals. You've paid a lot to bring me and my staff here. You want us to fight impossible odds with nonexistent equipment. If you also insist on your own organization of forces, I cannot accept the responsibility."

"I didn't say that."

Falkenberg shrugged. "If President Budreau so orders, and he would on your recommendation, I'll turn command over to anyone he names."

And he'd name Bradford, Hamner thought. I'd rather trust Falkenberg. Whatever Falkenberg does will at least be competently done; with Ernie there was no assurance he wasn't up to something, and none that he'd be able to accomplish anything if he wasn't.

But. "What do you want out of this, Colonel Falkenberg?"

The question seemed to surprise the colonel. "Money, of course." Falkenberg answered. "A little glory, perhaps, although that's not a word much used nowadays. A position of responsibility commensurate with my abilities. I've always been a soldier, and I know nothing else."

"And why didn't you stay with the CD?"

"It is in the record," Falkenberg said coldly. "Surely you know."

"But I don't." Hamner was calm, but the whiskey was enough to make him bolder than he'd intended to be, even in this camp surrounded by Falkenberg's men. "I don't know at all. It makes no sense as I've been told it. You had no reason to complain about promotions, and the admiral had no reason to prefer charges. It looks as if you had yourself cashiered."

Falkenberg nodded. "You're nearly correct. Astute of you." The soldier's lips were tight and his gray eyes bored into Hamner. "I suppose you are entitled to an answer. Grand Senator Bronson has sworn to ruin me for reasons you needn't know. If I hadn't been dismissed for a trivial charge of technical insubordination, I'd have faced a series of trumped-up charges. At least this way I'm out with a clean record."

A clean record and a lot of bitterness. "And that's all there is to it?"

"That's all."

It was plausible. So was everything else Falkenberg said. Yet Hamner was sure that Falkenberg was lying. Not lying directly, but not telling everything either. Hamner felt that if he knew the right questions he could get the answers, but there weren't any questions to ask.

And, Hamner thought, I must either trust this man or get rid of him; and to irritate him while keeping him is the stupidest policy of all.

The pipers came back in, and the mess president looked to Falkenberg. "Something more?" Falkenberg asked.

"No."

"Thank you." The colonel nodded to the junior officer. The mess president waved approval to the pipe major. Pipe major raised his mace, and the drums crashed. The pipers began, standing in place at first, then marching around the table. Officers shouted, and the room was filled with martial cries. The party was on again.

George looked for one of his own appointees and discovered that every Progressive officer in the room was one of his own. There wasn't a single man from Bradford's wing of the Party. Was that significant?

He rose and caught the eye of a Progressive lieutenant. "I'll let Farquhar escort me out, Colonel," Hamner said.

"As you please."

The noise followed them out of the building and

along the regimental street. There were more sounds from the parade ground and the camp beyond. Fires burned brightly in the night.

"All right, Jamie, what's going on here?" Hamner demanded.

"Going on, sir? Nothing that I know of. If you mean the party, we're celebrating the men's graduation from basic training. Tomorrow they'll start advanced work."

"Maybe I meant the party," Hamner said. "You seem pretty friendly with the other officers."

"Yes, sir." Hamner noted the enthusiasm in Jamie Farquhar's voice. The boy was young enough to be caught up in the military mystique. and George felt sorry for him. "They're good men," Jamie said.

"Yes, I suppose so. Where are the others? Mr. Bradford's people?"

"They had a field problem that kept them out of camp until late," Farquhar said. "Mr. Bradford came around about dinner time and asked that they be sent to a meeting somewhere. He spends a lot of time with them."

"I expect he does," Hamner said. "Look, you've been around the Marines, Jamie. Where are those men from? What CD outfits?"

"I really don't know, sir. Colonel Falkenberg has forbidden us to ask. He says that the men start with a clean record here."

Hamner noted the tone Farquhar used when he mentioned Falkenberg. More than respect. Awe, perhaps. "Have any of them served with the colonel before?"

"I think so, yes, sir. They don't like him. Curse the colonel quite openly. But they're afraid of that big sergeant major of his. Calvin has offered to whip any two men in the camp, and they can choose the rules. A few of the newcomers tried it, but none of the Marines would. Not one."

"And you say the colonel's not popular with the men?"

Farquhar was thoughtful for a moment. "I wouldn't say he was *popular*, no sir."

Yet, Hamner thought, Boris had said he was. Whiskey buzzed in George's head. "Who is popular?"

"Major Savage, sir. The men like him. And Captain Fast, the Marines particularly respect him. He's the adjutant."

"All right. Look, can this outfit fight? Have we got a chance after the CD leaves?" They stood and watched the scenes around the campfires. Men were drinking heavily, shouting and singing and chasing each other through the camp. There was a fist fight in front of one tent, and no officer moved to stop it.

"Do you allow that?" Hamner demanded.

"We try not to interfere too much." Farquhar said. "The colonel says half an officer's training is learning what *not* to see. Anyway, the sergeants have broken up the fight, see?"

"But you let the men drink."

"Sir, there's no regulation against drinking. Only against being unfit for duty. And these men are tough. They obey orders and they can fight. I think we'll do rather well."

Pride. They've put some pride into Jamie Farquhar, and maybe into some of those jailbirds out there too. "All right, Jamie. Go back to your party. I'll find my driver."

As he was driven away, George Hamner felt better about Hadley's future, but he was still convinced something was wrong; and he had no idea what it was.

IX

THE STADIUM HAD been built to hold one hundred thousand people. There were at least that many jammed inside it now, snd an equal number swarmed about the market squares and streets adjacent to it. The full CoDominium Marine garrison was on duty to keep order, but it wasn't needed.

The celebration was boisterous, but there wouldn't be any trouble today. The Freedom Party was as anxious to avoid an incident as the Marines on this, the greatest day for Hadley since Discovery. The CoDominium was turning over power to local authority and getting out; and nothing must spoil that.

Hamner and Falkenberg watched from the upper tiers of the Stadium. Row after row of plastisteel seats cascaded like a giant staircase down from their perch to the central grassy field below. Every seat was filled, so that the Stadium was a riot of color.

President Budreau and Governor Flaherty stood in the Presidential box directly across from Falkenberg and Hamner. The President's Guard, in blue uniforms, and the CoDominium Marines, in their scarlet and gold, stood at rigid attention around the officials.

The President's box was shared by Vice President Bradford, the Freedom Party opposition leaders, Progressive officials, officers of the retiring CoDominium government, and everyone else who could beg an invitation. George knew that some of them were wondering where he had got off to.

Bradford would particularly notice Hamner's absence. He might, George thought, even think the Second Vice President was out stirring up opposition or rebellion. Ernie Bradford had lately been accusing Hamner of every kind of disloyalty to the Progressive Party, and it wouldn't be long before he demanded that Budreau dismiss him.

To the devil with the little man! George thought. He hated crowds, and the thought of standing there and listening to all those speeches, of being polite to party officials whom he detested, was just too much. When he'd suggested watching from another vantage point, Falkenberg had quickly agreed. The soldier didn't seem to care too much for formal ceremonies either. Civilian ceremonies, Hamner corrected himself; Falkenberg seemed to like military parades.

The ritual was almost over. The CD Marine bands had marched through the field, the speeches had been made, presents delivered and accepted. A hundred thousand people had cheered, and it was an awesome sound. The raw power was frightening.

Hamner glanced at his watch. As he did the Marine band broke into a roar of drums. The massed drummers ceased to beat one by one until there was but a single drum roll that went on and on and on, until finally it too stopped. The entire Stadium waited.

One trumpet, no more. A clear call, plaintive but triumphant, the final salute to the CoDominium banner above the Palace. The notes hung in Hadley's air like something tangible, and slowly, deliberately, the crimson and blue banner floated down from the flagpole as Hadley's blazing gold and green arose.

Across the city uniformed men saluted these flags, one rising, the other setting. The blue uniforms of Hadley saluted with smiles, the red-uniformed Marines with indifference. The CoDominium banner rose and fell across two hundred light years and seventy worlds in this year of Grace; what difference would one minor planet make?

Hamner glanced at John Falkenberg. The colonel had no eyes for the rising banners of Hadley. His rigid salute was given to the CD flag, and as the last note of the final trumpet salute died away Hamner thought he saw Falkenberg wipe his eyes.

The gesture was so startling that George looked again, but there was nothing more to see, and he decided that he had been mistaken.

"That's it, then," Falkenberg snapped. His voice was strained. "I suppose we ought to join the party. Can't keep His Nibs waiting."

Hamner nodded. The Presidential box connected directly to the Palace, and the officials would arrive at the reception quickly while Falkenberg and Hamner had the entire width of the crowded Stadium to traverse. People were already streaming out to join the festive crowds on the grass in the center of the bowl.

"Let's go this way," George said. He led Falkenberg to the top of the Stadium and into a small alcove where he used a key to open an inconspicuous door. "Tunnel system takes us right into the Palace, across and under the Stadium," he told Falkenberg. "Not exactly secret, but we don't want the people to know about it because they'd demand we open it to the public. Built for maintenance crews, mostly." He locked the door behind them and waved expressively at the wide interior corridor. "Place was pretty well designed, actually."

The grudging tone of admiration wasn't natural to him. If a thing was well done, it was well done . . . but lately he found himself talking that way about CoDominium projects. He resented the whole CD administration and the men who'd dumped the job of governing after creating problems no one could solve.

They wound down stairways and through more passages, then up to another set of locked doors. Through those was the Palace courtyard. The celebrations were already under way, and it would be a long night.

George wondered what would come now. In the morning the last CD boat would rise, and the CoDominium would be gone. Tomorrow, Hadley would be alone with her problems.

* * *

"Tensh-Hut!" Sergeant Major Calvin's crisp command cut through the babble.

"Please be seated, gentlemen." Falkenberg took his place at the head of the long table in the command room of what had been the central headquarters for the CoDominium Marines.

Except for the uniforms and banners there were few changes from what people already called "the old days." The officers were seated in the usual places for a regimental staff meeting. Maps hung along one wall, and a computer output screen dominated another. Stewards in white coats brought coffee and discreetly retired behind the armed sentries outside.

Falkenberg looked at the familiar scene and knew the constabulary had occupied the Marine barracks for two days; the Marines had been there twenty years.

A civilian lounged in the seat reserved for the regimental intelligence officer. His tunic was a riot of colors; he was dressed in current Earth fashions, with a brilliant cravat and baggy sleeves. A long sash took the place of a belt and concealed his pocket calculator. Hadley's upper classes were only just beginning to wear such finery.

"You all know why we're here," Falkenberg told the assembled officers. "Those of you who've served with me before know I don't hold many staff councils. They are customary among mercenary units, however. Sergeant Major Calvin will represent the enlisted personnel of the regiment."

There were faint titters. Calvin had been associated with John Falkenberg for eighteen standard years. Presumably they had differences of opinion, but no one ever saw them. The idea of the RSM opposing his colonel in the name of the troops was amusing. On the other hand, no colonel could afford to ignore the views of his sergeants' mess.

Falkenberg's frozen features relaxed slightly as if he appreciated his own joke. His eyes went from face to face. Everyone in the room was a former Marine, and all but a very few had served with him before. The Progressive officers were on duty elsewhere—and it had taken careful planning by the adjutant to accomplish that without suspicion.

Falkenberg turned to the civilian. "Dr. Whitlock, you've been on Hadley for sixty-seven days. That's not very long to make a planetary study, but it's about all the time we have. Have you reached any conclusions?"

"Yeah." Whitlock spoke with an exaggerated drawl that most agreed was affected. "Not much different from Fleet's evaluation, Colonel. Can't think why you went to the expense of bringin' me out here. Your Intelligence people know their jobs about as well as I know mine."

Whitlock sprawled back in his seat and looked very relaxed and casual in the midst of the others' military formality. There was no contempt in his manner. The military had one set of rules and he had another, and he worked well with soldiers.

"Your conclusions are similar to Fleet's, then," Falkenberg said.

"With the limits of analysis, yes, sir. Doubt any competent man could reach a different conclusion. This planet's headed for barbarism within a generation."

There was no sound from the other officers but several were startled. Good training kept them from showing it.

Whitlock produced a cigar from a sleeve pocket and inspected it carefully. "You want the analysis?" he asked.

"A summary, please." Falkenberg looked at each face again. Major Savage and Captain Fast weren't surprised; they'd known before they came to Hadley. Some of the junior officers and company commanders had obviously guessed.

"Simple enough," Whitlock said. "There's no self-sustaining technology for a population half this size. Without imports the standard of livin's bound to fall. Some places they could take that, but not here.

"Here, when they can't get their pretty gadgets, 'stead of workin' the people here in Refuge will demand the Government do something about it. Guv'mint's in no position to refuse, either. Not strong enough.

"So they'll have to divert investment capital into

consumer goods. There'll be a decrease in technological efficiency, and then fewer goods, leadin' to more demands, and another cycle just like before. Hard to predict just what comes after that, but it can't be good.

"Afore long, then, they won't have the technological resources to cope even if they could get better organized. It's not a new pattern, Colonel. Fleet saw it comin' a while back. I'm surprised you didn't take their word for it."

Falkenberg nodded. "I did, but with something this important I thought I better get another opinion. You've met the Freedom Party leaders, Dr. Whitlock. Is there any chance they could keep civilization if they governed?"

Whitlock laughed. It was a long drawn-out laugh, relaxed, totally out of place in a military council. " 'Bout as much chance as for a 'gator to turn loose of a hog, Colonel. Even assumin' they know what to do, how can they do it? Suppose they get a vision and try to change their policies? Somebody'll start a new party along the lines of the Freedom Party's present thinkin'.

"Colonel, you will *never* convince all them people there's things the Guv'mint just *cain't* do. They don't want to believe it, and there's always goin' to be slick talkers willin' to say it's all a plot. Now, if the Progressive Party, which has the right ideas already, was to set up to rule strong, they might be able to keep something goin' a while longer."

"Do you think they can?" Major Savage asked.

"Nope. They might have fun tryin'," Whitlock answered. "Problem is that independent countryside. There's not enough support for what they'd have to do in city or country. Eventually that's all got to change, but the revolution that gives this country a real powerful government's going to be one bloody mess, I can tell you. A long drawn-out bloody mess at that."

"Haven't they any hope at all?" The questioner was a junior officer newly promoted to company commander.

Whitlock sighed. "Every place you look, you see problems. City's vulnerable to any sabotage that stops the food plants, for instance. And the fusion generators ain't exactly eternal, either. They're runnin' 'em hard without enough time off for maintenance. Hadley's operating on its capital, not its income, and pretty soon there's not goin' to be any capital to operate off of."

"And that's your conclusion," Falkenberg said. "It doesn't sound precisely like the perfect place for us to retire to."

"Sure doesn't," Whitlock agreed. He stretched elaborately. "Cut it any way you want to, this place isn't going to be self-sufficient without a lot of blood spilled."

"Could they ask for help from American Express?" the junior officer asked.

"They could ask, but they won't get it," Whitlock said. "Son, this planet was neutralized by agreement way back when the CD Governor came aboard. Now the Russians aren't going to let a U.S. company like AmEx take it back into the U.S. sphere, same as the U.S. won't let the Commies come in and set up shop. Grand Senate would order a quarantine on this system just like that." The historian snapped his fingers. "Whole purpose of the CoDominium."

"One thing bothers me," Captain Fast said. "You've been assuming that the CD will simply let Hadley revert to barbarism. Won't BuRelock and the Colonial Office come back if things get that desperate?"

"No."

"You seem rather positive," Major Savage observed.

"I'm positive." Dr. Whitlock said. "Budgets got cut again this year. They don't have the resources to take on a place like Hadley. BuRelock's got its own worries."

"But—" The lieutenant who'd asked the questions earlier sounded worried. "Colonel, what could happen to the Bureau of Relocation?"

"As Dr. Whitlock says, no budget," Falkenberg answered. "Gentlemen, I shouldn't have to tell you about that. You've seen what the Grand Senate did to the Fleet. That's why you're demobilized. And Kaslov's people have several new seats on the Presidium next year, just as Harmon's gang has won some minor elections in the States. Both those outfits want to abolish the CD, and they've had enough influence to get everyone's appropriations cut to the bone."

"But population control has to ship people out, sir," the lieutenant protested.

"Yes." Falkenberg's face was grim; perhaps he was recalling his own experiences with population control's methods. "But they have to employ worlds closer to Earth, regardless of the problems that may cause for the colonists. Marginal exploitation ventures like Hadley's mines are being shut down. This isn't the only planet the CD's abandoning this year." His voice took on a note of thick irony. "Excuse me. Granting independence."

"So they can't rely on CoDominium help," Captain Fast said.

"No. If Hadley's going to reach takeoff, it's got to do it on its own."

"Which Dr. Whitlock says is impossible," Major Savage observed. "John, we've got ourselves into a cleft stick, haven't we?"

"I said it was unlikely, not that it was impossible," Whitlock reminded them. "It'll take a government stronger than anything Hadley's liable to get, though. And some smart people making the right moves. Or maybe there'll be some luck. Like a good, selective plague. Now that'd do it. Plague to kill off the right people—but if it got too many, there wouldn't be enough left to take advantage of the technology, so I don't suppose that's the answer either."

Falkenberg nodded grimly. "Thank you, Dr. Whitlock. Now, gentlemen, I want battalion commanders and headquarters officers to read Dr. Whitlock's report. Meanwhile, we have another item. Major Savage will shortly make a report to the Progressive Party Cabinet, and I want you to pay attention. We will have a critique after his presentation. Major?"

Savage stood and went to the readout screen. "Gentlemen." He used the wall console to bring an organization chart onto the screen.

"The regiment consists of approximately two thousand officers and men. Of these, five hundred are former Marines, and another five hundred are Progressive partisans organized under officers appointed by Mr. Vice President Bradford.

"The other thousand are general recruits. Some of them are passable mercenaries, and some are local youngsters who want to play soldier and would be better off in a national guard. All recruits have received basic training comparable to CD Marine ground basic without assault, fleet, or jump schooling. Their performance has been somewhat better than we might expect from a comparable number of Marine recruits in CD service.

"This morning, Mr. Bradford ordered the Colonel to remove the last of our officers and noncoms from the Fourth Battalion, and as of this P.M. the Fourth will be totally under the control of officers appointed by First Vice President Bradford. He has not informed us of the reason for this order."

Falkenberg nodded. "In your estimate, Major, are the troops ready for combat duties?" Falkenberg listened idly as he drank coffee. The briefing was rehearsed, and he knew what Savage would answer. The men were trained, but they did not as yet make up a combat unit. Falkenberg waited until Savage had finished the presentation. "Recommendations?"

"Recommended that the Second Battalion be integrated with the First, sir. Normal practice is to form each maniple with one recruit, three privates, and a monitor in charge. With equal numbers of new men and veterans we will have a higher proportion of recruits, but this will give us two battalions of men under our veteran NCO's, with Marine privates for leavening.

"We will thus break up the provisional training organization and set up the regiment with a new permanent structure, First and Second Battalions for combat duties, Third composed of locals with former Marine officers to be held in reserve. The Fourth will not be under our command."

"Your reasons for this organization?" Falkenberg asked.

"Morale, sir. The new troops feel discriminated against. They're under harsher discipline than the former Marines, and they resent it. Putting them in the same maniples with the Marines will stop that."

"Let's see the new structure."

Savage manipulated the input console and charts swam across the screen. The administrative structure was standard, based in part on the CD Marines and the rest on the national armies of Churchill. That wasn't the important part. It wasn't obvious, but the structure demanded that all the key posts be held by Falkenberg's mercenaries.

The best Progressive appointees were either in the Third or Fourth Battalions, and there were no locals with the proper command experience; so went the justification. It looked good to Falkenberg, and there was no sound military reason to question it. Bradford would be so pleased about his new control of the Fourth that he wouldn't look at the rest; not yet, anyway. The others didn't know enough to question it.

Yes, Falkenberg thought. It ought to work. He waited until Savage was finished and thanked him, then addressed the others. "Gentlemen, if you have criticisms, let's hear them now. I want a solid front when we get to the Cabinet meeting tomorrow, and I want every one of you ready to answer any question. I don't have to tell you how important it is that they buy this."

They all nodded.

"And another thing," Falkenberg said. "Sergeant Major."

"Sir!"

"As soon as the Cabinet has bought off on this new organization plan, I want this regiment under normal discipline."

"Sir!"

"Break it to 'em hard, Top Soldier. Tell the Forty-second the act's over. From here on recruits and old hands get treated alike, and the next man who gives me trouble will wish he hadn't been born."

"Sir!" Calvin smiled happily. The last months had been a strain for everyone. Now the colonel was taking over again, thank God. The men had lost some of the edge, but he'd soon put it back again. It was time to take off the masks, and Calvin for one was glad of it.

X

THE SOUND OF fifty thousand people shouting in unison can be terrifying. It raises fears at a level below thought; creates a panic older than the fear of nuclear weapons and the whole panoply of technology. It is raw, naked power from a cauldron of sound.

Everyone in the Palace listened to the chanting crowd. The Government people were outwardly calm, but they moved quietly through the halls, and spoke in low tones—or shouted for no reason. The Palace was filled with a nameless fear.

The Cabinet meeting started at dawn and continued until late in the morning. It had gone on and on without settling anything. Just before noon Vice President Bradford stood at his place at the council table with his lips tight in rage. He pointed a trembling finger at George Hamner.

"It's your fault!" Bradford shouted. "Now the technicians have joined in the demand for a new constitution, and you control them. I've always said you were a traitor to the Progressive Party!"

"Gentlemen, please," President Budreau insisted. His voice held infinite weariness. "Come now, that sort of language—"

"Traitor?" Hamner demanded. "If your blasted officials would pay a little attention to the technicians, this wouldn't have happened. In three months you've managed to convert the techs from the staunchest support-

306

ers of this Party into allies of the rebels despite everything
I could do."

"We need strong government," Bradford said. His
voice was contemptuous, and the little half-smile had
returned.

George Hamner made a strong effort to control his
anger. "You won't get it this way. You've herded my
techs around like cattle, worked them overtime for no
extra pay, and set those damned soldiers of yours onto
them when they protested. It's worth a man's life to
have your constabulary mad at him."

"Resisting the police," Bradford said. "We can't permit that."

"You don't know what government is!" Hamner said.
His control vanished and he stood, towering above
Bradford. The little man retreated a step, and his smile
froze. "You've got the nerve to call me a traitor after all
you've done! I ought to break your neck!"

"Gentlemen!" Budreau stood at his place at the head
of the table. "Stop it!" There was a roar from the
Stadium. The Palace seemed to vibrate to the shouts of
the constitutional convention.

The Cabinet room became silent for a moment. Wea-
rily, Budreau continued. "This isn't getting us anywhere. I suggest we adjourn for half an hour to allow
tempers to cool."

There was murmured agreement from the others.

"And I want no more of these accusations and threats
when we convene again," President Budreau said. "Is
that understood?"

Grudgingly the others agreed. Budreau left alone.
Then Bradford, followed by a handful of his closest
supporters. Other ministers rushed to be seen leaving
with him, as if it might be dangerous to be thought in
opposition to the First Vice President.

George Hamner found himself alone in the room. He
shrugged, and went out. Ernest Bradford had been
joined by a man in uniform. Hamner recognized Lieutenant Colonel Cordova, commander of the Fourth Battalion of constabulary, and a fanatic Bradford supporter.
Hamner remembered when Bradford had first proposed

a commission for Cordova, and how unimportant it had seemed then.

Bradford's group went down the hall. They seemed to be whispering something together and making a point of excluding the Second Vice President. Hamner merely shrugged.

"Buy you a coffee?" The voice came from behind and startled George. He turned to see Falkenberg.

"Sure. Not that it's going to do any good. We're in trouble, Colonel."

"Anything decided?" Falkenberg asked. "It's been a long wait."

"And a useless one. They ought to invite you into the Cabinet meetings. You might have some good advice. There's sure as hell no reason to keep you waiting in an anteroom while we yell at each other. I've tried to change that policy, but I'm not too popular right now." There was another shout from the Stadium.

"Whole government's not too popular," Falkenberg said. "And when that convention gets through . . ."

"Another thing I tried to stop last week," George told him. "But Budreau didn't have the guts to stand up to them. So now we've got fifty thousand drifters, with nothing better to do, sitting as an assembly of the people. That ought to produce quite a constitution."

Falkenberg shrugged. He might have been about to say something, George thought, but if he were, he changed his mind. They reached the executive dining room and took seats near one wall. Bradford's group had a table across the room from them, and all of Bradford's people looked at them with suspicion.

"You'll get tagged as a traitor for sitting with me, Colonel." Hamner laughed, but his voice was serious. "I think I meant that, you know. Bradford's blaming me for our problems with the techs, and between us he's also insisting that you aren't doing enough to restore order in the city."

Falkenberg ordered coffee. "Do I need to explain to you why we haven't?"

"No." George Hamner's huge hand engulfed a water glass. "God knows you've been given almost no support the last couple of months. Impossible orders, and you've never been allowed to do anything decisive. I see you've stopped the raids on rebel headquarters."

Falkenberg nodded. "We weren't catching anyone. Too many leaks in the Palace. And most of the time the Fourth Battalion had already muddied the water. If they'd let us do our job instead of having to ask permission through channels for every operation we undertake, maybe the enemy wouldn't know as much about what we're going to do. Now I've quit asking."

"You've done pretty well with the railroad."

"Yes. That's one success, anyway. Things are pretty quiet out in the country where we're on our own. Odd, isn't it, that the closer we are to the expert supervision of the government, the less effective my men seem to be?"

"But can't you control Cordova's men? They're causing more people to desert us for the rebels than you can count. I can't believe unrestrained brutality is useful."

"Nor I. Unless there's a purpose to it, force isn't a very effective instrument of government. But surely you know, Mr. Hamner, that I have no control over the Fourth. Mr. Bradford has been expanding it since he took control, and it's now almost as large as the rest of the regiment—and totally under his control, not mine."

"Bradford accused me of being a traitor," Hamner said carefully. "With his own army, he might have something planned. . . ."

"You once thought that of me," Falkenberg said.

"This is very serious," Hamner said. "Ernie Bradford has built an army only he controls, and he's making wild accusations."

Falkenberg smiled grimly. "I wouldn't worry about it too much."

"You wouldn't? No. You wouldn't. But I'm scared, Colonel. I've got my family to think of, and I'm plenty scared." Well, George thought, now it's out in the open; can I trust him not to be Ernie Bradford's man?

"You believe Bradford is planning an illegal move?" Falkenberg asked.

"I don't know." Suddenly George was afraid again.

He saw no sympathy in the other man's eyes. And just who can I trust? Who? Anyone?

"Would you feel safer if your family were in our regimental barracks?" Falkenberg asked. "It could be arranged."

"It's about time we had something out," George said at last. "Yes, I'd feel safer with my wife and children under protection. But I'd feel safer yet if you'd level with me."

"About what?" Falkenberg's expression didn't change.

"Those Marines of yours, to begin with," George said. "Those aren't penal battalion men. I've watched them, they're too well disciplined. And the battle banners they carry weren't won in any peanut actions, on this planet or anywhere else. Just who are those men, Colonel?"

John Falkenberg smiled thinly. "I've been wondering when you'd ask. Why haven't you brought this up with President Budreau?"

"I don't know. I think because I trust you more than Bradford, and the President would only ask him . . . besides, if the President dismissed you there'd be nobody able to oppose Ernie. If you will oppose him that is—but you can stand up to him, anyway."

"What makes you think I would?" Falkenberg asked. "I obey the lawful orders of the civilian government—"

"Yeah, sure. Hadley's going downhill so fast another conspiracy more or less can't make any difference anyway . . . you haven't answered my question."

"The battle banners are from the Forty-second CD Marine Regiment," Falkenberg answered slowly. "It was decommissioned as part of the budget cuts."

Forty-second, Hamner thought for a second. He searched through his mental files to find the information he'd seen on Falkenberg. "That was your regiment."

"Certainly."

"You brought it with you."

"A battalion of it," John Falkenberg agreed. "Their women are waiting to join them when we get settled. When the Forty-second was decommissioned, the men decided to stay together if they could."

"So you brought not only the officers, but the men as well."

"Yes." There was still no change in Falkenberg's expression, although Hamner searched the other man's face closely.

George felt both fear and relief. If those were Falkenberg's men—"What is your game, Colonel? You want more than just pay for your troops. I wonder if I shouldn't be more afraid of you than of Bradford."

Falkenberg shrugged. "Decisions you have to make, Mr. Hamner. I could give you my word that we mean you no harm, but what would that be worth? I will pledge to take care of your family. If you want us to."

There was another shout from the Stadium, louder this time. Bradford and Lieutenant Colonel Cordova left their table, still talking in low tones. The conversation was animated, with violent gestures, as if Cordova were trying to talk Bradford into something. As they left, Bradford agreed.

George watched them leave the room. The mob shouted again, making up his mind for him. "I'll send Laura and the kids over to your headquarters this afternoon."

"Better make it immediately," Falkenberg said calmly.

George frowned. "You mean there's not much time? Whatever you've got planned, it'll have to be quick, but this afternoon?"

John shook his head. "You seem to think I have some kind of master plan, Mr. Vice President. No. I suggest you get your wife to our barracks before I'm ordered not to undertake her protection, that's all. For the rest, I'm only a soldier in a political situation."

"With Professor Whitlock to advise you," Hamner said. He looked closely at Falkenberg.

"Surprised you with that one, didn't I?" Hamner demanded. "I've seen Whitlock moving around and wondered why he didn't come to the President. He must have fifty political agents in the convention right now."

"You do seem observant," Falkenberg said.

"Sure." Hamner was bitter. "What the hell good

does it do me? I don't understand anything that's going on, and I don't trust anybody. I see pieces of the puzzle, but I can't put them together. Sometimes I think I should use what influence I've got left to get *you* out of the picture anyway."

"As you will." Falkenberg's smile was coldly polite. "Whom do you suggest as guards for your family after that? The Chief of Police? Listen."

The Stadium roared again in an angry sound that swelled in volume.

"You win." Hamner left the table and walked slowly back to the council room. His head swirled.

Only one thing stood out clearly. John Christian Falkenberg controlled the only military force on Hadley that could oppose Bradford's people—and the Freedom Party gangsters, who were the original enemies in the first place. Can't forget them just because I'm getting scared of Ernie, George thought.

He turned away from the council room and went downstairs to the apartment he'd been assigned. The sooner Laura was in the Marine barracks, the safer he'd feel.

But am I sending her to my enemies? O God, can I trust anyone at all? Boris said he was an honorable man. Keep remembering that, keep remembering that. Honor. Falkenberg has honor, and Ernie Bradford has none.

And me? What have I got for leaving the Freedom Party and bringing my technicians over to the Progressives? A meaningless title as Second Vice President, and—

The crowd screamed again. "POWER TO THE PEOPLE!"

George heard and walked faster.

Bradford's grin was back. It was the first thing George noticed as he came into the council chamber. The little man stood at the table with an amused smile. It seemed quite genuine, and more than a little frightening.

"Ah, here is our noble Minister of Technology and Second Vice President," Bradford grinned. "Just in time. Mr. President, that gang out there is threatening the city. I am sure you will all be pleased to know that I've taken steps to end the situation."

"What have you done?" George demanded.

Bradford's smile broadened even more. "At this moment, Colonel Cordova is arresting the leaders of the opposition. Including, Mr. President, the leaders of the Engineers' and Technicians' Association who have joined them. This rebellion will be over within the hour."

Hamner stared at the man. "You fool! You'll have every technician in the city joining the Freedom Party gang! And the techs control the power plants, our last influence over the crowd. You bloody damned fool!"

Bradford spoke with exaggerated politeness. "I thought you would be pleased, George, to see the rebellion end so easily. Naturally I've sent men to secure the power plants. Ah, listen."

The crowd outside wasn't chanting anymore. There was a confused babble, then a welling of sound that turned ugly. No coherent words reached them, only the ugly, angry roars. Then there was a rapid fusillade of shots.

"My God!" President Budreau stared wildly in confusion. "What's happening? Who are they shooting at? Have you started open war?"

"It takes stern measures, Mr. President," Bradford said. "Perhaps too stern for you?" He shook his head slightly. "The time has come for harsh measures, Mr. President. Hadley cannot be governed by weak-willed men. Our future belongs to those who have the will to grasp it!"

George Hamner turned toward the door. Before he could reach it, Bradford called to him. "Please, George." His voice was filled with concern. "I'm afraid you can't leave just yet. It wouldn't be safe for you. I took the liberty of ordering Colonel Cordova's men to, uh, guard this room while my troops restore order."

An uneasy quiet had settled on the Stadium, and they waited for a long time. Then there were screams and more shots.

The sounds moved closer, as if they were outside the Stadium as well as in it. Bradford frowned, but no one said anything. They waited for what seemed a lifetime as the firing continued. Guns, shouts, screams, sirens, and alarms—those and more, all in confusion.

The door burst open. Cordova came in. He now wore the insignia of a full colonel. He looked around the room until he found Bradford. "Sir, could you come outside a moment, please?"

"You will make your report to the Cabinet," President Budreau ordered. Cordova glanced at Bradford. "Now, sir."

Cordova still looked to Bradford. The Vice President nodded slightly.

"Very well, sir," the young officer said. "As directed by the Vice President, elements of the Fourth Battalion proceeded to the Stadium and arrested some fifty leaders of the so-called constitutional convention.

"Our plan was to enter quickly and take the men out through the Presidential box and into the Palace. However, when we attempted to make the arrests we were opposed by armed men, many in the uniforms of household guards. We were told there were no weapons in the Stadium, but this was in error.

"The crowd overpowered my officers and released their prisoners. When we attempted to recover them, we were attacked by the mob and forced to fight our way out of the Stadium."

"Good Lord," Budreau sighed. "How many hurt?"

"The power plants! Did you secure them?" Hamner demanded.

Cordova looked miserable. "No, sir. My men were not admitted. A council of technicians and engineers holds the power plants, and they threaten to destroy them if we attempt forcible entry. We have tried to seal them off from outside support, but I don't think we can keep order with only my battalion. We will need all the constabulary army to—"

"Idiot." Hamner clutched at his left fist with his right, and squeezed until it hurt. A council of technicians. I'll know most of them. My friends. Or they used to be. Will any of them trust me now? At least Bradford didn't control the fusion plants.

"What is the current status outside?" President
Budreau demanded. They could still hear firing in the
streets.

"Uh, there's a mob barricaded in the market, and
another in the theater across from the Palace, sir. My
troops are trying to dislodge them." Cordova's voice
was apologetic.

"Trying. I take it they aren't likely to succeed."
Budreau rose and went to the anteroom door. "Colonel
Falkenberg?" he called.

"Yes, sir?" Falkenberg entered the room as the President beckoned.

"Colonel, are you familiar with the situation outside?"

"Yes, Mr. President."

"Damn it, man, can you do something?"

"What does the President suggest I do?" Falkenberg
looked at the Cabinet members. "For three months we
have attempted to preserve order in this city. We were
not able to do so even with the cooperation of the
technicians."

"It wasn't my fault—" Lieutenant Colonel Cordova
began.

"I did not invite you to speak." Falkenberg's lips
were set in a grim line. "Gentlemen, you now have
open rebellion and simultaneously have alienated one
of the most powerful blocs within your Party. We no
longer control either the power plants or the food processing centers. I repeat, what does the President suggest I do?"

Budreau nodded. "A fair enough criticism."

He was interrupted by Bradford. "Drive that mob off
the streets! Use those precious troops of yours to fight,
that's what you're here for."

"Certainly," Falkenberg said. "Will the President sign
a proclamation of martial law?"

Budreau nodded reluctantly. "I suppose I have to."

"Very well," Falkenberg said.

Hamner looked up suddenly. What had he detected
in Falkenberg's voice and manner? Something important?

"It is standard for politicians to get themselves into a
situation that only the military can get them out of. It is

also standard for them to blame the military afterwards,"
Falkenberg said. "I am willing to accept responsibility
for enforcing martial law, but I must have command of
all government forces. I will not attempt to restore
order when some of the troops are not responsive to my
policies."

"No!" Bradford leaped to his feet. The chair crashed
to the floor behind him. "I see what you're doing!
You're against me too! That's why it was never time to
move, never time for me to be President, you want
control of this planet for yourself! Well, you won't get
away with it, you cheap dictator. Cordova, arrest that
man!"

Cordova licked his lips and looked at Falkenberg.
Both soldiers were armed. Cordova decided not to
chance it. "Lieutenant Hargreave!" he called. The door
to the anteroom opened wide.

No one came in. "Hargreave!" Cordova shouted again.
He put his hand on the pistol holstered at his belt. "You're
under arrest, Colonel Falkenberg."

"Indeed?"

"This is absurd," Budreau shouted. "Colonel Cordova, take your hand off that weapon! I will not have
my Cabinet meeting turned into a farce."

For a moment nothing happened. The room was very
still, and Cordova looked from Budreau to Bradford,
wondering what to do now.

Then Bradford faced the President. "You too, old
man? Arrest Mr. Budreau as well, Colonel Cordova. As
for you, Mr. Traitor George Hamner, you'll get what's
coming to you. I have men all through this Palace. I
knew I might have to do this."

"You knew—what is this, Ernest?" President Budreau
seemed bewildered, and his voice was plaintive. "What
are you doing?"

"Oh, shut up, old man," Bradford snarled. "I suppose you'll have to be shot as well."

"I think we have heard enough," Falkenberg said
distinctly. His voice rang through the room although he
hadn't shouted. "And I refuse to be arrested."

"Kill him!" Bradford shouted. He reached under his tunic.

Cordova drew his pistol. It had not cleared the holster when there were shots from the doorway. Their sharp barks filled the room, and Hamner's ears rang from the muzzle blast.

Bradford spun toward the door with a surprised look. Then his eyes glazed and he slid to the floor, the half-smile still on his lips. There were more shots and the crash of automatic weapons, and Cordova was flung against the wall of the council chamber. He was held there by the smashing bullets. Bright red blotches spurted across his uniform.

Sergeant Major Calvin came into the room with three Marines in battle dress, leather over bulging body armor. Their helmets were dull in the bright blue-tinted sunlight streaming through the chamber's windows.

Falkenberg nodded and holstered his pistol. "All secure, Sergeant Major?"

"Sir!"

Falkenberg nodded again. "To quote Mr. Bradford, I took the liberty of securing the corridors, Mr. President. Now, sir, if you will issue that proclamation, I'll see to the situation in the streets outside. Sergeant Major."

"Sir!"

"Do you have the proclamation of martial law that Captain Fast drew up?"

"Sir." Calvin removed a rolled document from a pocket of his leather tunic. Falkenberg took it and laid it on the table in front of President Budreau.

"But—" Budreau's tone was hopeless. "All right. Not that there's much chance." He looked at Bradford's body and shuddered. "He was ready to kill me." Budreau muttered. The President seemed confused. Too much had happened, and there was too much to do.

The battle sounds outside were louder, and the council room was filled with the sharp copper odor of fresh blood. Budreau drew the parchment toward himself and glanced at it, then took out a pen from his pocket.

He scrawled his signature across it and handed it to Hamner to witness.

"You'd better speak to the President's Guard," Falkenberg said. "They won't know what to do."

"Aren't you going to use them in the street fight?" Hamner asked.

Falkenberg shook his head. "I doubt if they'd fight. They have too many friends among the rebels. They'll protect the Palace, but they won't be reliable for anything else."

"Have we got a chance?" Hamner asked.

Budreau looked up from his reverie at the head of the table. "Yes. Have we?"

"Possibly," Falkenberg said. "Depends on how good the people we're fighting are. If their commander is half as good as I think he is, we won't win this battle."

XI

"GODDAMN IT, we won't do it!" Lieutenant Martin Latham stared in horror at Captain Fast. "That market's a death trap. These men didn't join to attack across open streets against rioters in safe positions—"

"No. You joined to be glorified police," Captain Fast said calmly. "Now you've let things get out of hand. Who better to put them right again?"

"The Fourth Battalion takes orders from Colonel Cordova, not you." Latham looked around for support. Several squads of the Fourth were within hearing, and he felt reassured.

They stood in a deep indentation of the Palace wall. Just outside and around the corner of the indentation they could hear sporadic firing as the other units of the regiment kept the rebels occupied. Latham felt safe here, but out there—

"No," he repeated. "It's suicide."

"So is refusal to obey orders," Amos Fast said quietly. "Don't look around and don't raise your voice. Now, glance behind me at the Palace walls."

Latham saw them. A flash from a gun barrel; blurs as leather-clad figures settled in on the walls and in the windows overlooking the niche.

"If you don't make the attack, you will be disarmed and tried for cowardice in the face of the enemy," Fast said quietly. "There can be only one outcome of that

319

trial. And only one penalty. You're better off making the assault. We'll support you in that."

"Why are you doing this?" Martin Latham demanded.

"You caused the problem," Fast said. "Now get ready. When you've entered the market square the rest of the outfit will move up in support."

The assault was successful, but it cost the Fourth heavily. After that came another series of fierce attacks. When they were finished the rioters had been driven from the immediate area of the Palace, but Falkenberg's regiment paid for every meter gained.

Whenever they took a building, the enemy left it blazing. When the regiment trapped one large group of rebels, Falkenberg was forced to abandon the assault to aid in evacuating a hospital that the enemy put to the torch. Within three hours, fires were raging all around the Palace.

There was no one in the council chamber with Budreau and Hamner. The bodies had been removed, and the floor mopped, but it seemed to George Hamner that the room would always smell of death; and he could not keep his eyes from straying from time to time, from staring at the neat line of holes stitched at chest height along the rich wood paneling.

Falkenberg came in. "Your family is safe, Mr. Hamner." He turned to the President. "Ready to report, sir."

Budreau looked up with haunted eyes. The sound of gunfire was faint, but still audible.

"They have good leaders," Falkenberg reported. "When they left the Stadium they went immediately to the police barracks. They took the weapons and distributed them to their allies, after butchering the police."

"They murdered—"

"Certainly," Falkenberg said. "They wanted the police building as a fortress. And we are not fighting a mere mob out there, Mr. President. We have repeatedly run against well-armed men with training. Household forces. I will attempt another assault in the morning, but for now, Mr. President, we don't hold much more than a kilometer around the Palace."

The fires burned all night, but there was little fighting. The regiment held the Palace, with bivouac in the courtyard; and if anyone questioned why the Fourth was encamped in the center of the courtyard with other troops all around them, they did so silently.

Lieutenant Martin Latham might have had an answer for any such questioner, but he lay under Hadley's flag in the honor hall outside the hospital.

In the morning the assaults began again. The regiment moved out in thin streams, infiltrating weak spots, bypassing strong, until it had cleared a large area outside the Palace again. Then it came against another well-fortified position.

An hour later the regiment was heavily engaged against rooftop snipers, barricaded streets, and everywhere burning buildings. Maniples and squads attempted to get through and into the buildings beyond but were turned back.

The Fourth was decimated in repeated assaults against the barricades.

George Hamner had come with Falkenberg and stood in the field headquarters. He watched another platoon assault of the Fourth beaten back. "They're pretty good men," he mused.

"They'll do. Now," Falkenberg said.

"But you've used them up pretty fast."

"Not entirely by choice," Falkenberg said. "The President has ordered me to break the enemy resistance. That squanders soldiers. I'd as soon use the Fourth as blunt the fighting edge of the rest of the regiment."

"But we're not getting anywhere."

"No. The opposition's too good, and there are too many of them. We can't get them concentrated for a set battle, and when we do catch them they set fire to part of the city and retreat under cover of the flames."

A communications corporal beckoned urgently, and Falkenberg went to the low table with its array of electronics. He took the offered earphone and listened, then raised a mike.

"Fall back to the Palace," Falkenberg ordered.

"You're retreating?" Hamner demanded.

Falkenberg shrugged. "I have no choice. I can't hold this thin a perimeter, and I have only two battalions. Plus what's left of the Fourth."

"Where's the Third? The Progressive partisans? My people?"

"Out at the power plants and food centers," Falkenberg answered. "We can't break in without giving the techs time to wreck the place, but we can keep any more rebels from getting in. The Third isn't as well trained as the rest of the regiment—and besides, the techs may trust them."

They walked back through burned-out streets. The sounds of fighting followed them as the regiment retreated. Civilian workers fought the fires and cared for the wounded and dead.

Hopeless, George Hamner thought. Hopeless. I don't know why I thought Falkenberg would pull some kind of rabbit out of the hat once Bradford was gone. What could he do? What can anyone do?

Worried-looking Presidential Guards let them into the Palace and swung the heavy doors shut behind them. The guards held the Palace, but would not go outside.

President Budreau was in his ornate office with Lieutenant Banners. "I was going to send for you," Budreau said. "We can't win this, can we?"

"Not the way it's going," Falkenberg answered. Hamner nodded agreement.

Budreau nodded rapidly, as if to himself. His face was a mask of lost hopes. "That's what I thought. Pull your men back to barracks, Colonel. I'm going to surrender."

"But you can't," George protested. "Everything we've dreamed of . . . You'll doom Hadley. The Freedom Party can't govern."

"Precisely. And you see it too, don't you, George? How much governing are we doing? Before it came to an open break, perhaps we had a chance. Not now. Bring your men back to the Palace, Colonel Falkenberg. Or are you going to refuse?"

"No, sir. The men are retreating already. They'll be here in half an hour."

Budreau sighed loudly. "I told you the military answer wouldn't work here, Falkenberg."

"We might have accomplished something in the past months if we'd been given the chance."

"You might." The President was too tired to argue. "But putting the blame on poor Ernie won't help. He must have been insane.

"But this isn't three months ago, Colonel. It's not even yesterday. I might have reached a compromise before the fighting started, but I didn't, and you've lost. You're not doing much besides burning down the city . . . at least I can spare Hadley that. Banners, go tell the Freedom Party leaders I can't take anymore."

The Guard officer saluted and left, his face an unreadable mask. Budreau watched him leave the office. His eyes focused far beyond the walls with their Earth decorations.

"So you're resigning," Falkenberg said slowly.

Budreau nodded.

"Have you resigned, sir?" Falkenberg demanded.

"Yes, blast you. Banners has my resignation."

"And what will you do now?" George Hamner asked. His voice held both contempt and amazement. He had always admired and respected Budreau. And now what had Hadley's great leader left them?

"Banners has promised to get me out of here," Budreau said. "He has a boat in the harbor. We'll sail up the coast and land, then go inland to the mines. There'll be a starship there next week, and I can get out on that with my family. You'd better come with me, George." The President put both hands over his face, then looked up. "There's a lot of relief in giving in, did you know? What will you do, Colonel Falkenberg?"

"We'll manage. There are plenty of boats in the harbor if we need one. But it is very likely that the new government will need trained soldiers."

"The perfect mercenary," Budreau said with contempt. He sighed, then sent his eyes searching around the office, lingering on familiar objects. "It's a relief. I don't have to decide things anymore." He stood and his shoulders were no longer stooped. "I'll get the family. You'd better be moving too, George."

"I'll be along, sir. Don't wait for us. As the Colonel says, there are plenty of boats." He waited until Budreau had left the office, then turned to Falkenberg. "All right, what now?"

"Now we do what we came here to do," Falkenberg said. He went to the President's desk and examined the phones, but rejected them for a pocket communicator. He lifted it and spoke at length.

"Just what are you doing?" Hamner demanded.

"You're not president yet," Falkenberg said. "You won't be until you're sworn in, and that won't happen until I've finished. And there's nobody to accept your resignation, either."

"What the hell?" Hamner looked closely at Falkenberg, but he could not read the officer's expression. "You do have an idea. Let's hear it."

"You're not president yet," Falkenberg said. "Under Budreau's proclamation of martial law, I am to take whatever actions I think are required to restore order in Refuge. That order is valid until a new President removes it. And at the moment there's no President."

"But Budreau's surrendered! The Freedom Party will elect a President."

"Under Hadley's constitution only the Senate and Assembly in joint session can alter the order of succession. They're scattered across the city and their meeting chambers have been burned."

Sergeant Major Calvin and several of Falkenberg's aides came to the door. They stood, waiting.

"I'm playing guardhouse lawyer," Falkenberg said. "But President Budreau doesn't have the authority to appoint a new president. With Bradford dead, you're in charge here, but not until you appear before a magistrate and take the oath of office."

"This doesn't make sense," Hamner protested. "How

long do you think you can stay in control here, anyway?"

"As long as I have to." Falkenberg turned to an aide. "Corporal, I want Mr. Hamner to stay with me and you with him. You will treat him with respect, but he goes nowhere and sees no one without my permission. Understood?"

"Sir!"

"And now what?" Hamner asked.

"And now we wait," John Falkenberg said softly. "But not too long . . ."

George Hamner sat in the council chambers with his back to the stained and punctured wall. He tried to forget those stains, but he couldn't.

Falkenberg was across from him, and his aides sat at the far end of the table. Communications gear had been spread across one side table, but there was no situation map; Falkenberg had not moved his command post here.

From time to time officers brought him battle reports, but Falkenberg hardly listened to them. However, when one of the aides reported that Dr. Whitlock was calling, Falkenberg took the earphones immediately.

George couldn't hear what Whitlock was saying and Falkenberg's end of the conversation consisted of monosyllables. The only thing George was sure of was that Falkenberg was very interested in what his political agent was doing.

The regiment had fought its way back to the Palace and was now in the courtyard. The Palace entrances were held by the Presidential Guard, and the fighting had stopped. The rebels left the guardsmen alone, and an uneasy truce settled across the city of Refuge.

"They're going into the Stadium, sir," Captain Fast reported. "That cheer you heard was when Banners gave 'em the President's resignation."

"I see. Thank you, Captain." Falkenberg motioned for more coffee. He offered a cup to George, but the Vice President didn't want any.

"How long does this go on?" George demanded.

"Not much longer. Hear them cheering?"

They sat for another hour, Falkenberg with outward calm, Hamner with growing tension. Then Dr. Whitlock came to the council room.

The tall civilian looked at Falkenberg and Hamner, then sat easily in the President's chair. "Don't reckon I'll have another chance to sit in the seat of the mighty," he grinned.

"But what is happening?" Hamner demanded.

Whitlock shrugged. "It's 'bout like Colonel Falkenberg figured. Mob's moved right into the Stadium. Nobody wants to be left out now they think they've won. They've rounded up what senators they could find and now they're fixin' to elect themselves a new president."

"But that election won't be valid," Hamner said.

"No, suh, but that don't seem to slow 'em down a bit. They figure they won the right, I guess. And the Guard has already said they're goin' to honor the people's choice." Whitlock smiled ironically.

"How many of my technicians are out there in that mob?" Hamner asked. "They'd listen to me, I know they would."

"They might at that," Whitlock said. "But there's not so many as there used to be. Most of 'em couldn't stomach the burnin' and looting. Still, there's a fair number."

"Can you get them out?" Falkenberg asked.

"Doin' that right now," Whitlock grinned. "One reason I come up here was to get Mr. Hamner to help with that. I got my people goin' round tellin' the technicians they already got Mr. Hamner as President, so why they want somebody else? It's workin' too, but a few words from their leader here might help."

"Right," Falkenberg said. "Well, sir?"

"I don't know what to say," George protested.

Falkenberg went to the wall control panel. "Mr. Vice President, I can't give you orders, but I'd suggest you simply make a few promises. Tell them you will shortly assume command, and that things will be different. Then order them to go home or face charges as rebels. Or ask them to go home as a favor to you. Whatever you think will work."

It wasn't much of a speech, and from the roar outside the crowd did not hear much of it anyway. George promised amnesty for anyone who left the Stadium and tried to appeal to the Progressives who were caught up in the rebellion. When he put down the microphone, Falkenberg seemed pleased.

"Half an hour, Dr. Whitlock?" Falkenberg asked.

"About that," the historian agreed. "All that's leavin will be gone by then."

"Let's go, Mr. President." Falkenberg was insistent.

"Where?" Hamner asked.

"To see the end of this. Do you want to watch, or would you rather join your family? You can go anywhere you like except to a magistrate—or to someone who might accept your resignation."

"Colonel, this is ridiculous! You can't force me to be president, and I don't understand what's going on."

Falkenberg's smile was grim. "Nor do I want you to understand. Yet. You'll have enough trouble living with yourself as it is. Let's go."

George Hamner followed. His throat was dry, and his guts felt as if they'd knotted themselves into a tight ball.

The First and Second Battalions were assembled in the Palace courtyard. The men stood in ranks. Their synthileather battledress was stained with dirt and smoke from the street fighting. Armor bulged under their uniforms.

The men were silent, and Hamner thought they might have been carved from stone.

"Follow me," Falkenberg ordered. He led the way to the Stadium entrance. Lieutenant Banners stood in the doorway.

"Halt," Banners commanded.

"Really, Lieutenant? Would you fight my troops?" Falkenberg indicated the grim lines behind him.

Lieutenant Banners gulped. Hamner thought the Guard officer looked very young. "No, sir," Banners protested. "But we have barred the doors. The emergency meeting of the Assembly and Senate is electing a new President out there, and we will not permit your mercenaries to interfere."

"They have not elected anyone," Falkenberg said.

"No, sir, but when they do, the Guard will be under his command."

"I have orders from Vice President Hamner to arrest the leaders of the rebellion, and a valid proclamation of martial law," Falkenberg insisted.

"I'm sorry, sir." Banners seemed to mean it. "Our Council of officers has decided that President Budreau's surrender is valid. We intend to honor it."

"I see," Falkenberg withdrew. He motioned to his aides, and Hamner joined the group. No one objected.

"Hadn't expected this," Falkenberg said. "It would take a week to fight through those guardrooms." He thought for a moment. "Give me your keys," he snapped at Hamner.

Bewildered, George took them out. Falkenberg grinned widely. "There's another way into there, you know. Major Savage! Take G and H Companies of Second Battalion to secure the Stadium exits. Dig yourselves in and set up all weapons. Arrest anyone who comes out."

"Sir."

"Dig in pretty good, Jeremy. They may be coming out fighting. But I don't expect them to be well organized."

"Do we fire on armed men?"

"Without warning, Major. Without warning. Sergeant Major, bring the rest of the troops with me. Major, you'll have twenty minutes."

Falkenberg led his troops across the courtyard to the tunnel entrance and used Hanmer's keys to unlock the doors. Falkenberg ignored him. He led the troops down the stairway and across, under the field.

George Hamner stayed close to Falkenberg. He could hear the long column of armed men tramp behind him. They moved up stairways on the other side, marching briskly until George was panting. The men didn't seem to notice. Gravity difference, Hamner thought. And training.

They reached the top and deployed along the passageways. Falkenberg stationed men at each exit and came back to the center doors. Then he waited. The tension grew.

"But—"

Falkenberg shook his head. His look demanded silence. He stood, waiting, while the seconds ticked past.

"MOVE OUT!" Falkenberg commanded.

The doors burst open. The armed troopers moved quickly across the top of the Stadium. Most of the mob was below, and a few unarmed men were struck down when they tried to oppose the regiment. Rifle butts swung, then there was a moment of calm. Falkenberg took a speaker from his corporal attendant.

"ATTENTION. ATTENTION. YOU ARE UNDER ARREST BY THE AUTHORITY OF THE MARTIAL LAW PROCLAMATION OF PRESIDENT BUDREAU. LAY DOWN ALL WEAPONS AND YOU WILL NOT BE HARMED. IF YOU RESIST, YOU WILL BE KILLED."

There was a moment of silence, then shouts as the mob realized what Falkenberg had said. Some laughed. Then shots came from the field and the lower seats of the Stadium. Hamner heard the flat snap of a bullet as it rushed past his ear. Then he heard the crack of the rifle.

One of the leaders on the field below had a speaker. He shouted to the others. "ATTACK THEM! THERE AREN'T MORE THAN A THOUSAND OF THEM, WE'RE THIRTY THOUSAND STRONG. ATTACK, KILL THEM!" There were more shots. Some of Falkenberg's men fell. The others stood immobile, waiting for orders.

Falkenberg raised the speaker again. "PREPARE FOR VOLLEY FIRE. MAKE READY. TAKE AIM. IN VOLLEY, FIRE!"

Seven hundred rifles crashed as one.

"FIRE!" Someone screamed, a long drawn-out cry, a plea without words.

"FIRE!"

The line of men clambering up the seats toward them

wavered and broke. Men screamed, some pushed back, dove under seats, tried to hide behind their friends, tried to get anywhere but under the unwavering muzzles of the rifles.

"FIRE!"

It was like one shot, very loud, lasting far longer than a rifle shot ought to, but it was impossible to hear individual weapons. "FIRE!"

There were more screams from below. "In the name of God—"

"THE FORTY-SECOND WILL ADVANCE. FIX BAYONETS. FORWARD, MOVE. FIRE. FIRE AT WILL."

Now there was a continuous crackle of weapons. The leather-clad lines moved forward and down, over the stadium seats, flowing down inexorably toward the press below on the field.

"Sergeant Major!"

"SIR!"

"Marksmen and experts will fall out and take station. They will fire on all armed men."

"Sir!"

Calvin spoke into his communicator. Men dropped out of each section and took position behind seats. They began to fire, carefully but rapidly. Anyone below who raised a weapon died. The regiment advanced onward.

Hamner was sick. The screams of wounded could be heard everywhere. God, make it stop, make it stop, he prayed.

"GRENADIERS WILL PREPARE TO THROW." Falkenberg's voice boomed from the speaker. "THROW!"

A hundred grenades arched out from the advancing line. They fell into the milling crowds below. The muffled explosions were masked by screams of terror.

"IN VOLLEY, FIRE!"

The regiment advanced until it made contact with the mob. There was a brief struggle. Rifles fired, and bayonets flashed red. The line halted but momentarily. Then it moved on, leaving behind a ghastly trail.

Men and women jammed in the Stadium exits. Others frantically tried to get out, clambering over the fallen, tearing women out of their way to push past, trampling each other in their scramble to escape. There was a rattle of gunfire from outside. Those in the gates recoiled, to be crushed beneath others trying to get out.

"You won't even let them out!" Hamner screamed at Falkenberg.

"Not armed. And not to escape." The Colonel's face was hard and cold, the eyes narrowed to slits. He watched the slaughter impassively, looking at the entire scene without expression.

"Are you going to kill them all?"

"All who resist."

"But they don't deserve this!" George Hamner felt his voice breaking. "They don't!"

"No one does, George. SERGEANT MAJOR!"

"SIR!"

"Half the marksmen may concentrate on the leaders now."

"SIR!" Calvin spoke quietly into his command set. The snipers concentrated their fire on the Presidential box across from them. Centurions ran up and down the line of hidden troops, pointing out targets. The marksmen kept up a steady fire.

The leather lines of armored men advanced inexorably. They had almost reached the lower tier of seats. There was less firing now, but the scarlet-painted bayonets flashed in the afternoon sun.

Another section fell out of line and moved to guard a tiny number of prisoners at the end of the Stadium. The rest of the line moved on, advancing over seats made slick with blood.

When the regiment reached ground level their progress was slower. There was little opposition, but the sheer mass of people in front of them held up the troopers. There were a few pockets of active resistance, and flying squads rushed there to reinforce the line. More grenades were thrown. Falkenberg watched the battle calmly, and seldom spoke into his communicator. Below, more men died.

A company of troopers formed and rushed up a stairway on the opposite side of the Stadium. They fanned out across the top. Then their rifles leveled and crashed in another terrible series of volleys.

Suddenly it was over. There was no opposition. There were only screaming crowds. Men threw away weapons to run with their hands in the air. Others fell to their knees to beg for their lives. There was one final volley, then a deathly stillness fell over the Stadium.

But it wasn't quiet, Hamner discovered. The guns were silent, men no longer shouted orders, but there was sound. There were screams from the wounded. There were pleas for help, whimpers, a racking cough that went on and on as someone tried to clear punctured lungs.

Falkenberg nodded grimly. "Now we can find a magistrate, Mr. President. Now."

"I—Oh my God!" Hamner stood at the top of the Stadium. He clutched a column to steady his weakened legs. The scene below seemed unreal. There was too much blood, rivers of blood, blood cascading down the steps, blood pouring down stairwells to soak the grassy field below.

"It's over," Falkenberg said gently. "For all of us. The regiment will be leaving as soon as you're properly in command. You shouldn't have any trouble with your power plants. Your technicians will trust you now that Bradford's gone. And without their leaders, the city people won't resist.

"You can ship as many as you have to out to the interior. Disperse them among the loyalists where they won't do you any harm. That amnesty of yours—it's only a suggestion, but I'd renew it."

Hamner turned dazed eyes toward Falkenberg. "Yes. There's been too much slaughter today. Who are you, Falkenberg?"

"A mercenary soldier, Mr. President. Nothing more."

"But—then who are you working for?"

"That's the question nobody asked before. Grand Admiral Lermontov."

"Lermontov? But you were drummed out of the Co-

Dominium! You mean that you were hired—by the admiral? As a mercenary?"

"More or less." Falkenberg nodded coldly. "The Fleet's a little sick of being used to mess up people's lives without having a chance to—to leave things in working order."

"And now you're leaving?"

"Yes. We couldn't stay here, George. Nobody is going to forget today. You couldn't keep us on and build a government that works. I'll take First and Second Battalions, and what's left of the Fourth. There's more work for us."

"And the others?"

"Third will stay on to help you," Falkenberg said. "We put all the married locals, the solid people, in Third, and sent it off to the power plants. They weren't involved in the fighting." He looked across the Stadium, then back to Hamner. "Blame it all on us, George. You weren't in command. You can say Bradford ordered this slaughter and killed himself in remorse. People will want to believe that. They'll want to think somebody was punished for—for this." He waved toward the field below. A child was sobbing out there somewhere.

"It had to be done," Falkenberg insisted. "Didn't it? There was no way out, nothing you could do to keep civilization. . . . Dr. Whitlock estimated a third of the population would die when things collapsed. Fleet Intelligence put it higher than that. Now you have a chance."

Falkenberg was speaking rapidly, and George wondered whom he was trying to convince.

"Move them out," Falkenberg said. "Move them out while they're still dazed. You won't need much help for that. They won't resist now. And we got the railroads running for you. Use the railroads and ship people out to the farms. It'll be rough with no preparation, but it's a long time until winter—"

"I know what to do," Hamner interrupted. He leaned against the column, and seemed to gather new strength from the thought. Yes. I do know what to do. Now. "I've known all along what had to be done. Now we can get to it. We won't thank you for it, but—you've saved a whole world, John."

Falkenberg looked at him grimly, then pointed to the bodies below. "Damn you, don't say that!" he shouted. His voice was almost shrill. "I haven't saved anything. All a soldier can do is buy time. I haven't saved Hadley. You have to do that. God help you if you don't."

XII

Crofton's Encyclopedia of Contemporary History and Social Issues (2nd Edition)

MERCENARY FORCES

PERHAPS THE MOST disturbing development arising from CoDominium withdrawal from most distant colony worlds (see *Independence Movements*) has been the rapid growth of purely mercenary military units. The trend was predictable and perhaps inevitable, although the extent has exceeded expectations.

Many of the former colony worlds do not have planetary governments. Consequently, these new nations do not possess sufficient population or industrial resources to maintain large and effective national military forces. The disbanding of numerous CoDominium Marine units left a surplus of trained soldiers without employment, and it was inevitable that some of them would band together into mercenary units.

The colony governments are thus faced with a cruel and impossible dilemma. Faced with mercenary troops specializing in violence, they have had little choice but to reply in kind. A few colonies have broken this cycle by creating their own national armies, but have then been unable to pay for them.

Thus, in addition to the purely private mercenary organizations such as Falkenberg's Mercenary Legion, there are now national forces hired out to reduce expenses to their parent governments. A few former colonies have found this practice so lucrative that the export of mercenaries has become their principal source of income, and the recruiting and training of soldiers their major industry.

The CoDominium Grand Senate has attempted to maintain its presence in the former colonial areas through promulgation of the so-called *Laws of War (q.v.)*, which purport to regulate the weapons and tactics mercenary units may employ. Enforcement of these regulations is sporadic. When the Senate orders Fleet intervention to enforce the Laws of War the suspicion inevitably arises that other CoDominium interests are at stake, or that one or more Senators have undisclosed reasons for their interest.

Mercenary units generally draw their recruits from the same sources as the CoDominium Marines, and training stresses loyalty to comrades and commanders rather than to any government. The extent to which mercenary commanders have successfully separated their troops from all normal social intercourse is both surprising and alarming.

The best-known mercenary forces are described in separate articles. See: *Covenant; Friedland; Xanadu; Falkenberg's Mercenary Legion; Nouveau Legion Etrangere; Katanga Gendarmerie; Moolman's Commandos . . .*

FALKENBERG'S MERCENARY LEGION

Purely private military organization formed from the former Forty-second CoDominium Line Marines under Colonel John Christian Falkenberg III. Falkenberg was cashiered from the CoDominium Fleet under questionable circumstances, and his regiment disbanded shortly thereafter. A large proportion of former Forty-second officers and men chose to remain with Falkenberg.

Falkenberg's Legion appears to have been first employed by the government of the then newly independent former colony of Hadley (*q.v.*) for suppression of civil disturbances. There have been numerous com-

plaints that excessive violence was used by both sides in
the unsuccessful rebellion following CoDominium withdrawal, but the government of Hadley has expressed
satisfaction with Falkenberg's efforts there.

Following its employment on Hadley, Falkenberg's
Legion took part in numerous small wars of defense and
conquest on at least five planets, and in the process
gained a reputation as one of the best-trained and most
effective small military units in existence.

It was then engaged by the CoDominium Governor
on the CD prison planet of Tanith.

This latter employment caused great controversy in
the Grand Senate, as Tanith remains under CD control.
However, Grand Admiral Lermontov pointed out that
his budget did not permit his stationing regular Marine
forces on Tanith owing to other commitments mandated
by the Grand Senate; after lengthy debate the employment was approved as an alternative to raising a new
regiment of CD Marines.

At last report Falkenberg's Legion remains on Tanith.
Its contract with the Governor there is said to have
expired.

Tanith's bright image had replaced Earth's on Grand
Admiral Lermontov's view screen. The planet might
have been Earth: it had bright clouds obscuring the
outlines of land and sea, and they swirled in typical
cyclonic patterns.

A closer look showed differences. The sun was yellow: Tanith's star was not as hot as Sol, but Tanith was
closer to it. There were fewer mountains, and more
swamplands steaming in the yellow-orange glare.

Despite its miserable climate, Tanith was an important world. It was first and foremost a convenient dump-
ing ground for Earth's disinherited. There was no better
way to deal with criminals than to send them off to
hard—and useful—labor on another planet. Tanith received them all: the rebels, the criminals, the malcon-
tents, victims of administrative hatred; all the refuse of
a civilization that could no longer afford misfits.

Tanith was also the main source of borloi, which the

World Pharmaceutical Society called "the perfect intoxicating drug." Given large supplies of borloi the lid could be kept on the Citizens in their Welfare Islands. The happiness the drug induced was artificial, but it was none the less real.

"And so I am trading in drugs," Lermontov told his visitor. "It is hardly what I expected when I became Grand Admiral."

"I'm sorry, Sergei." Grand Senator Martin Grant had aged; in ten years he had come to look forty years older. "The fact is, though, you're better off with Fleet ownership of some of the borloi plantations than you are relying on what I can get for you out of the Senate."

Lermontov nodded in disgust. "It must end, Martin. Somehow, somewhere, it must end. I cannot keep a fighting service together on the proceeds of drug sales— drugs grown by slaves! Soldiers do not make good slavemasters."

Grant merely shrugged.

"Yes, it is easy to think, is it not?" The admiral shook his head in disgust. "But there are vices natural to the soldier and the sailor. We have those, in plenty, but they are not vices that corrupt his ability as a fighting man. Slaving is a vice that corrupts everything it touches."

"If you feel that way, what can I say?" Martin Grant asked. "I can't give you an alternative."

"And I cannot let go," Lermontov said. He punched viciously at the console controls and Tanith faded from the screen. Earth, bluer and to Lermontov far more lovely, swam out of the momentary blackness. "They are fools down there," Sergei Lermontov muttered. "And we are no better. Martin, I ask myself again and again, why can we not control—anything? Why are we caught like chips in a rushing stream? Men can guide their destinies. I know that. So why are we so helpless?"

"You don't ask yourself more often than I do," Senator Grant said. His voice was low and weary. "At least we still try. Hell, you've got more power than I have. You've got the Fleet, and you've got the secret funds you get from Tanith—Christ, Sergei, if you can't do something with that—"

"I can urinate on fires," Lermontov said. "And little else." He shrugged. "So, if that is all I can do, then I will continue to make water. Will you have a drink?"

"Thanks."

Lermontov went to the sideboard and took out bottles. His conversations with Grand Senator Grant were never heard by anyone else, not even his orderlies who had been with him for years.

"Prosit."

"Prosit!"

They drank. Grant took out a cigar. "By the way, Sergei, what are you going to do with Falkenberg now that the trouble on Tanith is finished?"

Lermontov smiled coldly. "I was hoping that you would have a solution to that. I have no more funds—"

"The Tanith money—"

"Needed elsewhere, just to keep the Fleet together," Lermontov said positively.

"Then Falkenberg'll just have to find his own way. Shouldn't be any problem, with his reputation," Grant said. "And even if it is, he's got no more troubles than we have."

XIII

HEAT BEAT DOWN on sodden fields. Two hours before the noon of Tanith's fifteen plus hours of sunshine the day was already hot; but all of Tanith's days are hot. Even in midwinter the jungle steams in late afternoon.

The skies above the regiment's camp were yellow-gray. The ground sloped off to the west into inevitable swamp, where Weem's Beasts snorted as they burrowed deeper into protective mud. In the camp itself the air hung hot and wet, heavy, with a thick smell of yeast and decay.

The regiment's camp was an island of geometrical precision in the random tumble of jungles and hilltops. Each yellow rammed-earth barrack was set in an exact relationship with every other, each company set in line from its centurion's hut at one end to the senior platoon sergeant's at the other.

A wide street separated Centurion's Row from the Company Officers Line, and beyond that was the shorter Field Officers Line, the pyramid narrowing inevitably until at its apex stood a single building where the colonel lived. Other officers lived with their ladies, and married enlisted men's quarters formed one side of the compound; but the colonel lived alone.

The visitor stood with the colonel to watch a mustering ceremony evolved in the days of Queen Anne's England when regimental commanders were paid according to the strength of their regiments, and the

340

Queen's muster masters had to determine that each man drawing pay could indeed pass muster—or even existed.

The visitor was an amateur historian and viewed the parade with wry humor. War had changed and men no longer marched in rigid lines to deliver volleys at word of command—but colonels were again paid according to the forces they could bring into battle.

"Report!" The adjutant's command carried easily across the open parade field to the rigidly immobile blue and gold squares.

"First Battalion, B Company on patrol. Battalion present or accounted for, sir!"

"Second Battalion present or accounted for, sir." "Third Battalion present or accounted for, sir!"

"Fourth Battalion, four men absent without leave, sir."

"How embarrassing," the visitor said *sotto voce*. The colonel tried to smile but made a bad job of it.

"Artillery present or accounted for, sir!" "Scout Troop all present, sir!" "Sappers all present, sir!"

"Weapons Battalion, Aviation Troop on patrol. Battalion present or accounted for, sir!"

"Headquarters Company present or on guard, sir!"

The adjutant returned each salute, then wheeled crisply to salute the colonel. "Regiment has four men absent without leave, sir."

Colonel Falkenberg returned the salute. "Take your post."

Captain Fast pivoted and marched to his place. "Pass in review!"

"Sound off!"

The band played a military march that must have been old in the twentieth century as the regiment formed column to march around the field. As each company reached the reviewing stand and men snapped their heads in unison, guidons and banners lowered in salute, and officers and centurions whirled sabers with flourishes.

The visitor nodded to himself. No longer very appropriate. In the eighteenth century, demonstrations of the men's ability to march in ranks, and of the noncoms and officers to use a sword with skill, were relevant to battle capabilities. Not now. Still, it made an impressive ceremony.

"Attention to orders!" The sergeant major read from his clipboard. Promotions, duty schedules, the daily activities of the regiment, while the visitor sweated.

"Very impressive, Colonel," he said. "Our Washingtonians couldn't look that sharp on their best day."

John Christian Falkenberg nodded coldly. "Implying that they mightn't be as good in the field. Mr. Secretary? Would you like another kind of demonstration?"

Howard Bannister shrugged. "What would it prove, Colonel? You need employment before your regiment goes to hell. I can't imagine chasing escapees on the CoDominium prison planet has much attraction for good soldiers."

"It doesn't. When we first came things weren't that simple."

"I know that too. The Forty-second was one of the best outfits of the CD Marine—I've never understood why it was disbanded instead of one of the others. I'm speaking of your present situation with your troops stuck here without transport—surely you're not intending to make Tanith your lifetime headquarters?"

Sergeant Major Calvin finished the orders of the day and waited patiently for instructions. Colonel Falkenberg studied his bright-uniformed men as they stood rigidly in the blazing noon of Tanith. A faint smile might have played across his face for a moment. There were few of the four thousand whose names and histories he didn't know.

Lieutenant Farquhar was a party hack forced on him when the Forty-second was hired to police Hadley. He became a good officer and elected to ship out after the action. Private Alcazar was a brooding giant with a raging thirst, the slowest man in K Company, but he could lift five times his own mass and hide in any terrain. Dozens, thousands of men, each with his own strengths and weaknesses, adding up to a regiment of mercenary soldiers with no chance of going home, and an unpleasant future if they didn't get off Tanith.

"Sergeant Major."

"Sir!"

"You will stay with me and time the men. Trumpeter, sound Boots and Saddles, On Full Kits, and Ready to Board Ship."

"Sir!" The trumpeter was a grizzled veteran with corporal's stripes. He lifted the gleaming instrument with its blue and gold tassels, and martial notes poured across the parade ground. Before they died away the orderly lines dissolved into masses of running men.

There was less confusion than Howard Bannister had expected. It seemed an incredibly short time before the first men fell back in. They came from their barracks in small groups, some in each company, then more, a rush, and finally knots of stragglers. Now in place of bright colors there was the dull drab of synthetic leather bulging over Nemourlon body armor. The bright polish was gone from the weapons. Dress caps were replaced by bulging combat helmets, shining boots by softer leathers. As the regiment formed, Bannister turned to the colonel.

"Why trumpets? I'd think that's rather out of date."

Falkenberg shrugged. "Would you prefer shouted orders? You must remember, Mr. Secretary, mercenaries live in garrison as well as in combat. Trumpets remind them that they're soldiers."

"I suppose."

"Time, Sergeant Major," the adjutant demanded.

"Eleven minutes, eighteen seconds, sir."

"Are you trying to tell me the men are ready to ship out now?" Bannister asked. His expression showed polite disbelief.

"It would take longer to get the weapons and artillery battalion equipment together, but the infantry could board ship right now."

"I find that hard to believe—of course the men know this is only a drill."

"How would they know that?"

Bannister laughed. He was a stout man, dressed in expensive business clothes with cigar ashes down the

front. Some of the ash floated free when he laughed.
"Well, you and the sergeant major are still in parade
uniform."

"Look behind you," Falkenberg said.

Bannister turned. Falkenberg's guards and trumpeter
were still in their places, their blue and gold dress
contrasting wildly with the grim synthi-leathers of the
others who had formed up with them. "The headquarters squad has our gear," Falkenberg explained. "Sergeant Major."

"Sir!"

"Mr. Bannister and I will inspect the troops."

"Sir!" As Falkenberg and his visitor left the reviewing
stand Calvin fell in with the duty squad behind him.

"Pick a couple at random," Falkenberg advised. "It's
hot out here. Forty degrees anyway."

Bannister was thinking the same thing. "Yes. No
point in being too hard on the men. It must be unbear-
able in their armor."

"I wasn't thinking of the men," Falkenberg said.

The Secretary for War chose L Company of Third
Battalion for review. The men all looked alike, except
for size. He looked for something to stand out—a strap
not buckled, something to indicate an individual difference—but he found none. Bannister approached a
scarred private who looked forty years old. With regeneration therapy he might have been half that again.
"This one."

"Fall out, Wiszorik!" Calvin ordered. "Lay out your
kit."

"Sir!" Private Wiszorik might have smiled thinly, but
if he did Bannister missed it. He swung the packframe
easily off his shoulders and stood it on the ground. The
headquarters squad helped him lay out his nylon shelter cloth, and Wiszorik emptied the pack, placing each
item just so.

Rifle: a New Aberdeen seven-mm semi-automatic,
with ten-shot clip and fifty-round box magazine, both
full and spotlessly clean like the rifle. A bandolier of
cartridges. Five grenades. Nylon belt with bayonets,
canteen, spoon, and stainless cup that served as a pri-

vate's entire mess kit. Great-cloak and poncho, string net underwear, layers of clothing—

"You'll note he's equipped for any climate," Falkenberg commented. "He'd expect to be issued special gear for a non-Terran environment, but he can live on any inhabitable world with what he's got."

"Yes." Bannister watched interestedly. The pack hadn't seemed heavy, but Wiszorik kept withdrawing gear from it. First aid kit, chemical warfare protection drugs and equipment, concentrated field rations, soup and beverage powders, a tiny gasoline-burning field stove—

"What's that?" Bannister asked. "Do all the men carry them?"

"One to each maniple, sir," Wiszorik answered.

"His share of five men's community equipment," Falkenberg explained. "A monitor, three privates, and a recruit make up the basic combat unit of this outfit, and we try to keep the maniples self-sufficient."

More gear came from the pack. Much of it was light alloys or plastic, but Bannister wondered about the total weight. Trowel, tent pegs, nylon cordage, a miniature cutting torch, more group equipment for field repairs to both machinery and the woven Nemourion armor, night sights for the rifle, a small plastic tube half a meter long and eight centimeters in diameter—"And that?" Bannister asked.

"Anti-aircraft rocket," Falkenberg told him. "Not effective against fast jets, but it'll knock out a chopper ninety-five percent of the time. Has some capability against tanks, too. We don't like the men too dependent on heavy weapons units."

"I see. Your men seem well equipped, Colonel," Bannister commented. "It must weight them down badly."

"Twenty-one kilograms in standard g field," Falkenberg answered. "More here, less by a lot on Washington. Every man carries a week's rations, ammunition for a short engagement, and enough equipment to live in the field."

"What's the little pouch on his belt?" Bannister asked interestedly.

Falkenberg shrugged. "Personal possessions. Probably everything he owns. You'll have to ask Wiszorik's permission if you want to examine that."

"Never mind. Thank you, Private Wiszorik." Howard Bannister produced a brightly colored bandanna from an inner pocket and mopped his brow. "All right, Colonel. You're convincing—or your men are. Let's go to your office and talk about money."

As they left, Wiszorik and Sergeant Major Calvin exchanged knowing winks, while Monitor Hartzinger breathed a sigh of relief. Just suppose that visiting panjandrum had picked Recruit Latterby! Hell, the kid couldn't find his arse with both hands.

XIV

FALKENBERG'S OFFICE WAS hot. It was a large room, and a ceiling fan tried without success to stir up a breeze. Everything was damp from Tanith's wet jungle air. Howard Bannister thought he saw fungus growing in the narrow space between a file cabinet and the wall.

In contrast to the room itself, the furniture was elaborate. It had been hand carved and was the product of hundreds of hours' labor by soldiers who had little else but time to give their commanding officer. They'd taken Sergeant Major Calvin into a conspiracy, getting him to talk Falkenberg into going on an inspection tour while they scrapped his functional old field gear and replaced it with equipment as light and useful, but hand carved with battle scenes.

The desk was large and entirely bare. To one side a table, in easy reach, was covered with papers. On the other side a two-meter star cube portrayed the known stars with inhabited planets. Communication equipment was built into a spindly legged sideboard that also held whiskey. Falkenberg offered his visitor a drink.

"Could we have something with ice?"

"Certainly." Falkenberg turned toward his sideboard and raised his voice, speaking with a distinct change in tone. "Orderly, two gin and tonics, with much ice, if you please. Will that be satisfactory, Mr. Secretary?"

"Yes, thank you." Bannister wasn't accustomed to electronics being so common. "Look, we needn't spar

347

about. I need soldiers and you need to get off this
planet. It's as simple as that."

"Hardly," Falkenberg replied. "You've yet to mention money."

Howard shrugged. "I don't have much. Washington
has damned few exports. Franklin's dried those up with
the blockade. Your transport and salaries will use up
most of what we've got. But you already know this, I
suppose—I'm told you have access to Fleet Intelligence sources."

Falkenberg shrugged. "I have my ways. You're prepared to put our return fare on deposit with Dayan, of
course."

"Yes." Bannister was startled. "Dayan? You do have
sources. I thought our negotiations with New Jerusalem
were secret. All right—we have arrangements with Dayan
to furnish transportation. It took all our cash, so everything else is contingency money. We can offer you
something you need, though. Land, good land, and a
permanent base that's a lot more pleasant than Tanith.
We can also offer—well, the chance to be part of a free
and independent nation, though I'm not expecting that
to mean much to you."

Falkenberg nodded. "That's why you—excuse me."
He paused as the orderly brought in a tray with tinkling
glasses. The trooper wore battledress, and his rifle was
slung across his shoulder.

"Will you be wanting the men to perform again?"
Falkenberg asked.

Bannister hesitated. "I think not."

"Orderly, ask Sergeant Major to sound recall. Dismissed." He looked back to Bannister. "Now. You chose
us because you've nothing to offer. The New Demo-
crats on Friedland are happy enough with their base, as
are the Scots on Covenant. Xanadu wants hard cash
before they throw troops into action. You could find some
scrapings on Earth, but we're the only first-class outfit
down on its luck at the moment—what makes you think
we're *that* hard up, Mr. Secretary? Your cause in Washington is lost, isn't it?"

"Not for us." Howard Bannister sighed. Despite his

bulk he seemed deflated. "All right. Franklin's mercenaries have defeated the last organized field army we had. The resistance is all guerrilla operations, and we both know that won't win. We need an organized force to rally around, and we haven't got one." *Dear God, we haven't got one.* Bannister remembered rugged hills and forests, weathered mountains with snow on their tops, and in the valleys were ranches with the air crisp and cool. He remembered plains golden with mutated wheat and the swaying tassels of Washington's native corn plant rippling in the wind. The Patriot army marched again to the final battle.

They'd marched with songs in their hearts. The cause was just and they faced only mercenaries after defeating Franklin's regular army. Free men against hirelings in one last campaign.

The Patriots entered the plains outside the capital city, confident that the mercenaries could never stand against them—and the enemy didn't run. The humorless Covenant Scots regiments chewed through their infantry, while Friedland armor squadrons cut across the flank and far into the rear, destroying their supply lines and capturing the headquarters. Washington's army had not so much been defeated as dissolved, turned into isolated groups of men whose enthusiasm was no match for the iron discipline of the mercenaries. In three weeks they'd lost everything gained in two years of war.

But yet—the planet was still only thinly settled. The Franklin Confederacy had few soldiers and couldn't afford to keep large groups of mercenaries on occupation duty. Out in the mountains and across the plains the settlements were seething, and ready to revolt again. It would only take a tiny spark to arouse them.

"We've a chance, Colonel. I wouldn't waste our money and risk my people's lives if I didn't think so. Let me show you. I've a map in my gear."

"Show me on this one." Falkenberg opened a desk drawer to reveal a small input panel. He touched keys and the translucent gray of his desk top dissolved into colors. A polar projection of Washington formed.

There was only one continent, an irregular mass squatting at the top of the planet. From 25° North to the South Pole there was nothing but water. The land above that was cut by huge bays and nearly landlocked seas. Towns showed as a network of red dots across a narrow band of land jutting down to the 30° to 50° level.

"You sure don't have much land to live on," Falkenberg observed. "A strip a thousand kilometers wide by four thousand long—why Washington, anyway?"

"Original settlers had ancestors in Washington state. The climate's similar too. Franklin's the companion planet. It's got more industry than we do, but even less agricultural land. Settled mostly by Southern U.S. people—they call themselves the Confederacy. Washington's a secondary colony from Franklin."

Falkenberg chuckled. "Dissidents from a dissident colony. You must be damned independent chaps."

"So independent that we're not going to let Franklin run our lives! They treat us like a wholly owned subsidiary, and we are not going to take it!"

"You'll take it if you can't get somebody to fight for you," Falkenberg reminded him brutally. "Now, you are offering us transport out, a deposit against our return, minimum troop pay, and land to settle on?"

"Yes, that's right. You can use the return deposit to transport your noncombatants later. Or cash it in. But it's all the money we can offer, Colonel." And be damned to you. You don't care at all, but I have to deal with you. For now.

"Yeah." Falkenberg regarded the map sourly. "Are we facing nukes?"

"They've got some but so do we. We concealed ours in Franklin's capital to make it a standoff."

"Uh-huh." Falkenberg nodded. The situation wasn't that unusual. The CD Fleet still tried to enforce the ban for that matter. "Do they still have those Covenant Highlanders that whipped you last time?"

Bannister winced at the reminder. "Goddamn it, good men were killed in that fight, and you've got no right to—"

"Do they still have the Covenanters, Mr. Secretary?" Falkenberg repeated.

"Yes. Plus a brigade of Friedland armor and another ten thousand Earth mercenaries on garrison duty."

Falkenberg snorted. No one thought much of Earth's cannon fodder. The best Earth recruits joined the growing national armies. Bannister nodded agreement. "Then there are about eight thousand Confederate troops, native Franklin soldiers who'd be no match for our Washingtonians."

"You hope. Don't play Franklin down. They're putting together the nucleus of a damned good fighting force, Mr. Bannister—as you know. It is my understanding that they have plans for further conquests once they've consolidated their hold on New Washington."

Bannister agreed carefully. "That's the main reason we're so desperate, Colonel. We won't buy peace by giving in to the Confederacy because they're set to defy the CoDominium when they can build a fleet. I don't understand why the CD Navy hasn't put paid to Franklin's little scheme, but it's obvious Earth isn't going to do anything. In a few years the Confederates will have their fleet and be as strong as Xanadu or Danube, strong enough to give the CD a *real* fight."

"You're too damn isolated," Falkenberg replied. "The Grand Senate won't even keep the Fleet up to enough strength to protect what the CD's already got—let alone find the money to interfere in your sector. The shortsighted bastards run around putting out fires, and the few Senators who look ten years ahead don't have any influence." He shook his head suddenly. "But that's not our problem. Okay, what about landing security? I don't have any assault boats, and I doubt you've the money to hire those from Dayan."

"It's tough," Bannister admitted. "But blockade runners can get through. Tides on New Washington are enormous, but we know our coasts. The Dayan captain can put you down at night here, or along there . . ." The rebel war secretary indicated a number of deep bays and fiords on the jagged coast, bright blue spatters on the desk map. "You'll have about two hours of slack water. That's all the time you'd have anyway before the Confederate spy satellites detect the ship."

XV

ROGER HASTINGS DREW his pretty brunette wife close to him and leaned against the barbecue pit. It made a nice pose and the photographers took several shots. They begged for more, but Hastings shook his head. "Enough, boys, enough! I've only been sworn in as mayor of Allansport—you'd think I was Governor General of the whole planet!"

"But give us a statement," the reporters begged. "Will you support the Confederacy's rearmament plans? I understand the smelter is tooling up to produce naval armament alloys—"

"I said *enough*," Roger commanded. "Go have a drink." The reporters reluctantly scattered. "Eager chaps," Hastings told his wife. "Pity there's only the one little paper."

Juanita laughed. "You'd make the capital city *Times* if there was a way to get the pictures there. But it was a fair question, Roger. What are you going to do about Franklin's war policies? What will happen to Harley when they start expanding the Confederacy?" The amusement died from her face as she thought of their son in the army.

"There isn't much I can do. The mayor of Allansport isn't consulted on matters of high policy. Damn it, sweetheart, don't you start in on me too. It's too nice a day."

Hastings' quarried stone house stood high on a hill

above Nanaimo Bay. The city of Allansport sprawled
across the hills below them, stretching almost to the
high water mark running irregularly along the sandy
beaches washed by endless surf. At night they could
hear the waves crashing.

They held hands and watched the sea beyond the
island that formed Allansport Harbor. "Here it comes!"
Roger said. He pointed to a wall of rushing water two
meters high. The tide bore swept around the end of
Waada Island, then curled back toward the city.

"Pity the poor sailors," Juanita said.

Roger shrugged. "The packet ship's anchored well
enough."

They watched the 150-meter cargo vessel tossed about
by the tidal force. The tide bore caught her nearly
abeam and she rolled dangerously before swinging on
her chains to head into the flowing tide water. It
seemed nothing could hold her, but those chains had
been made in Roger's foundries, and he knew their
strength.

"It has been a nice day." Juanita sighed. Their house
was on one of the large greensward commons running
up the hill from Allansport, and the celebrations had
spilled out of their yard, across the greens, and into
their neighbors' yards as well. Portable bars manned by
Roger's campaign workers dispensed an endless supply
of local wines and brandies.

To the west New Washington's twin companion, Franklin, hung in its eternal place. When sunset brought
New Washington's twenty hours of daylight to an end it
passed from a glowing ball in the bright day sky to a
gibbous sliver in the darkness, then rapidly widened.
Reddish shadows danced on Franklin's cloudy face.

Roger and Juanita stood in silent appreciation of the
stars, the planet, the sunset. Allansport was a frontier
town on an unimportant planet, but it was home and
they loved it.

The inauguration party had been exhaustingly successful. Roger gratefully went to the drawing room while
Juanita climbed the stairs to put their sleepy children to
bed. As manager of the smelter and foundry, Roger had

a home that was one of the finest on all the Ranier Peninsula. It stood tall and proud—a big stone Georgian mansion with wide entry hall and paneled rooms. Now, he was joined by Martine Ardway in his favorite, the small conversation-sized drawing room.

"Congratulations again, Roger," Colonel Ardway boomed. "We'll all be behind you." The words were more than the usual inauguration day patter. Although Ardway's son Johann was married to Roger's daughter, the Colonel had opposed Hastings' election, and Ardway had a large following among the hard-line Loyalists in Allansport. He was also commander of the local militia. Johann held a captain's commission. Roger's own boy Harley was only a lieutenant, but in the Regulars.

"Have you told Harley about your winning?" Ardway asked.

"Can't. The communications to Vancouver are out. As a matter of fact, all our communications are out right now."

Ardway nodded phlegmatically. Allansport was the only town on a peninsula well over a thousand kilometers from the nearest settlements. New Washington was so close to its red dwarf sun that loss of communications was standard through much of the planet's fifty-two standard-day year. An undersea cable to Preston Bay had been planned when the rebellion broke out, and now that it was over work could start again.

"I mean it about being with you," Ardway repeated. "I still think you're wrong, but there can't be more than one policy about this. I just hope it works."

"Look, Martine, we can't go on treating the rebels like traitors. We need'em too much. There aren't many rebels here, but if I enforce the confiscation laws it'll cause resentment in the East. We've had enough bloody war." Roger stretched and yawned. "Excuse me. It's been a hard day and it's a while since I was a rock miner. There was once a time when I could dig all day and drink all night."

Ardway shrugged. Like Hastings, he had once been a miner, but unlike the mayor he hadn't kept in shape. He wasn't fat, but he had become a large, balding, round man with a paunch that spilled over his wide garrison belt. It spoiled his looks when he wore military uniform, which he did whenever possible. "You're in charge, Roger. I won't get in your way. Maybe you can even get the old rebel families on your side against this stupid imperialistic venture Franklin's pushing. God knows we've enough problems at home without looking for more. I think. What in hell's going on out there?"

Someone was yelling in the town below. "Good God, were those shots?" Roger asked. "We better find out." Reluctantly he pushed himself up from the leather easy chair. "Hello—hello—what's this? The phone is out, Martine. Dead."

"Those *were* shots," Colonel Ardway said. "I don't like this—rebels? The packet came in this afternoon, but you don't suppose there were rebels on board her? We better go down and see to this. You sure the phone's dead?"

"Very dead," Hastings said quietly. "Lord, I hope it's not a new rebellion. Get your troops called out, though."

"Right." Ardway took a pocket communicator from his belt pouch. He spoke into it with increasing agitation. "Roger, there is something wrong! I'm getting nothing but static. Somebody's jamming the whole communications band."

"Nonsense. We're near periastron. The sunspots are causing it." Hastings sounded confident, but he was praying silently. Not more war. It wouldn't be a threat to Allansport and the Peninsula—there weren't more than a handful of rebels out here, but they'd be called on for troops to go east and fight in rebel areas like Ford Heights and the Columbia Valley. It was so damn rotten! He remembered burning ranches and plantations during the last flareup.

"Goddamn it, don't those people know they lose more in the wars than Franklin's merchants are costing them?" But he was already speaking to an empty room. Colonel Ardway had dashed outside and was calling to the neighbors to fall out with military equipment.

Roger followed him outside. To the west Franklin flooded the night with ten thousand times Luna's best efforts on Earth. There were soldiers coming up the broad street from the main section of town.

"Who in hell—those aren't rebels," Hastings shouted. They were men in synthi-leather battledress, and they moved too deliberately. Those were Regulars.

There was a roar of motors. A wave of helicopters passed overhead. Roger heard ground effects cars on the greensward, and at least two hundred soldiers were running purposefully up the street toward his house. At each house below a knot of five men fell out of the open formation.

"Turn out! Militia turn out! Rebels!" Colonel Ardway was shouting. He had a dozen men, none in armor, and their best weapons were rifles.

"Take cover! Fire at will!" Ardway screamed. His voice carried determination but it had an edge of fear. "Roger, get the hell inside, you damn fool!"

"But—" The advancing troops were no more than a hundred meters away. One of Ardway's militia fired an automatic rifle from the house next door. The leather-clad troops scattered and someone shouted orders.

Fire lashed out to rake the house. Roger stood in his front yard, dazed, unbelieving, as under Franklin's bright reddish light the nightmare went on. The troops advanced steadily again and there was no more resistance from the militia.

It all happened so quickly. Even as Roger had that thought, the leather lines of men reached him. An officer raised a megaphone.

"I CALL ON YOU TO SURRENDER IN THE NAME OF THE FREE STATES OF WASHINGTON. STAY IN YOUR HOMES AND DO NOT TRY TO RESIST. ARMED MEN WILL BE SHOT WITHOUT WARNING."

A five-man detachment ran past Roger Hastings and through the front door of his home. It brought him from his daze. "Juanita!" He screamed and ran toward his house.

"HALT! HALT OR WE FIRE! YOU MAN, HALT!"

Roger ran on heedlessly.

"SQUAD FIRE."

"BELAY THAT ORDER!"

As Roger reached the door he was grabbed by one of the soldiers and flung against the wall. "Hold it right there," the trooper said grimly. "Monitor, I have a prisoner."

Another soldier came into the broad entryway. He held a clipboard and looked up at the address of the house, checking it against his papers. "Mr. Roger Hastings?" he asked.

Roger nodded dazedly. Then he thought better of it. "No. I'm—"

"Won't do," the soldier said. "I've your picture, Mr. Mayor." Roger nodded again. Who was this man? There had been many accents, and the officer with the clipboard had yet another. "Who are you?" he demanded.

"Lieutenant Jaimie Farquhar of Falkenberg's Mercenary Legion, acting under authority of the Free States of Washington. You're under military detention, Mr. Mayor."

There was more firing outside. Roger's house hadn't been touched. Everything looked so absolutely ordinary. Somehow that added to the horror.

A voice called from upstairs. "His wife and kids are up here, Lieutenant."

"Thank you, Monitor. Ask the lady to come down, please. Mr. Mayor, please don't be concerned for your family. We do not make war on civilians." There were more shots from the street.

A thousand questions boiled in Roger's mind. He stood dazedly trying to sort them into some order. "Have you shot Colonel Ardway? Who's fighting out there?"

"If you mean the fat man in uniform, he's safe enough. We've got him in custody. Unfortunately, some of your militia have ignored the order to surrender, and it's going to be hard on them."

As if in emphasis there was the muffled blast of a grenade, then a burst from a machine pistol answered by the slow deliberate fire of an automatic rifle. The battle noises swept away across the brow of the hill, but sounds of firing and shouted orders carried over the pounding surf.

Farquhar studied his clipboard. "Mayor Hastings and Colonel Ardway. Yes, thank you for identifying him. I've orders to take you both to the command post. Monitor!"

"Sir!"

"Your maniple will remain here on guard. You will allow no one to enter this house. Be polite to Mrs. Hastings, but keep her and the children here. If there is any attempt at looting you will prevent it. This street is under the protection of the Regiment. Understood?"

"Sir!"

The slim officer nodded in satisfaction. "If you'll come with me, Mr. Mayor, there's a car on the greensward." As Roger followed numbly he saw the hall clock. He had been sworn in as mayor less than eleven hours ago.

The Regimental Command Post was in the city council meeting chambers, with Falkenberg's office in a small connecting room. The council room itself was filled with electronic gear and bustled with runners, while Major Savage and Captain Fast controlled the military conquest of Allansport. Falkenberg watched the situation develop in the maps displayed on his desk top.

"It was so fast!" Howard Bannister said. The pudgy secretary of war shook his head in disbelief. "I never thought you could do it."

Falkenberg shrugged. "Light infantry can move, Mr. Secretary. But it cost us. We had to leave the artillery train in orbit with most of our vehicles. I can equip with captured stuff, but we're a bit short on transport." He watched lights flash confusedly for a second on the display before the steady march of red lights blinking to green resumed.

"But now you're without artillery," Bannister said. "And the Patriot army's got none."

"Can't have it both ways. We had less than an hour to offload and get the Dayan boats off planet before the spy satellites came over. Now we've got the town and nobody knows we've landed. If this goes right the first the Confederates'll know about us is when their spy snooper stops working."

"We had some luck," Bannister said. "Boat in harbor, communications out to the mainland—"

"Don't confuse luck with decision factors," Falkenberg answered. "Why would I take an isolated hole full of Loyalists if there weren't some advantages?" Privately he knew better. The telephone exchange taken by infiltrating scouts, the power plant almost unguarded and falling to three minutes' brief combat—it was all luck you could count on with good men, but it was luck. "Excuse me." He touched a stud in response to a low humming note. "Yes?"

"Train coming in from the mines, John Christian," Major Savage reported. "We have the station secured, shall we let it go past the block outside town?"

"Sure, stick with the plan, Jerry. Thanks." The miners coming home after a week's work on the sides of Ranier Crater were due for a surprise.

They waited until all the lights changed to green. Every objective was taken. Power plants, communications, homes of leading citizens, public buildings, railway station and airport, police station . . . Allansport and its eleven thousand citizens were under control. A timer display ticked off the minutes until the spy satellite would be overhead.

Falkenberg spoke to the intercom. "Sergeant Major, we have twenty-nine minutes to get this place looking normal for this time of night. See to it."

"Sir!" Calvin's unemotional voice was reassuring.

"I don't think the Confederates spend much time examining pictures of the boondocks anyway," Falkenberg told Bannister. "But it's best not to take any chances." Motors roared as ground cars and choppers were put under cover. Another helicopter flew overhead looking for telltales.

"As soon as that thing's past get the troops on the packet ship," Falkenberg ordered. "And send in Captain Svoboda, Mayor Hastings, and the local militia colonel—Ardway, wasn't it?"

"Yes, sir," Calvin answered. "Colonel Martine Ardway. I'll see if he's up to it, Colonel."

"Up to it, Sergeant Major? Was he hurt?"

"He had a pistol, Colonel. Twelve millimeter thing, big slug, slow bullet, couldn't penetrate armor but he bruised hell out of two troopers. Monitor Badnikov laid him out with a rifle butt. Surgeon says he'll be all right."

"Good enough. If he's able to come I want him here."

"Sir."

Falkenberg turned back to the desk and used the computer to produce a planetary map. "Where would the supply ship go from here, Mr. Bannister?"

The secretary traced a course. "It would—and will—stay inside this island chain. Nobody but a suicide takes ships into open water on this planet. With no land to interrupt them the seas go sixty meters in storms." He indicated a route from Allansport to Cape Titan, then through an island chain in the Sea of Mariners. "Most ships stop at Preston Bay to deliver metalshop goods for the ranches up on Ford Heights Plateau. The whole area's Patriot territory and you could liberate it with one stroke."

Falkenberg studied the map, then said, "No. So most ships stop there—do some go directly to Astoria?" He pointed to a city eighteen hundred kilometers east of Preston Bay.

"Yes, sometimes—but the Confederates keep a big garrison in Astoria, Colonel. Much larger than the one in Preston Bay. Why go twenty-five hundred kilometers to fight a larger enemy force when there's good Patriot country at half the distance?"

"For the same reason the Confederates don't put much strength at Preston Bay. It's isolated. The Ford Heights ranches are scattered—look, Mr. Secretary, if we take Astoria we have the key to the whole Columbia River Valley. The Confederates won't know if we're going north to Doak's Ferry, east to Grand Forks and on into the capital plains, or west to Ford Heights. If I take Preston Bay first they'll know what I intend because there's only one thing a sane man could do from there."

"But the Columbia Valley people aren't reliable! You won't get good recruits—"

They were interrupted by a knock. Sergeant Major Calvin ushered in Roger Hastings and Martine Ardway. The militiaman had a lump over his left eye, and his cheek was bandaged.

Falkenberg stood to be introduced and offered his hand, which Roger Hastings ignored. Ardway stood rigid for a second, then extended his own. "I won't say I'm pleased to meet you, Colonel Falkenberg, but my compliments on an operation well conducted."

"Thank you, Colonel. Gentlemen, please be seated. You have met Captain Svoboda, my Provost?" Falkenberg indicated a lanky officer in battledress who'd come in with them. "Captain Svoboda will be in command of this town when the Forty-second moves out."

Ardway's eyes narrowed with interest. Falkenberg smiled. "You'll see it soon enough, Colonel. Now, the rules of occupation are simple. As mercenaries, gentlemen, we are subject to the CoDominium's Laws of War. Public property is seized in the name of the Free States. Private holdings are secure, and any property requisitioned will be paid for. Any property used to aid resistance, whether directly or as a place to make conspiracy, will be instantly confiscated."

Ardway and Hastings shrugged. They'd heard all this before. At one time the CD tried to suppress mercenaries. When that failed the Fleet rigidly enforced the Grand Senate's Laws of War, but now the Fleet was weakened by budget cuts and a new outbreak of U.S.-Soviet hatred. New Washington was isolated and it might be years before CD Marines appeared to enforce rules the Grand Senate no longer cared about.

"I have a problem, gentlemen," Falkenberg said. "This city is Loyalist, and I must withdraw my regiment. There aren't any Patriot soldiers yet. I'm leaving enough force to complete the conquest of this peninsula, but Captain Svoboda will have few troops in Allansport itself. Since we cannot occupy the city, it can legitimately be destroyed to prevent it from becoming a base against me."

"You can't!" Hastings protested, jumping to his feet, shattering a glass ashtray. "I was sure all that talk about preserving private property was a lot of crap!" He turned to Bannister. "Howard, I told you last time all you'd succeed in doing was burning down the whole god-damn planet! Now you import soldiers to do it for you! What in God's name can you get from this war?"

"Freedom," Bannister said proudly. "Allansport is a nest of traitors anyway."

"Hold it," Falkenberg said gently.

"Traitors!" Bannister repeated. "You'll get what you deserve, you—"

"TENSH-HUT!" Sergeant Major Calvin's command startled them. "The Colonel said you was to hold it."

"Thank you," Falkenberg said quietly. The silence was louder than the shouts had been. "I said I could burn the city, not that I intended to. However, since I won't I must have hostages." He handed Roger Hastings a computer typescript. "Troops are quartered in homes of these persons. You will note that you and Colonel Ardway are at the top of my list. All will be detained, and anyone who escapes will be replaced by members of his family. Your property and ultimately your lives are dependent on your cooperation with Captain Svoboda until I send a regular garrison here. Is this understood?"

Colonel Ardway nodded grimly. "Yes, sir. I agree to it."

"Thank you," Falkenberg said. "And you, Mr. Mayor?"

"I understand."

"And?" Falkenberg prompted.

"And what? You want me to like it? What kind of sadist are you?"

"I don't care if you like it, Mr. Mayor. I am waiting for you to agree."

"He doesn't understand, Colonel," Martine Ardway said. "Roger, he's asking if you agree to serve as a hostage for the city. The others will be asked as well. If he doesn't get enough to agree he'll burn the city to the ground."

"Oh." Roger felt a cold knife of fear. What a hell of a choice.

"The question is," Falkenberg said, "will you accept the responsibilities of the office you hold and keep your damn people from making trouble?"

Roger swallowed hard. *I wanted to be mayor so I could erase the hatreds of the rebellion.* "Yes. I agree."

"Excellent. Captain Svoboda."

"Sir."

"Take the mayor and Colonel Ardway to your office and interview the others. Notify me when you have enough hostages to ensure security."

"Yes, sir. Gentlemen?" It was hard to read his expression as he showed them to the door. The visor of his helmet was up, but Svoboda's angular face remained in shadow. As he escorted them from the room the intercom buzzed.

"The satellite's overhead," Major Savage reported. "All correct, John Christian. And we've secured the passengers off that train."

The office door closed. Roger Hastings moved like a robot across the bustling city council chamber room, only dimly aware of the bustle of headquarters activities around him. The damn war, the fools, the bloody damned fools—couldn't they ever leave things alone?

XVI

A DOZEN MEN in camouflage battledress led a slim pretty girl across hard-packed sands to the water's edge. They were glad to get away from the softer sands above the highwater mark nearly a kilometer from the pounding surf. Walking in that had been hell, with shifting powder sands infested with small burrowing carnivores too stupid not to attack a booted man.

The squad climbed wordlessly into the waiting boat while their leader tried to assist the girl. She needed no help. Glenda Ruth wore tan nylon coveralls and an equipment belt, and she knew this planet and its dangers better than the soldiers. Glenda Ruth Horton had been taking care of herself for twenty-four of her twenty-six years.

White sandy beaches dotted with marine life exposed by the low tide stretched in both directions as far as they could see. Only the boat and its crew showed that the planet had human life. When the coxswain started the boat's water jet the whirr sent clouds of tiny sea birds into frantic activity.

The fast packet *Maribell* lay twelve kilometers off-shore, well beyond the horizon. When the boat arrived deck cranes dipped to seize her and haul the flat-bottomed craft to her davits. Captain Ian Frazer escorted Glenda Ruth to the chart room.

Falkenberg's battle staff waited there impatiently, some sipping whiskey, others staring at charts whose information they had long since absorbed. Many showed signs of seasickness: the eighty-hour voyage from Allansport had been rough, and it hadn't helped that the ship pushed along at thirty-three kilometers an hour, plowing into big swells among the islands.

Ian saluted, then took a glass from the steward and offered it to Glenda Ruth. "Colonel Falkenberg, Miss Horton. Glenda Ruth is the patriot leader in the Columbia Valley. Glenda Ruth, you'll know Secretary Bannister."

She nodded coldly as if she did not care for the rebel minister, but she put out her hand to Falkenberg and shook his in a thoroughly masculine way. She had other masculine gestures, but even with her brown hair tucked neatly under a visored cap no one would mistake her for a man. She had a heart-shaped face and large green eyes, and her weathered tan might have been envied by the great ladies of the CoDominium.

"My pleasure, Miss Horton," Falkenberg said perfunctorily. "Were you seen?"

Ian Frazer looked pained. "No, sir. We met the rebel group and it seemed safe enough, so Centurion Michaels and I borrowed some clothing from the ranchers and let Glenda Ruth take us to town for our own look." Ian moved to the chart table.

"The fort's up here on the heights." Frazer pointed to the coastal chart. "Typical wall and trench system. Mostly they depend on the Friedlander artillery to control the city and river mouth."

"What's in there, Ian?" Major Savage asked.

"Worst thing is artillery," the Scout Troop commander answered. "Two batteries of 105's and a battery of 155's, all self-propelled. As near as we can figure it's a standard Friedland detached battalion."

"About six hundred Friedlanders, then," Captain Rottermill said thoughtfully. "And we're told there's a regiment of Earth mercenaries. Anything else?"

Ian glanced at Glenda Ruth. "They moved in a squadron of Confederate Regular Cavalry last week," she said. "Light armored cars. We think they're due to move on, because there's nothing for them to do here, but nobody knows where they're going."

"That is odd," Rottermill said. "There's not a proper petrol supply for them here—where would they go?"

Glenda Ruth regarded him thoughtfully. She had little use for mercenaries. Freedom was something to be won, not bought and paid for. But they needed these men, and at least this one had done his homework. "Probably to the Snake Valley. They've got wells and refineries there." She indicated the flatlands where the Snake and Columbia merged at Doak's Ferry six hundred kilometers to the north. "That's Patriot country and cavalry could be useful to supplement the big fortress at the Ferry."

"Damn bad luck all the same, Colonel," Rottermill said. "Nearly three thousand men in that damned fortress and we've not a lot more. How's the security, Ian?"

Frazer shrugged. "Not tight. The Earth goons patrol the city, doing MP duty, checking papers. No trouble avoiding them."

"The Earthies make up most of the guard details too," Glenda Ruth added. "They've got a whole rifle regiment of them."

"We'll not take that place by storm, John Christian," Major Savage said carefully. "Not without losing half the regiment."

"And just what are your soldiers for?" Glenda Ruth demanded. "Do they fight sometimes?"

"Sometimes." Falkenberg studied the sketch his scout commander was making. "Do they have sentries posted, Captain?"

"Yes, sir. Pairs in towers and walking guards. There are radar dishes every hundred meters, and I expect there are body capacitance wires strung outside as well."

"I told you," Secretary Bannister said smugly. There was triumph in his voice, in contrast to the grim concern of Falkenberg and his officers. "You'll have to raise an army to take that place. Ford Heights is our only chance, Colonel. Astoria's too strong for you."

"No!" Glenda Ruth's strong, low-pitched voice commanded attention. "We've risked everything to gather the Columbia Valley Patriots. If you don't take Astoria now, they'll go back to their ranches. I was opposed to starting a new revolution, Howard Bannister. I don't think we can stand another long war like the last one. But I've organized my father's friends, and in two days I'll command a fighting force. If we scatter now I'll never get them to fight again."

"Where is your army—and how large is it?" Falkenberg asked.

"The assembly area is two hundred kilometers north of here. I have six hundred riflemen now and another five thousand coming. A force that size can't hide!" She regarded Falkenberg without enthusiasm. They needed a strong organized nucleus to win, but she was trusting her friends' lives to a man she'd never met. "Colonel, my ranchers can't face Confederate Regulars or Friedland armor without support, but if you take Astoria we'll have a base we can hold."

"Yes." Falkenberg studied the maps as he thought about the girl. She had a more realistic appreciation of irregular forces than Bannister—but how reliable was she? "Mr. Bannister, we can't take Astoria without artillery even with your Ford Heights ranchers. I need Astoria's guns, and the city's the key to the whole campaign anyway.

With it in hand there's a chance to win this war quickly."

"But it can't be done!" Bannister insisted.

"Yet it must be done," Falkenberg reminded him. "And we do have surprise. No Confederate knows we're on this planet and won't for—" he glanced at his pocket computer—"twenty-seven hours, when Weapons Detachment knocks down the snooper. Miss Horton, have you made trouble for Astoria lately?"

"Not for months," she said. Was this mercenary, this man Falkenberg, different? "I only came this far south to meet you."

Captain Frazer's sketch of the fort lay on the table like a death warrant. Falkenberg watched in silence as the scout drew in machine-gun emplacements along the walls.

"I forbid you to risk the revolution on some mad scheme!" Bannister shouted. "Astoria's far too strong. You said so yourself."

Glenda Ruth's rising hopes died again. Bannister was giving the mercenaries a perfect out.

Falkenberg straightened and took a brimming glass from the steward. "Who's junior man here?" He looked around the steel-riveted chart room until he saw an officer near the bulkhead. "Excellent. Lieutenant Fuller was a prisoner on Tanith, Mr. Bannister. Until we caught him—Mark, give us a toast."

"A toast, Colonel?"

"Montrose's toast, Mister. Montrose's toast."

Fear clutched Bannister's guts into a hard ball. Montrose! And Glenda Ruth stared uncomprehendingly, but there was reborn hope in her eyes. . . .

"Aye aye, Colonel." Fuller raised his glass. "He either fears his fate too much, or his desserts are small, who dares not put it to the touch, to win or lose it all."

Bannister's hands shook as the officers drank. Falkenberg's wry smile, Glenda Ruth's answering look of comprehension and admiration—they were all crazy! The lives of all the patriots were at stake, and the man and the girl, both of them, they were insane!

Maribell swung to her anchors three kilometers off-shore from Astoria. The fast-moving waters of the Columbia swept around her toward the ocean some nine kilometers downstream, where waves crashed in a line of breakers five meters high. Getting across the harbor bar was a tricky business, and even in the harbor itself the tides were too fierce for the ship to dock.

Maribell's cranes hummed as they swung cargo lighters off her decks. The air-cushion vehicles moved gracelessly across the water and over the sandy beaches to the corrugated aluminum warehouses, where they left cargo containers and picked up empties.

In the fortress above Astoria the officer of the guard dutifully logged the ship's arrival into his journal. It was

the most exciting event in two weeks. Since the rebellion had ended there was little for his men to do.

He turned from the tower to look around the encampment. Blasted waste of good armor, he thought. No
point in having self-propelled guns as harbor guards.
The armor wasn't used, since the guns were in concrete
revetments. The lieutenant had been trained in mobile
war, and though he could appreciate the need for control over the mouth of New Washington's largest river,
he didn't like this duty. There was no glory in manning
an impregnable fortress.

Retreat sounded and all over the fort men stopped to
face the flags. The Franklin Confederacy colors fluttered down the staff to the salutes of the garrison.
Although as guard officer he wasn't supposed to, the
lieutenant saluted as the trumpets sang.

Over by the guns men stood at attention, but *they*
didn't salute. Friedland mercenaries, they owed the
Confederacy no loyalty that hadn't been bought and
paid for. The lieutenant admired them as soldiers, but
they were not likable. It was worth knowing them,
though, since nobody else could handle armor like them.
He had managed to make friends with a few. Someday,
when the Confederacy was stronger, they would dis-
pense with mercenaries, and until then he wanted to
learn all he could. There were rich planets in this sector
of space, planets that Franklin could add to the Confederacy now that the rebellion was over. With the CD
Fleet weaker every year, opportunities at the edges of
inhabited space grew, but only for those ready for them.

When retreat ended he turned back to the harbor.
An ugly cargo lighter was coming up the broad roadway
to the fort. He frowned, puzzled, and climbed down
from the tower.

When he reached the gate the lighter had halted
there. Its engine roared, and it was very difficult to
understand the driver, a broad-shouldered seaman-
stevedore who was insisting on something.

"I got no orders," the Earth mercenary guardsman
was protesting. He turned to the lieutenant in relief.

"Sir, they say they have a shipment for us on that thing."

"What is it?" the lieutenant shouted. He had to say it again to be heard over the roar of the motors. "What is the cargo?"

"Damned if I know," the driver said cheerfully. "Says on the manifest 'Astoria Fortress, attention supply officer.' Look, Lieutenant, we got to be moving. If the captain don't catch the tide he can't cross the harbor bar tonight and he'll skin me for squawrk bait! Where's the supply officer?"

The lieutenant looked at his watch. After retreat the men dispersed rapidly and supply officers kept short hours. "There's nobody to offload," he shouted.

"Got a crane and crew here," the driver said. "Look, just show me where to put this stuff. We got to sail at slack water."

"Put it out here," the lieutenant said.

"Right. You'll have a hell of a job moving it though." He turned to his companion in the cab. "OK, Charlie, dump it!"

The lieutenant thought of what the supply officer would say when he found he'd have to move the ten-by-five-meter containers. He climbed into the bed of the cargo lighter. In the manifest pocket of each container was a ticket reading "COMMISSARY SUPPLIES."

"Wait," he ordered. "Private, open the gates. Driver, take this over there." He indicated a warehouse near the center of the camp. "Offload at the big doors."

"Right. Hold it, Charlie," Sergeant Major Calvin said cheerfully. "The lieutenant wants the stuff inside." He gave his full attention to driving the ungainly GEM.

The lighter crew worked the crane efficiently, stacking the cargo containers by the warehouse doors. "Sign here," the driver said.

"I—perhaps I better get someone to inventory the cargo."

"Aw, for Christ's sake," the driver protested. "Look, you can see the seals ain't broke—here, I'll write it in. 'Seals intact, but cargo not inspected by recip—' How you spell 'recipient,' Lieutenant?"

"Here, I'll write it for you" He did, and signed with his name and rank. "Have a good voyage?"

"Naw. Rough out there, and getting worse. We got to scoot, more cargo to offload."

"Not for us!"

"Naw, for the town. Thanks, Lieutenant." The GEM pivoted and roared away as the guard lieutenant shook his head. What a mess. He climbed into the tower to write the incident up in the day book. As he wrote he sighed. One hour to dark, and three until he was off duty. It had been a long, dull day.

Three hours before dawn the cargo containers silently opened, and Captain Ian Frazer led his scouts onto the darkened parade ground. Wordlessly they moved toward the revetted guns. One squad formed ranks and marched toward the gates, rifles at slope arms.

The sentries turned. "What the hell?" one said. "It's not time for our relief, who's there?"

"Can it," the corporal of the squad said. "We got orders to go out on some goddam perimeter patrol. Didn't you get the word?"

"Nobody tells me anythin'—uh." The sentry grunted as the corporal struck him with a leather bag of shot. His companion turned quickly, but too late. The squad had already reached him.

Two men stood erect in the starlight at the posts abandoned by the sentries. Astoria was far over the horizon from Franklin, and only a faint red glow to the west indicated the companion planet.

The rest of the squad entered the guardhouse. They moved efficiently among the sleeping relief men, and when they finished the corporal took a communicator from his belt. "Laertes."

On the other side of the parade ground, Captain Frazer led a group of picked men to the radar control center. There was a silent flurry of bayonets and rifle butts. When the brief struggle ended Ian spoke into his communicator. "Hamlet."

There was no answer, but he hadn't expected one.

Down in the city other cargo containers opened in darkened warehouses. Armed men formed into platoons and marched through the dockside streets. The few civilians who saw them scurried for cover; no one had much use for the Earthling mercenaries the Confederates employed.

A full company marched up the hill to the fort. On the other side, away from the city, the rest of the regiment crawled across plowed fields, heedless of radar alarms but careful of the sentries on the walls above. They passed the first line of capacitance wires and Major Savage held his breath. Ten seconds, twenty. He sighed in relief and motioned the troops to advance.

The marching company reached the gate. Sentries challenged them while others in guard towers watched in curiosity. When the gates swung open the tower guards relaxed. The officer of the watch must have had special orders . . .

The company moved into the armored car park. Across the parade ground a sentry peered into the night. Something out there? "Halt! Who's there?" There was only silence.

"See something, Jack?" his companion asked.

"Dunno—look out there. By the bushes. Somethin'— My God, Harry! The field's full of men! CORPORAL OF THE GUARD! Turn out the Guard!" He hesitated before taking the final step, but he was sure enough to risk his sergeant's scathing displeasure. A stabbing finger hit the red alarm button, and lights blazed around the camp perimeter. The sirens hooted, and he had time to see a thousand men in the field near the camp; then a burst of fire caught him, and he fell.

The camp erupted into confusion. The Friedland gunners woke first. They wasted less than a minute before their officers realized the alarm was real. Then the gunners boiled out of the barracks to save their precious armor, but from each revetment, bursts of machine-gun fire cut into them. Gunners fell in heaps as the rest scurried for cover. Many had not brought personal weapons in their haste to serve the guns, and they lost time going back for them.

Major Savage's men reached the walls and clambered over. Alternate sections kept the walls under a ripple of fire, and despite their heavy battle armor the men climbed easily in Washington's lower gravity. Officers sent them to the parade ground where they added their fire to that of the men in the revetments. Hastily set machine guns isolated the artillery emplacements with a curtain of fire.

That artillery was the fort's main defense. Once he was certain it was secure, Major Savage sent his invaders by waves into the camp barracks. They burst in with grenades and rifles ready, taking whole companies before their officers could arrive with the keys to their weapons racks. Savage took the Confederate Regulars that way, and only the Freidlanders had come out fighting; but their efforts were directed toward their guns, and there they had no chance.

Meanwhile the Earth mercenaries, never very steady troops at best, called for quarter; many had not fired a shot. The camp defenders fought as disorganized groups against a disciplined force whose communications worked perfectly.

At the fortress headquarters building the alarms woke Commandant Albert Morris. He listened in disbelief to the sounds of battle, and although he rushed out half-dressed, he was too late. His command was engulfed by nearly four thousand screaming men. Morris stood a moment in indecision, torn by the desire to run to the nearest barracks and rally what forces he could, but he decided his duty was in the communications room. The Capital must be told. Desperately he ran to the radio shack.

Everything seemed normal inside, and he shouted orders to the duty sergeant before he reallzed he had never seen the man before. He turned to face a squad of leveled rifles. A bright light stabbed from a darker corner of the room.

"Good morning, sir," an even voice said.

Commandant Morris blinked, then carefully raised his hands in surrender. "I've no sidearms. Who the hell are you, anyway?"

"Colonel John Christian Falkenberg, at your service. Will you surrender this base and save your men?"

Morris nodded grimly. He'd seen enough outside to know the battle was hopeless. His career was finished too, no matter what he did, and there was no point in letting the Friedlanders be slaughtered. "Surrender to whom?"

The light flicked off and Morris saw Falkenberg. There was a grim smile on the Colonel's lips. "Why, to the Great Jehovah and the Free States of Washington, Commandant. . . ."

Albert Morris, who was no historian, did not understand the reference. He took the public address mike the grim troopers handed him. Fortress Astoria had fallen.

Twenty-three hundred kilometers to the west at Allansport, Sergeant Sherman White slapped the keys to launch three small solid rockets. They weren't very powerful birds, but they could be set up quickly, and they had the ability to loft a hundred kilos of tiny steel cubes to 140 kilometers. White had very good information on the Confederate satellite's ephemeris; he'd observed it for its past twenty orbits.

The target was invisible over the horizon when Sergeant White launched his interceptors. As it came overhead the small rockets had climbed to meet it. Their radar fuses sought the precise moment, then they exploded in a cloud of shot that rose as it spread. It continued to climb, halted, and began to fall back toward the ground. The satellite detected the attack and beeped alarms to its masters. Then it passed through the cloud at fourteen hundred meters per second relative to the shot. Four of the steel cubes were in its path.

XVII

FALKENBERG STUDIED THE manuals on the equipment in the Confederate command car as it raced northward along the Columbia Valley road toward Doak's Ferry. Captain Frazer's scouts were somewhere ahead with the captured cavalry equipment and behind Falkenberg the regiment was strung out piecemeal. There were men on motorcycles, in private trucks, horse-drawn wagons, and on foot.

There'd be more walking soon. The captured cavalry gear was a lucky break, but the Columbia Valley wasn't technologically developed. Most local transport was by animal power, and the farmers relied on the river to ship produce to the deepwater port at Astoria. The river boats and motor fuel were the key to the operation. There wasn't enough of either.

Glenda Ruth Horton had surprised Falkenberg by not arguing about the need for haste, and her ranchers were converging on all the river ports, taking heavy casualties in order to seize boats and fuel before the scattered Confederate occupation forces could destroy them. Meanwhile Falkenberg had recklessly flung the regiment northward.

"Firefight ahead," his driver said. "Another of them one battery posts."

"Right." Falkenberg fiddled with the unfamliar controls until the map came into sharper focus, then activated the comm circuit.

"Sir," Captain Frazer answered. "They've got a battery of 105's and an MG Company in there. More than I can handle."

"Right. pass it by. Let Miss Horton's ranchers keep it under siege. Found any more fuel?"

Frazer laughed unpleasantly. "Colonel, you can adjust the carburetors in these things to handle a lot, but Christ, they bloody well won't run on paraffin. There's not even farm machinery out here! We're running on fumes now, and damned low-grade fumes at that."

"Yeah." The Confederates were getting smarter. For the first hundred kilometers they took fueling stations intact, but now, unless the patriots were already in control, the fuel was torched before Frazer's fast-moving scouts arrived. "Keep going as best you can, Captain."

"Sir. Out."

"We got some reserve fuel with the guns," Sergeant Major Calvin reminded him. The big RSM sat in the turret of the command caravan and at frequent intervals fondled the thirty-mm cannon there. It wasn't much of a weapon, but it had been a long time since the RSM was gunner in an armored vehicle. He was hoping to get in some fighting.

"No. Those guns have to move east to the passes. They're sure to send a reaction force from the capital, Top Soldier."

But would they? Falkenberg wondered. Instead of moving northwest from the capital to reinforce the fortress at Doak's Ferry, they might send troops by sea to retake Astoria. It would be a stupid move, and Falkenberg counted on the Confederates acting intelligently. As far as anyone knew, the Astoria Fortress guns dominated the river mouth.

A detachment of Weapons Battalion remained there with antiaircraft rockets to keep reconnaissance at a distance, but otherwise Astoria was held only by a hastily raised Patriot force stiffened with a handful of mercenaries. The Friedlander guns had been taken out at night.

If Falkenberg's plan worked, by the time the Confederates knew what they faced, Astoria would be strongly held by Valley Patriot armies, and other Patriot forces would have crossed the water to hold Allansport. It was a risky battle plan, but it had one merit: it was the only one that could succeed.

Leading elements of the regiment covered half the six hundred kilometers north to Doak's Ferry in ten hours. Behind Falkenberg's racing lead groups the main body of the regiment moved more ponderously, pausing to blast out pockets of resistance where that could be quickly done, otherwise bypassing them for the Patriot irregulars to starve into submission. The whole Valley was rising, and the further north Falkenberg went the greater the number of Patriots he encountered. When they reached the four-hundred-kilometer point, he sent Glenda Ruth Horton eastward toward the passes to join Major Savage and the Friedland artillery. Like the regiment, the ranchers moved by a variety of means: helicopters, GEM's, trucks, mules, and on foot.

"Real boot straps," Hiram Black said. Black was a short, wind-browned rancher commissioned colonel by the Free States Council and sent with Falkenberg to aid in controlling rebel forces. Falkenberg liked the man's dry humor and hard realism. "General Falkenberg, we got the damnedest collection in the history of warfare."

"Yes." There was nothing more to say. In addition to the confused transport situation, there was no standardization of weapons: they had hunting pieces, weapons taken from the enemy, the regiment's own equipment, and stockpiles of arms smuggled in by the Free States before Falkenberg's arrival. "That's what computers are for," Falkenberg said.

"Crossroad coming up," the driver warned. "Hang on." The crossing was probably registered by the guns of an untaken post eight kilometers ahead. Frazer's cavalry had blinded its hilltop observation radars before passing it by, but the battery would have had brief sights of the command car.

The driver suddenly halted. There was a sharp whistle,

and an explosion rocked the caravan. Shrapnel rattled off the armored sides. The car bounded into life and accelerated.

"Ten credits you owe me, Seregant Major," the driver said. "Told you they'd expect me to speed up."

"Think I wanted to win the bet, Carpenter?" Calvin asked.

They drove through rolling hills covered with the golden tassels of corn plants. Genetic engineering had made New Washington's native grain one of the most valuable food crops in space. Superficially similar to Earth maize, this corn had a growing cycle of two local years. Toward the end of the cycle hydrostatic pressures built up until it exploded, but if harvested in the dry period New Washington corn was high-protein dehydrated food energy, palatable when cooked in water, and good fodder for animals as well.

"Ought to be getting past the opposition now," Hiram Black said. "Expect the Feddies'll be pulling back to the fort at Doak's Ferry from here on."

His estimate was confirmed a half hour later when Falkenberg's comm set squawked into action. "We're in a little town called Madselin, Colonel," Frazer said. "Used to be a garrison here, but they're running up the road. There's a citizen's committee to welcome us."

"To hell with the citizen's committee," Falkenberg snapped. "Pursue the enemy!"

"Colonel, I'd be very pleased to do so, but I've no petrol at all."

Falkenberg nodded grimly. "Captain Frazer, I want the scouts as far north as they can get. Isn't there *any* transport?"

There was a long silence. "Well, sir, there are bicycles . . ."

"Then use bicycles, by God! Use whatever you have to, Captain, but until you are stopped by the enemy you will continue the advance, bypassing concentrations. Snap at their heels. Ian, they're scared. They don't know what's chasing them, and if you keep the pressure on they won't stop to find out. Keep going, laddie. I'll bail you out if you get in trouble."

"Aye, aye, Colonel. See you in Doak's Ferry."

"Correct. Out."

"Can you keep that promise, General?" Hiram Black asked.

Falkenberg's pale blue eyes stared through the rancher. "That depends on how reliable your Glenda Ruth Horton is, Colonel Black. Your ranchers are supposed to be gathering along the Valley. With that threat to their flanks the Confederates will not dare form a defense line south of Doak's Ferry. If your Patriots don't show up then it's another story entirely." He shrugged. Behind him the Regiment was strung out along three hundred kilometers of roads, its only flank protection its speed and the enemy's uncertainties. "It's up to her in more ways than one," Falkenberg continued. "She said the main body of Friedland armor was in the capital area."

Hiram Black sucked his teeth in a very unmilitary way. "General, if Glenda Ruth's sure of something, you can damn well count on it."

Sergeant Major Calvin grunted. The noise spoke his thoughts better than words. It was a hell of a thing when the life of the Forty-second had to depend on a young colonial girl.

"How did she come to command the Valley ranchers, anyway?" Falkenberg asked.

"Inherited it," Black answered. "Her father was one hell of a man, General. Got himself killed in the last battle of the first revolution. She'd been his chief of staff. Old Josh trusted her more'n he did most of his officers. So would I, if I was you, General."

"I already do." To Falkenberg the regiment was more than a mercenary force. Like any work of art, it was an instrument perfectly forged—its existence and perfection its own reason for existence.

But unlike any work of art, because the regiment was a military unit, it had to fight battles and take casualties. The men who died in battle were mourned. They weren't the regiment, though, and it would exist when every man now in it was dead. The Forty-second had faced defeat before and might find it again—but this time the regiment itself was at hazard. Falkenberg was gambling not merely their lives, but the Forty-second itself.

He studied the battle maps as they raced northward. By keeping the enemy off balance, one regiment could do the work of five. Eventually, though, the Confederates would no longer retreat. They were falling back on their fortress at Doak's Ferry, gathering strength and concentrating for a battle that Falkenberg could never win. Therefore that battle must not be fought until the ranchers had concentrated. Meanwhile, the regiment must bypass Doak's Ferry and turn east to the mountain passes, closing them before the Friedland armor and Covenant Highlanders could debauch onto the western plains.

"Think you'll make it?" Hiram Black asked. He watched as Falkenberg manipulated controls to move symbols across the map tank in the command car. "Seems to me the Friedlanders will reach the pass before you can."

"They will," Falkenberg said. "And if they get through, we're lost." He twirled a knob, sending a bright blip representing Major Savage with the artillery racing diagonally from Astoria to Hillyer Gap, while the main force of the regiment continued up the Columbia, then turned east to the mountains, covering two legs of a triangle. "Jerry Savage could be there first, but he won't have enough force to stop them." Another set of symbols crawled across the map. Instead of a distinctly formed body, this was a series of rivulets coming together at the pass. "Miss Horton has also promised to be there with reinforcements and supplies—enough to hold in the first battle, anyway. If they delay the Friedlanders long enough for the rest of us to get there, we'll own the entire agricultural area of New Washington. The revolution will be better than half over."

"And what if she can't get there—or they can't hold the Friedlanders and Covenant boys?" Hiram Black asked.

Sergeant Major Calvin grunted again.

XVIII

HILLYER GAP WAS a six-kilometer-wide hilly notch in the high mountain chain. The Aldine Mountains ran roughly northwest to southeast, and were joined at their midpoint by the southward stretching Temblors. Just at the join was the Gap that connected the capital city plain to the east with the Columbia Valley to the west.

Major Jeremy Savage regarded his position with satisfaction. He not only had the twenty-six guns taken from the Friedlanders at Astoria, but another dozen captured in scattered outposts along the lower Columbia, and all were securely dug in behind hills overlooking the Gap. Forward of the guns were six companies of infantry, Second Battalion and half of Third, with a thousand ranchers behind in reserve.

"We won't be outflanked, anyway," Centurion Bryant observed. "Ought to hold just fine, sir."

"We've a chance," Major Savage agreed. "Thanks to Miss Horton. You must have driven your men right along."

Glenda Ruth shrugged. Her irregulars had run low on fuel 180 kilometers west of the Gap, and she'd brought them on foot in one forced march of thirty hours, after sending her ammunition supplies ahead with the last drops of gasoline. "I just came on myself, Major. Wasn't a question of driving them, the men followed right enough."

Jeremy Savage looked at her quickly. The slender girl was not very pretty at the moment, with her coveralls streaked with mud and grease, her hair falling in strings from under her cap, but he'd rather have seen her just then than the current Miss Universe. With her troops and ammunition supplies he had a chance to hold this position. "I suppose they did at that." Centurion Bryant turned away quickly with something caught in his throat.

"Can we hold until Colonel Falkenberg gets here?" Glenda Ruth asked. "I expect them to send everything they've got."

"We sincerely hope they do," Jeremy Savage answered. "It's our only chance, you know. If that armor gets onto open ground . . ."

"There's no other way onto the plains, Major," she replied. "The Temblors go right on down to the Matson swamplands, and nobody's fool enough to risk armor there. Great Bend's Patriot country. Between the swamps and the Patriot irregulars it'd take a week to cross the Matson. If they're comin' by land, they're comin' through here."

"And they'll be coming," Savage finished for her. "They'll want to relieve the Doak's Ferry fortress before we can get it under close siege. At least that was John Christian's plan, and he's usually right."

Glenda Ruth used her binoculars to examine the road. There was nothing out there—yet. "This colonel of yours. What's in this for him? Nobody gets rich on what we can pay."

"I should think you'd be glad enough we're here," Jeremy said.

"Oh, I'm glad all right. In 240 hours Falkenberg's isolated every Confederate garrison west of the Temblors. The capital city forces are the only army left to fight—you've almost liberated the planet in one campaign."

"Luck," Jeremy Savage murmured. "Lots of it, all good."

"Heh." Glenda Ruth was contemptuous. "I don't believe in that, no more do you. Sure, with the Confederates scattered out on occupation duty anybody who could get troops to move fast enough could cut the Feddies up before they got into big enough formations to resist. The fact is, Major, nobody believed that could be done except on maps. Not with real troops—and he did it. That's not luck, that's genius."

Savage shrugged. "I wouldn't dispute that."

"No more would I. Now answer this—just what is a real military genius doing commanding mercenaries on a jerkwater agricultural planet? A man like that should be Lieutenant General of the CoDominium."

"The CD isn't interested in military genius, Miss Horton. The Grand Senate wants obedience, not brilliance."

"Maybe. I hadn't heard Lermontov was a fool, and they made him Grand Admiral. O.K, the CoDominium had no use for Falkenberg. But why Washington, Major? With that regiment you could take anyplace but Sparta and give the Brotherhoods a run for it there." She swept the horizon with the binoculars, and Savage could not see her eyes.

This girl disturbed him. No other Free State official questioned the good fortune of hiring Falkenberg. "The regimental council voted to come here because we were sick of Tanith, Miss Horton."

"Sure." She continued to scan the bleak foothills in front of them. "Look, I'd better get some rest if we've got a fight coming—and we do. Look just at the horizon on the left side of the road." As she turned away Centurion Bryant's communicator buzzed. The outposts had spotted the scout elements of an armored task force.

As Glenda Ruth walked back to her bunker, her head felt as if it would begin spinning. She had been born on New Washington and was used to the planet's forty-hour rotation period, but lack of sleep made her almost intoxicated even so.

Walking on pillows, she told herself. That had been Harley Hastings' description of how they felt when they didn't come in until dawn.

Is Harley out there with the armor? she wondered.

She hoped not. It would never have worked, but he's such a good boy. Too much of a boy though, trying to act like a man. While it's nice to be treated like a lady sometimes, he could never believe I could do anything for myself at all. . . .

Two ranchers stood guard with one of Falkenberg's corporals at her bunker. The corporal came to a rigid present; the ranchers called a greeting. Glenda Ruth made a gesture, halfway between a wave and a return of the corporal's salute and went inside. The contrast couldn't have been greater, she thought. Her ranchers weren't about to make themselves look silly, with present arms, and salutes, and the rest of it.

She stumbled inside and wrapped herself in a thin blanket without undressing. Somehow the incident outside bothered her. Falkenberg's men were military professionals. All of them. What were they doing on New Washington?

Howard Bannister asked them here. He even offered them land for a permanent settlement and he had no right to do that. There's no way to control a military force like that without keeping a big standing army, and the cure is worse than the disease.

But without Falkenberg the revolution's doomed.

And what happens if we win it? What will Falkenberg do after it's over? Leave? I'm afraid of him because he's not the type to just leave.

And, she thought, to be honest Falkenberg's a very attractive man. I liked just the way he toasted. Howard gave him the perfect out, but he didn't take it.

She could still remember him with his glass lifted, an enigmatic smile on his lips—and then he went into the packing crates himself, along with Ian and his men.

But courage isn't anything special. What we need here is loyalty, and that he's never promised at all . . .

There was no one to advise her. Her father was the only man she'd ever really respected. Before he was killed, he'd tried to tell her that winning the war was only a small part of the problem. There were countries on Earth that had gone through fifty bloody revolutions before they were lucky enough to have a tyrant gain control and stop them. Revolution's the easy part, as her father used to say. Ruling afterwards—that's something else entirely.

As she fell asleep she saw Falkenberg in a dream. What if Falkenberg wouldn't let them keep their revolution? His hard features softened in a swirling mist. He was wearing military uniform and sat at a desk, Sergeant Major Calvin at his side.

"These can live. Kill those. Send these to the mines," Falkenberg ordered.

The big sergeant moved tiny figures that looked like model soldiers, but they weren't all troops. One was her father. Another was a group of her ranchers. And they weren't models at all. They were real people reduced to miniatures whose screams could barely be heard as the stern voice continued to pronounce their dooms. . . .

Brigadier Wilfred von Mellenthin looked up the hill toward the rebel troop emplacements, then climbed back down into his command caravan to wait for his scouts to report. He had insisted that the Confederacy send his armor west immediately after the news arrived that Astoria had fallen, but the General Staff wouldn't let him go.

Fools, he thought. The staff said it was too big a risk. Von Mellenthin's Friedlander armored task force was the Confederacy's best military unit, and it couldn't be risked in a trap.

Now the General Staff was convinced that they faced only one regiment of mercenaries. One regiment, and that must have taken heavy casualties in storming Astoria. So the staff said. Von Mellenthin studied the map table and shrugged.

Someone was holding the Gap, and he had plenty of respect for the New Washington ranchers. Given rugged terrain like that in front of him, they could put up a good fight. A good enough fight to blunt his force. But, he decided, it was worth it. Beyond the Gap was open terrain, and the ranchers would have no chance there.

The map changed and flowed as he watched. Scouts

reported, and Von Mellenthin's staff officers checked the reports, correlated the data, and fed it onto his displays. The map showed well-dug-in infantry, far more of it than von Mellenthin had expected. That damned Falkenberg. The man had an uncanny ability to move troops.

Von Mellenthin turned to the Chief of Staff. "Horst, do you think he has heavy guns here already?"

Oberst Carnap shrugged. "*Weiss nicht*, Brigadier. Every hour gives Falkenberg time to dig in at the Gap, and we have lost many hours."

"Not Falkenberg," von Mellenthin corrected. "He is now investing the fortress at Doak's Ferry. We have reports from the commandant there. Most of Falkenberg's force must be far to the west."

He turned back to his maps. They were as complete as they could be without closer observation.

As if reading his mind, Carnap asked, "Shall I send scouting forces, Brigadier?"

Von Mellenthin stared at the map as if it might tell him one more detail, but it would not. "No. We go through with everything," he said in sudden decision. "Kick their arses, don't pee on them."

"*Jawohl*." Carnap spoke quietly into the command circuit. Then he looked up again. "It is my duty to point out the risk, Brigadier. We will take heavy losses if they have brought up artillery."

"I know. But if we fail to get through now, we may never relieve the fortress in time. Half the war is lost when Doak's Ferry is taken. Better heavy casualties immediately than a long war. I will lead the attack myself. You will remain with the command caravan."

"*Jawohl*, Brigadier."

Von Mellenthin climbed out of the heavy caravan and into a medium tank. He took his place in the turret, then spoke quietly to the driver. "Forward."

The armor brushed the infantry screens aside as if they had not been there. Von Mellenthin's tanks and their supporting infantry cooperated perfectly to pin down and root out the opposition. The column moved swiftly forward to cut the enemy into disorganized fragments for the following Covenanter infantry to mop up.

Von Mellenthin was chewing up the blocking force piecemeal as his brigade rushed deeper into the Gap. It was all too easy, and he thought he knew why.

The sweating tankers approached the irregular ridge at the very top of the pass. Suddenly a fury of small arms and mortar fire swept across them. The tanks moved on, but the infantry scrambled for cover. Armor and infantry were separated for a moment, and at that instant his lead tanks reached the mine fields.

Brigadier von Mellenthin began to worry. Logic told him the mine fields couldn't be wide or dense, and if he punched through he would reach the soft headquarters areas of his enemies. Once there his tanks would make short work of the headquarters and depots, the Covenanter infantry would secure the pass, and his brigade could charge across the open fields beyond.

But—if the defenders had better transport than the General Staff believed, and thus had thousands of mines, he was dooming his armor.

"Evaluation," he demanded. The repeater screen in his command tank swam, then showed the updated maps. His force was bunched up, and his supporting infantry was pinned and taking casualties. "Recommendation?"

"Send scouting forces," Oberst Carnap's voice urged.

Von Mellenthin considered it for a moment. Compromises in war are often worse than either course of action. A small force could be lost without gaining anything. Divided forces can be defeated in detail. He had only moments to reach a decision. "Boot, don't spatter," he said. "We go forward."

They reached the narrowest part of the Gap. His force now bunched together even more, and his drivers, up to now automatically avoiding terrain features that might be registered by artillery, had to approach conspicuous landmarks. Brigadier von Mellenthin gritted his teeth.

The artillery salvo was perfectly delivered. The brigade had less than a quarter-minute warning as the radars picked up the incoming projectiles. Then the shells exploded all at once, dropping among his tanks to brush away the last of the covering infantry.

As the barrage lifted, hundreds of men appeared from the ground itself. A near perfect volley of infantry-carried anti-tank rockets slammed into his tanks. Then the radars showed more incoming mail—and swam in confusion.

"*Ja*, that too," von Mellenthin muttered. His counter-battery screens showed a shower of gunk.

The defenders were firing chaff, hundreds of thousands of tiny metal chips which slowly drifted to the ground. Neither side could use radar to aim indirect fire, but von Mellenthin's armor was under visual observation, while the enemy guns had never been precisely located.

Another time-on-target salvo landed. "Damned good shooting," von Mellenthin muttered to his driver. There weren't more than five seconds between the first and the last shell's arrival.

The brigade was being torn apart on this killing ground. The lead elements ran into more mine fields. Defending infantry crouched in holes and ditches, tiny little groups that his covering infantry could sweep aside in a moment if it could get forward, but the infantry was cut off by the barrages falling behind and around the tanks.

There was no room to maneuver and no infantry support, the classic nightmare of an armor commander. The already rough ground was strewn with pits and ditches. High explosive antitank shells fell all around his force. There were not many hits yet, but any disabled tanks could be pounded to pieces, and there was nothing to shoot back at. The lead tanks were under steady fire, and the assault slowed.

The enemy expended shells at a prodigal rate. Could they keep it up? If they ran out of shells it was all over. Von Mellenthin hesitated. Every moment kept his armor in hell.

Doubts undermined his determination. Only the Confederate General Staff told him he faced no more than Falkenberg's Legion, and the staff had been wrong before. Whatever was out there had taken Astoria before the commandant could send a single message. At almost the same moment the observation satellite was killed over Allansport. Every fortress along the Columbia was invested within hours. Surely not even Falkenberg could do that with no more than one regiment!

What was he fighting? If he faced a well-supplied force with transport enough to continue this bombardment for hours, not minutes, the brigade was lost. His brigade, the finest armor in the worlds, lost to the faulty intelligence of these damned colonials!

"Recall the force. Consolidate at Station Hildebrand." The orders flashed out, and the tanks fell back, rescuing the pinned infantry and covering their withdrawal. When the brigade assembled east of the Gap, von Mellenthin had lost an eighth of his tanks, and he doubted if he would recover any of them

XIX

THE HONOR GUARD presented arms as the command caravan unbuttoned. Falkenberg acknowledged their salutes and strode briskly into the staff bunker. "Tensh-Hut!" Sergeant Major Calvin commanded.

"Carry on, gentlemen. Major Savage, you'll be pleased to know I've brought the regimental artillery. We landed it yesterday. Getting a bit thin, wasn't it?"

"That it was, John Christian," Jeremy Savage answered grimly. "If the battle had lasted another hour we'd have been out of everything. Miss Horton, you can relax now—the colonel said carry on."

"I wasn't sure," Glenda Ruth huffed. She glanced outside where the honor guard was dispersing and scowled in disapproval. "I'd hate to be shot for not bowing properly."

Officers and troopers in the CP tensed, but nothing happened. Falkenberg turned to Major Savage. "What were the casualties, Major?"

"Heavy, sir. We have 283 effectives remaining in Second Battalion."

Falkenberg's face was impassive. "And how many walking wounded?"

"Sir, that includes the walking wounded."

"I see." Sixty-five percent casualties, not including the walking wounded. "And Third?"

"I couldn't put together a corporal's guard from the

391

two companies. The survivors are assigned to headquarters duties."

"What's holding the line out there, Jerry?" Falkenberg demanded.

"Irregulars and what's left of Second Battalion, Colonel. We are rather glad to see you, don't you know?"

Glenda Ruth Horton had a momentary struggle with herself. Whatever she might think about all the senseless militaristic rituals Falkenberg was addicted to, honesty demanded that she say something. "Colonel, I owe you an apology. I'm sorry I implied that your men wouldn't fight at Astoria."

"The question is, Miss Horton, will yours? I have two batteries of the Forty-second's artillery, but I can add nothing to the line itself. My troops are investing Doaks Ferry, my cavalry and First Battalion are on Ford Heights, and the regiment will be scattered for three more days. Are you saying your ranchers can't do as well as my mercenaries?"

She nodded unhappily. "Colonel, we could never have stood up to that attack. The Second's senior centurion told me many of his mortars were served by only one man before the battle ended. We'll never have men that steady."

Falkenberg looked relieved. "Centurion Bryant survived, then."

"Why—yes."

"Then the Second still lives." Falkenberg nodded to himself in satisfaction.

"But we can't stop another attack by that armor!" Glenda Ruth protested.

"But maybe we won't have to," Falkenberg said. "Miss Horton, I'm betting that von Mellenthin won't risk his armor until the infantry has cleared a hole. From his view he's tried and run into something he can't handle. He doesn't know how close it was.

"Meanwhile, thanks to your efforts in locating transport, we have the artillery partly resupplied. Let's see what we can do with what we've got."

* * *

Three hours later they looked up from the maps. "That's it, then," Falkenberg said.

"Yes." Glenda Ruth looked over the troop dispositions. "Those forward patrols are the key to it all," she said carefully.

"Of course." He reached into his kit bag. "Have a drink?"

"Now?" But why not? "Thank you, I will." He poured two mess cups partly full of whiskey and handed her one. "I can't stay long, though," she said.

He shrugged and raised the glass. "A willing foe. But not too willing," he said.

She hesitated a moment, then drank. "It's a game to you, isn't it?"

"Perhaps. And to you?"

"I hate it. I hate all of it. I didn't want to start the rebellion again." She shuddered. "I've had enough of killing and crippled men and burned farms—"

"Then why are you here?" he asked. There was no mockery in his voice—and no contempt. The question was genuine.

"My friends asked me to lead them, and I couldn't let them down."

"A good reason," Falkenberg said.

"Thank you." She drained the cup. "I've got to go now. I have to get into my battle armor."

"That seems reasonable, although the bunkers are well built."

"I won't be in a bunker, Colonel. I'm going on patrol with my ranchers."

Falkenberg regarded her critically. "I wouldn't think that wise, Miss Horton. Personal courage in a commanding officer is an admirable trait, but—"

"I know." She smiled softly. "But it needn't be demonstrated because it is assumed, right? Not with us. I can't order the ranchers, and I don't have years of tradition to keep them—that's the reason for all the ceremonials, isn't it?" she asked in surprise.

Falkenberg ignored the question. "The point is, the men follow you. I doubt they'd fight as hard for me if you're killed."

"Irrelevant, Colonel. Believe me, I don't want to take this patrol out, but if I don't take the first one, there may never be another. We're not used to holding lines, and it's taking some doing to keep my troops steady."

"And so you have to shame them into going out."

She shrugged. "If I go, they will."

"I'll lend you a Centurion and some headquarters' guards."

"No. Send the same troops with me that you'll send with any other Patriot force." She swayed for a moment. Lack of sleep and the whiskey and the knot of fear in her guts combined for a moment. She held the edge of the desk for a second while Falkenberg looked at her.

"Oh damn," she said. Then she smiled slightly. "John Christian Falkenberg, don't you see why it has to be this way?"

He nodded. "I don't have to like it. All right, get your final briefing from the sergeant major in thirty-five minutes. Good luck, Miss Horton."

"Thank you." She hesitated but there was nothing more to say.

The patrol moved silently through low scrub brush. Something fluttered past her face; a flying squirrel, she thought. There were a lot of gliding creatures on New Washington.

The low hill smelled of toluenes from the shells and mortars that had fallen there in the last battle. The night was pitch dark, with only Franklin's dull red loom at the far western horizon, so faint that it was sensed, not seen. Another flying fox chittered past, darting after insects and screeching into the night.

A dozen ranchers followed in single file. Behind them came a communications maniple from the Forty-second's band. Glenda wondered what they did with their instruments when they went onto combat duty, and wished she'd asked. The last man on the trail was a Sergeant Hruska, who'd been sent along by Sergeant Major Calvin at the last minute. Glenda Ruth had been glad to see him, although she felt guilty about having him along.

And that's silly, she told herself. Men think that way. I don't have to. I'm not trying to prove anything.

The ranchers carried rifles. Three of Falkenberg's men did also. The other two had communications gear, and Sergeant Hruska had a submachine gun. It seemed a pitifully small force to contest ground with Covenant Highlanders.

They passed through the final outposts of her nervous ranchers and moved into the valleys between the hills. Glenda Ruth felt completely alone in the silence of the night. She wondered if the others felt it too. Certainly the ranchers did. They were all afraid. What of the mercenaries? she wondered. They weren't alone, anyway. They were with comrades who shared their meals and their bunkers.

As long as one of Falkenberg's men was alive, there would be someone to care about those lost. And they do care, she told herself. Sergeant Major Calvin, with his gruff dismissal of casualty reports. "Bah. Another trooper," he'd said when they told him an old messmate had bought it in the fight with the armor. Men.

She tried to imagine the thoughts of a mercenary soldier, but it was impossible. They were too alien.

Was Falkenberg like the rest of them?

They were nearly a kilometer beyond the lines when she found a narrow gulley two meters deep. It meandered down the hillsides along the approaches to the outposts behind her, and any attacking force assaulting her sector would have to pass it. She motioned the men into the ditch.

Waiting was hardest of all. The ranchers continually moved about, and she had to crawl along the gulley to whisper them into silence. Hours went by, each an agony of waiting. She glanced at her watch to see that no time had elapsed since the last time she'd looked, and resolved not to look again for a full fifteen minutes.

After what seemed fifteen minutes, she waited for what was surely another ten, then looked to see that only eleven minutes had passed altogether. She turned in disgust to stare into the night, blinking against the shapes that formed; shapes that couldn't be real.

Why do I keep thinking about Falkenberg? And why did I call him by his first name?

The vision of him in her dream still haunted her as well. In the starlit gloom she could almost see the miniature figures again. Falkenberg's impassive orders rang in her ears. "Kill this one. Send this one to the mines." He could do that, she thought. He could—

The miniatures were joined by larger figures in battle armor. With a sudden start she knew they were real. Two men stood motionless in the draw below her.

She touched Sergeant Hruska and pointed. The trooper looked carefully and nodded. As they watched, more figures joined the pair of scouts, until soon there were nearly fifty of them in the fold of the hill two hundred meters away. They were too far for her squad's weapons to have much effect, and a whispered command sent Hruska crawling along the gulley to order the men to stay down and be silent.

The group continued to grow. She couldn't see them all, and since she could count nearly a hundred she must be observing the assembly area of a full company. Were these the dreaded Highlanders? Memories of her father's defeat came unwanted, and she brushed them away. They were only hired men—but they fought for glory, and somehow that was enough to make them terrible.

After a long time the enemy began moving toward her.

They formed a V-shape with the point aimed almost directly at her position, and she searched for the ends of the formation. What she saw made her gasp.

Four hundred meters to her left was another company of soldiers in double file. They moved silently and swiftly up the hill, and the lead elements were already far beyond her position. Frantically she looked to the right, focusing the big electronic light-amplifying glasses —and saw another company of men half a kilometer away. A full Highlander Battalion was moving right up her hill in an inverted M, and the group in front of her was the connecting sweep to link the assault columns. In minutes they would be among the ranchers in the defense line.

Still she waited, until the dozen Highlanders of the point were ten meters from her. She shouted commands. "Up and at them! Fire!" From both ends of her ditch the mercenaries' automatic weapons chattered, then their fire was joined by her riflemen. The point was cut down to a man, and Sergeant Hruska directed fire on the main body, while Glenda Ruth shouted into her communicator.

"Fire Mission. Flash Uncle Four!"

There was a moment's delay which seemed like years. "Flash Uncle Four." Another long pause. "On the way," an unemotional voice answered. She thought it sounded like Falkenberg, but she was too busy to care.

"Reporting," she said. "At least one battalion of light infantry in assault columns is moving up Hill 905 along ridges Uncle and Zebra."

"They're shifting left." She looked up to see Hruska. The noncom pointed to the company in front of her position. Small knots of men curled leftward. They hugged the ground and were visible only for seconds.

"Move some men to that end of the gulley," she ordered. It was too late to shift artillery fire. Anyway, if the Highlanders ever got to the top of the ridge, the ranchers wouldn't hold them. She held her breath and waited.

There was the scream of incoming artillery, then the night was lit by bright flashes. VT shells fell among the distant enemy on the left flank. "Pour it on!" she shouted into the communicator. "On target!"

"Right. On the way."

She was sure it was Falkenberg himself at the other end. Catlike she grinned in the dark. What was a colonel doing as a telephone orderly? Was he worried about her? She almost laughed at the thought. Certainly he was, the ranchers would be hard to handle without her.

The ridge above erupted in fire. Mortars and grenades joined the artillery pounding the leftward assault column. Glenda Ruth paused to examine the critical situation to the right. The assault force five hundred meters away was untouched and continued to advance toward the top of the ridge. It was going to be close.

She let the artillery hold its target another five minutes while her riflemen engaged the company in front of her, then took up the radio again. The right-hand column had nearly reached the ridges, and she wondered if she had waited too long.

"Fire mission. Flash Zebra Nine."

"Zebra Nine," the emotionless voice replied. There was a short delay, then, "On the way." The fire lifted from the left flank almost immediately, and two minutes later began to fall five hundred meters to the right.

"They're flanking us, Miss," Sergeant Hruska reported. She'd been so busy directing artillery at the assaults against the ridge line that she'd actually forgotten her twenty men were engaged in a firefight with over a hundred enemies. "Shall we pull back?" Hruska asked.

She tried to think, but it was impossible in the noise and confusion. The assault columns were still moving ahead, and she had the only group that could observe the entire attack. Every precious shell had to count "No. We'll hold on here."

"Right, Miss." The sergant seemed to be enjoying himself. He moved away to direct the automatic weapons and rifle fire. How long can we hold? Glenda Ruth wondered.

She let the artillery continue to pound the right-hand assault force for twenty minutes. By then the Highlanders had nearly surrounded her and were ready to assault from the rear. Prayerfully she lifted the radio again.

"Fire Mission. Give me everything you can on Jack Five—and for God's sake don't go over. We're at Jack Six."

"Flash Jack Five," the voice acknowledged immediately. There was a pause. "On the way." They were the most beautiful words she'd ever heard.

Now they waited. The Highlanders rose to charge. A wild sound filled the night. MY GOD, PIPES! she

thought. But even as the infantry moved the pipes were
drowned by the whistle of artillery. Glenda Ruth dove
to the bottom of the gulley and saw that the rest of her
command had done the same.

The world erupted in sound. Millions of tiny fragments at enormous velocity filled the night with death.
Cautiously she lifted a small periscope to look behind
her.

The Highlander company had dissolved. Shells were
falling among dead men, lifting them to be torn apart
again and again as the radar-fused shells fell among
them. Glenda Ruth swallowed hard and swept the glass
around. The left assault company had reformed and
was turning back to attack the ridge. "Fire Flash Uncle Four," she said softly.

"Interrogative."

"FLASH UNCLE FOUR!"

"Uncle Four. On the way."

As soon as the fire lifted from behind them her men
returned to the lip of the gulley and resumed firing, but
the sounds began to die away.

"We're down to the ammo in the guns now, Miss,"
Hruska reported. "May I have your spare magazines?"

She realized with a sudden start that she had yet to
fire a single shot.

The night wore on. Whenever the enemy formed up
to assault her position he was cut apart by the merciless
artillery. Once she asked for a box barrage all around
her gulley—by that time the men were down to three
shots in each rifle, and the automatic weapons had no
ammo at all. The toneless voice simply answered, "On
the way."

An hour before dawn nothing moved on the hill.

XX

THE THIN NOTES of a military trumpet sounded across the barren hills of the Gap. The ridges east of Falkenberg's battle line lay dead, their foliage cut to shreds by shell fragments, the very earth thrown into crazy-quilt craters partly burying the dead. A cool wind blew through the Gap, but it couldn't dispel the smells of nitro and death.

The trumpet sounded again. Falkenberg's glasses showed three unarmed Highlander officers carrying a white flag. An ensign was dispatched to meet them, and the young officer returned with a blindfolded Highlander major.

"Major MacRae, Fourth Covenant Infantry," the officer introduced himself after the blindfold was removed. He blinked at the bright lights of the bunker. "You'll be Colonel Falkenberg."

"Yes. What can we do for you, Major?"

"I've orders to offer a truce for burying the dead. Twenty hours, Colonel, if that's agreeable."

"No. Four days and nights—160 hours, Major," Falkenberg said.

"A hundred sixty hours, Colonel?" The burly Highlander regarded Falkenberg suspiciously. "You'll want that time to complete your defenses."

"Perhaps. But twenty hours is not enough time to transfer the wounded men. I'll return all of yours— under parole, of course. It's no secret I'm short of medical supplies, and they'll receive better care from their own surgeons."

The Highlander's face showed nothing, but he paused. "You wouldn't tell me how many there be?" He was silent for a moment, then speaking very fast, he said, "The time you set is within my discretion, Colonel." He held out a bulky dispatch case. "My credentials and instructions. " 'Twas a bloody battle, Colonel. How many of my laddies have ye killed?"

Falkenberg and Glenda Ruth glanced at each other. There is a bond between those who have been in combat together, and it can include those of the other side. The Covenant officer stood impassively, unwilling to say more, but his eyes pleaded with them.

"We counted 409 bodies, Major," Glenda Ruth told him gently. "And—" she looked at Falkenberg, who nodded. "We brought in another 370 wounded." The usual combat ratio is four men wounded to each killed; nearly sixteen hundred Covenanters must have been taken out of action in the assault. Toward the end the Highlanders were losing men in their efforts to recover their dead and wounded.

"Less than four hundred," the major said sadly. He stood to rigid attention. "Hae your men search the ground well, Colonel. There's aye more o' my lads out there." He saluted and waited for the blindfold to be fixed again. "I thank you, Colonel."

As the mercenary officer was led away Falkenberg turned to Glenda Ruth with a wistful smile. "Try to bribe him with money and he'd challenge me, but when I offer him his men back—" He shook his head sadly.

"Have they really given up?" Glenda Ruth asked.

"Yes. The truce finishes it. Their only chance was to break through before we brought up more ammunition and reserves, and they know it."

"But why? In the last revolution they were so terrible, and now—why?"

"It's the weakness of mercenaries," Falkenberg explained crisply. "The fruits of victory belong to our employers, not us. Friedland can't lose her armor and Covenant can't lose her men, or they've nothing more to sell."

"But they fought before!"

"Sure, in a fluid battle of maneuver. A frontal assault is always the most costly kind of battle. They tried to force the passage, and we beat them fairly. Honor is satisfied. Now the Confederacy will have to bring up its own Regulars if they want to force a way through the Gap. I don't think they'll squander men like that, and anyway it takes time. Meanwhile we've got to go to Allansport and deal with a crisis."

"What's wrong there?" she asked.

This came in regimental code this morning." He handed her a message flimsy.

FALKENBERG FROM SVOBODA BREAK PATRIOT ARMY LOOTING ALLANSPORT STOP REQUEST COURT OF INQUIRY INVESTIGATE POSSIBLE VIOLATIONS OF LAWS OF WAR STOP EXTREMELY INADVISABLE FOR ME TO COMPLY WITH YOUR ORDERS TO JOIN REGIMENT STOP PATRIOT ARMY ACTIONS PROVOKING SABOTAGE AND REVOLT AMONG TOWNSPEOPLE AND MINERS STOP MY SECURITY FORCES MAY BE REQUIRED TO HOLD THE CITY STOP AWAIT YOUR ORDERS STOP RESPECTFULLY ANTON SVOBODA BREAK BREAK MESSAGE ENDSXXX

She read it twice. "My God, Colonel—what's going on there?"

"I don't know," he said grimly. "I intend to find out. Will you come with me as a representative of the Patriot Council?"

"Of course—but shouldn't we send for Howard Bannister? The Council elected him President."

"If we need him we'll get him. Sergeant Major."

"Sir!"

"Put Miss Horton's things on the troop carrier with mine. I'll take the Headquarters Guard platoon to Allansport."

"Sir. Colonel, you'll want me along."

"Will I? I suppose so, Sergeant Major. Get your gear aboard."

"Sir."

"It's probably already there, of course. Let's move out."

The personnel carrier took them to a small airfield where a jet waited. It was one of forty on the planet, and it would carry a hundred men; but it burned fuel needed for ammunition transport. Until the oil fields around Doak's Ferry could be secured it was fuel they could hardly afford.

The plane flew across Patriot-held areas, staying well away from the isolated Confederate strongpoints remaining west of the Gap. Aircraft had little chance of surviving in a combat environment when any infantryman could carry target-seeking rockets, while trucks could carry equipment to defeat airborne countermeasures. They crossed the Columbia Valley and turned southwest over the broad forests of Ford Heights Plateau, then west again to avoid Preston Bay where pockets of Confederates remained after the fall of the main fortress.

"You do the same thing, don't you?" Glenda Ruth said suddenly. "When we assaulted Preston Bay you let my people take the casualties."

Falkenberg nodded. "For two reasons. I'm as reluctant to lose troops as the Highlanders—and without the regiment you'd not hold the Patriot areas a thousand hours. You need us as an intact force, not a pile of corpses."

"Yes." It was true enough, but those were her friends who'd died in the assault. Would the outcome be worth it? Would Falkenberg *let* it be worth it?

Captain Svoboda met them at the Allansport field. "Glad to see you, sir. It's pretty bad in town."

"Just what happened, Captain?" Svoboda looked critically at Glenda Ruth, but Falkenberg said, "Report."

"Yes, sir. When the provisional governor arrived I turned over administration of the city as ordered. At that time the peninsula was pacified, largely due to the efforts of Mayor Hastings, who wants to avoid damage to the city. Hastings believes Franklin will send a large army from the home planet and says he sees no point in getting Loyalists killed and the city burned in resistance that won't change the final outcome anyway."

"Poor Roger—he always tries to be reasonable, and it never works," Glenda Ruth said. "But Franklin will send troops."

"Possibly," Falkenberg said. "But it takes time for them to mobilize and organize transport. Continue, Captain Svoboda."

"Sir. The Governor posted a list of proscribed persons whose property was forfeit. If that wasn't enough, he told his troops that if they found any Confederate government property, they could keep half its value. You'll see the results when we get to town, Colonel. There was looting and fire that my security forces and the local fire people only barely managed to control."

"Oh, Lord," Glenda Ruth murmured. "Why?"

Svoboda curled his lip. "Looters often do that, Miss Horton. You can't let troops sack a city and not expect damage. The outcome was predictable, Colonel. Many townspeople took to the hills, particularly the miners. They've taken several of the mining towns back."

Captain Svoboda shrugged helplessly. "The railway is cut. The city itself is secure, but I can't say how long. You only left me 150 troops to control eleven thousand people, which I did with hostages. The Governor brought another nine hundred men and that's not enough to rule *their* way. He's asked Preston Bay for more soldiers."

"Is that where the first group came from?" Glenda Ruth asked.

"Yes, Miss. A number of them, anyway."

"Then its understandable if not excusable, Colonel," she said. "Many ranches on Ford Heights were burned out by Loyalists in the first revolution. I suppose they think they're paying the Loyalists back."

Falkenberg nodded. "Sergeant Major!"

"Sir!"

"Put the Guard in battle armor and combat weapons.

Captain, we are going to pay a call on your provisional governor. Alert your men."

"Colonel!" Glenda Ruth protested. "You—what are you going to do?"

"Miss Horton, I left an undamaged town, which is now a nest of opposition. I'd like to know why. Let's go, Svoboda."

City Hall stood undamaged among burned-out streets. The town smelled of scorched wood and death, as if there'd been a major battle fought in the downtown area. Falkenberg sat impassive as Glenda Ruth stared unbelievingly at what had been the richest city outside the capital area.

"I tried, Colonel," Svoboda muttered. He blamed himself anyway. "I'd have had to fire on the Patriots and arrest the governor. You were out of communication, and I didn't want to take that responsibility without orders. Should I have, sir?"

Falkenberg didn't answer. Possible violations of mercenary contracts were always delicate situations. Finally he said, "I can hardly blame you for not wanting to involve the regiment in war with our sponsors."

The Patriot irregular guards at City Hall protested as Falkenberg strode briskly toward the Governor's office. They tried to bar the way, but when they saw his forty guardsmen in battle armor they moved aside.

The governor was a broad-shouldered former rancher who'd done well in commodities speculation. He was a skilled salesman, master of the friendly grip on the elbow and pat on the shoulder, the casual words in the right places, but he had no experience in military command. He glanced nervously at Sergeant Major Calvin and the grimfaced guards outside his office as Glenda introduced Falkenberg.

"Governor Jack Silana," she said. "The governor was active in the first revolution, and without his financial help we'd never have been able to pay your passage here, Colonel."

"I see." Falkenberg ignored the governor's offered hand. "Did you authorize more looting, Governor?" he asked. "I see some's still going on."

"Your mercenaries have all the tax money," Silana protested. He tried to grin. "My troops are being ruined to pay you. Why shouldn't the Fedsymps contribute to the war? Anyway, the real trouble began when a town girl insulted one of my soldiers. He struck her. Some townspeople interfered, and his comrades came to help. A riot started and someone called out the garrison to stop it—"

"And you lost control," Falkenberg said.

"The traitors got no more than they deserve anyway! Don't think *they* didn't loot cities when they won, Colonel. These men have seen ranches burned out, and they know Allansport's a nest of Fedsymp traitors."

"I see." Falkenberg turned to his Provost. "Captain, had you formally relinquished control to Governor Silana before this happened?"

"Yes, sir. As ordered."

"Then it's none of the regiment's concern. Were any of our troops involved?"

Svoboda nodded unhappily. "I have seven troopers and Sergeant Magee in arrest, sir. I've held summary court on six others myself."

"What charges are you preferring against Magee?" Falkenberg had personally promoted Magee once. The man had a mean streak, but he was a good soldier.

"Looting. Drunk on duty. Theft. And conduct prejudicial."

"And the others?"

"Three rapes, four grand theft, and one murder, sir. They're being held for a court. I also request an inquiry into my conduct as commander."

"Granted. Sergeant Major."

"Sir!"

"Take custody of the prisoners and convene a General Court. What officers have we for an investigation?"

"Captain Greenwood's posted for light duty only by the surgeon, sir."

"Excellent. Have him conduct a formal inquiry into Captain Svoboda's administration of the city."

"Sir."

"What will happen to those men?" Glenda Ruth asked.

"The rapists and murderer will be hanged if convicted. Hard duty for the rest."

"You'd hang your own men?" she asked. She didn't believe it, and her voice showed it.

"I cannot allow rot in my regiment," Falkenberg snapped. "In any event the Confederacy will protest this violation of the Laws of War to the CD."

Governor Silana laughed. "We protested often enough in the last revolution, and nothing came of it. I think we can chance it."

"Perhaps. I take it you will do nothing about this?"

"I'll issue orders for the looting to stop."

"Haven't you done so already?"

"Well, yes, Colonel—but the men, well, they're about over their mad now, I think."

"If previous orders haven't stopped it, more won't. You'll have to be prepared to punish violators. Are you?"

"I'll be damned if I'll hang my own soldiers to protect traitors!"

"I see. Governor, how do you propose to pacify this area?"

"I've sent for reinforcements—"

"Yes. Thank you. If you'll excuse us, Governor, Miss Horton and I have an errand." He hustled Glenda Ruth out of the office. "Sergeant Major, bring Mayor Hastings and Colonel Ardway to Captain Svoboda's office."

"They shot Colonel Ardway," Svoboda said. "The mayor's in the city jail."

"Jail?" Falkenberg muttered.

"Yes, sir. I had the hostages in the hotel, but Governor Silana—"

"I see. Carry on, Sergeant Major."

"Sir!"

"What do you want now, you bloody bastard?" Hastings demanded ten minutes later. The mayor was haggard, with several days' growth of stubble, and his face and hands showed the grime of confinement without proper hygiene facilities.

"One thing at a time, Mr. Mayor. Any trouble, Sergeant Major?"

Calvin grinned. "Not much, sir. The officer didn't want no problems with the Guard—Colonel, they got all them hostages crammed into cells."

"What have you done with my wife and children?" Roger Hastings demanded frantically. "I haven't heard anything for days."

Falkenberg looked inquiringly at Svoboda but got only a headshake. "See to the mayor's family, Sergeant Major. Bring them here. Mr. Hastings, do I understand that you believe this is my doing?"

"If you hadn't taken this city . . ."

"That was a legitimate military operation. Have you charges to bring against my troops?"

"How would I know?" Hastings felt weak. He hadn't been fed properly for days, and he was sick with worry about his family. As he leaned against the desk he saw Glenda Ruth for the first time. "You too, eh?"

"It was none of my doing, Roger." He had almost become her father-in-law. She wondered where young Lieutenant Harley Hastings was. Although she'd broken their engagement long ago, their disagreements had mostly been political, and they were still friends. "I'm sorry."

"It was your doing, you and the damned rebels. Oh, sure, you don't like burning cities and killing civilians, but it happens all the same—and you started the war. You can't shed the responsibility."

Falkenberg interrupted him. "Mr. Mayor, we have mutual interests still. This peninsula raises little food, and your people cannot survive without supplies. I'm told over a thousand of your people were killed in the riots, and nearly that many are in the hills. Can you get the automated factories and smelters operating with what's left?"

"After all this you expect me to—I won't do one damn thing for you, Falkenberg!"

"I didn't ask if you would, only if it could be done."

"What difference does it make?"

"I doubt you want to see the rest of your people

starving, Mr. Mayor. Captain, take the mayor to your quarters and get him cleaned up. By the time you've done that Sergeant Major Calvin will know what happened to his family." Falkenberg nodded dismissal and turned to Glenda Ruth. "Well, Miss Horton? Have you seen enough?"

"I don't understand."

"I am requesting you to relieve Silana of his post and return administration of this city to the regiment. Will you do it?"

Good Lord! she thought. "I haven't the authority."

"You've got more influence in the Patriot army than anyone else. The Council may not like it, but they'll take it from you. Meanwhile, I'm sending for the Sappers to rebuild this city and get the foundries going."

Everything moves so fast. Not even Joshua Horton had made things happen like this man. "Colonel, what is your interest in Allansport?"

"It's the only industrial area we control. There will be no more military supplies from off planet. We hold everything west of the Temblors. The Matson Valley is rising in support of the revolution, and we'll have it soon. We can follow the Matson to Vancouver and take that—and then what?"

"Why—then we take the capital city! The revolution's over!"

"No. That was the mistake you made last time. Do you really think your farmers, even with the Forty-second, can move onto level, roaded ground and fight set-piece battles? We've no chance under those conditions."

"But—" He was right. She'd always known it. When they defeated the Friedlanders at the Gap she'd dared hope, but the capital plains were not Hillyer Gap. "So it's back to attrition."

Falkenberg nodded. "We do hold all the agricultural areas. The Confederates will begin to feel the pinch soon enough. Meanwhile we chew around the edges. Franklin will have to let go—there's no profit in keeping colonies that cost money. They may try landing armies from the home world, but they'll not take us by surprise and they don't have *that* big an army. Eventually we'll wear them down."

She nodded sadly. It would be a long war after all, and she'd have to be in it, always raising fresh troops as the ranchers began to go home again—it would be tough enough holding what they had when people realized what they were in for. "But how do we pay your troops in a long war?"

"Perhaps you'll have to do without us."

"You know we can't. And you've always known it. What do you want?"

"Right now I want you to relieve Silana. Immediately."

"What's the hurry? As you say, it's going to be a long war."

"It'll be longer if more of the city is burned." He almost told her more, and cursed himself for the weakness of temptation. She was only a girl, and he'd known thousands of them since Grace left him all those years ago. The bond of combat wouldn't explain it, he'd known other girls who were competent officers, many of them—so why was he tempted at all? "I'm sorry," he said gruffly. "I must insist. As you say, you can't do without us."

Glenda Ruth had grown up among politicians and for four years had been a revolutionary leader herself. She knew Falkenberg's momentary hesitation was important, and that she'd never find out what it meant.

What was under that mask? Was there a man in there making all those whirlwind decisions? Falkenberg dominated every situation he fell into, and a man like that wanted more than money. The vision of Falkenberg seated at a desk pronouncing dooms on her people haunted her still.

And yet. There was more. A warrior leader of warriors who had won the adoration of uneducated privates—and men like Jeremy Savage as well. She'd never met anyone like him.

"I'll do it." She smiled and walked across the room to stand next to him. "I don't know why, but I'll do it. Have you got any friends, John Christian Falkenberg?"

The question startled him. Automatically he answered. "Command can have no friends, Miss Horton."

She smiled again. "You have one now. There's a condition to my offer. From now on, you call me Glenda Ruth. Please?"

A curious smile formed on the soldier's face. He regarded her with amusement, but there was something more as well. "It doesn't work, you know."

"What doesn't work?"

"Whatever you're trying. Like me, you've command responsibilities. It's lonely, and you don't like that. The reason command has no friends, Glenda Ruth, is not merely to spare the commander the pain of sending friends to their death. If you haven't learned the rest of it, learn it now, because some day you'll have to betray either your friends or your command, and that's a choice worth avoiding."

What am I doing? Am I trying to protect the revolution by getting to know him better—or is he right, I've no friends either, and he's the only man I ever met who could be— She let the thought fade out, and laid her hand on his for a brief second. "Let's go tell Governor Silana, John Christian. And let the little girl worry about her own emotions, will you? She knows what she's doing."

He stood next to her. They were very close and for a moment she thought he intended to kiss her. "No, you don't."

She wanted to answer, but he was already leaving the room and she had to hurry to catch him.

XXI

"I SAY WE only gave the Fedsymp traitors what they deserved!" Jack Silana shouted. There was a mutter of approval from the delegates, and open cheers in the bleachers overlooking the gymnasium floor. "I have great respect for Glenda Ruth, but she is not old Joshua," Silana continued. "Her action in removing me from a post given by President Bannister was without authority. I demand that the Council repudiate it." There was more applause as Silana took his seat.

Glenda Ruth remained at her seat for a moment. She looked carefully at each of the thirty men and women at the horseshoe table, trying to estimate just how many votes she had. Not a majority, certainly, but perhaps a dozen. She wouldn't have to persuade more than three or four to abandon the Bannister-Silana faction, but what then? The bloc she led was no more solid than Bannister's coalition. Just who would govern the Free States?

More men were seated on the gymnasium floor beyond the council table. They were witnesses, but their placement at the focus of the Council's attention made it look as if Falkenberg and his impassive officers might be in the dock. Mayor Hastings sat with Falkenberg, and the illusion was heightened by the signs of harsh treatment he'd received. Some of his friends looked even worse.

Beyond the witnesses the spectators chattered among themselves as if this were a basketball game rather than a solemn meeting of the supreme authority for three-quarters of New Washington. A gymnasium didn't seem a very dignified place to meet anyway, but there was no larger hall in Astoria Fortress.

Finally she stood. "No, I am not my father," she began. "He would have had Jack Silana shot for his actions!"

"Give it to 'em, Glenda Ruth!" someone shouted from the balcony.

Howard Bannister looked up in surprise. "We will have order here!"

"Hump it, you Preston Bay bastard!" the voice replied. The elderly rancher was joined by someone below. "Damn right, Ford Heights don't control the Valley!" There were cheers at that.

"Order! Order!" Bannister's commands drowned the shouting as the technicians turned up the amplifiers to full volume. "Miss Horton, you have the floor."

"Thank you. What I was trying to say is that we did not start this revolution to destroy New Washington! We must live with the Loyalists once it is over, and—"

"Fedsymp! She was engaged to a Feddie soldier!" "Shut up and let her talk!" "Order! ORDER!"

Falkenberg sat motionless as the hall returned to silence, and Glenda Ruth tried to speak again. "Bloody noisy lot," Jeremy Savage murmured.

Falkenberg shrugged. "Victory does that to politicians."

Glenda Ruth described the conditions she'd seen in Allansport. She told of the burned-out city, hostages herded into jail cells—

"Serves the Fedsymps right!" someone interrupted, but she managed to continue before her supporters could answer.

"Certainly they are Loyalists. Over a third of the people in the territory we control are. Loyalists are a majority in the capital city. Will it help if we persecute their friends here?"

"We won't ever take the capital the way we're fighting!" "Damn right! Time we moved on the Feddies." "Send the mercenaries in there, let 'em earn the taxes we pay!"

This time Bannister made little effort to control the crowd. They were saying what he had proposed to the Council, and one reason he supported Silana was because he needed the governor's merchant bloc with him on the war issue. After the crowd had shouted enough about renewing the war, Bannister used the microphone to restore order and let Glenda Ruth speak.

The Council adjourned for the day without deciding anything. Falkenberg waited for Glenda Ruth and walked out with her. "I'm glad we didn't get a vote today," she told him. "I don't think we'd have won."

"Noisy beggars," Major Savage observed again.

"Democracy at work," Falkenberg said coldly. "What do you need to convince the Council that Silana is unfit as a governor?"

"That's not the real issue, John," she answered. "It's really the war. No one is satisfied with what's being done."

"I should have thought we were doing splendidly," Savage retorted. "The last Confederate thrust into the Matson ran into your ambush as planned."

"Yes, that was brilliant," Glenda Ruth said.

"Hardly. It was the only possible attack route," Falkenberg answered. "You're very quiet, Mayor Hastings." They had left the gymnasium and were crossing the parade ground to the barracks where the Friedlanders had been quartered. Falkenberg's troops had it now, and they kept the Allansport officials with them.

"I'm afraid of that vote," Hastings said. "If they send Silana back, we'll lose everything."

"Then support me!" Falkenberg snapped. "My engineers already have the automated factories and mills in reasonable shape. With some help from you they'd be running again. Then I'd have real arguments against Silana's policies."

"But that's reason," Hastings protested. "You need the Allansport industry for your war effort. Colonel, it's a hell of a way to thank you for rescuing my family from that butcher, but I can't do it."

"I suppose you're expecting a miracle to save you?" Falkenberg asked.

"No. But what happens if you win? How long will you stay on the Ranier Peninsula? Bannister's people will be there one of these days—Colonel, my only chance is for the Confederacy to bring in Franklin troops and crush the lot of you!"

"And you'll be ruled from Franklin," Glenda Ruth said. "They won't give you as much home rule as you had last time."

"I know," Roger said miserably. "But what can I do? This revolt ruined our best chance. Franklin might have been reasonable in time—I was going to give good government to everyone. But you finished that."

"All of Franklin's satraps weren't like you, Roger," Glenda Ruth said. "And don't forget their war policies! They'd have got us sucked into their schemes and eventually we'd have been fighting the CoDominum itself. Colonel Falkenberg can tell you what it's like to be victim of a CD punitive expedition!"

"Christ, I don't know what to do," Roger said unhappily.

Falkenberg muttered something which the others didn't catch, then said, "Glenda Ruth, if you will excuse me, Major Savage and I have administrative matters to discuss. I would be pleased if you'd join me for dinner in the Officers' Mess at nineteen hundred hours."

"Why—thank you, John. I'd like to, but I must see the other delegates tonight. We may be able to win that vote tomorrow."

Falkenberg shrugged. "I doubt it. If you can't win it, can you delay it?"

"For a few days, perhaps—why?"

"It might help, that's all. If you can't make dinner, the regiment's officers are entertaining guests in the mess until quite late. Will you join us when you're done with politics?"

"Thank you. Yes, I will." As she crossed the parade ground to her own quarters, she wished she knew what Falkenberg and Savage were discussing. It wouldn't be administration—did it matter what the Council decided?

She looked forward to seeing John later, and the anticipation made her feel guilt. What is there about the man that does this to me? He's handsome enough, broad shoulders and thoroughly military—nonsense. I am damned if I'll believe in some atavistic compulsion to fall in love with warriors, I don't care what the anthropologists say. So why do I want to be with him? She pushed the thought away. There was something more important to think about. What would Falkenberg do if the Council voted against him? And beyond that, what would she do when he did it?

Falkenberg led Roger Hastings into his office. "Please be seated, Mr. Mayor."

Roger sat uncomfortably. "Look, Colonel, I'd like to help, but—"

"Mayor Hastings, would the owners of the Allansport industries rather have half of a going concern, or all of nothing?"

"What's that supposed to mean?"

"I will guarantee protection of the foundries and smelters in return for a half interest in them." When Hastings looked up in astonishment, Falkenberg continued. "Why not? Silana will seize them anyway. If my regiment is part owner, I may be able to stop him."

"It wouldn't mean anything if I granted it," Hastings protested. "The owners are on Franklin."

"You are the ranking Confederate official for the entire Ranier Peninsula," Falkenberg said carefully. "Legal or not, I want your signature on this grant." He handed Roger a sheaf of papers.

Hastings read them carefully. "Colonel, this also confirms a land grant given by the rebel government! I can't do that!"

"Why not? It's all public land—and that *is* in your power. The document states that in exchange for protection of lives and property of the citizens of Allansport you are awarding certain lands to my regiment. It notes that you don't consider a previous grant by the Patriot Government to be valid. There's no question of treason— you do want Allansport protected against Silana, don't you?"

"Are you offering to double-cross the Patriots?"

"No. My contract with Bannister specifically states that I cannot be made party to violations of the Laws of War. This document hires me to enforce them in an area already pacified. It doesn't state who might violate them."

"You're skating on damned thin ice, Colonel. If the Council ever saw this paper they'd hang you for treason!" Roger read it again. "I see no harm in signing, but I tell you in advance the Confederacy won't honor it. If Franklin wins this they'll throw you off this planet—if they don't have you shot."

"Let me worry about the future, Mr. Mayor. Right now *your* problem is protecting your people. You can help with that by signing."

"I doubt it," Hastings said. He reached for a pen. "So long as you know there isn't a shadow of validity to this because I'll be countermanded from the home world—" he scrawled his name and title across the papers and handed them back to Falkenberg.

Glenda Ruth could hear the regimental party across the wide parade ground. As she approached with Hiram Black they seemed to be breasting their way upstream through waves of sound, the crash of drums, throbbing, wailing bagpipes, mixed with off-key songs from intoxicated male baritones.

It was worse inside. As they entered a flashing saber swept within inches of her face. A junior captain saluted and apologized in a stream of words. "I was showing Oberleutnant Marcks a new parry I learned on Sparta, Miss. Please forgive me?" When she nodded the captain drew his companion to one side and the saber whirled again.

"That's a Friedland officer—all the Friedlanders are here," Glenda Ruth said. Hiram Black nodded grimly. The captured mercenaries wore dress uniform, green and gold contrasting with the blue and gold of Falkenberg's men. Medals flashed in the bright overhead lights. She looked across the glittering room and saw the colonel at a table on the far side.

Falkenberg and his companion stood when she reached

the table after a perilous journey across the crowded floor. Pipers marched past pouring out more sound.

Falkenberg's face was flushed, and she wondered if he were drunk. "Miss Horton, may I present Major Oscar von Thoma," he said formally. "Major von Thoma commands the Friedland artillery battalion."

"I—" She didn't know what to say. The Friedlanders were enemies, and Falkenberg was introducing her to the officer as his guest. "My pleasure," she stammered. "And this is Colonel Hiram Black."

Von Thoma clicked his heels The men stood stiffly until she was seated next to Falkenberg. That kind of chivalry had almost vanished, but somehow it seemed appropriate here. As the stewards brought glasses von Thoma turned to Falkenberg. "You ask too much," he said. "Besides, you may have fired the lands from the barrels by then."

"If we have we'll reduce the price," Falkenberg said cheerfully. He noted Glenda Ruth's puzzled expression. "Major von Thoma has asked if he can buy his guns back when the campaign is ended. He doesn't care for my terms."

Hiram Black observed drily, "Seems to me the Council's goin' to want a say in fixin' that price, General Falkenberg."

Falkenberg snorted contemptuously. "No."

He is drunk, Glenda Ruth thought. It doesn't show much, but—do I know him that well already?

"Those guns were taken by the Forty-second without Council help. I will see to it that they aren't used against Patriots, and the Council has no further interest in the matter." Falkenberg turned to Glenda Ruth. "Will you win the vote tomorrow?"

"There won't be a vote tomorrow."

"So you can't win," Falkenberg muttered. "Expected that. What about the war policy vote?"

"They'll be debating for the next two days—" she looked nervously at Major von Thoma. "I don't want to be impolite, but should we discuss that with him at the table?"

"I understand." Von Thoma got unsteadily to his

feet. "We will speak of this again, Colonel. It has been my pleasure, Miss Horton. Colonel Black." He bowed stiffly to each and went to the big center table where a number of Friedland officers were drinking with Falkenberg's.

"John, is this wise?" she asked. "Some of the Councillors are already accusing you of not wanting to fight—"

"Hell, they're callin' him a traitor," Black interrupted. "Soft on Fedsymps, consortin' with the enemy—they don't even like you recruitin' new men to replace your losses." Black hoisted a glass of whiskey and drained it at one gulp. "I wish some of 'em had been ridin' up the Valley with us! Glenda Ruth, that was some ride. And when Captain Frazer runs out of fuel, Falkenberg tells him, cool as you please, to use bicycles!" Black chuckled in rememberance.

"I'm serious!" Glenda Ruth protested. "John, Bannister hates you. I think he always has." The stewards brought whiskey for Falkenberg. "Wine or whiskey, Miss?" one asked.

"Wine—John, please, they're going to order you to attack the capital!"

"Interesting." His features tightened suddenly, and his eyes became alert. Then he relaxed and let the whiskey take effect. "If we obey those orders I'll need Major von Thoma's good offices to get *my* equipment back. Doesn't Bannister know what will happen if we let them catch us on those open plains?"

"Howie Bannister knows his way 'round a conspiracy better'n he does a battlefield, General," Black observed. "We give him the secretary of war title 'cause we thought he'd drive a hard bargain with you, but he's not much on battles."

"I've noticed," Falkenberg said. He laid his hand on Glenda Ruth's arm and gently stroked it. It was the first time he'd ever touched her, and she sat very still. "This is supposed to be a party," Falkenberg laughed. He looked up and caught the mess president's eye. "Lieutenant, have Pipe Major give us a song!"

The room was instantly still. Glenda Ruth felt the warmth of Falkenberg's hand. The soft caress promised

much more, and she was suddenly glad, but there was a
stab of fear as well. He'd spoken so softly, yet all those
people had stopped their drinking, the drums ceased,
the pipes, everything, at his one careless nod. Power
like that was frightening.

The burly Pipe Major selected a young tenor. One
pipe and a snare drum played as he began to sing. "Oh
Hae ye nae heard o' the false Sakeld, Hae ye nae heard
o' the keen Lord Scroop? For he ha' ta'en the Kinmont
Willie, to Haribee for to hang him up . . ."

"John, please listen," she pleaded.

"They hae ta'en the news to the Bold Bacleugh,
in Branksome Ha where he did lay,
that Lord Scroop has ta'en the Kinmont Willie,
between the hours of night and day.

He has ta'en the table wi' his hand,
he has made the red wine spring on hie.
Now Christ's curse be on my head, he said,
but avenged of Lord Scroop I will be."

"John, really."

"Perhaps you should listen," he said gently. He raised
his glass as the young voice rose and the tempo gathered.

"O is my basnet a widow's curch?
Or my lance the Wand o' the willow tree?
And is my hand a lady's lilly hand,
That this English lord should lightly me?"

The song ended. Falkenberg signaled to the steward.
"We'll have more to drink," he said. "And no more talk
of politics."

They spent the rest of the evening enjoying the party.
Both the Friedlanders and Falkenberg's mercenary officers were educated men, and it was a very pleasant
evening for Glenda Ruth to have a room full of warriors
competing to please her. They taught her the dances
and wild songs of a dozen cultures, and she drank far
too much.

Finally he stood. "I'll see you back to your quarters," Falkenberg told her.

"All right." She took his arm, and they went through the thinning crowd. "Do you often have parties like this?" she asked.

"When we can." They reached the door. A white-coated private appeared from nowhere to open it for them. He had a jagged scar across his face that ran down his neck until it disappeared into his collar, and she thought she would be afraid to meet him anywhere else.

"Good night, Miss," the private said. His voice had a strange quality, almost husky, as if he were very concerned about her.

They crossed the parade ground. The night was clear, and the sky was full of stars. The sounds of the river rushing by came faintly up to the old fortress.

"I didn't want it ever to end," she said.

"Why?"

"Because—you've built an artificial world in there. A wall of glory to shut out the realities of what we do. And when it ends we go back to the war." And back to whatever you meant when you had that boy sing that sinister old border ballad.

"That's well put. A wall of glory. Perhaps that's what we do."

They reached the block of suites assigned to the senior officers. Her door was next to his. She stood in front of it, reluctant to go inside. The room would be empty, and tomorrow there was the Council, and—she turned to him and said bitterly, "Does it have to end? I was happy for a few minutes. Now—"

"It doesn't have to end, but do you know what you're doing?"

"No." She turned away from her own door and opened his. He followed, but didn't go inside. She stood in the doorway for a moment, then laughed. "I was going to say something silly. Something like, 'Let's have a last drink.' But I wouldn't have meant that, and you'd have known it, so what's the point of games?"

"There is no point to games. Not between us. Games are for soldiers' girls and lovers."

"John—my God, John, are you as lonely as I am?"

"Yes. Of course."

"Then we can't let the party end. Not while there's a single moment it can go on." She went inside his room.

After a few moments he followed and closed the door.

During the night she was able to forget the conflict between them, but when she left his quarters in the morning the ballad returned to haunt her.

She knew she must do something, but she couldn't warn Bannister. The Council, the revolution, independence, none of them had lost their importance; but though she would serve those causes she felt apart from them.

"I'm a perfect fool," she told herself. But fool or not, she could not warn Bannister. Finally she persuaded the President to meet John away from the shouting masses of the Council Chamber.

Bannister came directly to the point. "Colonel, we can't keep a large army in the field indefinitely. Miss Horton's Valley ranchers may be willing to pay these taxes, but most of our people can't."

"Just what did you expect when you began this?" Falkenberg asked.

"A long war," Bannister admitted. "But your initial successes raised hopes, and we got a lot of supporters we hadn't expected. They demand an end."

"Fair-weather soldiers." Falkenberg snorted. "Common enough, but why did you let them gain so much influence in your Council?"

"Because there were a lot of them."

And they all support you for President, Glenda Ruth thought. While my friends and I were out at the front, you were back here organizing the newcomers, grabbing for power . . . you're not worth the life of one of those soldiers. John's or mine.

"After all, this is a democratic government," Bannister said.

"And thus quite unable to accomplish anything that takes sustained effort. Can you afford this egalitarian democracy of yours?"

"You were not hired to restructure our government!" Bannister shouted.

Falkenberg activated his desktop map. "Look. We have the plains ringed with troops. The irregulars can hold the passes and swamps practically forever. Any real threat of a breakthrough can be held by my regiment in mobile reserve. The Confederates can't get at us—but we can't risk a battle in the open with them."

"So what can we do?" Bannister demanded. "Franklin is sure to send reinforcements. If we wait, we lose."

"I doubt that. They've no assault boats either. They can't land in any real force on our side of the line, and what good does it do them to add to their force in the capital? Eventually we starve them out. Franklin itself must be hurt by the loss of the corn shipments. They won't be able to feed their army forever."

"A mercenary paradise," Bannister muttered. "A long war and no fighting. Damn it, you've got to attack while we've still got troops! I tell you, our support is melting away."

"If we put our troops out where von Mellenthin's armor can get at them with room to maneuver, they won't melt, they'll burn."

"You tell him, Glenda Ruth," Bannister said. "He won't listen to me."

She looked at Falkenberg's impassive face and wanted to cry. "John, he may be right. I know my people, they can't hold on forever. Even if they could, the Council is going to insist . . ."

His look didn't change. *There's nothing I can say*, she thought, *nothing I know that he doesn't, because he's right but he's wrong too. These are only civilians in arms. They're not iron men. All the time my people are guarding those passes their ranches are going to ruin.*

Is Howard right? Is this a mercenary paradise, and you're not even trying? But she didn't want to believe that.

Unwanted, the vision she'd had that lonely night at

the pass returned. She fought it with the memory of the party, and afterwards . . .

"Just what the hell are you waiting on, *Colonel* Falkenberg?" Bannister demanded.

Falkenberg said nothing, and Glenda Ruth wanted to cry; but she did not.

XXII

THE COUNCIL HAD not voted six days later. Glenda Ruth used every parliamentary trick her father had taught her during the meetings, and after they adjourned each day she hustled from delegate to delegate. She made promises she couldn't keep, exploited old friends and made new ones, and every morning she was sure only that she could delay a little longer.

She wasn't sure herself why she did it. The war vote was linked to the reappointment of Silana as governor in Allansport, and she did know that the man was incompetent; but mostly, after the debates and political meetings, Falkenberg would come for her, or send a junior officer to escort her to his quarters—and she was glad to go. They seldom spoke of politics, or even talked much at all. It was enough to be with him—but when she left in the mornings, she was afraid again. He'd never promised her anything.

On the sixth night she joined him for a late supper. When the orderlies had taken the dinner cart she sat moodily at the table. "This is what you meant, isn't it?" she asked.

"About what?"

"That I'd have to betray either my friends or my command—but I don't even know if you're my friend. John, what am I going to do?"

Very gently he laid his hand against her cheek. "You're

425

going to talk sense—and keep them from appointing Silana in Allansport."

"But what are we waiting for?"

He shrugged. "Would you rather it came to an open break? There'll be no stopping them if we lose this vote. The mob's demanding your arrest right now—for the past three days Calvin has had the Headquarters Guard on full alert in case they're fool enough to try it."

She shuddered, but before she could say more he lifted her gently to her feet and pressed her close to him. Once again her doubts vanished but she knew they'd be back. Who was she betraying? And for what?

The crowd shouted before she could speak. "Mercenary's whore!" someone called. Her friends answered with more epithets, and it was five minutes before Bannister could restore order.

How long can I keep it up? At least another day or so, I suppose. Am I his whore? If I'm not, I don't know what I am. He's never told me. She carefully took papers from her briefcase, but there was another interruption. A messenger strode quickly, almost running, across the floor to hand a flimsy message to Howard Bannister. The pudgy President glanced at it, then began to read more carefully.

The hall fell silent as everyone watched Bannister's face. The President showed a gamut of emotions: surprise, bewilderment, then carefully controlled rage. He read the message again and whispered to the messenger, who nodded. Bannister lifted the microphone.

"Councillors, I have—I suppose it would be simpler to read this to you. 'PROVISIONAL GOVERNMENT FREE STATES OF WASHINGTON FROM CDSN CRUISER INTREPID BREAK BREAK WE ARE IN RECEIPT OF DOCUMENTED COMPLAINT FROM CONFEDERATE GOVERNMENT THAT FREE STATES ARE IN VIOLATION OF LAWS OF WAR STOP THIS VESSEL ORDERED TO INVESTIGATE STOP LANDING BOAT ARRIVES ASTORIA SIXTEEN HUNDRED HOURS THIS DAY STOP PROVISIONAL GOVERNMENT MUST BE PREPARED TO

DISPATCH ARMISTICE COMMISSION TO MEET
WITH DELEGATES FROM CONFEDERACY AND
CODOMINIUM INVESTIGATING OFFICERS IM-
MEDIATELY UPON ARRIVAL OF LANDING BOAT
STOP COMMANDING OFFICERS ALL MERCE-
NARY FORCES ORDERED TO BE PRESENT TO
GIVE EVIDENCE STOP BREAK BREAK JOHN
GRANT CAPTAIN CODOMINIUM SPACE NAVY
BREAK MESSAGE ENDS' "

There was a moment of hushed silence, then the
gymnasium erupted in sound. "Investigate us?" "Goddamn CD is—" "Armistice hell!"

Falkenberg caught Glenda Ruth's eye. He gestured
toward the outside and left the hall. She joined him
minutes later. "I really ought to stay, John. We've got
to decide what to do."

"What you decide has just become unimportant,"
Falkenberg said. "Your Council doesn't hold as many
cards as it used to."

"John, what will they do?"

He shrugged. "Try to stop the war now that they're
here. I suppose it never occurred to Silana that a complaint from Franklin industrialists is more likely to get
CD attention than a similar squawk from a bunch of
farmers. . . ."

"You expected this! Was this what you were waiting
for?"

"Something like this."

"You know more than you're saying! John, why won't
you tell me? I know you don't love me, but haven't I a
right to know?"

He stood at stiff attention in the bright reddish-tinted
sunlight for a long time. Finally he said, "Glenda Ruth,
nothing's certain in politics and war. I once promised
something to a girl, and I couldn't deliver it."

"But—"

"We've each command responsibilities—and each
other. Will you believe me when I say I've tried to
keep you from having to choose—and keep myself from
the same choice? You'd better get ready. A CD Court

of Inquiry isn't in the habit of waiting for people, and they're due in little more than an hour."

The Court was to be held aboard *Intrepid*. The four-hundred-meter bottle-shaped warship in orbit around New Washington was the only neutral territory available. When the Patriot delegates were piped aboard, the Marines in the landing dock gave Bannister the exact honors they'd given the Confederate Governor General, then hustled the delegation through gray steel corridors to a petty officer's lounge reserved for them.

"Governor General Forrest of the Confederacy is already aboard, sir," the Marine sergeant escort told them. "Captain would like to see Colonel Falkenberg in his cabin in ten minutes."

Bannister looked around the small lounge. "I suppose it's bugged," he said. "Colonel, what happens now?"

Falkenberg noted the artficially friendly tone Bannister had adopted. "The Captain and his advisors will hear each of us privately. If you want witnesses summoned, he'll take care of that. When the Court thinks the time proper, he'll bring both parties together. The CD usually tries to get everyone to agree rather than impose some kind of settlement."

"And if we can't agree?"

Falkenberg shrugged. "They might let you fight it out. They might order mercenaries off planet and impose a blockade. They could even draw up their own settlement and order you to accept it."

"What happens if we just tell them to go away? What can they do?" Bannister demanded.

Falkenberg smiled tightly. "They can't conquer the planet because they haven't enough Marines to occupy it—but there's not a lot else they can't do, Mr. President. There's enough power aboard this cruiser to make New Washington uninhabitable.

"You don't have either planetary defenses or a fleet. I'd think a long time before I made Captain Grant angry—and on that score, I've been summoned to his cabin." Falkenberg saluted. There was no trace of mockery in the gesture, but Bannister grimaced as the soldier left the lounge.

Falkenberg was conducted past Marine sentries to the captain's cabin. The orderly opened the door and let him in, then withdrew.

John Grant was a tall, thin officer with premature graying hair that made him look older than he was. As Falkenberg entered, Grant stood and greeted him with genuine warmth. "Good to see you, John Christian." He extended his hand and looked over his visitor with pleasure. "You're keeping fit enough."

"So are you, Johnny." Falkenberg's smile was equally genuine. "And the family's well?"

"Inez and the kids are fine. My father's dead."

"Sorry to hear that."

Captain Grant brought his chair from behind his desk and placed it facing Falkenberg's. Unconsciously he dogged it into place. "It was a release for him, I think. Single-passenger flier accident."

Falkenberg frowned, and Grant nodded. "Coroner said accident," the Captain said. "But it could have been suicide. He was pretty broken up about Sharon. But you don't know that story, do you? No matter. My kid sister's fine. They've got a good place on Sparta."

Grant reached to his desk to touch a button. A steward brought brandy and glasses. The Marine set up a collapsible table between them, then left.

"The Grand Admiral all right?" Falkenberg asked.

"He's hanging on." Grant drew in a deep breath and let it out quickly. "Just barely, though. Despite everything Uncle Martin could do the budget's lower again this year. I can't stay here long, John. Another patrol, and it's getting harder to cover these unauthorized missions in the log. Have you accomplished your job?"

"Yeah. Went quicker than I thought. I've spent the last hundred hours wishing we'd arranged to have you arrive sooner." He went to the screen controls on the cabin bulkhead.

"Got that complaint signaled by a merchantman as we came in," Grant said. "Surprised hell out of me. Here, let me get that, they've improved the damned thing and it's tricky." He played with the controls until New Washington's inhabited areas showed on the screen. "OK?"

"Right." Falkenberg spun dials to show the current military situation on the planet below. "Stalemate," he said. "As it stands. But once you order all mercenaries off planet, we won't have much trouble taking the capital area."

"Christ, John, I can't do anything as raw as that! If the Friedlanders go, you have to go as well. Hell, you've accomplished the mission. The rebels may have a hell of a time taking the capital without you, but it doesn't really matter who wins. Neither one of 'em's going to build a fleet for a while after this war's over. Good work."

Falkenberg nodded. "That was Sergei Lermontov's plan. Neutralize this planet with minimum CD investment and without destroying the industries. Something came up, though, Johnny, and I've decided to change it a bit. The regiment's staying."

"But I—"

"Just hold on," Falkenberg said. He grinned broadly. "I'm not a mercenary within the meaning of the act. We've got a land grant, Johnny. You can leave us as settlers, not mercenaries."

"Oh, come off it." Grant's voice showed irritation. "A land grant by a rebel government not in control? Look, nobody's going to look *too* close at what I do, but Franklin can buy one Grand Senator anyway. I can't risk it, John. Wish I could."

"What if the grant's confirmed by the local Loyalist government?" Falkenberg asked impishly.

"Well, then it'd be OK—how in hell did you manage *that?*" Grant was grinning again. "Have a drink and tell me about it." He poured for both of them. "And where do you fit in?"

Falkenberg looked up at Grant and his expression changed to something like astonishment. "You won't believe this, Johnny."

"From the look on your face you don't either."

"Not sure I do. Johnny, I've got a girl. A soldier's

girl, and I'm going to marry her. She's leader of most of the rebel army. There are a lot of politicians around who think they count for something, but—" He made a sharp gesture with his right hand.

"Marry the queen and become king, uh?"

"She's more like a princess. Anyway, the Loyalists aren't going to surrender to the rebels without a fight. That complaint they sent was quite genuine. There's no rebel the Loyalists will trust, not even Glenda Ruth."

Grant nodded comprehension. "Enter the soldier who enforced the Laws of War. He's married to the princess and commands the only army around. What's your *real* stake here, John Christian?"

Falkenberg shrugged. "Maybe the princess won't leave the kingdom. Anyway. Lermontov's trying to keep the balance of power. God knows, somebody's got to. Fine. The Grand Admiral looks ten years ahead—but I'm not sure the CoDominium's going to *last* ten years, Johnny."

Grant slowly nodded agreement. His voice fell and took on a note of awe. "Neither am I. It's worse just in the last few weeks. The Old Man's going out of his mind. One thing, though. There are some Grand Senators trying to hold it together. Some of them have given up the Russki-American fights to stand together against their own governments."

"Enough? Can they do it?"

"I wish I knew." Grant shook his head in bewilderment. "I always thought the CoDominium was the one stable thing on old Earth," he said wonderingly. "Now it's all we can do to hold it together. The nationalsts keep winning, John, and nobody knows how to stop them." He drained his glass. "The Old Man's going to hate losing you."

"Yeah. We've worked together a long time." Falkenberg looked wistfully around the cabin. Once he'd thought this would be the high point of his life, to be captain of a CD warship. Now he might never see one again.

Then he shrugged. "There's worse places to be, Johnny," Falkenberg said. "Do me a favor, will you? When you get back to Luna Base, ask the admiral to see that all copies of that New Washington mineral survey are destroyed. I'd hate for somebody to learn there really is something here worth grabbing."

"OK. You're a long way from anything, John."

"I know. But if things break up around Earth, this may be the best place to be. Look, Johnny, if you need a safe base some day, we'll be here. Tell the Old Man that."

"Sure." Grant gave Falkenberg a twisted grin. "Can't get over it. Going to marry the girl are you? I'm glad for both of you."

"Thanks."

"King John I. What kind of government will you set up, anyway?"

"Hadn't thought. Myths change. Maybe people are ready for monarchy again at that. We'll think of something, Glenda Ruth and I."

"I just bet you will. She must be one hell of a girl."

"She is that."

"A toast to the bride, then." They drank, and Grant refilled their glasses. Then he stood. "One last, eh? To the CoDominium."

Falkenberg stood and raised his glass. They drank the toast while below them New Washington turned, and a hundred parsecs away Earth armed for her last battle.

Experience the bestselling worlds of

JERRY POURNELLE

DAVID DRAKE AND HIS FRIENDS

Let the bestselling author David Drake be your guide to excitement in strange new worlds of the distant future and mythic past. Meet some of the bravest, oddest, and most dangerous folk you can imagine.

Remember, with friends like these . . .

LACEY AND HIS FRIENDS

Jed Lacey is a 21st-century cop who plays by the rules. His rules. The United States of Lacey's day has imposed law and order with cameras that scan every citizen, waking or sleeping, and computers that watch the images for any hint of crime. Then it's Lacey's turn. He knows what mercy is, and pity. But he doesn't have either. Not for criminals. Not for victims. Not even for himself.

65593-0 • $3.50 _____

VETTIUS AND HIS FRIENDS

For centuries, Rome has ruled the civilized world, bringing peace and stability to a troubled age. But now, sorcerous powers gather, rousing the barbarians to battle, aiming to turn the Roman Pax into never ending chaos. Few men stand against the forces of Darkness. One is Vettius, an honorable soldier, but one as ruthless as the age demands. One other is Dama, a merchant whose favorite weapons aren't blade and shield, but wit and wealth. Two wildly dissimilar men, Vettius and Dama, bound only by their friendship, alike only in their determination that Rome— and civilization—shall not fail.

69802-8 • $3.95 _____